WRITER'S CRAMP

The elevator ground to a stop and Teresa pulled open the ancient steel grille. The doors were stuck, as usual. When she got them open, she got a clear view of what was inside.

A man's body was slumped against the back wall. He lay on his side, the left arm bent backward under him. His legs were grotesquely crooked. His right arm lay flat on the floor, palm upward. There was not much blood, except along the right side of the head and at the corner of the wide, straight mouth. There, a dark stream of blood had stained the chin, the throat, the bright-red silk scarf, and the lapel of the expensive gray overcoat. The man's brown hair was matted with blood and dirt, but the green-gold eyes were wide open. Teresa hadn't the heart to brush them shut. It seemed the worst kind of insult.

Bantam Crime Line Books offer the finest in classic and modern American mysteries.
Ask your bookseller for the books you have missed.

Rex Stout
The Black Mountain
Broken Vase
Death of a Dude
Death Times Three
Fer-de-Lance
The Final Deduction
Gambit
Plot It Yourself
The Rubber Band
Some Buried Caesar
Three for the Chair
Too Many Cooks

Max Allan Collins
The Dark City
Bullet Proof
Butcher's Dozen
Neon Mirage

Loren Estleman
Peeper
coming soon: Whiskey River

Dick Lupoff
The Comic Book Killer

Randy Russell
Hot Wire

V. S. Anderson
Blood Lies
King of the Roses

William Murray
When the Fat Man Sings
The King of the Nightcap
coming soon: The Getaway Blues

Eugene Izzi
King of the Hustlers
The Prime Roll
Invasions

Gloria Dank
Friends Till the End
Going Out in Style

Jeffery Deaver
Manhattan Is My Beat
Death of a Blue Movie Star

Robert Goldsborough
Murder in E Minor
Death on Deadline
The Bloodied Ivy
The Last Coincidence

Sue Grafton
"A" Is for Alibi
"B" Is for Burglar
"C" Is for Corpse
"D" Is for Deadbeat
"E" Is for Evidence
"F" Is for Fugitive

David Lindsey
In the Lake of the Moon

Carolyn G. Hart
Design for Murder
Death on Demand
Something Wicked
Honeymoon with Murder
A Little Class on Murder

Annette Meyers
The Big Killing
Tender Death

Rob Kantner
Dirty Work
The Back-Door Man
Hell's Only Half Full
Made in Detroit

Robert Crais
The Monkey's Raincoat
Stalking the Angel

Keith Peterson
The Trapdoor
There Fell a Shadow
The Rain
Rough Justice

David Handler
The Man Who Died Laughing
The Man Who Lived by Night
coming soon: The Man Who Would Be
F. Scott Fitzgerald

Jerry Oster
Club Dead
Internal Affairs

M. K. Lorens
Sweet Narcissus
Ropedancer's Fall
coming soon: Deception Island

Benjamin M. Schutz
A Tax in Blood
Embrace the Wolf
The Things We Do for Love

Monroe Thompson
The Blue Room

Diane Shah
As Crime Goes By

Meg O'Brien
The Daphne Decisions
coming soon: Salmon in the Soup

Paul Levine
To Speak for the Dead

ROPEDANCER'S FALL

M. K. Lorens

BANTAM BOOKS
NEW YORK · TORONTO · LONDON · SYDNEY · AUCKLAND

ROPEDANCER'S FALL

A Bantam Book / August 1990

*Grateful acknowledgment is made for permission to reprint an
excerpt from "The Love Song of J. Alfred Prufrock" in* Collected
Poems 1909–1962 *by T.S. Eliot, copyright 1936 by Harcourt
Brace Jovanovich, Inc., copyright © 1964, 1963 by T.S. Eliot,
reprinted by permission of the publisher.*

ISBN 0-553-28312-X

Published simultaneously in the United States and Canada

*Bantam Books are published by Bantam Books, a division of Bantam
Doubleday Dell Publishing Group, Inc. Its trademark, consisting of
the words "Bantam Books" and the portrayal of a rooster, is Regis-
tered in U.S. Patent and Trademark Office and in other countries.
Marca Registrada. Bantam Books, 666 Fifth Avenue, New York, New
York 10103.*

PRINTED IN THE UNITED STATES OF AMERICA

RAD   0 9 8 7 6 5 4 3 2 1

ROPEDANCER'S FALL

Chapter One

It was four o'clock on Friday afternoon, January 27, just the kind of New York day that drives faint hearts to seek the Florida Sunshine Tree for an extended stay. I was sitting in the office of my editor, old Cliff Munson, looking out the fifteenth-floor window of Garner and Sloan Publishing, and generally getting the ax. You see, Cliff wasn't exactly wild about my latest epic of crime, in which I'd replaced my old alter ego of thirty-odd years, the suave Gilded Age sleuth G. Winchester Hyde, with a new hero. I was rather fond of this newcomer, a fellow of Churchillean stature and stubbornly un-eighties proclivities, who liked old clothes, old chairs, old verse, old Scotch judiciously applied, and the occasional Turkish cigarette when he was ill at ease.

Cliff offered me a light and I inhaled deeply. "It's always a bad plan to write directly about yourself, Winnie," he said. "I just don't think the public's going to accept a man like you in the role of sleuth. Anyway, we've had sacks and sacks of mail asking you to bring Winchester Hyde back to life, you know that. I really think you should consider it."

Outside, the snow was coming down in Siberian strength. Cabs zoomed along with white frosting on their roofs, and from where I stood, it looked as if we were in for it, all right. And so was I. "You have to consider the marketplace," Cliff went on, a trace of regret in his voice. "I just don't think this new book will make it."

"It's fine to consider the marketplace," I said, "so long as that's not the only thing you consider. You're beginning to sound as if you're selling brussels sprouts around here, not

1

books. I think this book is good, Cliff, and I do have *some* claim to literary judgment, you know."

Cliff laughed. "Hell, I never said it wasn't good, you poor fish. And give me one of those smokes of yours." I did, and we sat back, filling the office with the sweet, faintly licentious fragrance of the Turkish Delights. "It's a new time, Winston," said Cliff at last. "I guess we've got to roll with the punches, if we don't want to go the way of the pterodactyls."

"I'm not so sure," I said thoughtfully. "I doubt it would've postponed the inevitable very long, if a pterodactyl had shopped round for a three-piece suit and an alligator briefcase and kept his beady eye on the marketplace." I stood up and looked out again at the falling snow. "Personally, I think I'd rather go down flapping."

I wasn't the only person looking out at the snow that late Friday afternoon. Across town, a friend of mine was also faced with a decision, but his plans were carefully laid. I'll tell you the story as I pieced it together from all kinds of sources after I became involved. And involved I was, whether the marketplace figured I was sleuth material or not.

From his window in the Danson Foundation for the Arts Building high above Rockefeller Center, John Falkner, my sometime friend and longtime adversary, was also keeping an eye on the storm. Down on the street the stuff was piling up on the golden shoulders of Prometheus, and already the skaters were abandoning their triple spins and double axels to hunt for cabs. John had to make his move now.

He checked his watch and punched a button on the desk. A moment later his formidable secretary, Miss Joan Plumb, quick-marched in without knocking. Plumb wore her white hair in a sleek pageboy, her ample form swathed in a corduroy jumper, and her face in an expression like John Calvin expounding the doctrine of original sin. Falkner had always figured she'd been staked out here to watch him, but he wanted no gimlet eyes around this afternoon. "Plumb," he said, "why don't you take off now? It's starting to pile up out there, and it'll be tough to get a cab if you hang around. Just phone the airline, will you, confirm me for the Philly flight tonight, and then you can go home."

Since Plumb never left before five-thirty, never arrived after eight, and had never taken a day off within recorded history, John's suggestion made her jittery. Probably he only wanted to head for the cocktail party down on the tenth floor, where the grant recipients were whooping it up. But he'd never bothered to get her out of the way before, and it made her determined to find out what was in the wind. Thanking him, she marched back to her own office, phoned the airline, and began to pull on a pair of thin plastic boots over her brown pumps. They were a tight fit, and while she tugged at them she had time to add up her thoughts.

All Plumb's loyalties were to the Dansons. Old Turner, now long dead, had hired her in 1948. His son Randolph, retired to perpetual golf in Savannah, had been the one love of her life, though he never knew it, and she his executive secretary, as indispensable as the family fortune. She'd taught the youngest Danson, Andrew, everything there was to know about how the Foundation worked, but when he took over from his father, he'd shunted her off to Public Relations to work for Falkner. Oh, she liked Andrew, you couldn't help doing that. He was pleasant and smiling and always a perfect gentleman, and he'd never cut her salary, though she was doing half the work she used to. Andrew had no children. His wife Cella was a difficult woman and his marriage a comfortless façade. There would be no more Dansons after him, and Miss Plumb wanted things to go well for Andrew. Still, she suspected him. She suspected the huge showy mechanism he'd made of the Foundation. She suspected the ranks of computers, she suspected public relations and cocktail parties and the succession of galas that were supposed to raise money but mostly seemed to spend it on Dom Perignon and Lobster Marinière. Plumb had for some time figured something not quite kosher was going on under her nose, and whatever it was, John Falkner seemed to have tumbled to it too. He ran far too many computer checks on applicants for grants, made phone calls to obscure towns in the Midwest, and sometimes disappeared for days delving into unexpected labyrinths in Washington, D.C.

And that was why, even though she finally had her boots on, Plumb decided not to go home early that afternoon.

Down on the tenth floor, in the cavernous, chandeliered Hospitality Room, the demure music of a string trio was being drowned out by the extremely loud voice of a young man barely past twenty, with close-cropped curly hair and John Lennon glasses. Shane McAuley was mad as hell and he didn't care who knew it. In fact, he wanted as many people as possible to know. He had Andrew Danson, the Grand Panjandrum himself, backed into the corner by the bar.

"He did a job on me," said the boy. "If they run that tape, I'm suing the fuck out of Falkner *and* this foundation."

Andrew Danson smiled slightly and lifted McAuley's emphatic forefinger off the lapel of his blue silk suit. "The Foundation underwrites John's talk show on PBS, Shane. It doesn't endorse his opinions. We don't control the questions he asks, or how he chooses to ask them. He's a man with strong points of view, surely you knew that going in?"

"Goddamn has-been, where the hell is he?" shouted McAuley at the walls.

"Shane, we're very proud of you here, you're one of our shining stars. We want to keep you happy. I'm sure WNYT will edit out anything—unpleasant, shall we say? With a little financial encouragement."

At fifty-five, Andrew Danson made the owlish twenty-two-year-old kid look badly out of shape. Danson was tall and lean, with clear, rather amused blue eyes and a head of white hair that did credit to his sixty-dollar styling job. He had an athlete's body with just a hint of thickness around the middle, and a deep St. Thomas tan that advertised his health like a billboard; not one of the guests milling around the mahogany bar doubted he could handle the half-squiffed kid without batting an eye. It was typical of him that he preferred a defter touch.

But McAuley wasn't going to be finessed. "You get the

sonuvabitch down here," he yelled. "Get Falkner the fuck down here, I got a couple things to say to him." McAuley was the youngest novelist ever to be nominated for the Pulitzer Prize. He had a reputation, all of six months old, to protect. "Get the old has-been screw-up down here, man," he said, and gave Danson a shove that put the whole scene in the morning papers, word for word.

A narrow-shouldered fellow in his thirties with a thin pencil moustache and thinner mouse-brown hair was watching the clash from beyond the bar, trying to decide whether to call Security. Dean Sommers decided against it. McAuley was the man of the hour since Andrew had wangled him that Pulitzer nomination, and you didn't hassle him without making the papers. Andrew didn't much like bad publicity, and whatever else he might think of his boss, a deeply buried part of Sommers still wanted to please and protect him. He looked inquiringly over at Andrew, waiting for a sign. Danson nodded. "Get John down here," he said quite calmly, straightening his jacket. "Please, Dean."

Upstairs, Plumb was about to get her hat and coat and conceal herself in the supply room connecting her office with the one next door, when the phone rang. It was her replacement in Danson's office, the vague, ubiquitous Mr. Sommers.

"For God's sake, Plumb," he said. His syllables were brittle and even, and he pronounced the word "Gawd" with what he seemed to think was an Ivy League accent, though she knew he came from Brooklyn. "Where's Falkner? Andy wants him. Right now. McAuley's raising hell at the party." His tone wasn't angry, it was carefully measured, but in spite of him, his voice rose now and then to a reedy tenor, thin as a pubescent boy's. "John assured us he'd be at the party. After all, visibility is his primary function here."

"I'll find out if he's in, shall I?" Plumb parried.

"Just get him downstairs in five minutes. Whatever he's done to Shane McAuley, he'd damn well better fix it up."

And Dean Sommers hung up the phone with a crash that made Plumb jump. When she looked up, Falkner was standing in the door of his inner office, his soft, fine hair blowing slightly in the draft from the ventilators.

"I heard," he said. "Thought you were gone. Picked up on my own line." The pale hazel eyes looked almost gold in the dull fluorescent light. He smiled at her rather shyly. He didn't smile often, and she warmed to him in spite of herself. "Guess it's my move," he said. "Visibility being my primary function."

"A person educated and promoted beyond his intelligence makes things unpleasant for everybody," Plumb announced crisply. "Dean Sommers is merely a sycophant and a bootlicker."

Falkner leaned tentatively, his fingertips on the edge of her desk. When he spoke, his voice was level and quiet, interior, as if his mind were talking to itself, a thing it rarely stopped doing. "They're a whole new species, Plummy," he said. "They keep their balls in numbered accounts, they bleed hundred dollar bills, and they own the goddamn world."

He strode determinedly out and the elevator doors closed behind him. But Plumb had barely time to get settled nicely at her peephole in the supply room before he was back again. Of course he'd never intended to go meekly down to that cocktail party as ordered. Plumb smiled grimly to herself as Falkner checked the closet to see if she'd taken her things and gone home. Finding the coat hook empty, he disappeared into his own office.

Down in the Computer Room on the second floor, a young woman was waiting for Falkner's call. Charlotte Stedman, as usual, had stayed at her terminal long after everyone else had checked out and gone. She was the workhorse of the office. When you wanted to know an entry code or the best way to access another system, it was Charlie you asked. The phone on her desk rang and she grabbed it. "Six eighty-three," she said. It was her operator number, the code under which she entered the computer banks. She had come to prefer it to her name.

Falkner's voice startled her with its cool, quiet control, even though she'd heard it often enough on the phone. "It's time," he said. "Wait for me in the Lobby." He paused for a second, sensing her nervousness. "It'll be all right," he told her, and waited another moment. She could hear his breath against the receiver, steady and soft. Then suddenly he hung up.

While Charlotte collected her things and went down to the Lobby, Falkner made two more calls. The first was to his ex-wife, Teresa, another old pal of mine. "Hi," said her throaty voice on the answering machine. "This is Teresa LaMagna. I'm probably at rehearsal, so leave me a message at the tone and I'll call you. Sorry I'm not here." Falkner rocked back in his leather chair, waiting for the tone, but when it sounded, he didn't speak. He held the receiver for a few moments, thinking, until the machine clicked and hung up on him. He considered dialing Teresa again. But he rang the Hospitality Room instead. Dean Sommers answered.

"Where the hell are you, John? McAuley's just gone storming out of here ready to lift your scalp, and Andy's in a mood to join him."

"Tell Andrew to get up to my office. Now. Tell him Dennis Weeks is here."

"What?" said Sommers sharply. Then he forced himself to relax his tone. "I can't order Andy around, you know that. Dennis Weeks?"

"Of the Hopewell Foundation. I'm sure he'll know the name, Dean," replied Falkner patiently. "Just tell him." And he hung up.

Next Falkner unlocked the three combination locks of a leather briefcase on his desk and took out a videotape cassette. He relocked the case, which contained a sheaf of papers and computer printouts. Then he put the tape into the video player attached to his TV and activated a sound-controlled timer. It would switch on when the office door closed behind Andrew Danson. Everything finished, Falkner stood looking round his office. He noticed the small photo of his ex-wife and his son Michael and shoved it into his coat pocket. Briefcase in hand, he went out, leaving the office door open wide.

But he didn't head for the hall elevators yet. He couldn't risk meeting Andrew Danson on the way up. Instead he went into the supply room, and Plumb just had time to duck behind the Xerox machine before he could spot her. He did get a whiff of her English lavender perfume, but he only smiled. So this was where the old girl baptized herself with that stuff.

Plumb crouched motionless as someone entered the outer office. By craning her neck over the Xerox and peering past Falkner's shoulder, she could just see the Man-from-Glad hair and Bain de Soleil complexion of Andrew Danson. He entered Falkner's office and Plumb heard the door shut with a clack. Almost immediately Falkner's voice could be heard from inside, though he was still there with her in the supply room. A tape recording, maybe a video. He made a lot of publicity videos for the Foundation; he even had one of those expensive cameras. As the tape went on, Falkner slipped quietly out and by the time Plumb emerged, the elevator was just closing behind him. She couldn't risk opening the inner office for a peek at Andrew, because the door always made a racket when you touched it. But she could certainly hear Falkner's voice on the tape.

"With the exception of a hundred thousand dollars given to eight well-known artists and writers in the Manhattan area, the entire fund of the Foundation during the past year, a total of almost five million dollars, has been given through grants recommended by twelve regional arts agencies, among them the Hopewell Foundation, under the control of Dennis Weeks, Kansas City, Missouri." Just another public relations blurb, thought Plumb, and hurried for the elevator, hoping to see where Falkner was headed next.

She might've been too late, but the snow, as predicted, made for the usual shortage of cabs. Falkner was still standing at the curb, right arm in the air, as cab after cab whizzed by him. A youngish woman, perhaps thirty-four, was standing beside him. The younger girls all blended into a blur for Miss Plumb, but this one was unforgettable, even though Plumb had no name to put with the face.

The young woman was short and a bit heavy for her height, but mainly memorable because of her ugliness. Her upper lip was too long, slightly simian, the mouth thin and wide, and the chin short and rounded. The nose was wide and flat, like the putty noses of clowns. Only Charlotte Stedman's eyes escaped her inheritance. They were wide-set and gray, round, intelligent, and clear as cold water. They seemed to have gotten into her face by accident.

Two kids with skates slung over their shoulders came by, giggling and whispering. Seeing Charlie, the boy pulled a monkey face, then duck-walked away down the street, terribly pleased with himself. Falkner looked down at Charlie's set, determined face. If she weren't quite so intelligent, he thought, it would've been a lot easier for her. As it was, she caught every sly nuance in the office chatter and registered every stare. Another cab sped by. "Damn," he said. "Do you mind walking? It's not very far." He smiled and took her arm. It was tense as strung wire.

They turned the corner and headed up Fiftieth Street, with Plumb hurrying about half a block behind them. There weren't many people on the street, and she had to hang back to make certain they didn't see her. She lost sight of them once or twice, but spied them again, turning into a place she knew quite well. It was a little Greek restaurant and bar, and she knew it because she went there every Friday night for a drink before she took the crosstown bus home to her East Side apartment, her ninety-year-old mother, and her two dogs. At least they were used to her in the Café Athene, and she knew her way around. Plumb yanked her fur toque tight around her ears and headed for the front door.

She found a booth by the window. It took her eyes a little while to adjust from the snow outside to the dim lights in the bar, but finally she spotted Falkner and Charlotte making their way between the tables to a phone near the cash desk. What kind of phone call did it take two people to make? And why not use the phones at the office? Plumb grabbed a handful of change and headed for the cigarette machine near the the phone. She stood fiddling with the levers and knobs, her ears nicely pricked up for whatever she might hear of the phone call.

Falkner had his back to her and he did all the talking. Charlie kept close, and pulled the receiver down so she could hear. "Don't be in a rush to make up your mind," Falkner was saying. "I'll be out of town all weekend, as you know. Think it over. But decide by Wednesday night. Call the number on the tape. I don't really think you can afford not to."

"Tell him about the computer check on Weeks," Charlie prompted, but John ignored her.

"I've got nothing to lose, Andrew," he said into the phone. You know that. Better than anybody."

Suddenly Falkner hung up. Plumb scurried back to her table, uncertain whether he'd seen her. His face wore an imperturbable half smile as he went to the bar and ordered a straight Scotch, then downed it without bothering to sit down. Charlie Stedman's anxious, ugly face was turned up toward him. "Is it really all right?" she said. "Can you really do it?"

Through the steamy window, Plumb watched them get into a cab outside. She wondered if this odd pair were lovers. It didn't seem to her very likely. Something in each of them seemed to be waiting for the other to slip off guard. There was gentleness in Falkner's careful attention, but nothing more. If the girl thought so, she was deluding herself. Plumb had done the same thing herself for years, with Randolph. She sighed, ordered a double gin and bitters, and determined to go back to the office and play that tape for herself. If the phone call had been blackmail, as it appeared, she would call dear silly Randolph and sound the alarm that would bring him back to take control—and naturally bring her back with him.

But when Plumb returned to the office she found nothing. She tried playing every cassette in the storage cabinet under the bookcase, and none was a copy of the one she'd heard played for Andrew. He'd obviously taken it with him. Nothing was left in the office but the uneasy shadows cast by the falling snow outside the window and the thin sigh of the ventilator. She studied the smooth, bare top of the rosewood desk, empty of papers, clutter, even the photo of Falkner's family. A sense of age and waste assailed Plumb, and she felt a shiver rise from the back of her neck and tighten her scalp. Sensibly, she decided she must've caught cold. But it was more. She thought of Falkner standing in the door watching her, and wondered for a second whether she'd made him up. Certainly there wasn't much evidence of his presence to be found here. "Visibility is his primary function," Dean Sommers had said. Though Joan Plumb didn't know it, she would never see John Falkner again.

Chapter Two

I've often wondered what would've happened if I'd stayed put under the covers that snowy Sunday morning after the debacle at my publisher's. If I'd ignored the phone, I mean. Ignored the racket when the TV went on in the guest room and reminded me that a teenage life form was camped in there. Ignored the blizzard, number twelve since Thanksgiving, that was still dumping snow on the little town of Ainsley, New York, perched on the Hudson bluffs, where I've lived for thirty years plus. Or even—fat chance—ignored the empty half of the bed where the warm shape of my Sarah should've been. At my age, verging on sixty-eight, it often seems the great question of life is how much of it you're prepared to ignore.

Personally, though, I've never mastered one dubious art at which Sarah's late father, old Erskine Cromwell, was truly accomplished. When he wished, Erskine could ignore anything. He treasured nothing but what he could buy, and regretted only what he couldn't. When Erskine woke up of an A.M., it was merely to a good breakfast. He carried no mortal baggage with him. He just ate.

But when I woke up that Sunday, it was different. Like Miss Plumb, I brought my old friends with me, and my old enemies too, and a nice dirty business it got the bunch of us into before we were done.

At the moment, though, I lay in bed pouting. Here I was, still smarting over Cliff Munson's rejection of the new book, and no Sarah to bully me out of it. I wanted her at home, you see, but neither of us is much of a hand at emotional blackmail, and I was determined to let her make the choice entirely freely. If she had to be off on another concert tour, so be it. Still, I ask you. There she was, in some chilly hotel bed up in Windsor, Ontario, and here was Yours Truly, Winston Marlowe Sherman, her faithful companion for going on thirty years of unwedded bliss, lying around with cold tootsies. It didn't seem to make much sense.

The TV was already blaring from the guest room when the phone rang. I lurched from the bed like a startled rhino and went thumping down the hall to answer it. "Mickey," I yelled through the guest room door, "turn that thing down; I'm on the phone!"

At last I grabbed the receiver and yelled "Hello? Sarah? Hello?" But all I got was the doleful buzz of the dial tone. "Blast Erskine," I growled, and banged the receiver down. Who else would've built a house where you've got to run the quarter mile just to pick up the telephone?

The TV seemed to be getting louder by the minute. "I am Earthman," it announced. "My mission is to prevent the Zarnags from surrounding Dr. Unitas and his semi-human assistant, Blotto—"

"For pity's sake, kiddo," I said, bursting through the door, "I thought they only ran *quiet* nonsense, like *Meet the Press*, on Sundays. Turn that thing down before you wake old Merriman." And then I saw the pair of them, my pal Eddie and the kid, cozy as you please, drinking cocoa with marshmallows melting on top and munching toast and raspberry jam. Eddie rents our old servants' quarters downstairs and devotes himself these days to the pursuit of happiness, bad clarinet playing, and crossword puzzles, instead of the teaching of Milton.

"You may come and watch with us, young Winnie," he said, "but you may only grumble during words from our sponsor."

I squeezed onto the bed beside him, nabbed the marshmallow off his cocoa, and began instead to watch Mickey. Not that the kid had any awesome personal charms, mind you. Since he'd pulled in on the Friday-night train, he hadn't managed more than two dozen complete sentences. But he was seventeen, he was my only godson, and I hardly knew him. I should've been his mentor, his Merlin, or at least his Dutch uncle, and I'd muffed the job.

Mickey's mother was Sarah's old friend from Juilliard, Teresa LaMagna, first cellist with the Manhattan Chamber Orchestra and a teacher of some regard at her alma mater. His father, on the other hand, was entirely my fault. If Teresa hadn't met him at our house, invited there as my old friend, John Falkner might never have married her, and the kid might've had a reliable father. Instead he got a prize-winning novelist who'd dried up after one book, drank a bottle of booze a day, and went into public relations for the Danson Foundation instead of writing. When he wasn't flitting around on tours to raise money, John was taping his talk show on PBS.

Eddie read my mind, as usual. "Not much like Johnny, is he?"

"Not to be like John Falkner could only be a blessing," I growled under my breath.

Mickey had Teresa's dark Italian eyes. John's were light hazel, wide and watchful, with a tinge of universal mistrust. Father and son had the same fine soft hair of dark reddish brown, and it kept falling over Mickey's forehead just as John's always did. The kid was growing into his father's height, too, just above six feet, except that John was straight as a rod and Mickey was more like a beanpole in a high wind. His chest caved inward and his narrow shoulders sagged as he leaned toward Earthman. He must've spent an awful lot of time staring at TV, because his skin had a pasty quality, like white paper under bad lights.

"I'm not exactly Daniel Boone myself," I told Merriman later, as we lugged the breakfast stuff downstairs. "But that kid ought to get outdoors more."

"You're sure he's not AWOL from that school of his?" Eddie doesn't approve of boarding schools in general, having himself been incarcerated at Groton during the Dark Ages. "All that sociological babble they trowel out. Problem children, indeed!" He kicked open the kitchen door with a vengeance.

The Wildwood School, from which Mickey had so far run away four times, was over in Jersey, not far from Princeton. If the kid was ever going to get through high school, it would have to be there. He'd tried everyplace else.

"Damn Falkner," I said. "The man was supposed to take Mickey to a Rangers game today and where is he? Off in Philadelphia, swilling booze at some cocktail party."

"Be fair, Winnie," Merriman told me, lighting up his old pipe and wheezing out a cloud of Captain Black. "John gave up the hard stuff three years ago, according to the press."

"You believe everything you read in *VIP* magazine. Anyway, the fact that he isn't a souse doesn't mean he's not a louse. I tried to warn Teresa not to marry the man," I muttered, diving my hands into the dishpan. "Nobody listens to me."

Then the phone rang again and I was about to dash out to the hall still dripping and answer it, when Mickey yelled from upstairs, "I got it, Doc!"

"My," said Eddie, "what a burst of energy! Is Teresa expected to phone from Connecticut, or what woke him up?" Thinking he'd be with Falkner for the weekend, Mickey's Mom had agreed to an out-of-town concert.

"She only said he had a weekend pass and had to be back at school by ten tonight." I peered out the window. "But with all this snow, I doubt if the trains are even running by now."

Mickey loped down the back stairs and came in for a landing. "It's some guy, Doc. I think it's Supernerd."

"Oh no," I groaned. "Tommy. He's been pestering me all week long about that television business." Thomas Van Doren Sheffield, Chairman of Arts and Letters at DeWitt Clinton College, never calls me at home. If he wants to know something, he sends out spies. If he has something to impart, he dictates a memo. But for some reason he was burning for me to appear on John Falkner's TV talk show. The invitation had arrived out of the blue a few weeks ago, and I'd been stalling ever since.

"Why not just do it?" prompted Eddie. "Surely it would boost sales of the new novel." I hadn't told him about my meeting with Cliff. I winced at the mere mention of the thing. Still in rejection-slip shock.

I went grumbling out to the hall and picked up the phone. "All right, Sheffield, what've I done now?"

"I need your help, Winston." I could hear the muffled roar of childish mayhem. Tommy's daughters, Frick and Frack, otherwise known as Tessa and Vanessa, were whooping it up. "It's about the *Bookends* program."

I didn't know how true the story of John's dry-out was, but we'd been feuding since before the divorce, and I had no intention of taking him on in public. "There isn't going to be a program with me on it, Thomas. I thought I told you that on Friday when you cornered me in the john."

"As a—a personal favor? To me?"

Well, our relationship doesn't run to favors, Tommy's and mine. We do deals, not favors. If Tommy wants something badly enough, it means I can roll back his constant *Anschluss* aimed at making me retire. Only some judicious blackmail had gotten him to give me the course I was teaching in mystery fiction. Pale substitute for the Shakespeare I'd made my life's work, but better than the weekly pinochle tournament at the Golden Oldies Club.

"I thought you could just mention the mystery fiction class, you know. That it was my idea for you to come out of semi-retirement and—"

"Your idea?" Now I saw where he was headed. "What're you after, Thomas? Faculty President? Dean of the College? Chancellor?"

"I just want to keep the job I have," he whispered.

"Oh come now, Sheffield. *I* may think you've infused a lot of eyewash into the curriculum with these sci-fi and film worship classes of yours, but—"

"Film Appreciation," he corrected.

"And I know they're cutting the budget. But surely—"

"There's talk of combining us with Social Sciences, Winston. It would be more cost effective, you see. And Leonard Costello, Hilda's husband? As Chairman over there, he'd have seniority. Over me." Hilda Costello is our dowdy High Priestess of Film.

"So you'd be a mere Indian instead of a chief," I said, with a certain relish. The prospect of old Tommy having to take his turn cleaning the grounds out of Mr. Coffee once a week like the rest of the braves was oddly appealing.

"And," he went on in funereal tones, "I'm not in favor with the Board just now."

"Speak up, Tommy. Did you say you're *not* in favor with the Board?"

"That's right."

"But Diana's daddy's on the Board of Trustees!" Lady Di, as she is known among the teepees of the rank and file, is Tommy's wife. And Daddy, we all figured, was the secret of Sheffield's meteoric rise to the Chairmanship. "Well, just put on a nice spread for the old boy. Turn on that Bostonian charm of yours."

"Oh, I wish it were that simple." Then his tone became all business. "I'm sorry, I can't talk anymore now, Winston. I really do wish you wouldn't phone me at home." And he hung up on me!

When I got back to the kitchen, Eddie was excavating my refrigerator. "You know," I told him, "I think Tommy's only running on one cylinder. He just hung up on me!" Eddie fished out some spaghetti and meatballs left from the War of 1812. I dumped them in the trash.

"You got any pizza or anything?" said Mickey. He was draped over a chair, delicately making pills out of a piece of bread.

Eddie looked at the kid, then winked at me. "I vote for pepperoni!" he cried.

"Merriman, if you eat that stuff, you'll be swilling Maalox for a month. Remember Blanche Megrim's Tuna Surprise?" The Divine Mrs. M. was Eddie's landlady, until her Surprise, her Perry Como records, and her eager attentions drove him to hide out with us.

"I shall throw caution to the winds," he declared, "and call the Venice Inn. They deliver, and it'll be entertaining watching that little red truck labor up our hill in the snow."

He went gleefully off to phone and I sent Mickey out for firewood. We were working together on an infant blaze in the huge stone living room hearth, when I took another stab at the Dutch uncle stuff.

"Kiddo, we haven't gotten together in a while. I'm glad you could come up this weekend."

He threw a random log onto the fire. "Sure."

"But I do wish you'd knock off the turtle imitation. I'd like to know you better, but I can't if you keep diving into your shell." I was getting frustrated.

He stood up and kicked a burning twig angrily back into the fire. "Why not just call up the goddamn school and get them to send you out my fucking file or something, okay? Save a little time. They think they know all about me, they ask all these fucking questions and they write this shit down and that's old Mickey, right? So just go read the fucking file and lemme alone!"

His feet were still thundering ferociously up the stairs as Merriman came in. "I thought we were making progress. What on earth have you done to him?"

"Nothing. He takes after his father more than I thought, that's all."

"I think you're scared of Johnny Falkner." He chuckled. "What was it he used to call your Hyde novels? Oh yes. Intellectual breakfast sausages, that was it."

"And I called him a flash in the pan and a performing flea for Andrew Danson. I'm going out in the hall now, to wait for that pizza where there's some peace and quiet," I said, and stalked out.

"Winston," Eddie called after me. "Do remember, there's something to be said for an absolutely perfect breakfast sausage. I'm exceptionally fond of them, myself."

Well, it wasn't long before peace and quiet were getting on my nerves and I found myself thinking of old Hyde and the book again. Though I wouldn't admit it to Cliff, I rather missed the old boy myself, not to speak of those civilized Gilded Age crimes of his. I could almost see him coming languidly up our drive, clad in opera cape and topper and twirling his gold and ebony cane. "Oh, take a hike, you old fraud," I said aloud.

And then I saw a real man coming up the drive, all

right, but it certainly wasn't G. Winchester Hyde. I hadn't seen him in years, but I knew him instantly. It was Mickey's father, John Falkner.

His feet clumped deliberately on the thick snow. He had broken his ankle as a kid and the bone had knit badly, leaving one leg slightly shorter than the other. He wore a built-up shoe to compensate, and the only thing you noticed was that he seemed to have a fear of falling, even on perfectly level ground. He was still slim, but broad in the shoulders and strong-chested, his stern bearing keeping his back very straight, the wide shoulders well back, and the head resolutely up. He wore a fashionably long, dark gray wool overcoat which was plainly expensive and perfectly cut. A red silk scarf at the neck showed just a flash of careful white collar and dark tie. There was no hat even in this blizzard, and his hair, not yet entirely gray at the age of fifty-seven, was stuck to his forehead with the wet, heavy flakes that carpeted the shoulders of his coat.

I, on the other hand, was still looking fetching in blue paisley pajama costume missing two buttons on the tummy, brown and red Tartan dressing gown with matching iron-on patches at each elbow—worn flapping open because I lost the belt in 1974—and balding corduroy bedroom slippers, run down on the sides. To top it off, my chicken-feather hair was still standing up from my night's resentful slumbers, and I hadn't shaved since Friday. I never do on weekends when Sarah's out of town, and who shaves in the middle of a blizzard, anyway?

"Merriman," I yelled, "get out here!"

"You rang, O Master?" He came scuffling out, opera slippers slapping.

"It's Falkner. He's halfway up the drive, dammit. I'm going upstairs."

"To shave, I presume?"

"No, not to shave. To disappear. You talk to him."

"Oh no you don't! This is your feud, you can stay down here and conduct it on your own. But he's staying to lunch with the neutral powers. I ordered a *large* pizza." And he opened the door to reveal me to John in all my glory.

Falkner paused a moment out on the terrace steps,

looking me over, pale eyes narrowed. "We got snowed out up in Philly," he said with a brief smile. I noticed a small cut on his upper lip. "Nobody showed up, so I thought I'd swing by and pick up the kid." Uncertainly, he offered me a gloved hand. "How are you, Winston?"

"You might as well come in," I said, "before we have to shovel out the front hall." And thus, unwillingly, I let John Falkner back into my life.

Later, over soggy pizza and a disreputable salad, John suggested driving Mickey back to school himself.

"And have you wrap my godson around a telephone pole in that flashy Jaguar of yours? Where is the thing, anyway, having itself polished by Nubian slaves? I didn't see it in the drive."

"You couldn't drive a reindeer up to this house, Winnie, it's buried in snow," said Eddie, kicking me under the table. "No. You'll stay here for the night, and by morning perhaps it will have let up. Surely the school will understand if you telephone?"

John looked over at Mickey and smiled ruefully. "Teresa's word is law over there. I'm pretty much a fifth-rate power."

"She told them not to believe him, whatever he says," Mickey snapped. "She didn't have any fucking right to do that."

"Mickey!" John said sharply. "She had a right." He paused, then went on with quiet amusement. "And if you want to use obscene language, do at least improve your vocabulary, will you?"

I had to bite my tongue to keep from laughing. Damn the man. Sometimes I still liked him. He turned to me. "If *you'd* phone them, Winston? Otherwise, I really think we *can* make it back to Manhattan at least."

"This joint should've been a hotel anyway, we've got enough empty rooms up there. Pick one."

So I capitulated with a bad grace and phoned the school, leaving name and phone number. The snow was getting finer by mid-afternoon, when I trudged up to my study, known to us as Prospero's Cave, to mark a dismal batch of essays. After a couple of hours, I wasn't surprised to look up and see Falkner watching me from the door. The gold pin had come out of his perfectly knotted tie, the tie itself dangled from his pants pocket, the built-up shoes were somewhere downstairs, and the coat was nowhere to be seen.

"Even smells the same up here," he said, sniffing. "Old Scotch, musty books, pencil shavings. Those Turkish cigarettes of yours." He smiled. "That was a hint, you know."

I offered him the packet and he limped cautiously into the room. It was dim and quiet, except for the snow blowing off the roof now and then and pelting the long rank of narrow windows. John's lighter flared in the shadows as he lit one of the Turkish Delights and sat down in the springless armchair beside my Commodore Vic-20. He exhaled with satisfaction and patted the old Commodore. "Don't tell me you've been converted to these damn things."

"Gift from the faculty. Inducement to retire."

"You?" He flashed the smile I'd grown not to trust, having seen him perform it for too many publicity pictures. Then, suddenly, it was gone. "How's my boy, Winnie?" he said soberly. "What's he like?"

"Why ask me?"

He ignored the question. "Is he tough enough?"

"For what?"

"To take what's coming to him."

"As we all do."

"Do we?"

"'The gods are just.'" I quoted the old Bard.

"Some of them. Some of them are on the take. I'd like Mickey to know the difference."

"I assume," I said, "that you set this up. Mickey's pass, your canceling out, suggesting me, then popping in. You invented the whole thing, didn't you?"

"I wanted him to get to know you. Anything wrong with that?"

"No. But the last time I invited him up here, you told me I was trying to alienate the kid's affections."

He spat out a crumb of tobacco. "I was probably drunk." Suddenly his fist smashed down onto the spineless keys of the Commodore. "Damn it, Winston. You sit here holed up in your den. Don't judge me, all right?" He got up and paced in front of my bookshelves, finally coming to rest at the long windows, the palms of his hands flat against the cold glass, his back to me.

"It's not a matter of judgment. I just don't think it's too smart to trust you."

"Because of what happened eight years ago?"

When Mickey was nine, John and the boy had set out to put a hundred bucks in the bank for Mickey's college fund. It was a routine invented by Teresa to get John alone with the boy at least once a week. When he wasn't traveling, John usually hid out with his bottle in the study. The story was that he was writing The New Novel, but that had been going on for years with no tangible result. Anyway, off they went to the bank, but instead of putting in the hundred, they drew out all four thousand. Next thing Teresa knew, she got a phone call from the Security boys at Kennedy Airport. They'd found her small son wandering around the Departures Building all by himself. Falkner was gone, the four thousand bucks were gone, and Mickey hadn't eaten since the previous night's dinner.

"I never know, do I, when you'll be phoning me from Tegucigalpa again?" I said. When he'd finally surfaced in Honduras, it'd been me John called to wire him the funds to get home. He could've got the plane fare from the Dansons, who seemed to feel these binges enhanced his publicity value, but for some reason he always came to me. It was the last straw. I'd sent the plane fare, and that was the final contact I'd had with John, except for the check he sent me two weeks later. I mailed a formal receipt, marked Paid in Full.

"All right. Don't trust me. That's even better." He spun round to face me, on the attack. It was a trick he'd perfected on TV. "Just be sure it's not the fact that I got the Pulitzer. Nor the fact that I have a real son, not a leftover kid they let me borrow and bring up." He was referring to David, of course, Sarah's younger brother, whom Sarah and I brought up after his mother took a powder when he was three. "A pseudo-wife you never married. And those pseudo-novels, those little formula whodunits you crank out year after year. You know you could do more." He flashed me that daring rotogravure smile again. He knew it drove me nuts. "You've never come near reality, have you? What are you afraid of?"

"Sarah is not a pseudo-anything, Falkner. Nor is David. And for your information, reality doesn't consist in the possession of vetting papers." I stopped for breath. "As for the books, I don't take advice from an author who wrote himself out by the age of twenty-nine and had to turn himself into a pitchman. Know what I think? I think you only got that Pulitzer for *The Human Abstract* because old Si Murdoch from Iowa City got himself on to the Prize Committee that year. And what's more, I think *you* think so too. You always have. You never believed you deserved that prize, and you haven't been able to write a book since."

The amber eyes never wavered. "It was a damn good book, though. Wasn't it?"

"Of course it was. What's that got to do with Pulitzer Prizes?" I had to look away from those eyes. "Why don't you prove me wrong? Write another one."

"I'll send you the manuscript. You ought to have it by Friday."

"I don't believe it. It doesn't exist." But I *wanted* to believe him.

"Read it on Saturday. Come on the show Sunday night and give the world your opinion."

"An old sausage grinder like me? Have you considered that I might just blow you out of the water from spite?"

He looked squarely at me. "No. Not for a minute."

"Of course I'll read it, then. Glad to."

"What about the show?"

"No, there I draw the line. No TV."

"Too bad. I wish you'd agreed. Please don't forget that."

He walked off down the long dark hall, footsteps a little unsteady in his stockinged feet. Night had closed in on us and I hadn't bothered switching on a lamp. I did so now and poured myself a hefty Haig and Haig, letting it attack my tongue before I swallowed. I was thinking of John's mother, Louise, and her old house where I'd rented a room while I did my graduate work at Iowa City. It was years before I met Sarah, and Louise Falkner's French-Canadian accent had seemed terribly exotic to an Iowa kid like me. After forty years of teaching high school French, Louise had died, oh, years ago now. I had loved her and walked away, and unlike Sarah, she had let me go without a fight. But suddenly I missed her, as I did all of us. I took another consoling swallow of booze and then I heard a sound out in the hall. Mickey sidled in, eyeing the Commodore.

"Mine's a Mackintosh," he said. "It can do a lot more stuff. That one's not state-of-the-art anymore."

"Well, neither am I."

He fiddled with the keys. "I just wanted to say good-bye, Doc. Didn't mean to act like a shit this morning."

"But you're not leaving till tomorrow."

"Dad's taking me out. Dinner and a movie." He still hung suspended. "This place? I figured it'd be the pits, you know. But it's okay. It's cool." He flashed me an exact replica of his father's on-camera smile. "Maybe next time I come, you'll have MTV, huh?"

Well, they took off soon afterward, and I waited around for Sarah to call. About eleven the phone finally rang. I thudded out to the hall and picked it up. "I tell you, old lady, we've got to put some more phones in this joint," I panted.

"You old fox," said a mushy male voice. Sheffield again! "I just wanted to thank you. *You* know." I could hear Diana, lead soprano of the Faculty Wives' Music Society, tuning up in the background. They were determined to subject us to an all-girl *My Fair Lady* in a few weeks. Tommy kept his voice down. "The *Bookends* program. I knew you'd give in."

"What do you mean, give in?"

"Weren't you watching? They announced it quite emphatically at the end of the show. 'Next Sunday's guest will be Winston M. Sherman, otherwise known as Henrietta Slocum, author of the Winchester Hyde mysteries.' And

Winston? I know you'd like the Shakespeare section back next term. I'll—well, I'll see what I can do. In return."

"But Tommy, I didn't agree to—"

"Have to have your little joke, don't you? You old fox!" And he chortled and hung up on me again.

Well, if Falkner thought he could paint me into a corner that easily, he had another think coming. I was rather looking forward to matching wits with him when he got back. Eddie toddled off to his quarters and I settled down in front of the living room fire to hone my wits. I lay back on the couch, sinking into the sags graven by my posterior over the years, and promptly fell asleep.

When I came to, Merriman was yanking me by the big toe. "Get up, Winnie!"

"Whatsamatter? Sarah? They called from Canada?"

"Nobody's called, that's the whole trouble. It's nearly four A.M. and John and Michael aren't back from dinner yet." He sat down by the embers of our fire. "And Winston, there's something else. Mickey's traveling bag? It's gone as well. It would appear they've taken a powder, the pair of them."

"Oh no," I groaned. It looked like Tegucigalpa all over again.

Chapter Three

The blizzard wore on. There were no classes the next day. Trains, planes, and buses had stopped running by noon on Sunday, and all the highways were closed. There seemed no way John could've got Mickey out of Ainsley, but they were gone, the pair of them. I'd had to phone Teresa, who was stuck in Connecticut, and tell her the news. "You okay?" I asked when I'd finished my tale.

I could hear her drag at a cigarette and exhale, then breathe in again. Funny. I was sure she'd given up smoking more than three years ago. "I ought to be used to this garbage by now," she said.

"I'm sorry, kiddo. It's my fault."

"I married the bastard, you didn't. What did he say to you, Winnie?"

"Talked about the new novel."

She laughed, a short, sharp bark. "There is no novel. We got married on that myth, remember? 'Once we're married, I'll be able to write.'"

"He was going to mail me a copy."

"When pigs can fly. He's taken the kid on another joy ride, is all." She inhaled deeply once more. "If he leaves Mickey high and dry again, I'll kill the sonuvabitch. I swear to God I will."

"I think we should hire someone," said Eddie. We were sitting at the kitchen table that afternoon, staring at the peanut butter jar. "I realize John is your friend and the son of your first love, and you don't want the police involved except as a last resort. But there are private detectives in life as well as fiction. Hire one, and I'll pay his price myself."

I dipped a Ritz in the Skippy and crunched it vengefully down. Nobody seemed to think I was suited for solving crimes. "Yes, all right. What does Lance Carmichael pay you for that remedial tutoring, about ten bucks a week?" Lance is a kid of the football persuasion, known to his fans as The Bulldozer. "What kind of gumshoe do you think you can get at that rate? I, on the other hand, work cheap. I didn't do so badly with that missing manuscript last spring, did I?"

"*We* didn't do so badly. But that was on our home ground, and I am not prepared to go cackling off to Honduras."

"What I don't understand is how they got out of town at the time they left here. Everything had shut down."

"I don't suppose you remember what time it was, naturally?" Merriman remembers the color of his socks on the first day of kindergarten; I, on the other hand, write notes, stick them in my pants pockets, and run them through the Maytag.

"I do," I said smugly. "It was seven-thirty, because I told John he'd have to eat fast to catch the eight o'clock show down at the Orion."

"Which he had no intention of catching." Eddie got up and went into his small sitting room off the kitchen, to return with legal pad and Bic pen. "Let's stick to good Winchester Hyde procedure. Make a list."

"Hyde is dead, dammit."

"So is Napoleon, but his Code lives on." He wrote down my first question and added another. "How did they get the boy's suitcase out of here without our seeing it?"

"Because it never was a suitcase, you fossil. Kids don't carry suitcases anymore. It was a nylon backback. Park-bench green."

"You're right, Hyde," he said. "Oops. Sorry. Rest in peace. At any rate, he could've strapped it on under his jacket. He was wearing one of those down-filled articles that make one into the Michelin Man, and thin as he is, we'd hardly have noticed a bit of extra padding."

"Was there ever a meeting in Philly, and did John duck out on it, send somebody in his place, or what? And he must've had luggage. Where did he leave it?"

"We'll try phoning the motels, but I doubt he'd stay in one of them," said Merriman. "As for Philadelphia, why not call his secretary at the Danson Foundation?"

I shook my head. I had more questions than I could possibly write down. "If John was going to nab Mickey, why not directly from the Wildwood School? Why here? He seems to want to involve me in his life again, Eddie. But why? I mean, that invitation to his TV show, for instance. I'm hardly in the league of the boys who show up there, am I? Arthur Miller, Saul Bellow, John Fowles. Those are the big boys, Merriman. And then he materializes here. I keep feeling as if I've been set up. I don't think he ever left this town. I think he's sitting on sombody's doorstep, having a good giggle. He wants to plague me, nudge me into something." I paused, somewhat reluctant to admit the rest of it. "But it's more than that. Up in the Cave yesterday? He wanted me to like him again. He wants to matter to me."

"And does he?"

"Yes. Dammit. Yes."

Eddie smiled. "What he's done to you, young Winnie, is to provide a mystery you can't resist. And he wants you to solve it on national television. Otherwise, why corner you into appearing?"

"Well," I growled, "it's working. I'm going to *be* on that show. I just hope he turns up himself."

By that night I still hadn't heard from Sarah. I tried her hotel in Windsor, and then Toronto, her next stop on the tour. But all I got at the Royal York Hotel was a polite Canadian voice saying, "Sorry, sir, Miss Cromwell's just gan oot."

Oot, was she? And not still oot, but just gan oot, at something past one A.M. What the devil was she up to? To tell you the truth, I was getting infernally sick of mysteries. Why hadn't I cranked out a nice uncomplicated bodice-ripper years ago instead of messing around in the snoop trade? What's more, I really missed my long subconscious chats with old Hyde. Eddie was asleep remarkably early for him, and I didn't want to wake him up, but I needed *somebody* to talk to. So I dialed the number of Sarah's brother David, back in Manhattan on hiatus from his TV series and shooting a film.

"Know anybody in Toronto, kiddo?" I asked him.

"A couple of people. Why?"

"Does Sarah know them?"

"No. They're theater types. Is anything the matter?" He sounded well and truly pooped. I shouldn't have called.

"Oh nothing. Just a midnight brainstorm." I told him about Mickey and John. "Do me a favor, will you, Davy? Ask around. See what you can learn about the Danson Foundation, how they operate."

"I thought you knew Andrew Danson."

"I met him years ago. When Hyde was in his heyday, Danson invited Sarah and me on one of those Hudson River cruises on his boat. You know how queasy I get on the water. Don't remember much else, not anymore."

"Maybe Sarah will. Why don't you ask her?"

"Yes," I grumbled. "If I can catch her."

During that night the snow stopped at last. The next day, Tuesday, passed in grading papers, since I had no Tuesday-Thursday classes, and another Toronto call that night got the same old response. Oot. It was nearly midnight and the wind was roaring in gusts up to sixty miles per hour when Eddie and I convened in my Cave with cups of steaming cider to lick our wounds and compare notes.

"According to Lance," he said, "no motelkeeper in Ainsley remembers anybody like Falkner, and certainly no Jaguars."

"What's The Bull got to do with this?"

"Oh. I assigned him to make all those boring phone calls. Fine exercise in verbal communication." He looked out at the blowing snow and shivered. "I don't see how the man got out of here. I tell you, I believe Johnny's a ropedancer."

"According to his secretary, that conference in Philly was real all right, and it wasn't canceled because of the storm. They still think he's there. Not due back till tomorrow some time. He had a reservation on Eastern's six o'clock flight Friday evening. Miss Plumb confirmed it herself. Pompous old twit. Sounds like the type who wears jackboots to the office and invades small countries on her lunch break."

"More rope tricks," said Merriman.

"What are you talking about?"

"Ropedancing," he said. "Levitation. When I was a little boy, back around the dawn of time, there was a circus that came through our town and in one of the sideshows was an Eastern gentleman who danced a rope. He would balance that rope on thin air and dance along it till the rope ran out, and when it did, he would dance for a while on the air itself. And at last he would simply disappear."

"And did he ever reappear?"

"I don't believe so," he said thoughtfully. "Perhaps he wasn't good enough at the dance." He was silent for a moment. "I do hope John is good enough for two."

Next day, the first of February, I sat up in my old coffin-shaped office on the third floor of Arts and Letters, smoking a Turkish Delight and listening to our Pakistani English-for-Foreign-Students man, little Krishnan Ghandour, on the subject of our chairman, Tommy Sheffield.

"A gentleman in his situation. Most improper, surely. The lady in Women's Studies, Miss Barnes-McGee. A terrible scandal." Krish frowned into his coffee mug.

"I'm surprised at you, Krishnan. Gossip isn't your style."

His great eyes opened wide. "Not gossip, sir. Fact, I am most afraid. Everyone on the faculty has been aware for months."

"Oh, I think you're making something out of nothing, the whole bunch of you. What could it amount to? A shared bowl of broccoli bisque in the Faculty Cafeteria?" Tommy didn't have the nerve for flaming infidelity.

"You know my feelings concerning the sanctity of the wedded condition, sir." He made it sound like a bad case of scurvy. Ever since Krish started his continuing search for a suitable wife, he never stops telling us how he feels. "And the two little girls, of course, very sad also. What shall be done with them, now that there will be divorce?"

"You mean Lady Di's actually filed for divorce?"

"Indeed. A most trying business, sir. Most sad. I feel it deeply."

After he trotted off to his final class of the afternoon, I settled down to make some notes, but my heart wasn't in it. I sat smoking and thinking. The pale winter sky peered in my window past the steel boxes they've filled our campus with, and I had a pang of nostalgia for the brick and white frame of Iowa, the wide sky and the fields disappearing beyond imagination. And then I was suddenly yanked out of my Edenic dream by Sheffield's voice in the hall.

"I think I ought to be with you. I mean, it's bound to be a shock, at his age."

"Shoo, Thomas." Merriman's voice.

I yanked the door open. "What's happened? It's Sarah, isn't it?"

"Be still, Winnie. Sarah has nothing to do with this." Eddie marched into the office, almost giving Tommy a nose job as he firmly closed the door in Our Leader's face. "Now," said Merriman. "Pour me a sizable whiskey out of that secret stash of yours. You may have some too. But not too much, because we have work ahead of us."

As I poured the stuff into our coffee mugs, I got a look at him. Eddie's generally a dapper little fellow who fancies Fair Isle sweater vests and gold watch fobs and things, and he's never appeared to my knowledge without his few hairs neatly combed. But here he was, wearing earmuffs over hair that stood almost straight up. He'd pulled off a ski mask, the kind the stickup artists favor, and another stocking cap dangled out of the pocket of one of his jackets. He was wearing three, so far as I could reckon, and at least one of them was mine, about eight sizes too large for him. "What're you got up for?" I said.

"This? Oh. Well. I had to hitch a ride over here with

young Lance, didn't I?" He pulled off the earmuffs and smoothed his hair.

"But The Bull rides a—"

"Motorcycle. My. Yes." And he downed the Scotch in one gulp. "Listen, Winston. Teresa's mother just phoned. We're needed in Manhattan. I've arranged with Tommy to drive us home for some things and then to the station. There's a train at half-past four we can just manage, if we're quick about it."

"Something happened to Mickey?"

"No. Mickey hasn't been heard from. No, Winnie. I'm afraid it's John. Wish there were some delicate way to put this. But there's nothing delicate about it. He's dead, Winston. Most brutally dead."

Chapter Four

Yuppification has made a lot of changes in Manhattan. The few remaining brownstone apartment buildings in midtown have been bought up by agents and producers as live-in tax write-offs. Old theatres and monuments of New York architecture have been totaled and replaced with towering versions of the Palais de Versailles, where the high rollers can stay above it all and let the rest of us eat cake. The pushcart vendors don't even bother to pause outside these stomping grounds of the mutual-funded, and the constant travelers with cardboard stuffed in their shoes blow past like yesterday's newspapers, to collect in what's left of the old New York.

Stuyvesant Hall is part of the old. To Teresa, it's more or less a second home. Stuyvesant Hall is the permanent base of the Manhattan Chamber Orchestra, in which she plays her cello. At the back of the Hall, reached by an alley entered from Thirty-eighth Street, is the Musicians' Entrance. Above and beside this basement-level doorway there's a concrete loading dock sloping up to the huge doors where deliveries are made at the back of the concert stage. In winter a canvas canopy stretches from the side of the loading ramp to the portico of the Musicians' Entrance, protecting the performers from the raw wind that roars down between the buildings. Under the canopy, late at night and in bad weather, live perhaps a half dozen oddly-assorted men and women. Rolled up in discarded carpets, closed into refrigerator cartons, they take turns over the steam vent from the boilers in the sub-basement, preferring their chances here to the murky warrens of the welfare hotels. Mostly they come and go with the weather, but Teresa, who arrived two hours early for her afternoon rehearsal that Wednesday, could've told you the names of all the regulars.

She'd left her mother Bea at home to mind the phone in case Mickey called. Mostly, though, he didn't. Like his father, he would stay away for days, hanging out with some friend whose parents were away or paid no attention, and then turn up on his mother's doorstep when he got bored.

As usual, Teresa had hardly slept; maybe some time alone with her cello in the practice cubicle she rented upstairs would calm her nerves. It was a cinch the cigarettes weren't helping. She was glad when Sugar George, one of the regular residents, came out to meet her.

"Where you been, Sugar?" she said. "You get busted again? I haven't seen you in a while." Sometimes he got into fights and wound up on Riker's Island. She didn't like thinking of him penned up.

"I been around," he said, his usual chatty self.

Sugar George was just past forty, like most of the Nam vets were by now. Under his camouflage jacket and a couple of layers of old sweaters, he was long-boned and muscular; his hair was dark and thick, whacked off unevenly just below his ears, and his eyes were round and light brown and absent, as if some part of him were still traveling. He was very strong and moved quickly, using his single crutch with skill. Sugar was missing the lower part of his left leg, and his left sleeve was pinned up at the elbow. He never spoke about what had happened to him, though everybody assumed it had been Da Nang or maybe the Delta.

"You're early today," said Teresa. During the day he was usually out "canning," collecting the aluminum cans he sold for sixty-five cents a pound to supplement his income from odd jobs. Sugar George wanted nothing to do with the welfare net. Nets in general weren't his cup of tea.

"Been here a hour already," he said. His accent was Louisiana or East Texas. He didn't talk about that either. "Too damn cold for reg'lar folks."

"Okay," she said briskly. "I got oranges today. You guys need your vitamin C." She gave him the red net bag of waxy fruit she was lugging. "What about green stuff?" Some lettuce, you want some lettuce tomorrow when I come down?"

"Nah. That salad bar down to McDonald's, they throw out real good stuff, if you don't sit around on your tail too long."

"They catch you digging in garbage, Sugar, they'll bust you." It was best not to work the Dumpsters at the chain restaurants, she knew. They threw out more, but they were quicker to complain to the cops or Social Services. They seemed to resent the salvaging of what they threw away, as if it were a personal insult. "You and Sonny come up to my place, I'll cook lasagna. Does Sonny like Italian?"

"Sonny and me," he said quietly, "we don't go uptown much." He took the bag of oranges from her and hooked it over his crutch.

Teresa watched him work his way through the alley, manipulating the crutch through the piles of snow more surely than she could move in her stylish, silly boots. She wondered, as she always did, what life he had cut loose from, and whether anyone had noticed him go. "My kid," she said abruptly.

Sugar stopped moving and she went on. "John took him on another binge. They've been gone since Sunday night."

"They'll be back."

"Maybe."

"They're reg'lar folks, like you. Gotta be someplace. Some people born to travel in this world, and some born to be someplace."

Teresa reached into her purse for change. "Sugar, you call me. Please. If you ever need something."

He only looked at her. "Thanks for the oranges, ma'am," he said, and walked away, leaving the coins in her hand. When the others gathered for the night, he would pass out the fruit, laughing softly to himself with pleasure, making sure Sonny got the biggest of the bunch. Sonny was tall, as slender and dark-haired as his friend. He went in and out of vets' hospitals and mental health clinics, and when he did, Sugar always disappeared for a while too, to hang out near whatever hospital it was this time, till they kicked Sonny loose.

Teresa hoped she hadn't made Sugar angry, offering him money. His pride was attached at random, and what scraps were left lurked in odd, unexpected places. His anger, though, stayed close to the surface. He'd been busted for battery a number of times, mostly when somebody pushed Sonny around. Sugar wielded that crutch like a deadly weapon as he danced on his one sound leg, defending his friend. Sonny got them into trouble with his poetry. He would stand on street corners reciting his poems, and if he picked the wrong corner he'd become the focus of a brawl. Sometimes he recited in English and sometimes in other languages, tongues he invented as he went along. It was then that he got checked into the vets' for a stay. Now Teresa remembered that she'd promised to bring him her old paperback of *Selected Poems of John Donne*, and she'd forgotten to give it to Sugar. That was why he'd been so anxious and so early, and why he'd stalked off that way. You couldn't forget Sonny if you wanted to keep right with Sugar George.

As Teresa picked up her cello and started for the entrance, a truck pulled into the alley and backed up to the loading ramp. On the side was a bar of musical notes and the name FREILING INSTRUMENTS. Two men got out and opened the rear doors of the truck. All she could later recall about the first man was that he was in his thirties, hefty, and wore a bushy brown moustache. The second man she knew. He was about fifteen years older, with a small, neat beard and short-clipped gray hair. His name was Andreas Freiling; she'd bought one of her cellos from him a few years ago. "Hello," she said.

Freiling looked up. "I beg pardon?" His voice seemed too loud. My God, she thought sadly, he's going deaf. To a man like Freiling, who hand-made and tuned some of the best baroque harpsichords and violoncellos outside Europe, deafness would be a brutal blow. Teresa raised her voice slightly.

"You don't remember me. I bought my cello from you. It's a wonderful instrument."

Freiling's scowl of concentration relaxed into a smile, and he bowed slightly. She'd remembered those fine Viennese manners that made him seem older than he was. "Ah, good. *Sehr gut.* Is a good cello?"

"Wonderful," she repeated. "Those are the instruments for Sunday's concert?" The younger man was unloading several crates, two smaller ones and one rather large, piano-sized, with which he needed Freiling's help. He kept his eyes averted from Teresa as she went on. "That's the harpsichord, isn't it? We've all been told how fine the tone is."

"Yes," he said. The younger man touched his arm impatiently. "Is good you like the cello, madame." And Andreas Freiling turned away. Teresa heard the strings inside the box jangle slightly as they moved the heavy crate toward the stage doors.

They were just wheeling it in as she stopped to shove the John Donne book into the old roll of carpet where Sonny usually slept. Then she made her way into the building. Inside the Musicians' Lounge, she took off her coat and put some coffee on to perk, then sat down on the cracked plastic couch to dig out her list of phone numbers. Since Sunday, she'd been telephoning everybody she could think of who might've seen her son. She made a routine of it when he ran away. So far it'd been no use, but she didn't intend to quit. She wondered how long it would take before she quit staring at faces that passed in bus windows, just in case they were Mickey.

"The hell with that," she said out loud, shaking off the mood. She lugged her cello out into the dimly lighted hall and punched the freight elevator button. Up in her practice room she would be free for a while.

The elevator ground to a stop and she pulled open the ancient steel grille. The doors inside were stuck, as usual. "Damn," she said. She laid the cello case down on the tiles and locked the grille open so she could pry the inner doors apart with her hands. When she got them open, she locked them and turned to pick up her cello. As she bent down, she got a clear view of what was inside.

A man's body was slumped against the back wall. He

lay on his side, the left arm bent backward under him. His legs were grotesquely crooked. His right arm lay flat on the floor, palm upward. There was not much blood, except along the right side of the head and at the corner of the wide, straight mouth. There, a dark stream of blood had stained the chin, the throat, the bright red silk scarf, and the lapel of the expensive gray overcoat. There was a long tear in the right coat sleeve. John Falkner's brown hair was matted with blood and dirt, but the green-gold eyes were wide open. Teresa hadn't the heart to brush them shut. It seemed the worst kind of insult. She merely sat down on the floor beside him and took his right hand, from which the rigor had already retreated. They must've sat that way together for a quarter of an hour before Ernie the janitor, his soap opera over, came out into the hall. It was Ernie, rather than Teresa, who first noticed that John was wearing neither shoes nor socks.

When the preliminary examination was conducted by the Medical Examiner's office, it was found that John's legs were broken in four places. There were seven breaks in the spine and ribs. The heart, lungs, and liver were crushed, and the skull fractured, though the face was reasonably undamaged. The bloodstream contained a hefty percentage of alcohol, as if he'd drunk at least a bottle of liquor not long before he died. In his coat pocket was a small gold-framed photograph, but there was no indication whatever of the whereabouts of his son Mickey.

Once Eddie'd told me everything he'd learned from Bea, the pair of us hardly spoke on the train into New York City. He sat beside me absently sucking on the pipe which the anti-smoking militia forbade him to light up. It made a dry, vacant sound, and he jabbed it into his vest pocket. "I didn't leave a message on the answering machine at home," he said at last. "Didn't want Sarah finding this out from a tape recording."

"She's probably heard about it already, wherever the hell she's hidden herself. By now it's all over the radio and TV."

"Oh yes," said Eddie. "The news hounds will be barking over this."

And we were both right. It was getting dark as we got out of a cab in front of Teresa's place on Seventy-sixth Street off Central Park West, but a number of people were still hanging around the steps. A young woman with round pink plastic glasses and frostbitten knees under a sausage casing of designer skirt stuck a mike in my face.

"What's your name? Are you a relative?" she demanded.

"My name is Ozymandias, King of Kings." I gave her my inscrutable Chessie Cat grin.

But Ms. Knees wasn't exactly up on her Percy Bysshe Shelley. "Mr. Mandias," she said into her mike, "what exactly is your relationship to the murder of John Falkner? Are you attached to the Police Department?"

"Not particularly," I said.

Eddie was trying to push his way through to the front door, but a kid with a Pentax was too much for him. "Oh for heaven's sake, Merriman," I said. "Come on." And I plowed through them full speed ahead. One of the many advantages of my size is that, like driving a Mack truck, it permits a degree of interpersonal intimidation.

After passing inspection by the cop at the door, we made our way up to Teresa's third-floor apartment. Beatrice, her mother, met us at the door, trailed by a young coplet. In the living room, an older cop was hitching the phone up to two separate tape recorders.

"You know about this stuff, Doc. What's with the two recorders?" Bea asked when we'd made our way to the kitchen.

"They must be hoping for a ransom call about Mickey," I said. "With two machines, they've got insurance."

"But hasn't Teresa informed them about John's escapades in the past?" Eddie poured himself a cup of Bea's strong, bitter coffee and laced it liberally with milk. "The boy may simply have been left behind somewhere, perfectly safe. What do the police think?"

Bea pulled her sweater closer around her, though it must've been ninety-five in there. "Half the time I get the feeling they think she did it herself."

"Nonsense," I said. I stirred three spoonfuls of sugar into my coffee. It didn't help. "Where is Teresa now?"

"In John's study, with the Big Cheese. Lieutenant Duffy." Bea wrinkled her nose. Clearly the man wasn't a popular favorite. "Doc," she said, "Mickey's a little brat sometimes. But he's my grandkid. You figure he's dead?"

She said it bluntly, in a toneless voice. Teresa's tiger cat, Wolfgang, came sauntering in to check us out and Bea swooped him up and sat stroking his back. "Damn cat," she muttered. If you were Bea, you didn't cry. You made coffee, you cleaned the icebox, you cursed the cat.

"There's been no ransom call, no call of any kind?" I asked her.

"Not that the boy's mother's told us," said a voice from the doorway.

Lieutenant Cornelius Patrick Duffy was the sort of fellow who makes me feel like Mount Rushmore when I fall in behind him in the checkout lane. He was small, wiry, and narrow-chested, with thinning peach-colored hair and the squint you get when you buy your contact lenses on sale. His tie was pre-tied, the crease in his double-knit slacks was stitched in, and the leather patches on his jacket were plastic, and peeling just a tad. Either he was a man after my own heart, or the kind who dealt in specious impressions, in which case we were in a lot of trouble here. "You're Winston Sherman," he informed me curtly, in a voice surprisingly big and deep for his size.

"And you, I presume, are the Big Cheese."

"Falkner a buddy of yours?"

"An old acquaintance, yes. Listen, Lieutenant. I think you ought to be told that John has a habit of—"

"Any enemies?"

"A good number, I imagine. Watch his show sometime."

"I have. Guy could be a real shit."

"John was abrasive," said Eddie, handing Duffy a cup of coffee. "He was very bright, imaginative, and his imagination was underused of late. He was opinionated, and that often creates friction. Particularly in the great vanilla spaces

of television. He did not suffer fools gladly. Especially in
official capacities," he added pointedly.

"Who in hell are you?" said Duffy.

"I am a highly informed and helpful taxpayer. Do drink
your coffee."

Duffy took a sip of Bea's coffee without milk or sugar,
blinked, and put the cup down. "Falkner took some pot
shots at you, didn't he?"

"Oh," I said, "I think we were about even in the pot-
shot department."

"WNYT told me you phoned the station Monday all
steamed up. Said he tricked you into being on his show.
That right?"

"John had pulled a fast one. Several. I was on my ear,
but not enough to kill him. Exactly how *was* he killed, anyhow?"

He ignored me as usual. "I'll leave a guy on the door
downstairs for twenty-four hours. The recorders on the
phone are automatic. Just don't use it unless you have to."
And he ambled out without a backward look.

"I believe the lieutenant is a bit automatic himself,"
said Eddie. "High on procedure and low on imagination."

"Maybe. Anyway, I'm phoning Lincoln when we get
over to David's." Detective Lincoln, first name, believe it or
not, Abe, helped us out when our David was attacked by a
deluded knife expert. Since then, I'd had a couple of
lunches with him when I was in town. Like my friend Lloyd
Agate up in Ainsley, Lincoln was a sound cop, a sensible
fellow who didn't mind a little give-and-take if it got the job
done.

When Duffy and his minions had all cleared out, I
went looking for Teresa. I found her in the living room with
a trim, bronzed fellow about John's age. I hadn't seen Andrew Danson since that tummy-churning cruise years ago,
but I recognized him in a minute. He was perched on the
edge of the couch beside Teresa, with his arm draped
around her. His blue eyes were intent on her face, his voice
kept carefully level. The words seemed to come out with a
little push, as if he were forcing himself.

"We're just wiped out, Teresa," he said, "all of us. Ever since the police called this afternoon. You have absolutely no idea how he might've been . . . killed?"

"No."

"John never let me get close to him. But I did respect him. Always. Please believe that. His work was absolutely unique. I always hoped there'd be another novel."

"There is," I said. Danson looked up, startled. I'd been standing in the kitchen doorway for fully five minutes and he hadn't noticed me. For a fellow of my heroic proportions, that's something of a coup.

"A new novel?" he said, smiling uncertainly. "He hadn't told me."

"He wouldn't be likely to, would he, Andrew?" Teresa stood up so as to walk out of his embrace.

He raised an eyebrow somewhat sheepishly. "Probably not, no." He turned back to me. "Haven't we met? I'm sorry but the name escapes me."

"Think of me as Henrietta Slocum."

"Of course. The Winchester Hyde mysteries. You're Winston Sherman. How's that lovely wife of yours? Clara, was it?"

Well, he knew damn well it was Sarah. She'd been at Amherst with Danson's wife Cella, a narrow-hipped, virginal post-post-deb, given, as I recalled, to twin sets and pearls and clumsy flirtations with deck hands. They'd kept up an uncertain correspondence over the years. "Sarah and I never married," I told him. "We're saving it for something to do in our old age."

"You and John were—"

"Old friends. Prehistoric."

He got up. "Teresa, if you need any help with arrangements—"

"Winston's taking care of them."

Danson bent to kiss her on the cheek and I saw her grow tense, braced for it as if he were going to punch her. Then he shook my hand. It was one of those handshakes you get from door-to-door salesmen, missionary preachers, and bookies, the kind that makes you feel they've been to Handshake School.

I let him out and came back to Teresa. It was dark outside as Danson's white limo drove away downstairs, and the block security guard at the Emily Dickinson School across the street was enshrined for the night in his glass-walled booth on the curb. Teresa sat at the piano looking out at him. "Old Harvey's looking for muggers," she said. "You know, I've lived in this city forty-nine years now, and I've never been mugged, never even come close. Now I know how it feels to get hit from behind."

She must, I thought, feel viciously handled. It seemed a conscious personal assault, putting John's body directly in her path. But who had it in for a cello player? "You've gotten it all at once today, kiddo," I said. I sat down on the piano bench beside her, and she fiddled with a chord. "I take it you and Danson aren't bosom pals."

"John didn't like him. Never said exactly why. But John didn't like a lot of people I did. I don't know. Andrew was always like that, like today. Considerate, mild, cultured. But wound too damn tight."

"Anybody hanging around Stuyvesant today? Anybody suspicious?"

"Some men unloading instruments. Nobody out of the way."

"And no one's contacted you?"

She struck a crashing chord. "Including Mick."

"How long since you spoke to John?"

"Thursday night he left a message on my machine, 'Going to Philly, can't take Mickey this weekend, how about Winston?' Friday night there was a blank call on my machine, somebody just let the tape run out. He did that sometimes, it might've been him. That's all."

"I mean really spoken, sat down and talked to him."

She leaned forward against the music rack, her head resting on her arm. "I don't remember. I'm sorry, Winston. I took a couple of sleeping pills. I think I'm zonking out here."

"But you never take sleeping pills," I said, surprised. She'd always shared Sarah's deep aversion to all pills and most doctors.

Her voice was shrill and her breathing sharp when she

replied. "Well, I did tonight, all right? I never had to identify my husband's mashed-up body before, either." She got up and pulled the drapes shut with a whoosh. Then she bent and kissed me on top of my head. "Sorry. I'm just tired. Thanks for coming."

"Like me to bunk on the couch tonight, kiddo?"

"If you slept on that couch all night, Winnie," she said, managing a smile, "I'd have to bring in heavy equipment to get you up in the morning."

And she disappeared into the bedroom, taking along everything I was sure she wasn't telling me about her dead husband and her missing son.

Eddie and I decided to walk the few blocks uptown to David's place on Eighty-ninth. I was tired, but I felt glad of the cold air, the snow scrunching underfoot, and the noise of traffic whizzing along the avenues. I was suddenly wide awake, as I always am in this city. The odd beauty of grimy old Manhattan is that of pure, concentrated energy, by turns violent, able to deaden the mind with unspecified fears, and electric, enlivening as a true and endless mystery. Now that I was here, I had no more doubts about what I had to do. How to do it was another, more complex question.

"You're not going to leave this to Lieutenant Duffy, are you?" said Eddie. "You're plotting to shove your oar in, I can always tell."

"I think," I told him, "it's already shoved."

Chapter Five

"How's Teresa?" asked David as he opened the door for Eddie and me. "I'd have come by, but I assumed the press would be swarming, and I'd only make matters worse." His recovery from the knifing that ruined half his face, plus his return to series TV, has set the news people onto Davy more than ever, and he's always dodging them.

"She's got me worried," I told him. "Knows more than she's telling, but I wasn't about to belabor the point tonight."

"I should hope not," said a voice behind me. It was low and set far down in the alto range, the words precise, with a crisp touch of Amherst. "Teresa's had quite enough today without you and your Sherlock Holmes impressions, you old ninny."

I took off my overcoat, arranged my ratty touring cap on top of it, and counted ten before I turned round. Sarah was ignoring my theatrics, busily pouring coffee for the four of us. Her long braid of dark hair was flipped over the shoulder of her ancient, baggy Aran sweater, the patched chinos rolled up above her shoes as usual. I was damned if I'd ask where she'd been for the past four days.

"Where have you been for the last four days?" she demanded. "I've phoned a dozen times. When you weren't out, it was busy, busy, busy. Oh, I did get that damned answer box, but you know I do not converse with electrical appliances."

Well, she was right, of course. When we weren't checking stations and motels and generally running around

47

like chickens in the rain, we'd been keeping the phone lines pretty busy ourselves. I began to explain, but she stopped me.

"David has just told me all about John's taking off with Mickey. But I was worried, you know. You might've telephoned my hotel."

"I did. You were out. In the middle of the night, no less."

"Oh, that," she said airily. "Who's for toast and sardines? I'm starved."

And I got no more out of her at all. I'd wanted to ask what she remembered of Andrew Danson and his wife Cella. I couldn't say exactly why, but his inordinately speedy condolence visit had struck a jarring note. But when we'd eaten and Eddie and I had told them all we knew about matters so far, Sarah stood up. "Right now, I'm phoning Teresa," she announced, "and then I shall march myself over there and stay the night."

"She didn't want anyone," I told her. "Said she'd taken sleeping pills."

"Ha!" she barked. "Well, that's a bald-faced lie. She was just trying to get rid of you and your questions. No. Whether she wants me or not, she's going to get me, and whatever she's hiding, I'll have it out of her by morning." She stomped off to the phone in the bedroom, with me hot on her heels.

"What about your concerts up north, Sarah?"

"The tour's officially over. I canceled the rest of it the minute I heard about John on the news." She picked up the phone and began to dial.

"I think we need a long talk, old girl."

"Not now. Teresa needs me more than you do tonight. You don't mind, do you, Win?" And in ten minutes she was off and away, whether I did or not.

When I got back to the living room, Merriman was pumping Davy, or trying to. "What's your impression of the Danson Foundation?" he asked. Silence.

David sat nursing a cup of frigid coffee, his long body wrapped round an antique Queen Somebody-or-Other chair which I knew was a gift from his estranged wife Alex.

Usually it serves as a sort of bookshelf, magazine rack, and clotheshorse, but tonight he'd cleared it off, which could only mean that Alex was in town from London and in danger of dropping in. "Kiddo," I said, nudging him with my foot, "you've been on that film set since six A.M. Turn in, and we'll talk in the morning."

He came to, having missed not a word. David's habit of concentration, developed in the midst of noisy rehearsals, is second only to his memory for exact words. "All I really know about the Danson Foundation is backstage chat. They get a lot of matching funds through the National Endowment, and they funnel them out through ten or twelve regional arts groups. They used to have a reputation for taking on total unknowns, and for being completely unbiased about style, content, and so on. But that was under old Randolph."

"The golfomaniac."

"Yes. He completely ignores the Foundation now. It's all changed since Andrew took over. Now you've got to do what Danson perceives as good for the arts in the 1990s."

"Oh yes," said Eddie. "They see themselves as quite the Ministry of Culture. Imbue the public with the true faith of post-modernism and keep on imbuing away till they know what's good for them."

"Meanwhile starving out the dissenters," I said, "and providing a comfy financial cushion for whatever's outrageous enough to impress the papers."

"Exactly," Eddie replied. "A gentleman who draped white sheets across a good portion of the lovely state of Vermont amidst great public outcry received a hefty grant, while a painter of realistic landscapes I know, very good one too, has applied repeatedly for modest sums and had his hands soundly slapped."

I pulled a wad of paper out of my pocket and flattened it out. "Who's this painter fellow?" I waited with pencil poised.

"Me," Eddie said with a grin.

"Well, it's about time you did something with those watercolors of yours."

"Oh, I didn't seriously expect results from the application, only I fancied a little painting trip somewhere would vary my subject matter, you know, and of course I can't afford it on my own chalk." He laughed. "I expect I'm a philistine, but when one thinks of mighty sums invested in cluttering up a lovely view with a lot of laundry and calling it art . . . well, let us say I am not a believer in the Gospel of Danson. It simply has no soul."

"You don't have to be a believer," David said. "Just a temporary hypocrite. Make a loud noise in the press and they'll get behind you."

"Evidently they're interested in publicity, and art only as an incidental," I said.

"A high media profile, as they say, to attract old chaps who're thinking of expiring and leaving their millions to the Danson endowment," said Eddie. "But John was their publicity man. Surely it wasn't his policy?"

"The policy is ego," said David. "Power. Collecting artists is the ultimate acquisitive trip. Trying to control what they do, break them to saddle." He drained his cup of cold coffee. "Sad thing is, it's done all the time. Christ, Michelangelo must've hated the Medici."

"There's one thing you're both forgetting. Publicity is a helluva smokescreen. With enough of it, and a little ingenuity, you can get away with murder," I said.

"You don't seriously suspect the Danson family of John's murder?" said Merriman. "I know you distrust plutocrats and oligarchs on principle, but they're an eminently respectable bunch. Fried chicken fortune, was it?"

"Frozen fried chicken. And I don't know what I suspect. But I've got a job for you, Merriman."

"If you wish me to become a temporary hypocrite, Winnie, there is no such animal. It's like eating peanuts. Once you start, you can't stop."

"Nonsense. You're going to visit the Danson Foundation, that's all. Stumble in, looking confused and doddering. Should be easy for you. Scrape an acquaintance with John's secretary, Miss Plumb."

"The lady who sounds like the Fifth Panzer Division?"

"Eddie ought to go as a prospective contributor," said David.

"Oh yes, people are always more receptive to a man with a hole in his pocket. Old money, I think. Baltimore. I'm disgustingly rich and I collect little-known masterpieces of the German Baroque." Merriman sighed. "Oh very well. But what is our leader planning for himself?"

"I'm going to see John," I said. I couldn't call him The Body. I half expected him to turn up alive and well, phoning me from the other side of the world. Until I saw him, I couldn't really believe in his death.

"I'll go with you, Winnie," said David. "I don't have another call on the film until early next week, when we wrap it up."

"That's not necessary. I can go alone."

He put a hand on my arm. "Let me."

I nodded. I had to admit I wasn't looking forward to that morgue downtown. "Thanks, kiddo. I'll get Lincoln to set it up for us."

"Oh," Eddie piped up all of a sudden. "I nearly forgot. Did you happen to watch John's show on Sunday night, David? It occurred to me there might've been something unusual said or done, considering recent events."

"I had a call that night, exterior they'd been waiting to shoot in the snow. So I missed the show too," said Davy. "But I put it on tape. Haven't looked at it yet."

"Who was the guest, do you know?"

"Shane McAuley, he wrote *Manhattan Underground*. Pulitzer nomination, great stuff with the book reviewers. Can a coked-up egomaniac find true love and a major publisher by networking his way through Danceteria—that sort of stuff. Bloody bore."

"You remember, Winnie, that thin little book? You saw it in B. Dalton and remarked, I believe, that any man who couldn't squeeze more than a hundred and fifteen pages out of a novel ought to be writing for the funny papers." Eddie winked at David. "Isn't young McAuley the boy they call King Brat?"

"Oh yes," I said. "Did John and King Brat have a dust-up?"

"There was something in the Books and People column of the *Times*. Apparently McAuley made quite a scene at some party the Dansons gave on Friday, and Sunday's show with John pretty much capped it," David told me.

"Oh hell," I said, exasperated. "The man made too damn many enemies. Why don't we just put the whole borough of Manhattan on our suspect list? They've probably all been on his show!"

It was getting pretty late by the time I finally telephoned Abe Lincoln at his place over in Queens. He kindly agreed to help out with a call to the morgue for me. "I figured you'd be in town, Doc," he said. "I saw your name in the paper. You were supposed to be on that show of his, weren't you? Too bad."

"He was an old friend, Linc. What can you give me?"

"Not much. I'm on Vice right now. Jeez, I hate Vice." He coughed, as if to hack the nasty taste out of his mouth before he went on. "But I did just happen to call up Cornelius Duffy, though. Just shoot the breeze."

"Oh, naturally. And?"

"The condition the guy was in when they found him, it looked like a car wreck or a fall. There was no glass ground into him, no car paint on the clothes or anything. So Duffy figures a fall. He'd like to have called it suicide or an accident, because of the booze, but somebody sure put the kibosh on that idea. Falkner didn't walk into that freight elevator by himself. He was put there, and that rules out suicide."

"But if they pushed him off a roof, or even if he fell, why go to such lengths to rule out suicide? Surely the killer would want it to look as if John jumped in a drunken depression, so there'd be no investigation."

"You're making one helluva big assumption, Doc. Maybe the killer wasn't the one who moved him."

"A friend who wanted to be sure it wasn't written off as a suicide? But who? Any idea how he was brought to Stuyvesant?"

"There were traces of sawdust and a splinter in his coat, yellow pine. Like the crates from some instruments that were delivered about the time he was found."

"So the delivery men brought him?"

"Maybe. But this old German guy has worked for the Chamber Orchestra for years. Repairs old instruments, builds stuff. A-one reputation in the business and no connection with Falkner. Andreas Freeling, his name is. No, wait. Freiling, F-R-E-I-L-I-N-G. Store over on Third. He's got an alibi for the time Falkner probably died anyway—he was staying overnight out on Staten Island."

"What was the time of death?"

"About two-thirty Wednesday morning. Freiling had this assistant. He had the old guy drop him off at a deli on Seventh after they left Stuyvesant around noon. Hasn't turned up since."

"Name?"

"Duffy didn't cough it up. Listen, Doc, you watch your step, okay? This guy did it once, and in for a penny, in for a pound, know what I mean?"

"In my case, several pounds," I said. But I got the idea.

Back in the living room, David was studying lines for the next shoot in the film. It was all about defectors and spies and secret arms deals, and David played the civilian caught in the middle. I'd read the script; his was the only part worth a hoot, and even that would take fine acting to conceal its predictability. "So, how's it going, kiddo?" I said, plonking down on the couch and putting my weary feet up.

He closed the script. "Eddie's right. Hypocrisy *is* like eating peanuts. I told myself I'd just keep this stuff up till I had enough money, and then go back to the real work." For David, real work was Shakespeare, classical theater. "But look at me. The medical bills are paid, Alex is actually talking about finding a cheaper flat, and here I still am, grinding out action movies and considered top candidate for next King of the Miniseries. I keep wondering if John told himself he'd quit when he had enough. I wonder if there *is* enough."

"You're no hypocrite. You work damn hard and you use your talent whatever you're doing. John buried his in a bottle for twenty-five years and couldn't pull it out again when he wanted it."

"You think the drinking made him stop writing?"

"Which came first, the chicken or the egg? Anyway, I can't be sure he ever really *did* stop." I told him about the new book. "If he got a chance to mail it, it may be waiting for me at home right now. Funny. I ran into Andrew Danson at Teresa's, and happened to mention it to him. Odd reaction. Maybe he's afraid he's one of the characters."

"I never knew John very well," said David. "I only really met him in *The Human Abstract*. It was required reading when I was at Columbia."

"Ah. Required reading. The kiss of death."

"But I loved it . . . He must've been an elusive man. Self-contained."

The kind, I thought, that David liked best to play on stage. I could tell he was getting involved, and remembering what had happened to him the last time we took on a real-life mystery—the knifing, followed by umpteen plastic surgeries and a wife who was still afraid to look at him—I didn't like it. Still, the best way to find out who'd killed John might be to get inside his mind, and I knew nobody could do that better than David.

He tossed the spy script onto the end table. "I want to research him, Winnie. As a part. Absorb him. Find out who he was, what made him tick."

"These people kill people," I said. "I don't want to risk you just because you're bored with this silly movie of yours."

"You don't really think I'm just amusing myself, do you?" He flared up for a moment. "He should've been left alone to work, not made into a media monkey, given that bloody prize before he was ready for it, and bribed into becoming Andrew Danson's tame genius. John was used, Winnie, and now he's been thrown away. I've seen it done too often. It's cheap and insidious and you can fall into it before you even realize. I've had to fight like hell to stay out of that hole myself. It makes me damned angry."

"I only hope," I said glumly, "that somebody hasn't thrown the boy away as well."

Like David, young Mickey Falkner was bored that chilly Wednesday night that began the month of February.

He'd been told to wait for his father's call, but there was no TV and no radio where he was, and nothing to do. He was miles from a newsstand, and he was tired of waiting. It had been three days. He had a telephone, but nobody answered at his father's apartment. There was no subway where Mickey was staying, but there were highways. He tried his father's place once more without success, and made up his mind. Then he did what he always did. Mickey took off.

He stood a long time on the shoulder of the snowy highway with his thumb sticking up before a produce truck headed for Manhattan finally stopped. "What the hell, a kid like you wants to hitch rides?" said the driver, a burly Greek called Demetrios. "You freeze you dumb ass off out here. Get in."

They hurtled along through the dark on the expressway, patches of ice gleaming on the pavement, the Hudson a ribbon of pewter visible now and then as they neared Manhattan and the Henry Hudson Parkway on the West Side. Demetrios had kept up a steady patter, but as they came into the city he fell silent. About 168th he said, "Look kid, you got some people? You got no people, you come home with me. To have no people in this world is lousy crap."

"My mom lives on Seventy-sixth," said Mickey.

The Greek eyed him narrowly. "You fulla crap. I say, what's your name, you tell me Charlie Brown, you think I'm dumb-ass. Charlie Brown is fulla crap."

"Look, just stop a second, I'll get out at Ninety-sixth, I'll walk the rest of the way, that's all I need."

"Nuts," said Demetrios. "My wife is lousy cook, she makes only Lipton soup. You come get some Lipton soup. You got nobody on Seventy-sixth, Charlie Brown."

He pulled up for an off-ramp, turned onto 125th, and squealed his brakes at a stoplight at Broadway. Three cabs whizzed through the light in the lane next to him, and Demetrios waved a fist at them, yelling in fruity Greek. When he looked over at the passenger's seat, Mickey was gone.

The Greek pulled away from the light, and Mickey was alone in the doorway of a garage. He hunched down low, making plans. He'd run away a lot, but he'd always gone to one of his buddies or to his Dad. He'd be okay, though, he told himself. He'd be cool. He had some cash his Dad had left with him. All you needed in this town was enough cash and you were cool. First thing he'd buy was something to eat.

He stuck to Broadway and his stomach was growling as he spotted a Hunan Chinese restaurant half a block down. Some kids about his age were hanging out around the doorway, and there were a lot of student types from Columbia inside. Mickey turned in, and so did the kids who'd been hanging out. He had cashew chicken and rice, and when he finished he felt better. He wasn't ready to go running to his Mom's yet. His Dad took off like this all the time and left him alone. His Dad knew he was cool. It was okay. You had to keep loose, and that was how his Dad liked it too. Loose and free.

He paid for the food and went into the john. He heard somebody come in behind him, and he didn't have time to turn around. His head hit the washbasin and somebody kicked him in the knee and he went down, then someone kicked him in the belly. He passed out cold, he told us later, and when he woke up his backpack was gone and so was his money. He sat rubbing his knee as he dug through the pockets of his jeans to see what they'd left him. He found two subway tokens, a wadded-up Kleenex, and half a stick of gum.

The Chinese kid at the cash desk was a hardnose and he took a subway token for a lousy quarter to use the pay phone. Mickey tried his Dad's number first, but there was still no answer. Then he called his mother, but he dialed a wrong number, and the phone kept his quarter. He'd just have to make it home on foot.

But it was a long hike from 110th, where he'd landed, to Seventy-sixth, and he was queasy from the kick in the stomach. He lost his Chinese dinner in an alley off 106th, but his head still ached where he'd hit it and his knee was swelling up now. He made it to the nearest subway entrance, used the one token he had left, and took the IRT that would stop at Seventy-ninth. He found a seat in a nearly empty car, but at Ninety-sixth two kids with a ghettobuster got on. They had it up too loud and it made his head worse. He leaned back in the seat and pulled his heavy jacket up around his ears.

Mickey didn't know whether he dozed off or just got spacy from the headache and the sick stomach, but when he woke up the car was about half full, the kids were gone, and the train was pulling into Times Square station. He'd gone far past his stop and when he got off, he was limping badly. He knew he couldn't walk back uptown tonight, it was too far. And nobody he knew lived midtown. Then he remembered his mother's practice room at Stuy. That was only a few blocks away. She worked late sometimes and it was just eleven. Even if she wasn't there, he might be able to talk his way in and use the phone, or sack out somewhere. He decided to give it a try.

Mickey turned off on Thirty-eighth and made his way painfully up the alley toward the back entrance of Stuyvesant Hall. There were still a couple of lights upstairs in the workrooms. Mickey had been here often enough to know his way around. He started for the back door when he heard a voice.

> *"Go and catch a falling star,*
> *Get with child a mandrake root,*
> *Tell me where all past years are*
> *Or who cleft the Devil's foot;*
> *Teach me to hear mermaids singing,*
> *Or to keep off envy's stinging*
> *And find*
> *What wind*
> *Serves to advance an honest mind."*

The voice paused and then went on. It was coming from a heap of old carpeting with torn edges.

> *"Fathers that wear rags*
> *Do make their children blind,*
> *But fathers that bear bags*
> *Shall see their children kind."*

A one-legged man with a crutch was standing over the steam vent. "That's just ol' Sonny," he said to the boy.

"'The only emperor is the emperor of ice cream,'" said the voice.

"He ain't nothin' to worry about, kid," said Sugar George.

Mickey started into the Musicians' Entrance, but Sugar stopped him. "They catch you sleepin' in there, they'll bust you good, boy, prob'ly cart you up to the Bronx Shelter. You wanna wind up way the hell up in the Bronx?" Mickey shook his head. "You can hang out here, though. They mostly let us alone out here. Want a orange?"

Mickey could make out the sleeping shapes of two or three other people among the clutter of cardboard and rugs under the canopy. "I was looking for my Mom. She works here."

"Cleaning lady? Nobody else here now. Only the night man, old Dom." Mickey just stared at the one-legged man. Sugar George seemed to hover in midair as he searched his pockets for the orange he had left and finally found it. Watching him made Mickey dizzy. "He's tough, too, old Dom," said George, handing him the orange. "If I was you, I wouldn't try him on." He sat down on a chair with a broken back. "Leg hurt you, boy?"

"No," said Mickey. His head felt woozy and he wanted to throw up again.

"You can't lie no better'n that, kid, don't make a career out of it," said Sugar with a laugh. "Get over here and park. Sonny! Get out here, we got us some company."

An arm stuck out of the carpet, then a leg, and finally a tall, dark-haired man in his late thirties stood, looking suspiciously at Mickey. He came up close, nose to nose, and his wide eyes probed the boy. "'I have measured out my life with coffee spoons,'" he said fiercely.

"'Tiger, tiger burning bright/ In the forests of the night,'" said Mickey. It was the only poem he could remember.

Sonny's wide, full mouth broke into a smile that went from ear to ear.

"Who beat you up, boy, your Daddy?" said Sugar. He wrapped some snow in a rag and put it on Mickey's bruised head, then ran his fingers over the swollen knee and tried moving the leg. "What's your Mama's name?"

"Teresa," Mickey said, "Teresa LaMagna. Teresa Falkner." He'd never gotten used to her having a different name. "I thought she might still be here."

"No," snapped Sugar George. "She ain't. Nobody here, I told you that."

"We gotta go, Sugar." Sonny jumped up. "We can't stay here, I told you. We gotta find a better place. Cops'll come back."

"Shut up, Sonny."

"'I am thy father's spirit, doomed to walk the night,'" Sonny wailed.

"I said shut up. Just shut the hell up." Dancing on his crutch, Sugar George grabbed a washing-machine carton and shoved it toward Mickey. "You can sleep in here to-night."

But Sonny pushed past him, almost knocking him off his precarious balance. "'Darkness and devils!'" he cried. "'Saddle my horses, call my train together.'" He ran off down the alley, yelling into the dark.

Sugar pulled himself up and took off after him, making good time in the snow. "Sonny, damn it!" he shouted. "I'm sorry, okay?" Then he yelled back to Mickey. "You eat that orange, you hear me? Stay put now."

Mickey's body ached too much to go anywhere. Exhausted and dizzy, he crawled inside the newspaper-padded carton and pulled the flap shut over his head. It smelled funny, but the steam from the vent made it damp and faintly warm, and at least he wouldn't freeze to death. He began to peel the orange, but in a few minutes it fell out of his hand and he was asleep. He remembered nothing else clearly for a long time, except once the voice of Sonny nearby in the darkness:

> "I should have been a pair of ragged claws,
> Scuttling across the floors of silent seas."

"Shut up now, Sonny," crooned Sugar George. "Just shut up now."

Chapter Six

When I got up next morning, I found David in front of the TV set, watching the tape of last Sunday night's *Bookends* show. John's long silences as young Shane McAuley reeled out the current literary party line were far more intriguing than anything King Brat had to say. The Infant Phenomenon looked more like fifteen than twenty-one, and the red rims of his eyes made me suspect he had more up his nose than between his ears.

"Of course," he said, "art is a lot of crap. What it's all about today, is money. You find out what people will buy and sell it to them, if the price is right."

Falkner let him have the silence for a beat or two. Then the questions began in earnest. "How much money were you paid for *Manhattan Underground,* Mr. McAuley?"

"Million dollars advance."

"And that was, I believe, the largest advance ever paid for a first novel?"

"Right. It was a hot property. It had all the elements."

"The elements people want? Or the elements they will pay for?"

"We fed the plot lines, characters, all that crap, of the past ten Pulitzer Prize winners into our computers up in New Haven, and that gave us the scenario. Frequency of violence, frequency of sex between main characters, ratio of conversational passages to description, average length compared to current estimates of attention span in the medium consumer group." The boy smiled, his blue eyes half closed

61

in deep self-satisfaction. "We knew we had a marketable product."

John's pale eyes never flickered, never left McAuley's smug face. "You say you know what people want. Which people, Mr. McAuley?"

"People who buy books. People who spend money."

"But initially that money comes not through the reading public, but through editors, doesn't it? Unless they are willing to buy, none of the rest of us will ever see a book. It ceases to exist in any practical way."

"Oh sure. Right."

"So you were, in fact, writing not for readers but for editors." The heavy brows were lowered in concentration, the body motionless, expressing no more than the secret, toneless voice. "You were writing for the million dollars, were you not?"

"What's the matter with that?"

"How many editors of so-called literary fiction are left in New York?"

"I don't know."

"Guess. Regular publishers of literary fiction, not just the token noncategory book once or twice a year. Fifteen? Twelve? Ten full-time editors who could afford your opinion of yourself?"

"Ten. Maybe ten. What's the difference?" The smug look had turned angry and sullen.

"Oh, there is a difference, Mr. McAuley. Because tomorrow three of the remaining houses regularly publishing nonformula literary fiction are conglomerating. That will leave eight editors."

"So?"

"So you are writing for an audience of eight people. You went to Yale, didn't you?"

The kid relaxed. "Oh, right. My professor in the Creative Writing Program was just super, he—"

"Submitted your first novel to a friend of his at Seabury House, didn't he? Who also went to Yale, I believe. How many of those eight members of your audience would you estimate went to Yale, Harvard, Dartmouth, Sarah Lawrence, Princeton, the Iowa Workshop, and so on?"

"Probably—"

"Where they were taught by people who went to Yale, Harvard, Dartmouth, Sarah Lawrence, Princeton, the Iowa Workshop, and so on?"

"Well, sure—"

"Who had friends among those eight editors who also went to Yale, Harvard, Dartmouth, Sarah Lawrence, Princeton, the Iowa Workshop, and so on?"

"I don't see what this has to do with my book."

"Oh. Well. What it means is that you are writing for an audience of eight people, all of whom are almost exactly like you. An inbred intellectual society with eight members, dictating the taste of a vast reading public. Narrowing its options until they disappear."

"Look, I don't have to put up with this shit—"

"What it means is that literature has become a private club from which those who do not know the rules, or who choose to break them, or who cannot pay the price of being discreetly manipulated into success, are quietly but most efficiently blackballed. Doesn't it, Mr. McAuley? What it means is, that yours is not a literature of mind or, God forbid, of conviction. It is a literature of greed."

"You go to hell, Falkner!" The kid stood up and swayed for a moment beside his chair. The excitement was too much for the punished membranes in his nose and it began to bleed. He swiped at it with his sleeve. "You has-been bastard, you go to hell!"

John merely smiled. "Now *that*," he said quietly," is a private club with an open membership list."

McAuley took a step toward him. The screen went black, then the camera switched on again, wavering wildly between John and the Brat. Falkner knew the punch was coming and he waited it out, braced so hard that when the kid's hand shot out and connected with his face, he hardly moved. The strength of the blow knocked his head back for a moment, but no more. He straightened up and faced the camera again, his upper lip bleeding sightly. Blood was streaming down McAuley's face, though John hadn't touched him.

"Thank you for joining us," Falkner said quietly. "One

last thing. Please remember that by next week there will be another conglomeration, and it will be an audience of four. Good night."

David switched the machine off. Already he seemed to have absorbed John's manner. He spoke quietly, half to himself. "He wanted that punch. He couldn't really have won without it. It made McAuley look like exactly what he is."

"John's always figured his quick success was nothing but old-boy politics. He thought he had something to expiate. Now he's finally said his piece."

"What I don't understand is why they ran it. It must've been taped early, because John wasn't in New York that night, he was up at your place."

"Yes," I said, "why didn't they just edit out the nasties?"

"I know a girl over at WNYT. Myra Fish, remember her? I'll give her a call."

"Might as well add her to the list," I told him. "But Davy, what did John expect *me* to do next Sunday night, make his apologies or what?"

"I think he'd come back to haunt you if you did," said David.

Later that morning, as the lunchtime traffic was picking up in the hallways of the Danson Building, Joan Plumb flipped through the pile of manila folders on her desk and opened one of them for the hundredth time. She stared through her Ben Franklin glasses at the photo clipped to the various applications, recommendations, and evaluation forms that made up Charlotte Stedman's personnel record. The ugly face and ungainly body concealed a past of academic honors and fine work experience, clearly a first-rate mind, but once she'd joined the Danson computer force, Charlie had simply gotten stuck. Steady performance, even excellence, but no advancement. Plumb had mentioned the fact to the head of Personnel. Young blow-dried Bruce Barrington had hemmed and hawed and finally told her he felt Charlie shouldn't be promoted to a job in which she'd have to deal with other executives, potential donors, or, heaven forbid, sensitive applicant artists. Her public image, it seemed, was not what the Foundation wished to project. "You mean," Plumb had said sharply, "that the child's too ugly to be given what she's earned." And she stalked away, leaving Barrington with his ears turning a rare fuchsia and his office staff gaping. Sometimes Miss Plumb's voice was very loud.

Back in her own office, Plumb had suddenly remembered all those computer checks on the grant applicants that Falkner had ordered. Plumb never threw anything away, and she didn't trust the principle of the floppy disk. Now the printouts were on her desk, and she had time to go through them. She spread out the green-and-white striped sheets on the worktable. Each one carried a code indicating which computer operator had performed the check. Without exception, Falkner's sheets carried the same number: 683.

Plumb picked up the phone and punched the number of the Computer Office. "I'd like Operator Six eighty-three," she said.

"Sorry," said the young man, "Six eighty-three's not in today. Called in sick. Want another operator?"

"What is the name?" said Plumb.

"Name?"

"I assume Operator Six eighty-three has a form of human nomenclature. A name."

"Oh. Sure. Stedman. Charlie Stedman."

"Excuse me," said a cultivated voice from the doorway. "I think I'm completely lost. Idiotic of me, I know, but it is such a conundrum, this building, don't you think? Modern architecture, I mean, well, the corridors seem to go every which way, don't they, like cats from a sack. Oh dear, here I am rattling on like sixty, and I haven't told you what I want. I'm looking for Mr. John Falkner's office, if it's in this hemisphere."

"This is Mr. Falkner's office," said Plumb, hanging up the phone, "but—"

"Oh? Oh, thank goodness." The small, rather delicate man came inside and perched on the chair nearest the door. He was in his seventies, Plumb decided, but young for his age. She was only sixty-one, but a difference of age was interesting. He was very well-dressed, too, except for those earmuffs sticking out of his coat pocket. "My name is Edward Merriman, and I am here to see John Falkner. Came all the way up from Baltimore, in this awful snow. Devil of a climate up here, don't you think? I have an appointment. Haven't I?"

"I'm sorry," she told him, "but I'm afraid you've had a long trip for nothing. Mr. Falkner died yesterday."

"Oh my. Oh dear. What was it, heart? Too much of this jogging and jiggling business? He seemed well when we spoke about my little endowment."

"I'm afraid the police are calling it murder. They were in here most of this morning, making a mess of things . . . I could direct you to the Endowments Office."

"Murder? Dear Lord." He took a deep breath and stood up. "Well, if that's the case, I think we'd better just have lunch, don't you?" And he shooed Plumb into her coat and out the door.

They made their way through streets streaming with snow-melt. The weather had turned warm for Ground Hog Day, and the sun was bright, as Eddie led Plumb to a small, quiet English-style tearoom on a side street. Over the steak-and-kidney pie, she told nice Mr. Merriman from Baltimore all about Falkner's mysterious reappearance in the Stuyvesant Hall elevator.

"What a strange place to find him! Not a musician at all, was he?"

"No, but his wife is. Ex-wife, actually, but he never called her that. Always 'my wife.'"

"Divorce is a social myth for some people. Like a vaccination that simply doesn't take, don't you know."

"Oh yes. Whenever she had a concert in the City, he would ask me to get him tickets."

"In the plural?"

"Well, no. Just the one ticket. He always went alone."

"Poor fellow. Lying murdered in a place he must've known so well. Shocking."

"Well I must say," Plumb said in a discrete undertone,

"I wasn't as surprised as I might've been. Before last Friday."

"What happened on Friday?"

He seemed fascinated and she spread her wings a bit. "I'm not quite sure, but I think he may've been blackmailing someone." She didn't mention Andrew Danson. "I heard him on the telephone, arranging some sort of, well, rendezvous, for Wednesday night. And it's odd, you know, because he was in Philadelphia on the night they say he was killed, Tuesday night, or early Wednesday morning."

"Perhaps he never went to Philadelphia at all."

"Oh yes. He must have. I checked the airline this morning. A round-trip ticket, both halves used as reserved. He left Friday at six P.M. and returned at noon on Tuesday. And his hotel reservation was used as well. He checked into the Liberty Plaza Hotel in Philadelphia at seven-fifteen on Friday night, had room-service dinners each night, and checked out early on Tuesday morning."

"But that's impossible," cried Merriman, getting dirty looks from a brigade of blue-haired dowagers.

"Nevertheless," said Plumb firmly. "Perhaps his friend has an explanation. Miss Stedman."

"Friend? Miss What Stedman? I mean who. I mean, has she a Christian name?"

"Charlotte. I've heard the other girls call her Charlie." Plumb spoke with distaste. The epicene nickname was their way of dealing with Charlotte's appearance; if you couldn't avoid an ugly woman, you simply made her into a man. "She works in our Computer Office, and she's run a great many searches for Mr. Falkner. She was with him when he made the call."

Eddie grinned at her. "Miss Plumb, you are a peach," he said. "What else do your little gray cells contain? I can't resist a mystery, you know."

"Well, there was a recording. Videotape, I think. It was playing in his office, but when I went in later to tidy up and put it away, it was gone." Again she failed to mention Andrew.

"What was on the tape? Hear anything?"

"It seemed to be just another public relations tape. Nothing important. How much the Foundation had given in grants, how much through the Hopewell Foundation, that sort of thing." She watched him closely. He was too old for a policeman or a private detective. But he certainly wasn't what he pretended to be. His questions were too specific and persistent for a mere curious mystery buff.

"Odd though, that a perfectly ordinary tape should disappear. What's this Hopewell bunch, haven't heard of them."

"Oh, they're very reputable. Headquartered in Kansas City, headed by Mr. Dennis Weeks. I remember his name was included on the tape, quite specifically. We give a great deal of endowment money through them to arts groups and individuals in the Midwest."

"Weeks lives in Missouri, does he?"

"Well, I believe he does come into Manhattan now and then. He keeps a place here."

Eddie poured her a second cup of tea. "Where would that be? Surely you'd know, in your trusted position. Perhaps you've even met him?"

When she'd been Randolph's secretary, Plumb had met everyone who came in and out of the Foundation, but those days were long gone. "Well," she had to admit, "no, I haven't. Mr. Weeks deals directly with Mr. Danson's office through Dean Sommers."

"And who is Dean Sommers when he's at home?"

"Andrew Danson's private secretary," she said carefully.

"May I venture to guess that you don't like him much?"

"You may. He's a very efficient young man, constantly reorganizing things. I find the two a contradiction. With procedures in a constant shuffle, forms changing every week, nothing much ever gets done."

And, thought Eddie, with the help in a continual pickle, nobody would have time to notice if nasty business was going on under his nose.

"Also," said Plumb, "Mr. Sommers is bland. No quirks, no habits. Coffee with too much milk. It has no flavor, it's merely tepid and rather muddy." She peered at Eddie. "I mistrust blandness. You, for instance, are not in the least tepid."

Eddie smiled. "Oh let's be wicked and have a Napoleon with our tea, shall we?" He signaled the waitress, then turned back to Plumb. "And now, you clever thing, I shall pull off my false whiskers and tell you the truth. And you are going to find me the address of Dennis Weeks. May I call you Joan?"

"I am worn out from scintillating like the dickens all morning long," said Eddie, stretching himself out on David's couch that afternoon. "Miss P. not only told me all, she invited me home to Thirty-fourth Street to meet the Aged Parent and the two Scotch terriers."

"What about this Charlotte Stedman? I wonder if Mickey or Teresa knew John had a girlfriend."

"Perhaps she wasn't one." He rummaged in his coat pocket. "According to the phone book, she lives in one of those buildings near the Metropolitan Museum, just across the park from Teresa's place. High-priced neighborhood."

"Computer people make the stuff in sackfuls if they're any good. The real puzzler is who used those airline tickets, and who checked into the Liberty Plaza. Certainly wasn't John."

"And what was on that disappearing tape."

"Anything else in Miss P.'s memory bank?"

"John's car is still missing, so she tells me. And his briefcase. Our friend Duffy was about to check LaGuardia's long-term parking at last bulletin. Oh, and it was the photo from John's desk that was found in his coat pocket. Miss P. noticed it missing on Friday afternoon, when the blackmail call was made."

"I'm sorry, but nothing's making me buy the idea of John as a blackmailer."

"No. I don't know what rope Johnny was dancing, but blackmail wasn't tied to the end of it. That takes a dull, sordid mind."

Eddie sat up as David came out of the bedroom, selected a copy of John's book, *The Human Abstract*, from his shelves, and departed without a word to either of us. "How was our boy at the morgue today, Winnie?" said Merriman.

"Not chatty, but who would be?" I knew how David had felt. I'd only been inside such a place once before, looking for a missing person. I'd been lucky, because all the body bags had contained strangers, and Davy, my missing person, had turned up alive. But today it had been different. I could still hear John's voice goading me: "You've never come near reality. What're you afraid of?" Well, you couldn't get much nearer than this.

John had always had an uncanny knack for putting his finger on my soft spots. Maybe he'd been right. When reality got in my way, I took off my glasses. When life got complicated, I hauled out a bit of moldy verse to beat it down.

When we left the morgue, I'd felt aged and deflated, a mildly foolish old fraud. I'd looked over at David, walking beside me. He wasn't my kid brother, my brother-in-law, or my son. When I introduced him to strangers, I still had to bob and weave about our relationship. When he was young, I'd sometimes passed myself off as his father just to save explanations. Pseudo-son, John had said. I was beginning to realize why I'd pushed my friend away. It had had nothing to do with booze or irresponsibility or phone calls from Tegucigalpa. I'd forgiven lesser friends far worse. No. Eddie, too, had been right. I was a bit afraid of John Falkner and his unswerving, uncomfortable truth. Even now that he was dead.

Eddie yanked me back to the present. "I don't think you should let David involve himself, Winnie. Not wise. I have every faith in him, but he hardly knows himself anymore. All that plastic surgery, I mean, and after those dreadful scars. Even I can notice a vague difference, if I allow myself to look closely at his face. Let him sort all that out before he dives into this business and hurts himself. It's one thing playing spies in the movies. It's another playing this sort of part."

"Even if I asked him to lay off, you don't really think he would, do you? He's hooked, just like the rest of us."

Eddie got up and poured me a drink. "Did you learn anything from seeing John today?"

"What puzzles me is those feet. I'd almost say they'd been wiped clean, or even washed before he was left in that elevator. Aside from a little sawdust out of the crate they brought him in, there was nothing. Not a thread. No lint from his socks between his toes. Not even a stray piece of callus or a little grime from perspiration."

"Perhaps he'd just had a bath. Or been in bed."

"With his overcoat on?" It had begun to remind me of the plot of my poor rejected novel. I realized now that I'd written myself into a corner in that book. I didn't want to do the same thing with this mystery of John's.

Eddie was watching me with that look of his, like a fussy and elderly robin listening for a worm. "You have another case of your sciatica coming on, haven't you?" he said. "I recognize the telltale greenish tinge around the eyes."

"I'm just pooped," I said. "Think I'll have a nap before dinner."

"In broad daylight? I've known you for thirty-five years. You never nap in the daylight hours."

"Well, maybe I ought to change a few of my rules," I said.

And I was about to stretch out and indulge my case of the blues, when in whizzed Sarah, hair streaming in wisps from under her knitted cap, wool cape flapping around her.

"I know I shouldn't have let her out of my sight," she said, "but I wanted to visit Mr. Freiling's shop myself, I mean, you and your tin ear, and I do speak German, so I made certain she was lying down and I left a note for Bea, because *she* was gone, she had to stock up the refrigerator, you know Teresa never keeps a thing but ice in it, and Winston, how do you bail somebody out of jail for heaven's sake?" She stopped with a gasp like the Goodyear blimp taking on air, and sat down, plop, on the couch, barely missing my head.

"Has Mickey been arrested?"

"No, no, you ninny, it's Teresa!" She jumped up again. "The fool went to John's apartment and broke the police tapes. She's been arrested for tampering with evidence!"

Chapter Seven

"What do you want me to do, Duffy, indenture myself to you for seven years? I told you I'd be responsible for her, and that's what I mean." It'd taken me two solid hours of browbeating, but with the help of Lieutenant Duffy's empty stomach, I just about had him convinced not to press charges. None of us had had dinner, it was past nine, and I could hear his tum making noises like the Long Island Special going through a tunnel.

"Okay," said the little man at last, "she can go. But if I catch her anywhere near that apartment of Falkner's again before we're finished in there, I'm filing charges, understand? I don't care whose mama she is, evidence is evidence. So just keep her the hell out of my way."

"What the devil were you doing breaking that tape and waltzing in there?" I roared.

It was after ten now, but we finally had Teresa back at her apartment. She sat like a small fortified island in the sea of music stands and orchestra scores, one hand laid on the glossy wood of her cello. "I told you," she said. "I told Duffy. I was looking for Mickey."

"Trash!" said Sarah, kicking a footstool in frustration. "The police had been inside the place, and the seal hadn't been broken since they left. Mickey couldn't have been there. What did you think you'd find?"

"I don't know, all right?" Teresa's face looked tense and forced, the eyes larger and more luminous than usual. "I thought I might get an idea where he took my kid." And she clamped her lips so tight you'd need an oyster knife to pry them open.

I'd wandered over to where the double recording equipment was set up. It was reel-to-reel tape, the kind I'm used to at school. I bent to examine the reel. Then I came over and sat opposite Teresa.

"When did they call?" I said. "While Sarah and Bea were out, I'd guess. You'd have needed time to erase that bit of tape and rewind it by hand."

"What're you talking about, Win?" said Sarah.

"That tape. It's been wound back by hand. It's not tight, the way it should be if it's just run through the machine normally. And both recorders have been rewound about the same number of inches. What did they want, Teresa? I think you'd better come clean."

Bea slammed her hand down on the table, sloshing coffee out of her cup. "You think I got no rights here, Teresa? Mickey's my kid too. What the hell is going on?"

"Nothing, Ma. Calm down. Winston, I've had enough. Lay off."

"Not yet, kiddo. I called the Wildwood School today and talked to Mickey's roommate. He says you and John came to see Mickey, the two of you together, the weekend before last. You told me you couldn't remember the last time you'd seen John."

"All right, that's it," said Teresa angrily. "Winston, I owe you one for Duffy. But go home. Ma called you up, you can help Ma. Take her home to Brooklyn, tuck her in. But leave me the hell alone!"

"Teresa," Sarah said, "you have known me for a long time. If you don't trust me when you're in real trouble, there's no point going on. Is there?" She picked up her cape, jammed her hat over her ears, and walked out, slamming the door behind her.

As we walked back to Davy's through the slushy snow that was freezing into miniature glaciers on the crosswalks, Sarah kept up a marathon pace, and I had to struggle to stay beside her. "You know it's not a matter of trusting you, kiddo," I told her. "Till the boy's safe, she doesn't think she has a choice."

But it was no consolation. Sarah marched on in total silence.

That night we bunked on the pull-out couch in David's living room. I don't know, maybe it was the half inch of mattress between me and the steel springs. Maybe it was the faint drift of voices that carry up from the moving city streets at all hours, no matter how high the high-rise, or the omnipresent sense of possible danger even in locked rooms, the fear of somehow being taken unawares, that made me travel in and out of sleep without ever losing consciousness entirely. Whatever it was, though, Sarah and I shared it all that night. Just after the clock on Davy's desk clanged three, she turned over and put her hand on my chest.

"You're not sleeping either," she said.

"Adrenaline. Two hours with the Delectable Duffy."

"Win. I didn't say it earlier. But I think somebody followed me when I left the instrument shop this afternoon."

I'd been concerned with David's involvement and hadn't given Sarah's a thought. She isn't the sort of woman who likes being worried about. "What did he look like, this tail of yours?"

"I couldn't see his face, he was half a block away. A red ski parka, short, sort of dumpy."

"Who tails people in a red jacket?" Either he was an idiot or he'd wanted her to spot him.

"I dodged around, in and out of shops, and there he was, half a block behind me again. Finally I flagged a cab and lost him."

"Well, I don't know what we can do, except see if he turns up again, and try to figure out what he wants. Did you learn anything from Freiling?"

"Not much. He's Austrian, from Salzburg. He's about fifty, I'd say, a little hard of hearing. I don't think he had anything to do with John's death."

"Don't think so, or don't want to?"

She was quiet a moment. "Both." She laughed. "His helper's name, if you'd believe it, is Thomas Mann."

"Like the Nobel Prize winner? No. I wouldn't believe it. Patently phony."

I hauled myself up off the killer mattress, sat down in the only chair I wasn't afraid I'd break, and lighted a Turkish Delight. "Sarah, what do you know about Andrew Danson that I don't?"

"Such as?"

"Still married to Cella?"

"Yes." She moved around the living room in the dark and came, finally, to sit tailor fashion on the floor beside my chair. "Poor Cella."

"Why poor? I always thought she was pretty well-heeled, even pre-Danson."

"Oh she was. Very old money, railroads, I think, and then oil later on. The sort of people who're brought up not to think about money because it's too, too vulgah. They ignore it the way you do water out of a tap."

"Till the well runs dry. Did it?"

"Not really. But there was some trouble. They almost had to sell her father's old company, Kenwood Enterprises. Of course they still have Andrew's money. And what he'll get from his father when he dies."

"Not the same, though, is it? All that vulgar fried chicken. Look, why don't you give Poor Cella a ring, have lunch tomorrow."

"She wouldn't come, Win. She doesn't go out."

"What, never?"

"Not for several years now. I haven't seen her since the reunion in 'seventy-two. They have a penthouse in that awful high-rise, Gallup Tower, at Fifty-third and Madison. She never leaves that place. Andrew's hired a lady companion for her, I'm told."

"An invalid, is she?"

"I think she's afraid. She's hiding out."

"Paranoia?"

Sarah lay down flat on the floor. "I don't know. Paranoia is imaginary fear. I'm not sure that in this city it's possible to invent a danger that doesn't actually exist."

"Not easy for Danson," I said, looking down at Sarah's relaxed, confident body and picturing her cowering in some empty room at home. It was hard to imagine, but I didn't expect he'd exactly counted on it either. "Any kids?"

"No. She had a miscarriage not long after the wedding. After that I think she more or less gave up."

"I seem to recall watching Cella trying to make sheep's eyes at a sailor on that yacht of theirs. That a common pattern?"

Sarah laughed. "She was dreadful at it, wasn't she? I thought she was trying to make Andrew jealous."

"Does she see people? Would she see us?"

"I don't know. I could try."

"Call her tomorrow."

"What do you expect to find out?"

"Whatever I can."

Sarah got up and fumbled around in the dark, clanking glasses. In a minute she was back with two stiff Scotches. "Now," she said, "about Toronto."

I sank an inch lower in the chair, took a belt of the Scotch, and braced myself. "Let's have it. What's been going on?"

"I saw Maureen. Well, almost saw her."

The name took a minute to register. "You mean our Mo? David's mother Mo?" Maureen Fitzroy had been Erskine's second wife, who'd escaped her difficult marriage in the arms of a Cuban trumpet player when the kid was too little even to remember her.

"You know she used to be an actress? Well, I was reading the theater page of the *Globe and Mail* in my hotel up in Windsor, and there she was, Maureen Fitzroy, featured in some dreadful play at this little Toronto theater off Yonge Street. So when I got there, naturally I had to try and track her down."

"But you didn't succeed?"

"By the time I got there the miserable play had already folded. They had a Toronto address for her, but then I heard about John, and that was that. Do you think I ought to tell David?"

"Of course you should, but not right now. At the moment I doubt if he'd even hear you."

"He's so quiet, Win. Just like after the slashing. I'm worried about him."

"He's bored with his movie, and John's a much more interesting part, that's all." I spoke with more confidence than I felt. "He needs to get away from it for a while. Maybe if I phoned Alex?"

Sarah shrugged and lit one of my cigarettes. "At least he could have a day with Gemma." Gemma is David's small daughter. Now that Alex was in town, so was she. "He mustn't think we're cooking things up, Winston, he'll be furious."

Better furious, I thought, than in over his head.

Next morning, I took the early train back to Ainsley by myself to teach my Friday class and see if that promised manuscript of John's had arrived in the mail. Before I left, though, I issued a proclamation to Sarah and the others. "From now on, it's strictly Noah's Ark around here, you lot. Everybody two by two, nobody goes out alone. I don't care who you go with, but not alone. That fellow in the red suit isn't Santa, you know."

"And who, O Master, are you taking with you?" asked cheeky old Merriman.

Well, I curled my lip at him, but I kept my eyes open for dumpy red-clad strangers on the train home. The closest I came was a squad of Moose Lodge brothers in matching red velvet blazers. I found out, though, that I didn't much like looking over my shoulder constantly. I got home just after nine that morning with a crick in my neck, feeling worn and grimy. Lowering myself onto the hall bench, I switched on the answering machine.

The first voice was Lloyd Agate's. Lloyd, a veteran of my Remedial Composition class and a Detective Lieutenant with the local fuzz, is a sturdy friend and a fine source of official knowledge. "Doc," he said after the beep, "I got some good stuff for you. Stop by." I was still sighing over his prose style as the second message began, a voice I didn't know.

"This is Brother Felix at the Monastery of the Renunciation. Mr. Falkner asked me to speak with you. Could you please come up?"

The Renunciation Brothers are a Moldavian order famous for their work with addicts of all kinds, particularly alcoholics, and their monastery sits high on our river bluffs among a grove of pines. So the story of John's dry-out was true after all, and he'd chosen my hometown to do it in.

The third call was even shorter. "Weeks," said a muffled voice, "five-five-five, eight-nine-six-two."

"Weeks?" I said out loud. "Who the hell's Weeks?" Then I remembered what Eddie had relayed from Miss Plumb about the Hopewell Foundation in Kansas City and their chairman, Dennis Weeks. I dialed the number.

The phone rang three times and then there was a click, another answering machine kicking into operation. The same muffled voice. "Have the Weeks file by Monday morning," it growled. "I'll find you." Click.

I made record time pedaling my bike through the mucky streets to the Cop House, where Agate sat behind his desk champing one of his famous Tootsie Rolls. "Lloyd," I said, "how much do you know? Will you start, or shall I?" I rescued a stack of files as he knocked them off his desk.

"Thanks," he said, taking the Tootsie Roll out of his mouth and unsticking his tongue from his teeth. He tossed the files into a basket. "Well, first off, we got John Falkner's Jag." He chuckled. "New York cops called me up, some hot dog named Duffy. Seems to think you're a shady character and I'm a sap."

"Where was the car?"

"Up at the Monastery. Falkner left it when he dropped off his kid with them."

"So that's where he left Mickey! Let me use your phone, Lloyd, I'll call his mother."

"He's gone, Doc. Took off Wednesday night. That's when they called me. I figured you must be in the City, but I didn't have a number."

I grabbed a pad and scribbled several for him. "So after Mickey heard the evening news about his father, he ran?"

"Couldn't have heard. You check in with those monks up there, you're incommunicado for the duration. Falkner was pretty much a regular up there, I guess. Checked in late Friday night and took off sometime Monday, after the tracks were cleared. One of the brothers drove him in and out of town in the Jeep."

"Then he really didn't go to Philly. But who checked into the Liberty Plaza Friday night? Because somebody certainly did."

"That's what Duffy said. So I called the Liberty myself and got a description of the guy from the night clerk. Duffy hadn't gotten around to him yet." The heady musk of professional pride was in the air. Put-downs about small-town cops are a burr under Lloyd's saddle. "Desk clerk says the guy was crippled. Um, handicapped."

"John had a limp, but only when he wasn't wearing his built-up shoes."

"No, I mean really handicapped. The guy was missing most of one leg, used a crutch. Half an arm gone too. Know him?"

"Not yet, but I have a feeling I may before long." I told Lloyd about the strange message on my machine and the phone number I'd called. "I'm sure it's the same as the call Teresa erased. But why call me?"

"May've been watching Mrs. Falkner's place. May be some other connection, somebody who knew you were a friend of his. Whatever they want, they may've bumped off Falkner to get it. I'll put a car on your block, in case he decides to have a look for himself. And gimme that phone number you called, I'll get an address to go with it."

"How's your trusty computer, Lloyd? I could use a little information on this Weeks and an Austrian named Andreas Freiling. You can access the Customs and Immigration people, can't you?"

"I could, if I wasn't locked out of the Computer Room right now. Seems I accidentally erased a couple case files." He grinned and blushed. "I'll see who I can bribe, though. You still bake those German-chocolate brownies, do you?"

Lloyd agreed to meet me on his lunch hour and drive me up to visit Brother Felix. Meantime, I made a raid on the magazine stacks in the Clinton College Library.

In a two-year-old copy of *Money Matters*, I found what

I'd hoped for. The author had researched and compared the funding and investments of several large arts foundations, including the Danson. According to the article, the Danson Foundation had begun with a huge endowment from old Turner, the original frozen-chicken king, and had made some cautious and fruitful blue chip investments under Randolph. Since Andrew's accession to the throne, though, they'd invested heavily in Kenwood Enterprises, Cella Danson's father's old firm, which had lost money steadily since the oil shortage of the seventies. I could find nothing solid about the current state of Kenwood. The money poured into the company hadn't helped its stock much, though. The Dow quoted Kenwood at a quivering six per share.

Glancing through a few copies of the Foundation journal, *American Muse*, I noticed that Andrew Danson had a real penchant for parties. If he was supposed to be running the fried chicken business, I didn't see where he found the time. Here was Danson on his famous yacht out in Long Island Sound, fairly awash with Beautiful People, there he was in the roof garden of his penthouse. I looked through a dozen pages and found no mention of Poor Cella, let alone a photo. And then I turned page twelve and there was a shot of our David in dinner jacket and black tie, champagne glass in hand, knockout wife Alex beside him glittering in white satin, laughing at some funny of Danson's. The caption read, "Actor David Cromwell and his wife, British model Alexandra Hemmings, join Andy at the annual New Year's Gala." No wonder Davy was getting involved. He probably knew Danson better than I did.

I began to look at Danson with the camera's eye. There was something planned about him, something a little theatrical. He had managed the gala and managed the photograph, and even managed the way Alex's head was tilted back and her drift of fine red hair caught the light just as the camera clicked. Nothing about the man was noticeable, and that in itself was odd. Look at five out of six people on the street, and you'll find something to remember—a scar, a big nose, ears like Dumbo. Danson seemed touched up. A man with a chaotic and hopeless private life, he had made a profession of control. Precise and careful, never out of hand, no impulses allowed. He was a mask, long and painstakingly constructed.

"I'm damned," I said to myself, and closed the magazine. And there, at a table between some book stacks, nicely entwined with Ms. Allison Barnes-McGee, I spotted our leader, Chairman Thomas Van Doren Sheffield. "Well I *am* damned," I said, and whipped out my specs for a better view. They were sharing a large art book, as well as one of The Mizz's shapely knees, and Tommy sat surreptitiously nuzzling her fingertips. She looked up, saw me, rapidly untangled herself and whispered something in his ear. Then she was off with a cloud of dust and a hearty Heigh-O Silver.

By that time, though, I only had eyes for the stiff, furry thing that was making its home on Sheffield's balding dome. I've seen hairpieces and hairpieces, but this one must've been bought mail order from Taiwan. The color didn't match what was left of his hair, but worst of all, nothing disturbed the stuff. No draft tickled it, no sweat from his brow made it wilt. It just roosted up there, waiting for take-off.

I toddled over to his table and he slammed the art book shut. *The Nudes of Peter Paul Rubens,* in living color. Tommy's idea of hard-core porn, no doubt. "Have you joined some sect demanding penitential headgear, Thomas, or what is that on your upper slopes?" I peered down at the thing over my glasses.

"It's a hairpiece," he said. "I thought it might give me better rapport with—"

"Oh, from what I've seen I think your rapport's just dandy. Tommy, we need to have a serious talk, but I haven't got time right now. I'll phone you at home."

"Oh. I'm—I'm not *at* home. I'm not living at home, I mean."

So Lady Di had actually chucked him out on his ear. "Where can I reach you, then? At the home of La Mizz, I presume?"

"Actually, I'm staying at the—the Roman Holiday Motel. Temporarily. Until things are—"

"Finished? Because that's what you're about to be, if

you don't wise up." And I left him to his mid-life crisis. From what I could see, he was in it up to his cheap Dynel.

I had visited the Monastery of the Renunciation only once before, when Davy was a kid and I took him up to their annual Fun Fair. Like the Dansons, the good brothers needed to raise money now and then, but their scale ran more to baked goods and homemade potholders. Today though, there were no tents set up on the lawn between the modest wood and stone buildings. Half a dozen cars were parked in a snow-covered lot and the community Jeep was near the door of the *dor toir*, in the shelter of a small grove of pines and hickories. We found Brother Felix in the kitchen with a calico apron wrapped around him, washing stacks of monastic dishes. I felt right at home in the kitchen, naturally, and grabbed a dish towel to pitch in while we talked. Having foregone his own lunch, Lloyd was soon installed at the scrubbed pine table with a plate of leftover chicken pot pie, still steaming hot.

"Mr. Falkner left me some instructions," said Brother Felix. He was a slender, thirtyish man dressed not in the medieval cowl I'd expected but in rumpled gray sweat pants and an old cardigan. "I wanted to fulfill them as soon as possible. I thought he was being overdramatic at the time, but he must've known what might happen to him. He asked me to give you two packages. One is a manuscript, and the other is a videotape, or so he told me. He asked me, if anything should keep him from picking them up, to give them to you before the weekend, and to take his son to you. I'm only sorry that I failed where the boy is concerned. Has Michael been heard from at all?"

"Not yet," I told him. "But at least we know he's on his own and he wasn't kidnapped. Or was he? Could anyone have got in here and nabbed him?"

"As you can see, we're a walled community, and our front gates are electronically locked at five-thirty. After that, you have to phone ahead so that one of us can open them for you. There were a number of guests in residence over the weekend. No one reported hearing or seeing anything unusual. No. I believe Michael left of his own accord."

"Did John come here often?"

"When he felt he needed us. You know about his drinking, I take it." I nodded. "Three years ago, he spent several months here. You didn't know that?"

"We hadn't been—well, in touch, for a while."

"I see. He wasn't an easy man to reach. Still, he left you his son. He must've trusted you."

"Were you good friends?"

"We had certain things in common." Brother Felix smiled. "We were both drunks." He put away a huge stack of plates and then sat down at the table. "I stopped drinking three years ago, when I came here. At the same time as John. I never left. John—well, he never managed to give it up entirely. Perhaps if he'd stayed on here. But there was too much pulling at him. Too much unresolved anger. And love. I didn't have a son, you see, and he did. So he would come and go as he felt he had to."

Lloyd dropped his fork on the floor and bent to pick it up. "Did he say who he was afraid of?" he asked, cleaning the fork with his napkin. "What he figured might happen to him?"

"Not specifically. But he wanted his son safe. And I failed him." Brother Felix handed Lloyd a clean fork. "Perhaps there's some answer in the things he left for you."

"Was there anything like a file, a bunch of papers?" I asked.

"No, I'm afraid not. Only the things I was to give you, wrapped in brown paper."

"Did he ever mention a man called Weeks?"

"No. We talked mostly about books. If it's connected with his work, we never discuss business matters here. It's part of the addiction, more or less." He sat staring at the table. "Please. I won't be at ease until I know about the boy. I feel deeply responsible. Is there anything at all I can do?"

"I think so. One thing. Can you perform a funeral service here, Brother?"

When we'd discussed the arrangements, I felt better, as if I'd found a way to get John home again, to something like the peaceful illusion I chose to remember as Iowa. I understood why he'd kept coming back here, why he'd chosen this place to leave Mickey. It was a much better hideout than Cella Danson's penthouse could ever be.

I sat silent, the manuscript and tape on my lap, as Lloyd drove us back down the hill. "I checked on that phone number, Doc," he said at last. "You called an answering machine in Room Two-oh-nine of the Seven Pines Motor Inn. Rented to an Al Zadravic. He paid in advance for a week, cash. Hasn't checked out yet. No prints on the machine, it'd been wiped. We'll keep an eye on the place." He paused, considering me quizzically. "You going to let me see that video?"

"Of course. But I've got to catch the three o'clock train back to New York right after class."

"Matter of fact, I'll be in New York myself. Got the weekend off, and I promised Bev dinner and a show, night at a real hotel. So I'll be available. In case you should want to run that tape."

"Fine," I said. I'm always glad to hear Lloyd's two cents' worth. "But isn't all that pretty rich on a cop's salary, dinner, theater, hotel and all?"

He laughed. "I didn't say what kind of a hotel, now did I?"

Chapter Eight

For most of Thursday, Mickey Falkner lay in the cardboard carton beneath the shelter at Stuyvesant Hall. Now and then he woke, but his head throbbed and his stomach felt too sick to care what he did. Sugar George came once, peeled the forgotten orange and made him suck the juice out of it, but the flesh was like straw and Mickey drifted back to sleep, chill and numb. Again he woke and Sonny was beside him, piling him with rugs as the cold got deeper through the night. It wasn't until Friday noon, about the time Lloyd and I were sitting in Brother Felix's clean, steamy kitchen, that Mickey crawled stiffly out of the box at last. His knee was still sore and swollen, but his head was finally clear. He found Sonny munching a hamburger bun and suddenly realized how hungry he was.

"Breakfast," said Sonny, flashing one of his extra-strength smiles. "Sugar got 'em at McDonald's."

"Yeah?" A McD.L.T. would hit the spot right now.

"They throw them in the garbage when they get stale. Only a couple, three days old, is all. Here." He tossed over a half-full plastic bag of the buns.

"There's no burgers in them, man," said Mickey.

Sonny laughed and chomped off another bite. "Use your imagination, kid. Go on. Eat it. Hamburger's good for you, don't you know that." He laughed again. Sonny had a quick, warm laugh, and it made Mickey feel better. He'd never eaten garbage before, but he took a bun and stuffed half of it in his mouth at once.

87

"Where'd the other guy go?" said the boy, pulling himself up onto the broken chair near the steam vent.

"Sugar George? He's out on recon. We gotta find another place. It was an eight-ball operation from the beginning. I tried to tell him, but he's a hardhead, you can't tell him anything."

"Was he in the War, or what? Sugar George, I mean."

Sonny stopped and stared at Mickey, his tongue caught between wide, half-parted lips. He glared down the alley, then turned back to the boy. "Damn it," he said, and began to pace back and forth, arms swinging, with the liquid gait of a constant walker. "Damn it, kid, I told you to watch for booby traps. Now look at you. You're all the hell screwed up."

"Where's Sugar George?" Mickey asked again.

Sonny continued to pace. "They fragged him. Bastards fragged him. Never saw it coming. He never does. I told him." He put an arm around Mickey and lifted him gently, helping him put weight slowly on the bad knee. Sonny was very strong, and it surprised the boy. "We gotta bug out, kid. They're moving up. It's okay. I'm gonna get you back okay."

Mickey had no idea where they were going, but when Sonny moved, he moved too. They started down the alley and got almost to the opening on Thirty-eighth when Sugar swung around the corner. He paused, propped on his crutch, and studied Sonny's earnest, open face. "Loo-tenant Emerson!" he roared suddenly. "Where the hell you think you're taking that recruit?"

"Field hospital, sir." Sonny saluted sharply. "Booby trap. Damn kids pay no attention to the training. Never get it straight."

"Field hospital's this way, Lieutenant," said Sugar. "I'll take point."

Once out of the alley and onto Thirty-eighth, they stopped at a demolition site and Sugar fished a piece of half-rotted two-by-four out of a Dumpster. He fitted it under Mickey's arm. "Make better time that way," he said.

"Where we going?" Mickey struggled to keep up with Sugar's rhythmic bounce and Sonny's rolling progress. It was past the noon rush now, but traffic was still pretty heavy, even on the sidewalks.

"Got us a different place for a while. Better. No cops."

"What they want you for, man? Drugs or what?"

Sugar laughed softly. "Nah. Ain't that kind of sugar, kid."

"What's cops doin' around Stuy, anyhow?"

Sonny glanced at him, eyes narrowed. "Found a dead guy in the elevator. Couple days back," said Sugar.

"Jesus. Who was he?"

But Sugar ignored him, and marched straight on, heading them west toward Times Square. When a truck passed or traffic got crazy, Sonny would crouch low behind the railings and garbage cans or dodge into doorways, pulling Mickey with him. He threw his body over the kid to protect him from the bursting shells, the rockets, the fiery fog of napalm. And then, as soon as the enemy had passed, they would go on.

Mickey thought he could feel people staring from buildings, from passing cars and limos. Some of them laughed at Sonny and the laughter bothered the boy. "What's he do that stuff for anyhow?" he asked Sugar.

"Old Sonny knows a goddamn war when he sees one." And they marched on.

Just off Seventh Avenue, at the back door of Times Square, a girl called to Sugar from the door of a building where half a dozen kids were hanging out on the steps. Sugar stopped and she ran out to him. She had a fresh black eye and her hair was messed up. "Nita, honey, I told you already what you gotta do," said Sugar. "I told you I'd take you again."

"I know," she told him. "Only I'm scared, though. He can find me anyplace. Jesus. Sugar, can't you make me ten years old again?" And she put her arms around him and held on.

"How old is she?" asked Mickey when they began to move once more.

"Dunno. Maybe fifteen." Sugar glanced at him. "Never seen a hooker before, boy?"

"Oh. Sure," he said. But that was mostly on TV, where

they wore low-cut blouses and leather minis and always looked about forty-five. They'd passed a dozen Nitas today. Mickey began to remember them, one by one.

"Nita, she came up from Winston-Salem, her and her little sister. Didn't care much for their Daddy, so they took off. Sister got lost someplace. Forget her name now."

"Who's she scared of?"

"Goddamn pimp." Sugar stopped, balancing for a moment on Mickey's shoulder. "Look, kid. I figure you can make it home on that knee now. Where's your Ma live?"

"Up on Seventy-sixth. Other side of the Park."

Sugar dug some money out of his fatigue jacket. "You take this. Catch you a bus. Uptown kid like you got no damn business hanging out down here. Go on home to your Ma, boy, 'fore they sell you for dog meat."

There were a lot of cabs as they crossed Eighth Avenue, but Mickey didn't hail one. Something kept him with Sugar and Sonny. These were the people his father would always drift toward, seeking them out wherever he happened to wake up in the morning. Mickey had found a new kind of school, and for once in his life, he liked it.

Across Forty-third and halfway down the block toward Ninth, an alley cut through between two old tenements slated for removal. One of them had condemned signs on the front and all the windows had plywood or tin nailed over them from the inside. When they were opposite the alley, Sugar stopped and took Mickey by the shoulder again. "Okay, kid, you're on your own. This is where we get off. Get it? I got no room for kids." Mickey only stared. "I don't want no pukin' kids on my tail, understand?" George was shouting. "So just take off. That money will get you home."

"I don't want your fuckin' money!" Mickey shouted back.

But Sugar didn't pay any attention. Sonny had gone on alone, taking the point himself. He was across Forty-third now and heading up the alley beside the condemned tenement, with loping steps about two feet long. "Aw Jeez," said Sugar, "look at that damn fool go. Sonny, dammit! Wait up!" But Sonny didn't slow up at all. "Loo-ten-ant!" yelled Sugar, and stepped into the street.

It was then that Mickey noticed a small car pulling away from the curb and heading for Ninth. It was an old Toyota, dark green and not in great shape. The sun visor was pulled down in front of the driver's face, and all Mickey could see was something bright red, a sleeve, a shoulder.

Sugar was in the middle of the street now, concentrating on Sonny. He couldn't move as fast as usual on the crutch because the snow-melt had frozen and left rough islands of solid ice several inches thick in spots. The green car was headed straight for him. Even when he moved past the middle of the street, the car swerved, aimed straight at him.

"Hey!" yelled Mickey. Sugar looked up in time to see the Toyota coming, but his footing gave way and he dropped the crutch. It slid toward the gutter and he stood helpless, balanced on his one sound leg, waiting and unable to move unless he crawled. And that Sugar George wouldn't do. "Hey!" Mickey yelled again. He knew he couldn't make it across the street in time to knock Sugar out of the way, like you saw guys doing all the time on TV. Instead he picked up his two-by-four crutch and threw it like a javelin at the side of the green Toyota. It made a heavy, wicked thud as it bounced off the rear door. The car zigzagged, screeching crazily, then straightened, and when it had roared by, Sugar George lay in the gutter beside his crutch.

Sonny, halfway down the alley, broke into a loping run. By the time Mickey had hobbled across the street, Sonny had his friend in his arms and was carrying him up the alley toward the rear of the condemned tenement.

"We gotta get an ambulance, man!" Mickey said, tugging at him. "You shouldn't move him."

"*No hospitals!*" shouted Sonny fiercely. In the alley, he kicked hard at a board across one basement window, then tried another. It gave way. Gently he laid Sugar down on the wet bricks of the alley, crawled in through the cellar window, and put his arms out. "Give me a hand, kid," he said from the dark.

Mickey got his hands under Sugar George's body and when he touched the stump of arm, he barely noticed. He lifted, and Sonny guided his friend's limp body into the darkness. Mickey crawled through after them, the money Sugar had given him still shoved into his pants pocket.

A little light leaked into the cellar where the boards had been kicked off. There were rags and broken bottles and old beer cans and paper cartons from pizza and Chinese takeouts. They weren't the first ones to use the place, you could be sure of that. Somebody had even put hinges on one of the window boards so it swung in and out like a cat flap, though nothing looked different from outside. There were a couple of cans of Sterno and a half-burnt candle. Mickey found some fairly dry cardboard boxes and tore them up for Sugar to lie on. Sonny fished some matches and a paperback out of his jacket and put them on a shelf while he lighted the candle and one of the Sterno cans. Mickey took off his jacket and covered Sugar with it. Then all he could do was wait while Sonny ran his hands delicately over George's body, first the back and leg, then the chest, belly, arm, and finally the head. There was some blood on the face where he'd rolled against the curb and knocked himself out. The rest seemed to be just scrapes, but Mickey was still scared. "Go get some snow, kid," said Sonny.

Mickey had to go all the way back to the street to find clean snow. He looked around for Sugar's crutch, but the cars had run over it and it was in three pieces. He put two handfuls of snow together into a hard ball and carried it back.

Sonny was crouched down on his heels beside the can of Sterno, and Sugar was half sitting, leaning against the cellar wall. "I've seen him worse," Sonny told the kid. "He didn't get hit. He fell. He'll be okay."

"Who was in that car?" Mickey wished he'd gotten the license number, but that was TV stuff too. TV was a lot of crap when you got down to it. In real life you never got the license number.

"Take off, kid," Sugar said. He moved a little, winced, and leaned back again.

"I'm callin' the paramedics." Mickey got up and started for the window.

"Nah. I just got the crap knocked outa me, 's all. No doctors. Cops come with doctors. Put you where it's good for you. Never did like what's good for me." He looked up at Mickey and the words were mean but the voice wasn't. "Get the hell outa here, kid. Think I want some dumb little uptown brat hanging around? Go on, now."

"Okay," said Mickey, "okay, but I'll be back, all right? I'll be back pretty soon."

As he crawled out the window flap, he could hear Sonny's voice where he knelt beside his friend in the dim light. "'I think we are in rats' alley,'" he chanted. "'Where the dead men lost their bones.'"

The same Thursday night that Mickey spent in Sugar George's carton, David spent rereading John's only published novel, *The Human Abstract*. He had it on his mind all Friday morning, especially the main character, Max Fleming. Max was the resident demon John must've had looking over his shoulder, just as I've always had old Hyde, and Davy couldn't get rid of him so easily either. Max Fleming walked around with him all that morning and he was still hanging around at lunchtime. David's friend Myra Fish from WNYT noticed his preoccupation.

"So," she asked, "it's a bad space, David? The divorce is going through, or what?"

"No, no divorce. Yet."

"Alex should make up her mind. Either she sticks it out or not. The woman flits. This I can't stand."

"At least she's here, and not on the other side of the Atlantic." He munched his bagel. "I've been thinking a lot about John."

"Who isn't? But at least you didn't say 'poor John.' People should not patronize the dead. Only the living, if they deserve it." She stirred her tea thoughtfully. "I was on the control board when they taped that show with Shane McAuley. We had ten minutes dead air by the time we edited out all the actionable stuff. Only somebody switched the tapes and they ran the original. Great, wasn't it?" She smiled.

"My, my, I wonder who could have switched them?"

She shrugged. "You know me. I was always a shit. I

figured America deserved better than a ten-minute filler on the mating habits of the sand crab."

"If the brass find out, little Myra's out on her ear, my love."

"So. Let 'em eat worms."

"Do you think McAuley could've been angry enough to kill John?"

"King Brat? Nah." She took a forkful of raw spinach and spiked a mushroom. "With an Uzi maybe, from a safe distance, in front of ten guys from the international press handpicked by his agent. This kid does diddly without big media value, I'm telling you. He wanted an apology after the show, but yesterday his agent calls us up, Mr. Sunshine. His book sales are up thirty percent since the show." She snorted. "Anyway, he's got an alibi, I happen to know. The night John got killed, little Shane was in the lockup. He slugged some guy at Purple People, that punk club downtown. They couldn't talk the guy out of pressing charges. You don't read the papers, honey?" She shook her head. "If they hadn't moved his body like they did, I'd almost say John walked off some roof by himself, you know."

"Depressed?"

"It's too neat a word. We shared cabs sometimes. Once I stayed. No come-ons or anything, he wasn't like that. It wasn't planned. He was . . . uncertain. I'd say shy, but that doesn't seem to apply to John either. Halfway through the night, I knew nothing was going to happen. It didn't. I stayed anyway."

"And the next morning he pretended to be sleeping till you were gone." David's eyes closed.

"How did you know that?"

"A guess. It's a scene in *Human Abstract*. Max Fleming spends the night with a girl he's shared a cab with but he's too—"

"Sonuvabitch," said Myra in amazement. "I'd forgotten that. He was playing a scene."

"No," David told her gently. "I think he was living one."

"But didn't Max Fleming—"

"He committed suicide. Yes."

* * *

David took his time getting back across town that afternoon, stopping off to pick up little Gemma and take her to watch the skaters on Wollman Rink. It was past four when he got to Seventy-sixth Street. He'd meant to see Teresa ever since Wednesday night, and now the press had moved along to a subway stabbing down on Second Avenue. So David decided to stop off on his way home. What he didn't know was that the cops had at last released John's body, and Teresa and her mother had gone to sign the papers.

As promised, the cops were no longer on guard at the front door. David glanced up and saw that a light was on in Teresa's front window, but when he rang the entry buzzer, nobody answered. Finally he tried the handle and found it unexpectedly open.

Well now. If you've lived in any city in the late twentieth century, you know that a door is always supposed to be locked. And one that should be and isn't makes the hackles stand up on the back of your neck. David had heard all my warnings about our chum in the red ski parka, but as usual, he ignored me. No traveling in pairs for him. Now, though, he wished he'd brought the U.S. Marines.

But being David, he pushed open the entry door anyway, and went inside. He went safely up the stairs and was starting to drop his guard until he saw that the door of Teresa's apartment was standing wide open. The lock had been pried off and part of the door frame was hanging in jagged splinters.

David stepped cautiously inside. There was no sound except the rustling of papers in the draft from the open door. The floor was littered with torn orchestral scores, and bits of sheet music paved the carpet. Teresa's prized concert cello, the work of Andreas Freiling, lay on the floor with a jagged hole through its belly, the bow in two pieces beside it. On the wall behind the sofa something had been scrawled in Day-Glo orange paint. It was the single word, WEEKS!

Wolfgang the cat had escaped the marauder and taken up a post on the top bookcase shelf above the piano. He'd been stuck there all during the visit of the first strange human, and now he was damned if there wasn't another one. He was getting plenty tired of it, and he had a yen for his bowl of Friskies out in the kitchen. With a leap like Nijinsky, he dived off the shelf and landed on the bass keys of the piano, which he usually favored. David whirled around as if he'd been shot, his back turned to the open door. Suddenly something much larger than Wolfgang came flying through the air and landed on him, kicking and flailing and pounding his shoulders, head, and neck.

And that was just about where I came in. "I dropped to the floor," David told me as he rubbed his bruised bean with an ice cube. "Finally I shook our friend here off, but I whacked my fool loaf on the coffee table and put my own lights out."

Mickey, the Unidentified Flying Object, was grubby and even skinnier than I remembered. His jacket was missing, his face was bruised along the jaw, and he seemed to favor one foot. But he was here and he was alive. "I figured you were the guy that broke in," he told David. "I just saw you from behind."

"Never mind that, Mickey," I said. "Where the devil have you been since Wednesday night?"

"Around. I been okay. Listen, there's this guy, he got hurt. He needs help. I promised I'd be back."

He was already up and would've been out the door again, except that I'd parked in front of it. "Not just yet, kiddo. Sit down."

"Look, this guy's hurt and I promised, man, he's—"

"Mickey, I know your father left you with Brother Felix up at the Monastery, and he told you to wait there till he called."

"Yeah." The kid was back in the old sullen posture, slumped down, staring at his Adidas. "He didn't call. I guess he took off. But it's okay, though. It's cool."

"Mickey," David asked him, "have you seen any TV or read a paper in the last few days?"

"News is a lotta crap," he said. He looked steadily up at me. "Has something happened to my Mom, or what?"

"If you mean this mess, no," said David. "She must've

been out by the time all this happened. There's a note for
Sarah stuck to the fridge."

Mickey looked from one of us to the other. "You guys
know where my Dad is, don't you?"

"Mickey. Kiddo." There was no euphemism for John's
kind of death, even if I'd wanted one. "He's dead."

He sat still. His eyes were fixed on the floor in front of
him. "How?"

"We think somebody killed him. He was found in the
elevator at Stuyvesant Hall. By your mother."

His mouth tightened a little and I could hear his
breathing, sharp but regular. "Who did it?"

"We don't know. Maybe the same person who broke in
here. Maybe not."

Then he was silent again. He showed none of the predictable emotions. But neither had John. I recalled him at
Louise's funeral in the scorching Iowa August, trailing like a
somnambulist through the garrulous ceremonies of his
mother's death. Grief gave him no bonds with the rest of us;
it merely made him more alien. All you could do was hang
around, hang on, till it was over.

At last Mickey got up and moved toward the door. "I
promised this guy," he said. "You coming, or not?"

"I've got my car downstairs," said David. "Let's go."

On the way across town Mickey told us the tale of his
travels. He left huge gaps, but one thing was clear. If he was
okay, it was thanks to his two new friends. It was the part
about the green Toyota with the red-coated driver that bothered me, naturally. It was all just too much coincidence.
Whoever these two fellows of Mickey's were, I was sure
they had some connection with John's death and the mysterious Weeks file.

When we pulled into the alley off Forty-third and
Eighth, I knew instantly what the connection was. The two
men were making their way toward Forty-second. One was
propped on a length of iron pipe for a crutch, and he was
missing part of an arm and part of a leg. David barely had
time to switch off the engine before Mickey was out of the
car and running. "Hey!" he yelled. "Wait up!"

Sonny turned, lighting up with an ear-to-ear smile, but Sugar George went doggedly on. Mickey caught up with him and yanked at his shoulder. "You said you might know my Mom. You did. You knew the dead man was my Dad. Didn't you? Why didn't you answer me? You knew! You killed my Dad, you bastard! You lousy bastard!" He started to pound at Sugar's chest, but the man hardly seemed to notice. Angry tears streamed down the kid's face, but he kept on pounding, until David pulled him away. Sugar just turned back toward the street. "Come on, Loo-ten-ant," I heard him say. "We gotta get outa this damn town and travel."

"Where to?" I shouted. The alley was an echo chamber. "Not Philadelphia again, I hope?"

We made quite a sight half an hour later as we all trooped through David's building and squeezed into the elevator. Mickey had a patina of three day's assorted grime. David had the beginning of his usual five o'clock shadow. Sugar and Sonny wore fatigue jackets, but not the chi-chi kind, and their fragrance didn't come from Yves St. Laurent either. I tried to help out by puffing a Turkish Delight on the way up, but that didn't seem to placate a beige female leashed to a pair of equally beige pooches. When the elevator stopped, she charged down the hall muttering "Actors," tore into her apartment, and barricaded her door.

Once inside David's place, Sonny wandered around the living room, scanning the books on the shelves with great attention, while Sugar sat isolated in Alex's antique chair, bracing himself for the third degree. I rather wanted to give it to him, too, but I kept remembering that Mickey might not have been here if it weren't for George and his cardboard box.

"Of course it was you on the plane and at the Liberty Plaza Hotel," I said, as we got down to cases.

"I told John it wasn't gonna work," said George.

"If you didn't kill my Dad, why didn't you tell me about him? If you were his friend, why didn't you tell me?" Mickey couldn't hold out any longer.

"It was Sonny liked him. Sonny don't like a lot of people." He glanced up at his friend. "John would come down for the music. When your Ma played at the Hall. He'd bring a bottle, slip out back afterward, pass it around, just hang out with us." He laughed. "Gonna write a book about old Sonny, that's what he always said."

"Why did John want you to go to Philly in his place?"

"He said this scam was going down. Where he worked. Mixed up, I don't know. He didn't always make a lotta sense when he was juiced. Anyhow, he didn't trust them, and he wanted a chance to get the kid outa the way. That's all I know."

"So he shipped Mickey off to me, and tried to cover his tracks by making the Danson people think he was in Philadelphia, as planned. Only he sent you instead. Then he doubled back and put the boy into even deeper hiding at the Monastery. Who was it he didn't trust? Did he give a name?"

"Nah. Had a partner, though."

"The guy in the green car?" asked Mickey.

"Charlie. That's the only name he said."

"Charlotte Stedman, the computer wiz?" David looked at me.

I shrugged. "Fits with what Plumb told Eddie." I turned back to George. "You took a big risk going in his place, if someone was laying for him. Why did you do it?"

"Bucks. Me and the Lieutenant could use a little travelin' cash. John gave me two hundred bucks. We can get us down to Baton Rouge on two hundred bucks."

"You're sure he never said anything more about this scam? Who else was involved?" He wasn't the kind of man who gave things away quickly. I kept at him.

"Look," he said, "I don't know what the hell he was into, okay?"

"But somebody thinks you do. Who was in that green car? Weeks? Danson?"

"Only thing I know, John found something fishy over there. Something to do with vets. MIAs, he told us."

Suddenly Sonny ducked beneath the desk, arms over

his head, feet tucked under him in the kneehole. David got up and moved slowly toward him, on hands and knees.

"Ever heard of Dennis Weeks?" I continued my questioning.

"Nope."

"Did he think Danson was behind this funny business at the Foundation?"

"'There's ne'er a villain dwelling in all Denmark,'" Sonny shrieked, "'but he's an arrant knave.'"

"Shut up, Lieutenant! I told you already. Just shut up," shouted Sugar George.

David was on his knees in front of the desk now. "'There needs no ghost, my lord, come from the grave,'" he said, offering Sonny a hand, "'to tell us this.'"

"'Consent to swear.'" The lines from *Hamlet* were out of sequence, but not quite random. Sonny selected them on some principle of his own. A hand came from under the desk to take David's. Then a head and shoulders followed, and Sonny crept out, looking wide-eyed from one side of the living room to the other.

"'Propose the oath, my lord.'" David drew him out, grasping his forearms, till they were kneeling face to face.

"'Never to speak of this that you have seen. Swear by my sword.'" Sonny held up his hands before his face, crossed at the wrists like the hilt of a sword, or like a man in handcuffs, and offered them to David.

Then David did what I've seen him do on stage with a prop sword. He took the hands in his, pulled them to his lips, and kissed them where they crossed. It was a gentle gesture, a sign of human fidelity. And Sonny returned it in kind. He brushed his right hand delicately over the not-quite-perfect side of David's face, as if he were looking for something he couldn't find.

"Tell me," said David softly. "You have something to tell me."

Sonny knelt, watching him with wide, soft eyes. "'The Prince of Darkness is a gentleman,'" he said abruptly. Then he got up and plonked down on the couch, observing radio silence.

"What's his name?" said David, still on his knees. He was looking intently up at Sonny's face.

"Vince," Sugar said uncertainly. It'd been a long time since anybody but cops and shrinks wanted Sonny's real name. "Vince Emerson."

David stood up. "You're staying here now. The two of you. Till this is over."

"Sonny don't like houses."

"Sonny doesn't, or you don't?"

"He can stay by himself then. I gotta split."

Mickey stood up. "Sonny won't stay without you. You just want to make him go."

"If that sweetheart in the red jacket tracks you down again, your friend will be right in the middle," I said.

"You can't tell Sonny what to do. It's not fuckin' fair," said the kid. He picked up a glass ashtray and pitched it across the room. It struck the bricks in front of the fireplace and shattered. Suddenly Emerson dived off the couch and tackled Mickey, flattening him onto the rug. He threw his own long, fluid body over the boy and covered him, shoulders hunched to protect himself.

"Kill-fire!" he screamed. "Kill-fire!"

Sugar George got up and lowered himself beside them. He put his hand on Sonny's hard, tense back and stroked him gently. "Okay, Son'," he said. "It's okay. It was a drill, that's all."

Emerson's body was tight and twitching and he turned wild-eyed on Sugar at the first faint touch and swung out at him. His fist connected and Sugar slammed back against the coffee table, but he never took his hand off Sonny's back. Finally Sonny began to relax, and Mickey crawled out from under. They sat there on the floor, their arms around Sonny, the kid on one side, and Sugar, a trickle of blood running down from a cut beside his eye, on the other. "Okay, Lieutenant," said Sugar George. "It's okay." He looked up at David. "You don't want him here, man."

"The hell I don't," said David firmly.

Chapter Nine

We phoned Eddie, who, with Sarah for protection, was once again on a visit to Plumb's office. Bea had gone back to Brooklyn, but they managed to intercept Teresa and take her home to the ransacked apartment, where Lieutenant Duffy and his minions were already scraping orange paint samples off the wall. I'd phoned him to report the break-in, and I could tell the little Irishman was getting frustrated. When Teresa, Sarah, Eddie, Wolfgang the cat and his impedimenta at last arrived at David's, they were herded by a small, seething son of Erin. And it was Yours Truly that Duffy zeroed in on.

"I thought we understood each other, Sherman," he growled. "You shoulda brought this kid straight to the Precinct, not up here. And what about these two?" He indicated Sugar and Sonny. "They coulda been kidnappers, you ever think of that?"

"But they're not, are they, Lieutenant Huffy? They're just concerned citizens."

"Or accessories. I called the Liberty Plaza this morning and got a description of the guy that called himself Falkner." He waggled a meaningful finger at George.

"It's not illegal to take an all-expense-paid trip to Philadelphia, is it?"

He laid his dainty paw on Sonny's shoulder. "I wanna talk to both these guys. This one first." And in a moment the two of them had disappeared into the bedroom, leaving George to wait his turn.

Teresa, taking after her mother, eschewed the traditional teary-eyed reunion. Maybe she'd invested in too many of them in the past when the boy had turned up unhurt. But she certainly didn't hesitate to land on him with both feet.

"When is this crap going to stop, Mickey, this taking off on the lam? You think you're gonna spend your life that way, throw the world in the toilet and take off for another planet?"

"Africa," he said.

"What?" said his mother sharply.

"We were going to Africa. Me and Dad. He was gonna quit that fuckin' job and we were gonna take off. For good."

Teresa sat down. "I see," she said.

All of us were quiet. Even Wolfgang, still trapped in his kitty carrier, had stopped cursing under his whiskers.

"I was gonna tell you."

"Oh. Nice of you."

"When we were ready."

"I see."

"I figured you'd say no."

"I always do. Don't I?"

"Yeah. A lot." He came to sit with her. "I didn't think he'd really take me. Not really. So I didn't say anything. Because he was always talking about stuff and we never did any of it. I didn't believe him much. Anymore." For almost ten sentences he'd forgotten to throw in his pet obscenity. "Only I didn't want him to know I didn't. So I just kinda went along."

Teresa put her arms around him. "Goddamn it, Mick," she said.

There was a pause, and Sarah charged into the breach. "All right now. I simply cannot bear any more of this. Before that measly little man with the made-up tie comes back in here, tell us who this Weeks person is and what's going on."

"So far as John knew," said Teresa, "Weeks doesn't exist." She got up and lighted a cigarette. "At least not in the present tense. You were right, Winnie. I did get a phone call and erase it from that tape. Somebody'd phoned me a couple of times, even before John died." She took one puff and tossed the cigarette into the fireplace. "The guy kept talking about Mickey. He knew what school he went to, he knew about your place. Just cute little hints, you know. But when Mick disappeared, I was sure they had him. So I went over to John's place to try and find the file he was keeping on Weeks. That's what they kept asking for.

"That Sunday Mickey's roommate told you about, when John and I showed up at Wildwood together? He'd asked me to come up that day. He said he was leaving the Danson Foundation, going to California."

"Not Africa?"

"No. He wanted to be sure Mickey was okay. Asked a lot of stuff about the money and the insurance. It was strange. He hated talking business, he left it all to his lawyer, Sandor Hoffman. Well. John drove me home that night. I didn't ask him to go."

"I didn't know you were seeing him again," said Sarah.

"It wasn't a regular thing. But you know John, he wandered around a lot at night, looking for somebody to talk to. A few times lately, it was my place. Oh, don't look like that, Mickey. All right, I slept with your father. If you don't want to hear it, go out in the kitchen. You think you can take off for Africa, you ought to be old enough to find out. Marriage and love don't always live the same length of time. Sometimes one plays out too soon, sometimes the other."

"If you still loved him, why did you divorce him?" Mickey demanded. "Why couldn't you live together?"

"Because he was going down the drain, and I didn't want to watch."

"He wasn't. He didn't drink anymore."

"Not when you were around, no. He managed that much."

"Kid," said George, "she's right. He was past quitting the stuff."

"What do you fuckin' know about it?" shouted Mickey. He stood up and squared off at Sugar George, who was propped against the mantelpiece. "You know shit, man." He poked a finger two, three times, against the man's chest. And then all of a sudden Mickey was flat on his back on the rug.

Sugar got his balance back. "I know, kid," he said.

"Because I got him home a couple times. I mopped puke off his shoes. He was your Dad. Why the hell does he have to be perfect?" He looked over at Teresa. "Sorry I punched him. I'll do it again, though." She nodded.

"So," I said, "now that we've got that over with, what did John tell you about Weeks?"

"He said he'd found a glitch in the Foundation's grant-giving procedures. It took him a long time to add it all up. He kept recommending people for grants, but they were never awarded. So he began to check into things, run down the histories of some of the grant applicants."

"With the help of Miss Charlotte Stedman, in the Computer Room," said Eddie. Today's visit to Plumb's office had netted him a hefty box of printouts, now stashed beside his chair.

"Right," Teresa went on. "Anyway, John found out that a few controversial people were getting juicy grants and making big news, but almost all the other individual applicants got refused. Everything went through the regional agencies, like Hopewell. There were twelve of them, but the money wasn't evenly spread around. Hopewell and a couple of others, one in Mississippi and one out in Oregon, I think, sent in three fourths of the approved applications."

"And there was no Dennis Weeks in Kansas City?"

She shook her head. "John flew out there just before Christmas. The Hopewell Foundation address turned out to be a mail drop at a trailer court."

"What about the MIAs?" said Sugar. They used MIAs for part of the scam, he told me and Sonny that."

"Okay," said Teresa. "So, Charlie Stedman cross-checks a dozen different files with the official bio the Danson office has. He was born in Blair, North Dakota, that much checks out. There was a real Dennis Weeks. He went to Princeton from 'sixty-three to 'sixty-six. Okay too. Now we get the good stuff. The official bio says Weeks left school in 'sixty-six and went to London to study art at the Slade School. Only the Slade never heard of him. But the Army did. Selective Service says Dennis Weeks got his one-A notice in March 1966 and was inducted in August. He went down in a Huey crash in North Vietnam in February 1970. MIA since then."

"No living family, naturally."

"Of course not, it would've queered the whole thing. But John talked to a guy in North Dakota who was in his platoon in Nam. Weeks's father died about a year after the Huey went down."

"What advantage was there in using a real person?" asked Sarah. "Why not just make someone up, so no one would know anything about him?"

"Because," Mickey told her, "if part of the stuff was true, and anybody stumbled on to it in the computers and started checking, they'd be more likely to give up if the first part checked out okay."

"But Johnny didn't give up," said Eddie.

"No," said Teresa. "It mattered to him. That's why I didn't tell him about those calls I got. I hadn't seen anything matter to him in a long time."

"So what we have," I said, "is a phony agency, or maybe three agencies, fronted by semi-real people whose existing records will discourage investigation, through which somebody can drain off the entire Danson endowment and all the matching funds and bequests a little at a time, using computer transfers. The money comes out of the Danson pocket, goes into the mythical Weeks pocket through phony grant applications that account for the drain. When the money is paid out to those fake applicants, it sifts right through the nonexistent Weeks pocket into—where, would you guess?"

"Anywhere with numbered accounts, and no disclosure treaties with our Treasury Department about criminal funds," said David. "The Caymans, Liechtenstein, Panama."

"But it couldn't just go straight into a numbered account. They'd make a couple of transfers, in case they were audited. And they'd bury all the records in the computer bank on a private program with an entry code nobody knew except the one who kept track of the money they skimmed off." Mickey was getting excited now, and knowledge was leaking out of him. As I'd suspected, he was smarter than he ever let his teachers know.

"Most foundations invest their endowments," I said.

"Why not put the bucks into some legitimate business, and transfer it from there? Organized crime and the intelligence community do it all the time, I'm told. So long as you keep the fake grants the same size as the fund transfers, the books balance, the paperwork—or computerwork—adds up. Down the mousehole, and nobody knows." Kenwood Enterprises, Cella Danson's father's old firm, sounded to me like a fine mousehole. "Mickey, how would you trace a money transfer like that from the outside?"

"Send in a mouse," he said with a grin. "Make out a grant application approved by Weeks, and that should trigger the cash transfer. After that, just monitor."

"In other words," said Eddie, "let X equal a nonexistent applicant."

"Kiddo," I said, putting my arm on Mickey's shoulder. "Could you chase that mouse for us, the one your Dad must've used to find those numbered accounts? Could you do it again?"

"Maybe. Why? What good will it do?"

"It might tell us part of what your Dad had in that file of his, and that might help us use it against whoever killed him."

"How are you going to recognize the name of John's trace applicant?" said David.

"Maybe John gave me some kind of clue to it." He'd involved me so carefully that I knew he must've planned this part as well. Somewhere, I already had the name of his trace through the computers.

"I'd need to access a big system, with a lot of tie-ins," said Mickey.

"The Frumious Bandersnatch!" cried Eddie. "Surely that would do." We'd nabbed Lewis Carroll's name for our local college monster, the computer that eats all my exam scores and is always "down" when I want my monthly paycheck.

"Could you use the college system, kiddo?"

"Probably," Mickey said judiciously. "But I'd have to look it over to know."

"Okay," I said. "I think I can get you in, with a little arm-twisting."

"But what about these?" groaned Eddie, indicating the box of printouts. "I have diddled about with every kind of code from Boy Scout Special to the OSS, but this gibberish eludes me. And there is no Weeks file among them, not that I can ferret out."

"I don't think John would've left it on a computer," I said, "no matter how clever the code was. He didn't trust the things. No, I think it exists in very ordinary, tangible form somewhere, and if we're clever enough, we can find it. Any ideas?"

They all looked as blank as I felt. All this computer stuff was giving me a stomachache, to be honest. I was far from sure that, being the compuphobe I'm proud to be, I'd ever be able to unravel the crime that had led somebody to murder my friend. But looking at the long faces around me, I made a stab at rallying the troops. "'Once more unto the breach' you lot," I said. "Merriman, keep at those printouts. Sort out all the Hopewell grants and see if any of the names ring a bell. Mickey can help you figure them out. And then list the amounts of the grants to compare with fund transfers when we attack the Frumious Bandersnatch back home. Teresa, why don't you take that injured cello of yours to Andreas Freiling and see what kind of reaction you get to a few judicious hints about his assistant? George, you with us, or not?"

He studied Teresa and the kid. "Okay," he said, though not without a tinge of misgiving.

"Then go with Teresa. I don't want her buzzing around alone."

Sarah had been quiet a long time, and I knew she had something on her mind. Now she came out with it. "I still don't see," she said, "why it was necessary to invent a character based on Dennis Weeks. Computer embezzlement is nothing new, after all, it's done all the time. Why not simply make the investments directly from the Danson pocket, as you put it, into some money laundry bought for the purpose, and then into the Swiss accounts, or wherever they are? Why complicate a simple crime with this elaborate fiction?"

"Perhaps the complication was as much an attraction as

the crime," said Eddie. "Isn't it true that people who are involved with computer manipulations view the intricacy of the patterns as a sort of art form?"

"It was more than a computer manipulation," said David. "They created a person, as Sarah said. A new character. They even began a plot. They sent him to art school. Very specific school at that . . . But I'm making too much of it, I suppose."

"Maybe. Maybe not." I turned to Sarah. "Now, what about—"

"I phoned Cella Danson this morning, my dear old nag, and you and I are invited to afternoon tea tomorrow. Her companion was delighted. But I refuse to go with you in that grubby old touring cap of yours. I shall buy you a respectable hat tomorrow morning. So there."

I didn't have a chance to protest, because just then Lieutenant Duffy came out of the bedroom, herding Sonny. Sugar George looked at them nervously, but Sonny was smiling, as usual. "Okay," said Duffy to George, "you next." He shook his head as Sonny sat down on the floor.

"This guy a smartass, or what?" Duffy inquired. "I say, 'What's your name,' he tells me Phlebas the Something."

"Oh," I said, "you mean Phlebas the Phoenician. 'Phlebas the Phoenician, a fortnight dead . . .'"

"'Forgot the cry of gulls,'" Sonny continued, "'and the deep sea swell/ And the profit and loss.'"

"That supposed to be some kind of a crack?" said the pugnacious litle Irishman.

"No, Lieutenant Stuffy," I told him. "It's T. S. Eliot. Fellow wrote a few little poems in his misspent youth, before he took to Broadway musicals." But to tell you the truth, Sonny's quotations had begun to sound to me like clues. Oh hell, *everything* had begun to sound like a clue!

Duffy merely curled his lip. "Sounds like a lotta crapola to me," he declared.

> *Twit, twit, twit*
> *Jug jug jug jug jug jug*
> *So rudely forced*
> *Tereu,*"

said Sonny.

Chapter Ten

Mickey and Teresa would stay the night at David's, along with George and Sonny, who were used to bunking on the carpet. Sarah, Eddie, and I phoned ahead to Bert the desk clerk at my favorite hotel, the dear old creaky Battersea, and trundled along there once Duffy had retreated with his tail between his legs. I suppose I was hard on him, but Duffy seemed more concerned with keeping me out of his peach-colored hair than with finding out who'd killed John, and his patience with me was no thinner than mine with him.

That's why I was especially pleased to see Lloyd Agate waiting for me in the Battersea's moth-eaten plush and mahogany lobby. Somehow I'd had an idea this might be his choice in New York hotels. While the others checked in, I toddled over to him. He dumped the *Times* off his lap and stood up.

"I remembered you liked this place. Bev thinks it's quaint."

"The Battersea?" I remembered the place from the old days of formal tea in the Salon and Swiss waiters in the Dining Room. "Where is the missus?" I asked, looking round with rising paranoia. Bev Agate and her formidable little daughter Sylvia have both had classes in the martial arts. Whenever they cross my path, I expect them to yell "Hai-yah!" and crash through a door.

"Bev? She went to some play. *Jogging to Calcutta*, that was it. Just this one guy in it, they want forty-five bucks a ticket. At that price I wouldn't enjoy it." He grinned. "Besides, I kinda had other plans."

And so we convened up in our room. Eddie was next door, already buried in printouts, with the adjoining door wide open so as not to miss anything. I filled Lloyd in on the events of the afternoon and the information Teresa had given us.

"Okay," he said, "so what we got is a genuine fiddle. Real scam."

"But who's the violinist?"

"Not Miss Plumb," piped up Eddie from next door. "I indemnify her."

"Besides," I said, "she's not in a position to pull it off, is she? Since she's no longer the power behind the throne."

"Who is Andrew's assistant now?" asked Sarah.

"Milky fellow named Sommers," called Eddie. "Dean Sommers. Appeared out of the ether some eight years ago and was clasped to the bosom of the mighty Andy D." The papers scrunched and he appeared in the door. "Efficiency mad, apparently, keeps the entire staff conveniently off balance."

"This guy have access to Danson's papers?" asked Lloyd.

"As executive secretary, certainly. A rubber stamp with Danson's John Henry, access to all the computer what-nots, whatever he liked."

"All right, then," said Sarah. She had Eddie's famous legal pad before her, and she ruled three lines down the page, heading the columns Motive, Means, and Opportunity—the Big Three of crime. "Sommers, Dean. Means and opportunity. Motive?"

"Power, greed, usual stuff. He sounds the type. Power worshipers are often the bland, vague sort. And I'm sorry, Merriman, but I think we have to put Miss Plumb down too. After all, there isn't much she doesn't know about the workings of that joint. She's entirely capable of heisting Danson's rubber stamp. And she has a better motive even than Sommers to make the Foundation look bad, or even go broke."

"Yes. She *was* demoted from the Executive Suite," said

Sarah. "And she's not a forgiving woman. Did you see how she glared at me when we walked in together this afternoon, Eddie?"

"Jealousy," I said. "She's got a terminal crush on Merriman." He gave me a dirty look, but I forged on. "Besides, she may need money. Supporting the Aged Parent."

"And the two dogs, let us for heaven's sake not overlook the dogs as a motive," Merriman said, attempting withering scorn. He marched back to his room and shut the door. In a moment, he stuck his head in again. "Oh, blast you. Very well. Put her on the list. Phooey!" And he popped back again.

"Who else we got, inside the Foundation?" said Lloyd.

"Charlotte Stedman," Sarah suggested. "She certainly had means and opportunity. Teresa says she's the best computer person they have. Those people can do almost anything with a machine. They actually killed a friend of mine. She went down in January to pay her real estate taxes and they informed her she'd been dead since the Fourth of July." She shivered and took a sip of coffee. "I wouldn't be surprised if you and I aren't officially married on somebody's damn computer."

"Horrors!" I said. "Would that be so bad?"

"It would if somebody did it by poking the wrong silly button."

Lloyd turned a nice pink, as he always does at mention of our state of mortal, though tender, sin. "Charlotte Stedman had two out of three. What about motive for her?"

"I don't see one. If she was part of the scheme, why help John figure everything out and get evidence?" Sarah objected.

"Throw him off the track. Put him on to somebody else's neck. Keep an eye on how much he knew. Feed him fake information."

Sarah sighed and wrote it down.

"What about Dandy Andy?" I said. "He lost a lot of money investing in his wife's father's company. Maybe he decided to put it back out of the Foundation funds, and then some."

"Okay. He'd sure have the other two, means and opportunity. It's all his ball game."

"And don't forget John himself," said Eddie's voice. There he was in the doorway again. "He hated his job, and probably Danson, from what we've heard. He disliked everything the Foundation stood for these days, the phony avant-gardism, the lack of content, the media madness. They used him shamelessly, Winnie, you know they did. They wanted nothing from him but his reputation and his ability to make news by his outspoken opinions. What better motive could anyone have had to ruin them?"

"He sure had himself a computer wiz," said Agate. "This Miss Stedman. So long as she was on the job, he had means and opportunity."

"And he was a fiction writer, Win," said Sarah. "It would explain the elaborate business with Weeks, the invention of a mythical person."

I shook my head. "John was not a thief. No." The others looked at one another, one of those looks people exchange in the presence of the senile, the simple, and the chronically stubborn. I fumed and charged on. "And anyway, if he did it all himself, who had a motive to push him off a roof? Or do you think he decided to commit suicide after piling up millions for his old age and planning a trip to Africa? No. Whoever killed John had a lot to lose if this Weeks information came out. Somebody still wants that file. Somebody wants to eliminate Sugar George. How do you square all that?"

"He's quite right," Eddie admitted. "This feverish search for the file doesn't point to John at all."

"I'm putting him down on the list," said Sarah. "We can't make exceptions, and the possibility remains, even if it's marginal."

"After all," Eddie said thoughtfully, "what crime comes down to is character. All this listing doesn't consider a personal ethic, or the shreds of compassion or—if I may be so archaic—honor. I believe John had that. Honor amounts to an inviolable sense of self. There are certain things you simply won't do, not from some sentimental code, but because they would destroy who you are, how you define yourself. You become a criminal if the definition is too rigid, madly egocentric, or if there is no real definition."

"And we know far too little about the characters of this lot," I said. "I wish we could find a way to get them on our home turf for a while, get to know them."

"You're assuming," said Lloyd, looking troubled, "that the killing was done by whoever worked the fiddle."

"Surely it's probable. To keep John from making it public."

"Maybe. But what about the guy who unloaded those crates?"

"Ah, the elusive Thomas Mann. Did you get a chance to run Freiling through the computer, Lloyd?"

"I got it right here," he said, and pulled a crumpled print sheet from his pocket. "Andreas Viktor Freiling, born Salzburg, Austria, 1935. Parents moved to Bern, Switzerland, 1938, returned to Austria, 1949. He emigrated to the U.S. in 1963. Parents deceased, one sister, Magdalena Freiling Ritter, two years older, one half brother, Martin Peter Freiling, fifteen years younger. Quite a gap there. Kid brother's still in Austria, according to this."

"That would make the younger brother about David's age," said Sarah.

"And about the age of Freiling's mysterious assistant," Eddie reminded her.

"Could Thomas Mann have been the man in the red parka who followed you?"

"Well, as you know, I didn't see him very closely, but Teresa said the assistant was big and hefty, and our Santa is short, pudgy, not muscular-looking at all. I doubt it, Win, really I do."

"I'll see what else I can dig up on the brother," said Agate. "But there's a couple other people. This guy Sugar George, for one."

"Why would he want to kill John?"

"Money," said Agate. "Same reason he went to work for him."

"And there's another motive, Win," Sarah said quietly. "Did you notice the way he looked at Teresa? I think she's the real reason he got involved with John."

"You think she helped organize his trip to Philly?"

"No, you blind old bat, I think he did it because he

loves her and she was still in love with Johnny. Looking after him when he was drunk, cleaning him up, all that. He did what he could to make her fond of him, because he thought he couldn't approach her. But he must've hated every minute of it. Maybe he hated John, too." She sat watching us. "Oh, don't look like that. Men! Honestly. It's as good as you and your mysterious Austrian half brothers."

"But does the guy have an alibi?" Lloyd's cop brain pulled us back from personalities to procedures. "When did he get back from this mission to Philly?"

"The noon flight on Tuesday," Merriman told him glumly. "No alibi in that. And of course you cannot accept poor Sonny's word as corroboration. He would prevaricate to His Holiness the Pope if George were to ask him."

"Mickey says he has a lot of friends on the street. Maybe one of them can give him an alibi."

"Well, Teresa certainly has one," said Sarah. "She was at her mother's in Brooklyn all Tuesday night and didn't leave until almost nine on Wednesday morning. That's hours after John was killed."

"She had a damn good motive," said Lloyd, "if she found out Falkner was going to disappear for good with her kid."

"Yes," Eddie said, "and if we aren't to believe George's friend, we must also cast doubt on the word of Teresa's mother."

I sat there biting my tongue. I couldn't mention what Teresa had said to me on the phone—"I'll kill the sonuvabitch myself." Oh, I knew I should, but I couldn't. I really knew she hadn't been serious, after all. But there in the back of my head was the ghost of Hyde, the old son-of-a-sea-cook, clicking his tongue and muttering curses in one of his nine languages.

"Let's see that confounded list," I said. Sarah handed it over. "Damn thing's all question marks," I grumbled. "And the Foundation's full of people we don't even know who might be just as guilty."

"Look," said Lloyd, "first we gotta find *where* the guy was killed. Then find this guy Mann, or whoever he is. If he moved the body, he must at least know where it happened and probably how. Number three, find the file on Dennis

Weeks, and see if we can use it to bring the murderer out. The guy in the red jacket hasn't had much luck finding it, and he's getting worried. We just gotta push hard enough on the right spot and he'll make a move."

I sighed. "I don't know, Lloyd. Maybe we ought to leave it to Stuffy Duffy after all." I hated the idea of knuckling under to the little guy with the double-knit underwear, but I felt as if I were swimming through oatmeal. Or jogging to Calcutta.

"Hang tough, Doc," said Lloyd. "Let's get a look at that tape first, and you read the new book Brother Felix gave you. I'll see what I can worm out of Duffy."

Suddenly there was a loud hammering on the door. Mrs. Agate's determined soprano could've been heard in Yonkers. "Lloyd, I know you're still in there. You know what time it is? I'm giving you five before I lock myself in the bedroom." And I heard the clatter of tiny hooves as Bev marched her five-foot-one down the hall.

Lloyd got up, knocked over his cup of coffee and stepped on Eddie's foot as he made haste for the door. When he'd gone, Merriman sat massaging his instep. "You know, Winnie, there's one way to find out who killed John."

"Don't you dare say it, Eddie," cried Sarah.

"All right, then *I* will. We've all been thinking it all night anyway," I told her. "The only way to smoke this fellow out is to become as interesting to him as John was. Become a threat to him."

"A target, you mean. And go off a roof in the process. No, Win, this sleuthing business has gone far enough. You are neither of you Sam Spade." Sarah went into the bathroom and slammed the door. Soon I could hear the shower running at about the speed of the Snake River Falls.

"She's quite right, of course," said Merriman meekly. "Damn fool idea."

"And if I tried it, I'd probably wind up living in the Roman Holiday Motel." I puffed thoughtfully on a Turkish Delight. "Still, it's rather a shame. Probably would've worked."

What I didn't know was that our David had already had the same idea, and there was no Sarah around to tell him no.

Chapter Eleven

I spent the rest of that night, my second in a row with no sleep, reading John's manuscript. It wasn't funny-paper length, like the Infant Phenomenon's opus, but I got through it before first light. It was called *The Dance of a One-Legged Soldier*, and it detailed a day and night in the life of one Vince Oakes. Vince was just under forty, slept in a rolled-up carpet hidden in a basement landing, and scrounged through the garbage cans of the downtown party animals for his food. Shattered by a nameless war, Vince's mind was a dust heap for the fragments of Western culture, intermixed with very real memories of battle death, of child enemies lined up and shot in ditches on orders from the Man Upstairs. When I'd finished reading, and Vince Oakes lay frozen to death on the steps of the Public Library, I switched off the lamp and sat thinking for a long time. It seemed to me a fine book, perhaps even a great one, about sentient human life relentlessly undermined by brutality and fraud and mindless consumption. But that was what the reviewers would say. Mostly, it was about waste, not least the waste of John himself. No matter how he'd soaked himself with booze, he'd never been able to stop thinking. Not even, I was certain, during that last, long fall. I knew him. Even going over the edge, he'd have been thinking all the way.

I went in and stood naked under the coldest shower I've ever taken in my life and looked at myself, bulbous and cranky and ill-equipped for anything but what I've done for years—writing, teaching, teasing the brain with mortal puzzles. But risking what John had finally been pushed to, the extinguishing of W. M. Sherman? Sarah was right. I wasn't brave enough. I cared too much for me. I finally understood just how much John had despised himself. That phone call Plumb had overheard hadn't been blackmail, it'd been a dare, just as he'd dared young King Brat to punch him. John hadn't given a damn what happened to him. Instead, he'd come to me and made me give a damn again.

And he'd been right about me, too. All my life I had evaded ultimate realities. I had managed to approximate the great risks of living—marriage, fatherhood, professional success, artistic creation—without ever quite confronting them. Despair and self-loathing had given Johnny a kind of courage I would never have, an ability to dance on the edge of death. But there was another thing John had also known about me. Once I'm in a fight, I'm in for keeps. And that was why he'd given me his book to fight for.

Next morning Sarah went off to shop for my new hat and Eddie was once again up to his elbows in printouts. All alone, I rode the creaky elevator down to the old Salon, where I spied Lloyd Agate and his wife Bev having breakfast. At their table was the Dazzling Duffy, with Lincoln at his side munching an English muffin. I was about to skulk to a table a safe distance away, where I might consume cholesterol and nitrites, but Lloyd waved at me. "Over here, Doc," he yelled, tipping over the salt shaker with his sleeve.

Mrs. Agate smiled as I approached. "Don't look so worried, Dr. Sherman. You can have Lloyd for the morning. But if he's not waiting for me after I'm finished at Macy's and Lord & Taylor, I'm moving on to Saks for the afternoon, and you can foot the bill. After that, there's always Tiffany's. Bye now." And off she went.

I parked and ordered my eggs and bacon. When I looked up from the menu, Duffy was sitting there smiling at me. Well, I didn't much like that, I can tell you. I must've looked pretty nervous, because Lloyd nudged Lincoln and they both started to laugh. "Okay," I said, "what's the matter, soap on my nose?"

"Duffy's figured out who you are," Lloyd replied.

"Who am I?"

"Henrietta Slocum," said Duffy. "Jeez, I figured the old girl pegged out after that last book. When Hyde bought it under the streetcar and all? Take my advice, Doc, you fix the guy up. Maybe he lived through it, and now he solves these crimes from this wheelchair."

"I think that one's been done on TV," I told him with a sigh. Avoiding fans like Duffy is exactly why I've been writing incognito for thirty years.

"I been reading those Hyde books since I was ten," he declared. "I love the guy. What a style! Man, would I love to handle a cane like he does! Hell, I figured you probably wrote some high-brow crap, you know, being a professor and all."

He dug out a tattered book. It was the very first Hyde to have come out in paper, *Death of a Gilded Lily.* "Put your John Hancock on that, will you, Doc?" His necktie was slipping, and one end of the plastic tab stuck out from under his collar. But I didn't tell him. I was rather flattered. "This one's a collector's item now," he said, landing me back on earth with a thud. "Autograph makes it worth more on the market."

"Market?"

"Sure," he said brightly. "I go to a lot of flea markets."

"Duffy's been telling us about the case," said Lincoln, while I choked on my eggs.

"Yeah. Oh, by the by, your pal Sugar George has an alibi for the time Falkner was killed. Actually, Lincoln here came up with it," said the little man grudgingly.

"He was over at Covenant House, you know, down on Forty-first? He took this kid Nita over there, her pimp had busted her up. He hung around till she got settled down, then he took off. He was there from one-thirty till almost four. Falkner got killed at two-thirty. So . . ." Abe Lincoln spread marmalade on his muffin with a certain satisfaction, and glanced at Duffy. "You know Covenant House, Doc?"

"It's a sort of shelter, isn't it? Runaways, abused kids, that kind of thing."

"The New York sex industry hates that guy's guts, that

priest over there. Anyway, I stop in there since I'm on Vice once, twice a night. This guy George Antoine, he brings i⟩ kids all the time. He's okay."

"So it's Antoine, is it? But why Sugar George?"

"He used to be a musician. Jazz and blues. Piano, think. And Sugar George Lemon was the name of this ol⟨ blues man, had one leg."

"Ah. And what about Sonny?"

"According to George and this Nita, he staked himsel⟩ out on the sidewalk to keep an eye out in case the pimⱷ tried anything. They do sometimes. Nobody inside sav⟨ him, but George says he was still outside when he left a four o'clock. We'll settle for it, for now anyway."

Duffy finished his coffee and got up. "It's this Week⟨ guy we want to get hold of. Name on Mrs. Falkner's wall.

"Wouldn't we all," I said blandly. As Duffy walke⟨ away, I considered the faces of my two cops. "You didn't fi⟩ him in on John's theory and the fraud at the Danson Foun⟨ dation, did you?"

"Just hearsay so far," said Lincoln. "Wouldn't want t⟨ bug the guy."

"Besides, a nice juicy murder bust would get you of Vice for good. Stealing the collar, I think you call it?"

He laughed. "You do on TV. I call it sweet revenge Duffy hotdogged me out of a couple of good busts las⟨ month."

"Well, I suppose in that case you want to come alonⱢ and see that tape John left."

Agate looked a bit embarrassed. "I already invited him. Doc," he confessed, and dunked his tie in his scramble⟨ eggs.

Teresa, Mickey, and George had gone to lug the bro⟨ ken cello to Freiling's shop. But Sonny let us in when w⟨ got to the apartment. He was washed and combed an⟨ wearing only the usual layers of clothing. He looked ver⟨ young and self-consciously new. He seemed quite at hom⟨ around David, who was just on his way out as we arrived. "⟩ thought you didn't film till Monday," I said. "Don't you want to hang around and watch this?"

Use Your Powers of Deduction!

Follow these clues to the "World of Mystery," and enjo
Agatha Christie like you've never enjoyed her before!

Clue #1—The World's Greatest Mysteries!

Intrigue…murder…deception! No one does it like Dame Agatha!
Now savour her most cunning tales of mystery and mayhem in *The
Agatha Christie Mystery Collection*.

Clue #2—Beautiful Volumes!

These are collector's editions—not available in any bookstore.
Bound in sturdy, simulated leather of rich, Sussex blue, set off with
distinctive gold embossing in the finest Victorian tradition. Covers a
densely padded—elegant on the shelf, and exquisite to the touch!

Clear, easy-on-the-eye type makes reading a pleasure again! These
are stories to be enjoyed. And owning them shows your appreciatio
of fine books.

Clue #3—Fabulous FREE Book.
Fabulous FREE Read!

Get *The New Bedside, Bathtub & Armchair Companion to Agatha
Christie* as your FREE GIFT just for previewing *The Agatha Christie
Mystery Collection*. Over 360 pages filled with story plots (but *never*
the endings!), photos, facts about Agatha's life, and the many movies an
plays of her work. This $12.95 value is yours to keep *absolutely free*,
no matter what!

You also get *And Then There Were None* free for 15 days to read and
enjoy. Here's your chance to sample *The Agatha Christie Mystery
Collection* without risk—enjoy this classic "whodunit," then decide
for yourself if you wish to keep it.

No Obligation—EVER!

It all adds up! Send for your no-risk preview of *And Then There Were
None*. Enjoy it *free* for 15 days! We'll send your Agatha Christie
Companion free, and start your *Agatha Christie Mystery
Collection* right away. Each volume in the Collection
arrives with the same *free 15 day preview. No*
minimum number of books to buy. No
obligation. *You may cancel
at any time!* Mail the
reply card today!

"I played it last night," he said. "Hope you don't mind. Oh, by the way, you're to call Myra Fish at WNYT. I said I thought you wanted to go ahead with the show, but she'd better talk with you. See you later. Sonny will be fine." He breezed out.

"But where are you headed? Alex's?"

"Bye," he said as the elevator doors closed.

The two cops settled into chairs facing the TV as I switched on the tape player. The first shot was an empty chair. Evidently John had shot the tape alone, probably at the WNYT studio. It was a large, dim space with no other furniture. In a moment, he appeared and took his place in the chair. He sat with his feet flat on the floor, his hands braced against his knees in a peculiarly military posture, his back very straight, as always. He looked like a man being court-martialed.

"Good evening, ladies and gentlemen," he said. "Welcome to *Bookends*. Our guest this evening is the author of a new novel. So far, it is unpublished. In fact, there is considerable doubt that it will ever be."

He looked down, momentarily, seeming confused. Then he stood up, scanning the room as if there were a live audience and any one of them might be out to get him. Finally he looked straight at the camera again and abruptly sat down.

"Thirty years ago, our author won a prize, the Pulitzer Prize for Fiction, when he was hardly more than a boy. He believed in prizes. Nobel Prizes, Pulitzer Prizes, prizes in Crackerjack boxes. Where he came from, that was what you saw when you closed your eyes. White and beautiful, the always-possible, just out of reach. The golden apple of the sun. The Bright Light. The Big Prize." He smiled, and I noticed the cut lip King Brat had given him.

"But our author grew up quickly. In fact, he did it all in one week. He became mistrustful. Because what he found out was, that he was a piece of literary meat. Somebody'd bought him the Bright Light. And it wasn't light at all. It was made out of money.

"On the committee for the Pulitzer Prize there were, in that year, four gentlemen. One was the author's old pro-

fessor from Iowa, Simon Murdoch. He was himself an author, but it'd been years, oh, many years, since he'd written
a book, and he needed money. Two of the other judges had
agreed to vote for a book by an old man publishing his last,
probably his finest, piece of work. And the fourth man, the
fourth judge, was Andrew Danson."

John got up and walked around behind the chair, pacing back and forth. For the first time he seemed to be drifting, inside himself, and disoriented. He had forgotten that
the stationary camera couldn't follow him, and his image
flashed by, caught, and then was torn away as he paced,
talking to himself.

"The Dansons had a great deal of money and they gave
a lot of it to the arts. So as a reward, young Andrew was put
on the committee that year. But he didn't care who won. It
only mattered that whomever he voted for should get the
prize, so that Andrew Danson would have control of the
committee, and power in the arts. Because power was what
mattered. It would carry over and become power over a
thousand other committees and boards and panels. And you
got it with money.

"So Andrew Danson began to buy votes, and the first
one he bought was Simon Murdoch's. Wouldn't Murdoch
like a sizable grant to go on with his own writing? Danson
could arrange that. Murdoch had almost given up hope, but
Danson could buy that for him, too, why not? You see, Andrew Danson had decided the old novelist's last master-
piece would gain him nothing if it were chosen. He wanted
somebody he could make his own, somebody unknown.
And Simon Murdoch proposed our author instead."

John's pacing had stopped and he stood behind the
chair again. It was then that I realized he'd been limping.
He must not be wearing shoes! He went on, hands resting
on the chair back with more than a casual pressure.

"And then Andrew Danson bought himself the third
vote, the crucial one. One of the other two judges had a
mistress, and the mistress had a brother, and that brother
was a painter. Not a very good painter, but a penniless one.
So Andrew Danson said that if the judge would vote with
him and with Simon Murdoch, he would see to it that the

seedy artist brother got a grant, too. And so our author, our author of one book, got his prize. The Crackerjack toy. And he went out with his old professor to celebrate.

"Well, old Simon Murdoch wasn't very proud of what he'd pulled off. He got drunk, you see, couldn't manage his vodka. And he spilt the beans. He told our callow author what the Bright Light was made of. And what did our author do? Did he give the prize back? Did he tell, of all absurdities, the truth? Well, no. Because he'd grown up. There weren't any more possibilities, there was only profit and loss. So what he did was, he drank. Liberally. Sometimes he'd take trips, trying to work again, but of course he couldn't, because now he had betrayed himself. He was a dodger, an Artful Dodger. Only he had to live. So he went to work for Andrew Danson, because Danson owned him anyway. And he never wrote another book. Until now."

He stopped, breathing deeply. He loosened his tie and removed his jacket, and I could see that his shirt was soaked with sweat. Still the amber eyes roamed suspiciously around the room, evading the implacable eye of the camera.

"One day he went into a bookstore, to look for his old book. But it wasn't there anymore, it wasn't even in print anymore. It had disappeared. He was a ghost. Not marble nor the gilded monuments of princes shall outlive this powerful rime, unless it isn't cost-effective. In a strange way, being a ghost set him free of the past. He felt he could begin again. He called his new book *The Dance of a One-Legged Soldier*, and when it was finished, he took it to his old publisher. But nobody there remembered him. Nobody had read his first book. They were children, most of them. Clever children. Because they knew what would make money, what would turn on the Bright Light. They watched wars like cartoon specials on TV, when they wanted to feel love, hate, pain, something, *something*, they bought some and put it up their noses, and when it was gone they bought some more, because there wasn't anything you couldn't buy. Well. The children told our author that his book would never make it in the market. Which they said was aimed at a mental age of twelve. Or sometimes fifteen. That was what would make more money than anything else. And money has a life of its own. We make it and we use it, but we can't control it. So if money says we have a mental age of twelve, then that is what we must have. And if you believe the children, it will be true. And that, ladies and gentlemen, *that* is the prize in *your* box of Crackerjacks."

And he stepped out of the frame.

Agate got up and switched off the machine. "Jesus," he said softly.

And then I looked at Sonny. He sat hugging his ankles, hunched against the arm of the couch and rocking gently back and forth. The clarity of his words startled me.

"Is it a good book?"

"Yes."

"Will people read it?"

"He can't tell you that, Sonny," said Lloyd.

"No. I can't. Maybe we've created a taste for junk. Maybe I've helped it along myself. But I think we can still tell the difference. And I'm damn well going to see that we get the chance to try."

I went to the phone in the hall and called Myra Fish at WNYT. "This is Winston Sherman," I said. "I've got a tape your *Bookends* audience ought to see. But I can guarantee you that the station manager won't let it pass without a fight."

She thought for a minute. Then she said, "Okay, listen. You still doing the show tomorrow night?"

"You bet."

"All right. We run a disclaimer. Opinions are those of Mr. Falkner, just like always. It's saved the station's butt more than once. So you just introduce it, a little bio, the way John used to. I promise no cuts, no bleeps."

"Won't you lose your job?"

"Maybe." There was a long silence. "But even getting canned you got advantages. I've waited five years to baptize my bozo producer with a wine spritzer. Can you believe, this guy drinks fizzy wine?" She laughed, but it didn't last long. "I'm glad you're doing the show, Doc. Somebody's gotta kick ass for the guy. And who knows? Maybe you'll become a star."

We hung up and I'd barely gotten back to the living room when the phone rang. I thought Myra had changed her mind, but it turned out to be Sandor Hoffman, John's attorney.

"Dr. Sherman," he said, "I'm just calling to tell you I've got it all set up according to the will. You can get into his apartment any time now, to sort through the papers. Whenever you're ready."

I was fogged. "What're you talking about?"

"I'm sorry. I assumed you knew, you're John's executor."

"But that arrangement was made years ago. Didn't he change it?"

"Not a line. And the police are through with his place, so I imagined you'd be wanting to inform yourself about the bills on the estate and so on, before the actual transfer of everything to his son. By the way, I understand the funeral's to be up in Ainsley?"

"Yes. At the Monastery of the Renunciation. If you like, you're welcome to stay at our place, plenty of room."

"Thanks. I may take you up on it. There are a couple of things I'd like to talk over with you."

"Such as?"

"Such as John's recent interest in numbered bank accounts. Sorry, Doctor, I've got a client on hold. We'll talk more on Monday."

Sandor Hoffman hung up, and I stood for a moment alone in the hallway, the receiver dangling from my hand. How little of John I had really understood when I marked him paid-in-full and sent him packing. And how little of myself. Now he was teaching me that I, too, had something to expiate.

I shook myself and hung up the phone. If I'd misjudged John, so be it. He had underestimated me, and that made us about even. The only thing I knew for sure was that the new novel was the biggest asset in John's estate, and I was its executor. And marketplaces are only as good as you make them. I intended to see that book published.

* * *

That same morning, Teresa and Mickey, with Sugar George in attendance, took a cab over to Third Avenue. They found Andreas Freiling in his workshop, applying the first layer of varnish to a violoncello. He rubbed his hands on a rag smelling of paint thinner, reached into his shirt pocket to turn up the hearing aid attached to his left ear, and hurried toward the counter. Teresa cast an eagle eye round the place, but she saw no sign of any assistants, with or without red parkas. Mickey laid her cello case on the counter and opened it.

"I'm afraid I have a patient for you," she said.

Andreas bent over the brutalized cello. He put out an uncertain hand and touched the battered body. Something—probably the crowbar that had pried Teresa's front door open—had struck the cello at its fullest point, making a jagged wound from which splinters of wood still bearing their beautiful finish stuck out at bizarre angles. The neck, too, had been broken and the strings hung slack and voiceless from their tuning pegs. Even the bow had been snapped in half. Inside the body, on the unbroken back, there was a small label. It pictured a violin and bow, and next to them, the single word: FREILING. Andreas looked up at Teresa. "Mine," he said.

"It was."

He straightened, staring at her, and then at George and the boy. His voice shook with fury. "What kind of bastard does such things to my music?" He locked on to George. "You?"

"If I did it, would I come here with her?"

"You are a man with anger. The eyes."

Teresa intervened. "Someone broke into my house. I think he also killed my husband. I saw you that day, just before I found his body. Yesterday they did this. Can you fix it?"

"Fix?" It was like showing Leonardo the "Mona Lisa" slashed to ribbons and asking him to fix it.

"Repair."

He continued to stare at her a moment longer. "How

dare he," he said. "*Er hat keine Seele*, a man who does this. He has no soul. He tempts God." Gently, he closed the case. "Madame," he said. "Please allow me to present you with another cello."

"I couldn't do that. It's kind of you, but it's out of the question."

"Please, madame." His hands straight at his sides, he drew himself to attention. "To atone for this bastard. Things must be balanced in the world. You will come into the back and select what is best."

"Let's compromise. I'll give you half the price. Otherwise I can't accept your kindness. As you say, a balance."

"Very well," he agreed, and led her into the back room.

Sugar George wandered around the shop and finally sat down at one of the pianos Freiling used for tuning. His fingers rested on the treble keys, but didn't really strike them at first. Mickey amused himself trying to play "Chopsticks" on the bass keys, but Sugar ignored him and began "The St. Louis Blues." Mickey shut up to listen. The strong fingers wound in and out of the melody like wind in the branches of a tree, touching it here, rising above it there. There was no bass, of course, but the treble was enough, it was like clear water over clean sand. When he tired of the first tune, he switched to another, Billie Holiday's "God Bless the Child." And again the fingers wove and embroidered, round and round the tune. Mickey listened and watched in silence, and when George finally looked up, Freiling and Teresa were standing beside him.

Andreas took the strong, high-boned face between the flats of his two hands. "Not only can I not hear, I also cannot see. I mistook an artist." He bowed slightly and let Sugar go. "For this I apologize." He turned to Teresa. "You chose well, madame. Will you take the cello now?"

"Perhaps your assistant could deliver it? What was his name, Martin, wasn't it?"

Andreas stalled, pretending to turn up his hearing aid again. "I beg pardon, madame?"

"Your assistant, Martin, perhaps he could deliver it."

"I have no longer an assistant. I will bring it myself."

"On second thought, I believe we can manage it now," she said.

When they got outside, the three stopped to flag a cab. "That guy's lying," said Mickey. "He heard what you said, about Martin. He was figuring out what to say."

"Kid," said George, "you get your Mama back home. Don't make no stops, hear me. Take her to David's."

"Mick," Teresa said, "take a cab. I'm staying."

"You think he'll go looking for Martin? I wanna stay too."

"He's a man with a lot on his mind," said Sugar. "Just wanna see where it takes him to, 's all. You go on with the boy, ma'am."

"No," she said flatly. "Mickey's taking this cello back to David's. It's in the way here."

"Like me, you mean." Mickey scowled as a cab pulled up for them.

"Kid, you wouldn't be half bad, you let your brains catch up with your mouth." George tried to ease Teresa toward the cab, but she shoved Mickey in, and Sugar gave up and loaded the cello in beside him. The cab took off.

"If he goes, he'll have to lock the shop first. Come on. There's a coffee shop across the street where we can see the front door." She led the way across Third Avenue. "And jeez, will you quit calling me ma'am?"

They got a booth by the front window with a clear view of Freiling's place and ordered coffee. Teresa sat watching George.

"I'm not going to tell you how good you are. You damn well know it."

"Half good."

"I could get you work. I know a guy. Little jazz place on a Hundred and Tenth."

"I find my own work."

"Dishwashing? Sweeping out? People shouldn't throw themselves away."

His eyes flashed, the dark brows lowered. "This friend of yours, he gonna saw his piano in half for me, ma'am? He gonna put up a screen around it so's I don't spook out the customers, ma'am? He gonna put a sign out front says, One-Arm Gimp Appearing Nightly?"

"You go to hell," she said. "I didn't have to watch John, I don't need to watch you." She slid out of the booth and stood up, letting her hand rest for a minute on the remnant of his arm. "But if you want me, I'll be over there."

She'd just settled into another booth across the aisle when George saw Freiling turn the OPEN sign in his front window to read CLOSED and pull down the blinds. He was up and out of the booth in a second, but he paused beside her. "He's moving, Teresa. You can come or not."

When they hit the sidewalk, she wasn't more than half a dozen steps behind him. And not more than fifty yards behind her, though she didn't notice, was our friend in the red parka.

George and Teresa got across Third Avenue and around the corner just in time to see Andreas Freiling come out of the back door of his shop and hotfoot it down the alley toward a maroon sedan. Freiling got in and started the engine. Just then George heard footsteps and glanced behind him. A dumpy, hurtling figure in red, with matching ski mask hastily pulled on, was jogging full tilt and almost on top of them.

"Look out!" yelled George, and pushed Teresa aside. She fell into some empty cardboard cartons and plastic trash bags, and the jogger changed directions. George took a swing with his crutch but missed, and the jogger kept coming, forcing him against the brick wall of a building. Red Jacket was wielding a six-foot length of two-by-four that would've felled both George and Teresa from behind if they hadn't seen it coming. As it was, the jogger had George pinned against the wall, the two-by-four smashing his ribs. His crutch was lying a few feet away, useless.

Teresa picked herself up, scrambled into the mucky alley and grabbed the crutch, a new steel one she'd bought him herself in gratitude for his helping Mickey. She swung it round and whacked Red Jacket a sound blow across the forearms. He dropped the two-by-four and staggered, but didn't fall. Sugar made a grab for the top of the ski mask, but he didn't have much breath left, and Teresa hung onto the tail of the red parka. But Red Jacket managed to turn round and slug blindly at her, catching her nicely along the ear. Teresa lay still in the muck, stunned and woozy, and Red Jacket took off down the alley.

George got his crutch and offered her a hand up. "You look like hell, ma'am," he said, pointing, "but you ain't bad hand-to-hand."

"Neither are you," she told him. "For a one-arm gimp."

And all they had to show for their morning's work was a two-by-four, a ringing in Teresa's ear, and a nice set of bruises on George's ribcage. Had Andreas Freiling called Red Jacket to run interference for him, or to keep an eye on them? Whatever he'd done, they'd certainly lost the Austrian. For all they knew, he might've been on his way back to Salzburg by now, with or without the mysterious Thomas Mann.

Chapter Twelve

Saturday was Miss Plumb's day off, and one of her mother's card parties was going on in the living room as she pulled on her outdoor things and snuck out the door. In her pocket was the address of a building called The St. Claire, between Madison and Fifth at Sixty-ninth. It housed the apartment of Charlotte Stedman, and when Plumb checked on Dennis Weeks's New York address for Eddie, she'd found that it, too, was in The St. Claire.

When she got off the bus, Plumb realized she needed an excuse to invade Charlie's premises and question her. What should it be? Something that would evoke sympathy, and force the woman to be hospitable whether she wanted to or not.

Plumb strode into snowy Central Park and looked round for a garbage bin, then sat down on a bench and went through her purse. She stuffed her trusty police whistle into her coat pocket and squirreled her wallet away in a place that shall remain nameless. Then she pulled off her famous fur toque and stuffed it and the purse into the garbage can. Next she scouted out the biggest, wettest snowbank she could find, waited until nobody was in sight, and simply tipped herself over into the snow head first. She rolled around a bit, just to be sure she was properly messy, and at last emerged, dripping wet, sodden-haired, her neat brown coat covered with snow and mud and dead leaves.

The St. Claire, Charlotte Stedman's building, was fairly tall for the area, having thirty-five floors, each containing four large square flats with neatly landscaped balconies. These went all the way round the building, one on each of the four sides. Plumb made a thoroughly piteous sight as she trudged, in soggy, squelching shoes, up the pink marble front steps. The lobby was elegant with Moorish tiles and brass openwork, and she stood in a corner gently oozing, hoping the doorman wouldn't chuck her out. But he was busy talking to a small dapper gentleman with an overcoat and a pair of fuzzy earmuffs. Plumb wiped the drips out of her eyes and was mildly surprised to recognize Merriman.

Well, naturally she didn't want him to see her in that state, but she *did* want to hear what was being said. So Plumb sloshed over to one of the fancy brass lattices and took cover, eavesdropping mightily.

"Oh I do sympathize," Merriman was saying. "I expect they keep you hopping day and night, don't they?"

"Aw, we got a night man, but you know how it is."

"Not up-and-coming, is he?"

"Guy don't speak much English, see. People want a cab, they want a paper, they got a problem, he can't handle it. So who they gonna call?" He pointed to his shiny brass buttons.

Eddie looked round the lobby for a fountain. He was sure he could hear something dripping. "Awfully busy here on the night shift, is it?"

"People here are pretty quiet. Old building. Nothing flashy."

"Expensive? I mean to say, if I wanted to rent—"

"Ah, not a chance, buddy. These places, they're leased for life, I can't remember the last time one of them opened up. 'Course, lot of the people who lease 'em don't even live in 'em, maybe once, twice a year for a couple weeks."

"This night man of yours, was he on duty last Tuesday night, Wednesday morning?"

"Gleich? With his lousy American, we only use the guy when there's not much traffic in the lobby here. Wind came up that night, it was like the South Pole out there, nobody goin' out. Yeah, he was on."

"Gleich?" Eddie spelled it. "Sounds German. What's the first name?"

"Marty. Martin. I got nothin' against the guy being Kraut, only he takes off, and now I'm pullin' a shift and a half. Ain't been back since Thursday night."

"But he *was* here on Wednesday and Thursday nights, then?"

"Yeah. And Tuesday night, too, like I said."

"Tell me, does Mr. Dennis Weeks use his apartment much, or does he sublet?"

"Nah. Weeks just gets his mail here, mostly. Up on thirty-two we got three outa four empty. His place and two others. Right now, come to think, the whole damn floor's empty. Mrs. Salisbury's in France this winter. Not a soul up there. But you can forget about a sublet."

"One last thing," Plumb heard Eddie say. "Martin Gleich. Does he by any chance wear a red ski parka?"

"No sir. Blue, I think. Yeah. Bright blue."

"Thank you so much," said Eddie, and whizzed round the corner of the lattice. He stopped short, looking Plumb over. "Do excuse my mentioning it, Miss P., but you're puddling, rather. Shall we go upstairs together, or do you prefer to confront Charlotte Stedman alone?"

Plumb took his arm and they squished off to the elevator. Eddie noticed her missing pocketbook. "I presume you were not *really* mugged and are simply being fiendishly clever," he said airily. "Terribly spiffy building, isn't it? Lovely tilework and things. Art Deco detail. Only the rich can afford the survival of the past." He sighed. "Seems too much for a Charlotte Stedman, computer ace or not."

Plumb smiled at him triumphantly. "It is. The lease is owned by Randolph Danson. I knew I remembered the address when I looked it up, and then I checked Randolph's holdings. He has several apartments, some leased through the Foundation, and some personal."

"Does the Foundation own this Weeks place up on thirty-two as well?"

"It isn't in the record of holdings," she said. "Oh, here we are." They had arrived on the thirtieth floor. Charlotte Stedman's flat was at the front of the building, looking down onto Sixty-ninth Street. Eddie rang the buzzer, and an eye appeared at the peephole.

"It's Joan Plumb, from the Foundation," said Miss P. "I'm so sorry to barge in on you, but I knew you were in this building. Could you help me?" She added a nice quaver to her usual Marine topkick delivery. "Oh dear. I'm afraid I've just been mugged!"

The door opened. Charlie Stedman smiled uncertainly at the pair of them. "Come on in," she said. "Are you hurt? Take your coat off and sit down. It looks like you've broken a heel. Is your ankle sprained?"

"No dear, it's just the muck. If I could just use your powder room, I'll clean myself up." She paused. "Oh. My manners. This gentleman interrupted my mugger, or I don't know what would've become of me. Mister . . . ?"

"Filbert," said Eddie. "Like the nut."

"And this," said Plumb, "is Charlotte Stedman, one of our brighter people at the Danson Foundation."

"The bathroom's right through there," said Charlie. She paused a moment before she asked, "How did you know I lived here?" She looked a bit off balance, which was exactly what Plumb had hoped for.

"Oh, poor Mr. Falkner had your address on his desk file, dear. I was going through it yesterday, sorting things out before the new man comes in down in your department."

"New man?" She stared at Plumb, caught herself, then relaxed.

"Why yes. To run the Computer Office. Oh, do excuse me now, I'm dripping all over the carpet." She oozed off through the bedroom.

"And a lovely carpet it is, too," said Eddie. "Tabriz, I believe?"

"You know Persian rugs?"

"Oh, not to speak to. Just a nodding sort of acquaintance. Lovely things here, if I may remark. You must enjoy entertaining in such a nice, open room."

Charlie's ugly face seemed to conceal nothing. "People don't come here," she said bluntly. "I don't know much of anybody."

"Dreadful thing about that Mr. Falkner of yours."

"Yes." She sat fiddling with a small malachite paperweight, picking it up and putting it down on the table beside her.

"All over the papers. Rather spectacular death."

"Yes."

"And you knew the fellow well?"

"No. The Foundation's huge."

"Still. He had your name and address."

"I ran some computer checks for him now and then. He phoned me at home once."

"Probably the sort of fellow who writes every little thing down. Personally, I prefer to activate the gray matter. Do you like computer work?"

From the bedroom, Plumb couldn't hear the answer, because she had her head stuck under the bed. Methodically, she checked the closet, the chairs, and every corner of bedroom and bath, including the shower stall, but nowhere did she spot a man's shoes and socks. The murderer would've disposed of them by now, but if they'd been lovers, Falkner might've been surprised here by his killer and dragged off before he had time to finish getting dressed.

Finding nothing, Plumb cleaned herself up at the bathroom sink and then opened the medicine chest. No pack of contraceptives, no diaphragm, nothing to indicate a love affair, or even the hope of one. It looked just like her own medicine cabinet at home. There was only one bottle of prescription medicine. Plumb read the label carefully. "C. Stedman. Take one at bedtime, to induce sleep." Whatever the girl was involved in, it was taking its toll on her nerves.

It was then that she remembered the man with the red jacket that Mr. Merriman had warned her about. He was supposed to be short and dumpy, just like Charlie. She went to the closet and opened it again, hoping not to find what she was looking for. She emerged from the bedroom in high spirits. Not a red jacket in sight.

"Names are beastly things," Eddie was saying. "I, for instance, am nothing like a Gilbert Filbert. Sounds like an advertisement for a salted nut company, don't you know?" He laughed uncomfortably. Dithering is always Eddie's way out of awkward social situations, and this was certainly one. He'd never met a girl as gauche and self-conscious as Charlotte Stedman. Yet there was something about her he liked. She sat in a rather outsized wing chair, her short legs barely touching the floor, listening to his silly chatter with unfailing politeness. Her eyes followed him steadily, intelligently, and when she ventured to laugh, it seemed to surprise her. He found he enjoyed making her laugh.

"Shall I tell you what?" he said gently. "You are nothing like a Charlotte. If I were to name you again, I should call you Marina."

"From the Shakespeare play," she said, "or the boat dock?" The laugh came from her again, deep, soft, and too unexpected to be coy.

"Oh, the daughter of Pericles, my dear," said Eddie with a smile. "The nice little girl who was miraculously saved from drowning."

Just about the time Eddie and Plumb left The St. Claire, Sarah and I were making one of our infrequent forays into the Lifestyles of the Rich and Famous. She was done up in her old gray flannel skirt and some blouse or other, along with those high-heeled shoes she saves for funerals and wedding receptions. I, I regret to say, was wearing my new hat. The thing was a sort of muddy tweed, made of some soft stuff you could've run a herd of buffalo over without changing its shape. The brim flapped around my ears, and my undomesticated hair stuck out beneath it like fringe on a tablecloth. I got a look at myself in the mirrored façade of the fabled Gallup Tower, where the Dansons lived. I looked like a rhino balancing a cupcake on his head.

In a moment more, we were inside the elevator, being observed by the electronic eye of a roving security camera. "If I scratch my behind," I asked Sarah, "do bells go off at the Pentagon?"

"You're supposed to be admiring the carpet and the wall covering, you goop." She stroked the stuff on the elevator walls, a fairly unrepulsive paisley. For a paisley. "My God, I think it's real silk."

"Looks like an Edwardian smoking room," I grumbled. "All we need is a good cigar and a bottle of Scotch."

"Here." She spied a button on the wall and punched it. A little door opened. Inside a tiny leather-lined compartment was a mahogany tray with a selection of airline-sized booze bottles, but not of airline vintage. None of the wine was domestic and none of the booze was less than middle-aged. There were two glasses—not plastic, either—and a lever to one side read PRESS HERE FOR ICE.

"Which one brings on the dancing girls?"

Sarah punched another button. Two sliding doors parted to reveal a TV screen. She hit another button. Another choice of levers was revealed, controlling four tape decks marked Classical, Pop, Jazz, and Rock. As we zoomed past the fifty-third floor, we got what Sarah said was Handel. She slammed the little door shut. "Can they hear what we're saying, do you think?"

"Probably." I lighted a Turkish Delight and blew a cloud of smoke at our Eye in the Sky.

Sarah stood glaring at the thing. "I should like you to know," she told it, "that this is an extremely bad recording of Handel's *Water Music*. That's all."

We'd now reached the sixty-fifth floor, which was the Danson penthouse. The elevator doors opened directly into a sort of entry hall, about the size of the main gallery of the Louvre, with almost as much statuary. It was Southeast Asian or perhaps Chinese. Bronze and golden Buddhas nestled inscrutably among the fronds of potted banana trees that reached up to a domed glass roof thirty-five feet above our heads. I knew what kind of trees they were, because there were real live bananas on them.

We stood among the little fat-bellied gods, half expecting some burnt-out case from a Graham Greene novel to accost us. What we got was a smiling little blue-eyed blonde in a business suit, who materialized from the underbrush.

"I'm Tiffany Faber," she said, "Cella's companion. It's so nice to have you here. Cella's in the Wellness Room. Shall we go through?"

She led the way past a living room the size of Avery Fisher Hall, done in Chinese red and black, with lots of lacquer cabinets and several ornate ivories on display pedestals. The next room was apparently Danson's tribute to the rococo. It was the dining room, where pink-bottomed cherubs flew across a frescoed ceiling, keeping their collective eye on the inlaid parquetry dining table built to accommodate the House of Lords. Now I knew where Civilization As We Knew It had gone. Danson bought it with his Gold Card and squirreled it away.

"We're just having a cholesterol check," said Tiffany. Her roots were the color of old dishwater, and her real name, I figured, was probably Edna Mae.

"Is Cella ill, then?" Sarah sounded worried. "Maybe we shouldn't have come."

"Oh no. But we all have to be aware of our bodies these days, don't we?"

"Do we?" I said. I mean, what do all these tests accomplish? Six extra months in the Rip Van Winkle Golden Years Village eating imitation egg yolks and low-fat yogurt?

Cella Danson certainly didn't seem to be palely loitering. She was robust and rosy, approaching my own proportions, and she looked in better health than Edna Mae. But she was hooked up to a computer, and the thing was typing out some sort of score on her as we came in. The room was filled with the paraphernalia of Wellness. There was a rowing machine, an exercise bike, the health computer with built-in blood pressure cuff and direct tie-ins to three major hospitals. There was a treadmill, a small bar with a blender that was zapping out some greenish-yellow, yeasty-looking liquid I assumed was good for you, and a row of large glass jars containing fruits, nuts, berries, and herbs of the field.

Cella wore a pair of bright purple jogging pants rolled up to her knees, a Roman-striped silk shirt, and a pair of grubby white tennies with argyle socks sticking out of them. Her hair was thick and sandy gray, tied back with a purple scarf.

"How are we coming now, Cella?" said the girl.

"Unhook me, Gertrude, and bring us some coffee." Cella ripped the page off the printer, studied it for a moment, then wadded it up.

"Now Cella. Cook has some nice herbal tea for you."

"I said coffee, damn it. And the Napoleon brandy. Pronto." She turned on the treadmill and climbed aboard as Tiffany flounced away. "I get my jollies picking on her, but she's not so bad," panted Cella. She did a few laps around the Western Hemisphere on the treadmill, shut it off, and stuck a stethoscope in her ears. She sat listening to her excited heart thumping away for a few moments, then, seeming satisfied, she put the stethoscope aside and attached herself to the blood pressure cuff. "How'd you like the Road to Mandalay out front?" She crowed, delighted with her joke.

"It's very . . . striking."

"I keep telling Andy he ought to put the Raffles Bar under that banana tree." She monitored the reading on the computer.

"Are you fond of Oriental art?" asked Sarah.

"No. That's Andy's territory. This is mine."

"And never the twain shall meet?"

"Only when absolutely necessary. Oh, I don't have anything against old Andy. We just bore the hell out of each other. Have for years."

"But you didn't divorce."

"No. No need to. I didn't mind if Andrew shopped around. He wanted kids. I didn't have any. He's got two, by my count." She paused, enjoying the shock waves. Then she unwrapped the blood pressure cuff, went over and poured the green goo into a glass, and belted it down. She gave me an owlish look. "You don't shock easy, do you, honey?"

"Nope. Who was their mother?"

"Darlene. Darlene Something. I used to hear him on the phone with her. She ran a travel agency over in Brooklyn. He bought them a house, used to spend a couple nights a week there. Take them on regular vacations."

"Can't remember Darlene's other name?"

"Z. Something with Z. Zab-Something. Zag-Something."

There aren't that many surnames starting with Z, and two in one week was too much to believe. "Zadravic?" I said. It had been Al Zadravic, you remember, who rented that room at the Motor Inn in Ainsley and left me the ultimatum on an answering machine.

"Zadravic? Maybe. I don't remember."

I didn't believe her. No matter how much her husband bores her, no woman is likely to forget the last name of the mother of his two illegitimate kids. Not even Cella Danson. "What were their first names, these kids?"

"Girl was Paula, I remember that. Now what was the boy? Something wimpy."

"Al? Alvin, maybe. Albert."

"No."

The coffee and brandy arrived and Cella played hostess, but she refilled her own glass with more of the green goo. When Tiffany had bustled out again, she winked at us. "She's Andy's, not mine, you know. I got her for him when Darlene died. Cancer. He was a helluva mess."

"Cella," Sarah finally said, "don't you ever go out?"

"Oh, no."

"Come out with us. Come to dinner."

"Couldn't."

"There's nothing to be afraid of."

"I know. I just don't like it."

"Don't like what."

"Things. Things have happened. I have to stay here."

"What? What's changed?"

"Oh," she said. "Almost everything. There's almost nothing left." She smiled. "Besides, I don't need to go out. Come in here."

She led the way through a door into a small adjoining room. The place was filled with radios, shortwaves, microwaves, satellite hookups. "I can pick up Peking on this sucker. And this one? I can listen to the Russian embassy talking to Afghanistan. It's better than Andy's painting. Ever see any of Andy's paintings?" We shook our heads. "Lousy van Gogh. Ever hear him play the violin?" We shook our heads again. "Just lousy."

"Did he study art?"

"And music. Right before he wrote his novel."

"Andrew? A novel? Who's his publisher?"

"Bernaby, Freeman and Miles."

"I'm impressed."

"Don't be. He couldn't sell the thing, so he bought a publishing company." She considered me carefully. "Is Andy in a mess?"

"We think he may be. Somebody at the Foundation is draining off funds. Does Andrew still own Kenwood Enterprises?"

"Papa's old company? It was in trouble a couple of years back. But it's all right now. Isn't it?"

"Presumably. Andrew doesn't spend much time with business. Who runs the companies, Kenwood and the fried chicken business?"

"Ask Pops," she said. "I mean Randolph. He knows more than he lets on. You'll have to have him kidnapped to get him off the golf course, but he'll know." Suddenly she shot up out of her chair. "Dean, that's it. I knew it was something wimpy."

"Dean? Not Dean Sommers?"

"No." She shook her head positively. "Dean Zadravic."

"But names," I told Sarah in the cab back to the Battersea, "can be changed."

"Never mind that now." She took my hand, a thing she doesn't often do in public. "Did you miss not having children of our own, Win?"

"I had all I could do with David, thanks very much, when you were off touring Europe."

"Be honest now. Never once wished he were yours? Ours. Not just my baby brother?"

"All right. I thought about it. Didn't you?"

"Yes. But I don't think I could've stood it if you'd shopped around."

"How do you know I didn't?"

"Because you are a man with a code, my dear. Never knuckle under, never dance to another man's tune, and never do unnecessary damage."

"And I don't think I could've stood it if you'd decided to talk to the world by radio." I decided to chance it. "Just one little thing, old girl, while you're keenly aware of my virtues. About this pusillanimous headgear."

"Oh. That."

She leaned forward and slid back the glass between us and the cabbie. "Excuse me, señor. Could you use a perfectly good hat? It's nearly new. Really."

David had spent most of the afternoon watching The St. Claire from the Park. He'd seen Eddie and Plumb come and go, and once he'd ventured into the lobby himself. He was getting into character. Now, about the time we were having supper, David was far downtown in a little dive called Freddie's. He'd never been there before, and he'd never go in again. He'd only come in now to use the phone. Like John, he had a phone call to make. And being an actor, he required a set. He dialed the number of Dean Sommers's loft in SoHo. When he spoke, his voice was unlike himself, lower pitched and a little scratchy.

"This is Dennis Weeks," he said. "I thought you'd like to know I was in town."

Sommers was quiet. Then he said angrily, "Who the hell is this?"

"Dennis Weeks. Shall I spell it? Dennis Weeks, of Kansas City."

"What do you want?" The young man was in control, but barely. In early middle age, his voice could not escape a tinge of adolescent treble.

"I'll let you know that in a day or so. I'll be calling again. Count on it. And do have a pleasant evening," said David, and hung up the phone.

Chapter Thirteen

The next day was Sunday, and the snow was sinking into that terminal mush Manhattan thinks of as spring. Windows were left open, to waft the scent of Italian Sunday dinners along West Fourth Street in the Village, as Mickey, Teresa, and I made our way to John's apartment. Red Jacket was nowhere in sight, but my guard was up as I marched stolidly along, a grumpy and suspicious invasion force in an aged tweed overcoat designed by Omar the Tentmaker.

I knew I ought to be glad of the chance to go through John's papers without the scrutiny of the Delightful Duffy, but something in me was queasy at the idea. I kept thinking that in a comparatively few years someone would probably be doing the same for me, rooting round my Cave, making neat piles of my ancient rough drafts, casting an eagle eye at my check stubs. It made me want to go straight home and burn everything.

John's was a garden apartment with wrought iron grill-work over the doors and windows that gave the place a rather French Quarter flair. I stood in the middle of the small living room and tried to remember. "It's exactly the same, isn't it? As when you two were first married."

"Yes," said Teresa. "Emotionally, he never moved out. Even after we took the place uptown, he kept this lease and sublet. Then when we split up, he just came back."

I was remembering the two of them here, Teresa sawing away at her cello, and John, not drunk but nicely mellow, listening from the front stoop for Madame Zorah the Clairvoyant—who lived next door and played the violin in her birthday suit—to join in. I woke up when Mickey came in from the kitchen, where he'd been slamming cupboard doors.

"I told you guys. There's no booze in here. I told you he quit."

"He didn't drink at home anymore," Teresa said. "He'd buy a bottle and take it somewhere. He could drink anywhere, he was an expert at it. The park. Staten Island Ferry."

"Or Stuyvesant Hall," I said. "You knew he went to all your concerts."

She was quiet. "No. I didn't."

"Never missed one, according to Miss Plumb."

"Some divorce," she said quietly. "I watched his show. Every week."

Mickey was sitting at John's desk, fiddling with a typewriter. It was one of those electronic jobs, the ones that balance your checkbook and make plane reservations in their spare time. It seemed odd, considering John's disgust with such electronic mind crutches. "I didn't know John typed."

"He didn't. He used a typist over on Tenth Street. When there was anything to type."

"What's that stuff?" Next to the machine were several small objects that looked like ribbon cartridges.

"Extra memory tapes," said Mickey. He plugged one into the side of the machine and switched it on. The thing had a little display screen on the front, where any sensible typewriter keeps its tabulator bar. Mickey punched a few buttons, apparently at random, and the screen lit up. It whirred and hiccupped, beeped twice, flashed its print wheel around, and stopped. A phrase appeared on the display screen.

MEMORY ENGAGED. SCAN, PRINT, EDIT, ERASE?

"Scan," Mickey typed.

READY, it reported, and giggled twice. A sentence began to run slowly across the screen.

TERESA, it read. NOT YET A BREACH, BUT AN EXPANSION.

Mickey stopped the machine. "What's that mean?"

"It's a poem. John Donne." I quoted for him.

> *"Our two souls therefore, which are one*
> *Though I must go, endure not yet*
> *A breach, but an expansion,*
> *Like gold to airy thinness beat."*

"I love the line," said Teresa. "But it always sounds a little suicidal to me."

"It's another one of his damn clues, that's what it is. Go on, Mickey."

Another sentence ran across the screen. WINSTON. REMEMBER THE BANISHMENT OF POSTHUMUS.

"Who's Post Humus?" said the kid.

"From Shakespeare," said Teresa. "*Cymbeline*, isn't it, Winnie?"

"Yes. Posthumus is banished in the very first scene. He gives his wife a bracelet to remember him by while they're apart. John hand out any bracelets lately?"

"Never. With the cello, I can't wear the damn things, they bang around."

I took John's Shakespeare off the shelf. It was an old, dog-eared copy of the G. B. Harrison edition, just like mine. I'd given it to him for his college graduation and he'd kept it ever since. I flipped the thin, cheesy pages to the back, and *Cymbeline*. Nothing. I shook it, but nothing fell out, and there was nothing slipped inside the loose binding along the spine.

The kid turned the tape on again. MICKEY, it read. SORRY ABOUT AFRICA.

We spent another two hours at the apartment, going through the filing cabinet, the papers, and the books. After we'd taken every book off its shelf, shaken it out and replaced it, without a sign of the Weeks file, we called it quits. Teresa was determined to take her place for the Sunday afternoon concert at Stuyvesant Hall, and we were all pleasantly surprised when Mickey elected to go with her. I put them into a cab, then headed back to the Battersea by bus, trying to decipher the quotation and the reference to *Cymbeline*.

So far as I could recall, John and I had never discussed the play. Quite honestly, I've always thought it must've been cranked out one weekend when the Bard's latest bill for a doublet and hose was past due. Posthumus. A poor but worthy gentleman, exiled for having ideas above his station. For daring the powers that be. Children might be posthumus, books might be posthumus. *Dance of a One-Legged Soldier* would be. Had he known that? Had he meant to die? Teresa had said it. The Donne quotation sounded prophetic. *"Though I must go."* But John was always going, always taking off. *Mickey. Sorry about Africa.* He'd known they weren't going to Africa and the boy would be disappointed again, but had he known he would be dead, or had he thought he'd be somewhere else? Suppose John had merely meant to disappear, go into exile like Posthumus, or even fake his own death. But the death Teresa had seen in that elevator was no fake. Words were spinning, humming, echoing in my mind, and not just John's most recent clues either. I hadn't stopped thinking of the odd phrases Sonny had put together. *"The Prince of Darkness is a gentleman." "Phlebas the Phoenician, a fortnight dead." "Never to speak of this that you have seen." "Forgot the cry of gulls, and the deep sea swell/ And the profit and loss."*

I was still rattling around in a literary maze when I found Merriman in my room at the hotel, immersed in reading John's manuscript. He looked up when I came in. "Sarah asked me to tell you she's gone to have tea with someone fairly mighty in Actors' Equity, and will meet you at WNYT for the taping at seven. David has lines to study, but will also be on hand. As for me," he said, with that smug grin on his map that means he has a juicy secret, "I've got a surprise for you, young Winnie."

"What's she doing with Actors' Equity?" And then I remembered Maureen and the episode in Toronto. Equity might help Sarah track her down, or at least give her an agent's name. And being Sarah, she wouldn't just phone the office. She always starts up top and works down.

Merriman was waving a piece of paper at me. "You old

goopus, pay attention! After you left, I dipped into this new novel of Johnny's. Well, naturally it struck me at once."

"Well for pity's sake strike me with it, will you?" I lowered myself into a chair and kicked off my loafers. New York isn't built for a man with bunions.

"I've found John's control. I knew he must've run one absolutely foolproof name through the computer, someone he knew didn't exist because he'd made him up. Here it is." He handed me a printout sheet. "Vincent Oakes. The hero of this new book of his. And he put the clue straight into your hands. I should feel flattered, if I were you."

I squinted at the printout on Oakes. Everything was right. Age forty-two, born Darby, Pennsylvania, attended Boston College, graduated 1967, married 1965, divorced 1966. All those things could be cross-checked and found to be fictional, of course, but I knew enough about bureaucracies to doubt they would be, and so did John. I've sat on the Scholarship Committee at school for some years—reluctantly, because committees in general give me the pip—and I know we rarely doubt the basic facts of an application. What we really pay attention to are the letters of recommendation. Let's face it, we've become a society of political maneuverers, from nursery school to funeral chapel. At Clinton, a letter from Joe Dogsbody at Yale recommending his favorite student, Toadsquat, will get immediate attention from Tommy Sheffield, who knew Dogsbody back at the frat house. And at the Danson Foundation, the recommending signature of the reputable Weeks was enough to get attention for the most fictional of applicants. Particularly with Charlotte Stedman to field any fly balls that might be hit. So there it was, signed on the dotted line. "Application approved, Andrew Danson, November twelfth, 1987," I read.

"So the money was paid out to Vincent Oakes last December. They probably assumed, if they caught it at all, that Oakes was one of their own phonies, and simply passed it through," Eddie said.

"I still don't see how it could work on a grand scale without somebody catching on. It's so pervasive. There'd have to be somebody in cahoots in every department from Accounting to Applications to Xerography."

Eddie looked sober. "I do. Charlotte Stedman. When every department is computerized and the computers are centralized in one bank, whoever runs them runs the lot. And, as I understand it, if the program is complex enough, it's very seldom actually audited or evaluated, because the auditor would have to recreate the program for himself, and each one is unique. A clever programmer could create one so complex that the auditor gives up in frustration and simply takes his—or her—word for it. And even I would've been inclined to trust Miss Stedman. As apparently Johnny did."

"You think she was working both for John and for the bad guys?"

"Unless Danson or Sommers, or some unknown factor, is better at computers than she is. And I doubt that." He got up and began to whiz around the room, as he always does when he gets excited.

"So the money comes out of the Foundation," I said, "and disappears into, say, Kenwood Enterprises. It's an ideal money laundry. Old, respectable family business, solvent but in danger of shipping water, open for mysterious investors. Oh, will you light somewhere, you're making me airsick."

"Where is Kenwood Enterprises headquartered?"

"Don't know, but I can guess. Manhattan, with branches in the Bahamas, the Caymans, Montserrat, maybe Monaco or Liechtenstein."

"All providing worry-free banking for the criminal-on-the-go."

"There are still a lot of things that need checking out." I shook my head. "Damn waste of time, this TV show tonight. I could be ferreting my way into that Weeks place at The St. Claire."

Eddie had paused behind my chair and I could feel something tickling my neck. I slapped at it. It turned out to be the two ends of Merriman's aged silk necktie with the green stripes. "What the hell are you doing, preparing to strangle me?" I swatted at him again, but he had the thing around my cranium.

"I am measuring your noggin," he said. "I wish to be able to ascertain how much your hat size will increase, once you've become a star of the little screen."

Well, I didn't feel much like a star, I can tell you. Shortly after six that evening, Myra Fish delivered me to a small, ceramic-tiled room the color of an aquarium where I was told by a little miss with most of Max Factor's spring line on her cheekbones to climb into a sort of dentists' chair for "makeup." I emerged powdered and reflectionless, and they even sprayed my specs with some goo to keep them from "burning the lens." I had to wear them, you see, to read the cue cards Myra had prepared with a capsule version of John's life on them.

We entered the huge and drafty studio. I looked around carefully. At one end was a mess of folding chairs, behind the large, heavy camera. At the other end was a sort of set, a simple desk and two reasonably comfortable chairs. But neither of them was the chair John had used on his last tape. I spotted Sarah in one of the folding chairs off-camera, and just as we began, David joined her. Myra was waving her cue cards at me and making signs. Five, four, three, two, one. Then she pointed at me.

For a second, I froze. I seemed to be swimming, but there wasn't any water, and I could feel people staring at my knees. Then I read the first line of the cue card. "Good evening, ladies and gentlemen. My name is Winston Sherman."

"Oh for pity's sake," I grumbled. Had I been reduced to being told my own name? I ignored the cards and went on.

"As most of you probably know, John Falkner won't be with us in the studio, but he'll be here, in a sense. In a moment I'll show you a tape he left, his last show. But I'd like a word or two first, just as his friend."

I got up and moved around a little, and Myra kept

making frantic gestures to the cameraman to follow me. "I knew John's mother," I said. "She was a teacher, and I wanted to be one, and she spoke French, and I didn't. Still don't. And she rented rooms, and I needed one. She had this boy. Not a very talkative kid. Read a lot of books, big ones. When I first met him he was gulping down *War and Peace*, I think, and when he finished it he just started over at the beginning and read it through again. Anyway, I was young, and he was younger. I went away and he went to college. He wrote a book, and it won a prize. And then for a long time he became what's called a public man. If he were here, I might have some things to say to him—that I'm sorry for our years of silence and estrangement, but not for our fights, because they were damn fine fights and I enjoyed every one of them and so did he. That I resent the way he pulled the wool over my eyes, but pulling it off is the best jigsaw puzzle I've ever worked." I paused. Nobody made a sound.

"I think I'd like to tell him that something in the weather of the world seems to have turned against men like John and replaced them with brats and opportunists and left the rest of us with not much to read. Not much to open our eyes to and say, Ah, that's the stuff. That's the real old stuff out of the crusty bottles at the back. I wish I could tell you when this spell of weather's going to change. I can't. But John's been doing his bit to help it along. This is the tape he left for you. He'd want us to think about it. I hope we still remember how."

I was bone tired when we left, and I walked along between Sarah and Davy without saying a word for a long time. All I wanted to do was go back to the hotel and conk out till morning, when we'd all be going home to Ainsley for the funeral. I missed it badly just then, the big old house, the trees, the sense of the everyday. I think I even missed Hilda Costello and her feed-sack dresses and dopey Tommy Sheffield calling me an old fox. But we'd promised to meet Teresa and Mickey at David's after the show for a drink and a late supper with them and George and Sonny, who were still camping there.

The gods of the parking space were with us, and David found one only a block from the apartment. We were walking along, still maintaining radio silence, when we got in viewing range of David's front steps. The door opened and out came Sugar, moving at a good pace on his new crutch. He saw us, no doubt recognized my unmistakable profile, and took off in the opposite direction, headed toward Central Park West, where the ten o'clock traffic was just picking up. Somewhere behind us, I heard a car start its engine. Then Sonny came out of the building, loping along in that loose-jointed way of his. On the corner, he caught up to Sugar, and they seemed to be arguing.

We were too far away to hear anything. In the lights at the corner I saw Sonny catch at his friend's arm, and then George pushed him away with an angry shove that made Sonny stagger. George seemed to want nothing except to get away from him. Maybe the incident with the jogger the day before had spooked him and he felt he had to get away before Sonny got caught in the middle, as Teresa had. Whatever his reasons, he started into CPW against the light, dodging between the lanes of moving traffic, balancing precariously as cars and cabs and buses whizzed by honking madly. David began to run, and so did Sarah, but I could only toddle doggedly forward. In a minute I felt someone beside me. It was the kid Mickey, and Teresa was close behind him.

"What's going on?" I asked her.

"He wouldn't tell me," she panted. "He just got his stuff and took off."

Then I saw the car I'd heard earlier. It picked up speed as it passed us, going down the narrow tunnel of parked vehicles on both sides of the street, heading for CPW. It was a small car, and dark, and I couldn't see the driver. And then Sonny dashed out into the busy street after his friend. David didn't have time to get to him before he was standing a lane away from George, turning confusedly against the shafts of oncoming light and balancing precariously on the narrow white line between the lanes. "Okay, Lieutenant!" yelled Sugar George. "Don't move. Stay on the line. Mines. Just stay on the line."

The car made the turn; I could see it was dark green as it passed under the bright lights at the corner. David dodged into the street and I felt Mickey grab my arm and hang on. I couldn't hang onto anything. Now I knew how those ropedancers of Eddie's felt when the rope ran out. There they were in the street, the three of them, all dark and young and enough alike to have been brothers, a lane of traffic between each one as they tried to make it to the park side. And there was the green Toyota heading straight at them. Then blessedly it swerved, missing David by a couple of hairs and some exhaust fumes. When the lanes cleared, Sonny had made it to his friend, and David was about to join them and find out what was going on.

But then the car I *hadn't* seen, the one right behind the green Toyota, swerved round the corner with its brakes screeching. It was light gray, a neat, newish sedan, and that's all I registered before I saw Sonny shove George down onto the curb. He spun round in the car lights, balancing his feet carefully, exactly according to orders, along the white line. For a second he froze, staring.

Then there was a soft thump. Not much of a sound for the end of a long, long war.

Chapter Fourteen

"Have the Weeks file by Monday. I'll find you." That had been the ultimatum of the voice on my answering machine, the unknown Al Zadravic. I'd phoned Lincoln and asked him to check the Hall of Records, and even though it was Sunday, he'd pulled it off. Dean Sommers had officially changed his name, Albert Dean Zadravic, to Dean Sommers on his eighteenth birthday, just as he was about to enter Harvard's School of Business. If it was Sommers who'd planted the answering machine in Room 209 of the Seven Pines Motor Inn, he'd be likely to make his move while we were all at John's funeral, up at the Monastery.

But to my surprise, along with the few friends and relatives who sat in deep concentration during the Mass was the urbane figure of Andrew Danson, and with him a younger man I didn't know. I scribbled a note and passed it to Miss Plumb, who was sitting with Eddie. "Who's the man with Danson?"

"Dean Sommers," she wrote, and passed it back to me.

He was perhaps thirty-two or -three, and if today I had to pick him out of a crowd, even after all that's happened, I'd find it rough going. Some generations, like mine, fight their way more or less out of the egg. Some grow like Topsy. The young man with Danson appeared to have been cloned. Someone had worked hard teaching him how to move along the surface of the world extracting and storing its treasure, leaving not the slightest track, only to disappear at last, indistinguishable from any other ant. He might've been managing a Kmart or running the Ainsley franchise of Buddy

155

Burger. It wouldn't matter, so long as the guiding principle was tasteless, faceless unanimity.

But at least with Sommers here in the Chapel, he couldn't be breaking into my Cave looking for the Weeks file. I relaxed and looked over the rest of the mourners. Myra was there, and a group from the college, bless their hearts, and of course Lloyd Agate. And there was one absolute surprise. If there was anybody I knew who never took the risk of encountering mortality in its ultimate form, it was David's wife Alex. But there she was, long red-bronze hair braided like Sarah's and pinned up under the plain black hat. And the face that's made Estée and Helena and Max so many bucks was almost without makeup. Alex looked shy and girlish and distinctly unlike her usual daunting self. She had her arm through David's and she kept it there resolutely, even when we all sat down for the sermon.

The burial service was without incident, except for a reporter who tried to climb the wall to snap a picture. When it was over and the prior had retreated to his office, we milled aimlessly around the churchyard. I felt awkward, as I always do at funerals, and I was about to sneak off to David's car and kick off my shoes in the backseat, when I caught sight of Danson and his son making for the white limo. Andrew stopped to speak to Teresa, and I zeroed in to head Sommers off.

"I'm Winston Sherman," I said, sticking out my paw.

"I know. I saw John's show last night."

"He certainly knew how to bear a grudge," I said. "But then, I imagine you're used to artistic temperaments, working for Andrew."

"I'm afraid they're not something I care to get used to."

"Bourgeois affectations?"

"Ineffective resource management. Anger is counterproductive." His eyes were very clear gray and oddly still. He didn't even blink, and kept maintaining eye contact with me. Even when I looked away, I looked back to find him still locked on to me. Probably a management technique. I decided to *make* him blink.

"Oh, by the way, how did you enjoy the Seven Pines

Motel, Mr. Zadravic? But then I don't suppose you spent the night, did you, just drove in and set things up."

Well he did blink, just barely. But another nervous habit surfaced instead. A couple of strong white teeth emerged from under the neat Bus. Ad. moustache and bit down hard on his lower lip, until a fine line of blood outlined it. He ran his tongue over it carefully. "Stop calling me, damn you," he said under his breath. "I won't pay."

"Calling? Me call you? I've never—"

"Do you think I'm a fool?"

"Far from it. But I do think you're the most tightly packaged man I've ever met, and packages wrapped too tightly have a way of coming apart at the seams. Why did you change your name? Zadravic not upmarket, was it, not quite Harvard material? It reeked a bit of onions and Polish sausage and sweaty armpits. Albert your grandfather's name? What was he, construction worker, truck driver, stevedore?"

And then Andrew Danson came up to us. Sommers escaped quickly into the limo.

"Winston," Andrew said, "I hear you're quite the TV star. WNYT informs me they've gotten over a thousand calls since the show."

"John's doing, not mine."

Andrew leaned against his car. "It was true, about the Pulitzer. Publicly, I'll deny it. But it was true. He never forgave me for it."

"Did you actually expect him to?"

"I made no excuses. I was young. I wanted power. I got it the only way anybody does. I bought it. I'm only sorry John found out."

"Of course, if he hadn't, it would've been dandy, is that your logic?" I shook my head. "Did John ever confront you about it?"

"Years ago. Oh yes. I've still got the capped tooth to prove it." He dragged the back of his hand across his eyes, as if his head ached. "I think he stayed with the Foundation mainly to punish me. It worked."

"Not as well as that phony Pulitzer did on him."

"You mean his burnout? That would've happened anyway."

"You ought to win a prize for casuistry, Danson, you're an expert at self-delusion."

"I tried to convince him that what I did had nothing to do with him. It was between me and the Danson Foundation Board. They didn't take me seriously as management material, not after Pops. You know my father?"

"By reputation."

He laughed softly. "If it hadn't been for old Plumb, he'd have run the whole thing into the ground. John was a means to an end. To prove to them I could be a force in the arts community."

"Somehow I don't imagine John found that motive overly comforting."

Danson opened the car door. "Odd thing is, Winston— neither did I."

I was just watching the limo pull away when a couple of fellows in Italian suits and Gucci loafers came up to me. The bald one, tall and built like Eddie's clarinet, offered his hand.

"Sandor Hoffman, Professor. John's attorney. Call me Sandy. We spoke on the phone, remember? And this is Jeremy McKaye. The investment man I sent John to about those numbered accounts."

McKaye, as short as Sandy Hoffman was tall, spoke with the remnant of a Scots burr. "I caught you on the box last night," he said. "Verra moving, that little chat of yours."

"Please, both of you," I told them, "join us at the house for coffee before you go back to the city. I need to talk to you."

Like one organism, they checked their Rolexes. Then they exchanged nods. "Fine," said Sandy. "We've got some things to clear up too."

I felt a touch on my arm. It was Alex. She led me aside, into a small greenhouse near the Chapel.

"I'm worried about David," she said. "Last night he called me after the accident. If it *was* an accident. Anyway, he sounded so shaken. He'd answered all those questions, that insufferable man Duffy. And they kept poor George all night long, trying to break down his resistance. Drug tests, psychological tests, the lot. Duffy thinks he knows something and won't tell. At any rate, D. was alone, and he sounded dreadful, so I took a taxi over there. Sometime during the night I woke up and heard him talking on the phone. He was using a voice. You know. Not his own, an acting voice. A little like the one from *Richard the Third*, but more gravelly. He only said one sentence, and then hung up. 'Dennis Weeks, I'll call again.'"

"Oh Lord, so that's what Sommers was talking about. Listen Alex, whatever you do, get David to bring you down to the house before you go back to New York. I've got to talk to him right away."

"There's no time, Winston, he's got a film shoot this afternoon, the last bit of his movie. We'll only just make it on time as it is."

"Damn it! All right. Then tell him, well, tell him I've got a plan of my own and he mustn't do anything to mess it up till I've filled him in."

"What sort of plan?"

"I wish I knew." I stood looking at her. Since David's plastic surgeries, none of us had seen much of Alexandra, and neither had David. She'd been afraid of his scars and the memory of the slashing, which she'd witnessed, and though there'd been a minor rapprochement between them, nothing had been settled before she took off with Gemma for London. Now that she was back, she seemed entirely changed. "Thanks for coming, kiddo," I said. "And for ratting on David."

She smiled. "Kiddo? I don't think you've called me that before. I take it as rather high praise." She started to go, then turned back. "And I shall make every effort to rat on him again, should the need arise."

When I came out again into the Monastery close, a woman in a long brown skirt was just taking her life in her hands for a drive to the station with our local cabbie, Frieda Fritz. "Somebody ought to warn that poor woman and give her a ride," I told Sarah as I joined her.

She looked round. "What poor woman?"

"Over there, heading for the Yellow Peril."

Sarah stared and grabbed my arm. "That's him!" she said. "The size and height. And I'd know that duck walk anywhere!"

"Him? Him who?"

"That woman getting into the cab is the man in the red parka!"

"Merriman," I roared across the close, "who was that lady?"

He spun round like a startled squirrel. "That? Why, Charlotte Stedman, the computer wiz."

An hour later we were gathered in our living room before a bright fire, as the weather began to worsen outside. After a stop at his office for the latest bulletins from Manhattan, Agate, who can never pass up a chance at my cooking, joined us for a late lunch. "Duffy's boys found both those cars early this morning. The green Toyota was ditched up in the South Bronx. Stripped, naturally, engine and all. Prints all over the sucker, a bunch of them known juvies, car strippers, parts thieves. Can you identify the Stedman woman as the driver?"

"No, of course not. When I saw her, she was on foot," said Sarah.

"Teresa, was she the jogger with the two-by-four?"

"I don't know. To tell the truth, I could identify that two-by-four a lot easier than the jogger. But one thing I don't understand. He—or she—could've broken George's neck with that thing, but she didn't. She could've run the three of them down on Central Park West, but she didn't, she just aimed at them and then swerved away."

"That's what she did before, the day George got hurt," Mickey chimed in. "Then she drove away."

"So," said Eddie, "you feel the red jacket may've been worn on purpose, to make her conspicuous as a threat, and scare us off, without doing real harm?"

Agate nodded. "Begins to look like it. I'd say you've got more than one person making threats. The Stedman woman, Dean Sommers, who made the phone calls, and whoever broke into Mrs. Falkner's—Miss LaMagna's, I mean—apartment. Might be three people, or just the two. And then there's that assistant of Freiling's, the guy we figure moved the body."

"You said before that Duffy found *both* cars, Lloyd."

"Yeah. The gray car that hit Sonny was parked up by the Cloisters. Somebody spotted the blood on the front grille and the busted headlight and called the cops. Blood types and skin traces match. But it was wiped clean of prints, even the jack and the hood-latch lever. Reported stolen first thing this morning. Registered to a corporation."

"Not Kenwood Enterprises?" I saw Jeremy McKaye perk up and listen.

Lloyd nodded. "It wasn't checked out to anybody at the time."

"Not officially. But it's Danson's company, either he or Sommers could've got hold of it."

Sandy Hoffman spoke up for the first time. "I knew John was afraid, but I didn't take it seriously. When we had lunch a week ago, he seemed terribly nervous. He insisted on walking to the restaurant, in and out of stores, through back doors. Like a le Carré novel. I assumed he'd had a couple. His behavior had been a bit odd lately anyway."

"In what way?"

"At times disoriented. Absent. You had to drag him back to you. Forgetful, too, but then he always did forget what he didn't care to bother with. Only he'd completely erase things, his car for instance. Once he telephoned me to ask if he'd left it at my place. He'd simply forgotten it and taken a cab home."

"That day you had lunch, did you see any red parkas on the horizon?"

"No. Not that I remember," said Sandy after a minute's thought.

"Martin Gleich, the doorman at Charlotte Stedman's building, wears a blue jacket," said Eddie.

"The guard at the school across the street from my place, you know, Winnie, old Harvey? He told me a guy in a blue jacket was hanging around the block the day my place was broken into," Teresa volunteered.

"So we now have two German immigrants, both missing, both named Martin, if our surmise is correct and Freiling's younger brother *is* his mysterious assistant. Could he also be Gleich, the doorman at The St. Claire?" asked Eddie.

"Lemme make a phone call," said Lloyd, and disappeared into the hall.

"What do you know about Kenwood Enterprises, Mr. McKaye?" I asked.

"I know it appears to be a money laundry for a verra nice little fraud," replied Jeremy McKaye. "My firm handles the Foundation's investments. Ordinarily we keep everything confidential. But we're not priests. What I need to know now is whether to go to the Securities and Exchange people straightaway. I don't wish to lose the Foundation account, but I cannot afford to be tarred with the same brush if there's monkey business under way."

"Did John have evidence of the fraud in black and white?"

"Oh, aye, indeed. Photostated birth certificates, Army records, even college transcripts for this man Weeks. And a number of computer traces, one in particular, a fellow he'd invented and sent through the system."

"Vincent Oakes?"

"I believe that was the name, yes. Quite a nice fat file it was. John did everything but handcuff himself to the thing. He wanted me to use my firm's facilities to follow the path of the money after it was paid out to his Vincent Oakes. Naturally it was all computerized transfers."

"Let me try it out," I said. "Danson pays out a grant through the computer, but it goes into a general slush fund, liquid funds, where it's easy to transfer out as a general investment. He waits a few weeks, then has you invest the money in Kenwood."

He nodded. "I've tried several times to get Andrew to sell out that silly stock, but he claimed sentimental grounds, because of his wife. Well, one can't dispute that sort of thing. But it was a bottomless pit. To tell the truth, I'd begun to be suspicious even before John came to me, but I closed my eyes to it. The customer is always right, you know."

"Where are the numbered accounts?"

"Kenwood has several foreign offices, and one happens to be in Montserrat, which has no disclosure treaty with us. From there the money was spread out to Liechtenstein, the Channel Islands, and Monaco."

"Shall I ask? How much?" I braced myself.

"Judging by the Kenwood investments over the last five years, around fifteen million." He looked worried. "A good bit of that is federal matching funds, you know, National Endowment monies. He's siphoned off not only the trust, but public monies as well, and that makes it a federal crime. Frankly, I'd go to Securities and Exchange this afternoon, but there's nothing illegal about numbered accounts per se. What I need is John's file. Clear evidence."

"Miss Plumb," I said, "don't you think Randolph might be able to help us now? Maybe it's time to give him a call."

"I telephoned him three times yesterday and each time he was unavailable. I know where *he* is, all right. He's at that silly country club of his down in Georgia, knocking little white balls around some cow pasture."

"He couldn't be involved, could he? In the fraud, I mean," asked Sarah.

Plumb gave her a murderous look. "Certainly not. I *know* Randolph. But you must know him, too, Edward—he's on the Board of Trustees of your college."

"*My* college?" said Eddie. "Clinton College?"

"Yes. He was given an honorary doctorate and a permanent seat on the Board there, oh, twenty years ago now."

My beady eyes lit up. A plan was forming in my mind that would transfer the main players into my court for what I hoped would be the match point. "Miss Plumb, when's the next fund-raiser at the Foundation?"

"That would be the Valentine's Gala. Why?"

"Because Randolph's going to be there in person. And the Gala's going to be held at Clinton College, right here in Ainsley. Do you think you can bully him into it?"

"It's only a few days until Valentine's. Randolph will take some convincing. Edward will have to come with me. I'm flying to Savannah tomorrow." And she planted her feet firmly on the floor, bracing for takeoff.

Eddie turned a little pale. "Me? Oh, really, I don't think—"

"It's a dandy idea, Merriman. You can go as Sheffield's personal faculty representative," I said. "I'll tell him about it later."

"That's settled then," said Plumb as Eddie gnashed her teeth behind her back. "You may call for me at noon, Edward. I'll make reservations for two." And she marched out to get her coat.

Sarah went off to warm up the old Volks and take Plumb to the station, so she missed Lloyd's revelation when he got back from his phone call. "Just got hold of Lincoln," he said. "He's been running a check on that kid brother of Freiling's. If you guys are right and he's the missing assistant, Immigration wants him. If it's Martin Freiling, he's here illegally. He's on the Deny Entry list. Belonged to some screwy bunch over in Vienna, called Red Thursday."

"I remember Red Thursday," said Myra. "We ran a BBC special about middle-aged terrorist groups. They blew up a bunch of stuff back in the sixties; once they even killed a guy."

Everybody fell silent at this revelation, and in the lull Sandor Hoffman and his friend McKaye made their farewells. I trailed them for one last question. "What about the IRS and Social Security? Why haven't they caught on yet?"

"A good computer man could simply erase the records of the payments," said the Scot.

"So they may be gone for good if we can't find John's file?"

"It depends. If the operator actually took apart the program bit by bit, backtracked, and eradicated the records, yes, they're gone. If he merely erased, to allow the program to stand in case they ran through another batch of frauds, the information can be reconstructed. It's still there, just— obliterated."

"Sort of electronic Wite-Out. Scrape it off and read the message underneath."

"Right you are. You'd need a dedicated hacker to uncover it. But it could be done."

"Let me try, Doc." Mickey was standing behind me.

"You'd need the entry codes into the main system at the Foundation," said McKaye.

"If you sprint for it, kiddo, you can catch Miss Plumb before she gets away. If anybody can get them for you, she can." He took off, hot on her heels.

Late that afternoon, after the last can of film had been shot for David's spy flick, round about the time I was sitting with Eddie in the Faculty Lounge at school, refereeing a grudge cribbage match between Krish and Hugh (Tess of the D'Urbervilles) Jonas, our doleful Hardy professor, an unknown man walked into the lobby of The St. Claire. He was, or seemed to be, just past forty, tall and slim, with dark hair graying only slightly. He wore a neat beard and moustache and a pair of tinted glasses that suggested vision problems, as did his uncertain walk. He moved slowly through the lobby, assisted by his companion, a man who had one whole leg and one whole arm. The bearded man carried a small, elegant suitcase with the initials D.W. on the side.

"Help you, sir?" asked the doorman.

"Yes. Which way are the elevators?" said D.W. He looked round dimly, just in time to save himself from stumbling over a statue of Venus. The doorman reached out protectively.

"What apartment did you want, sir? I'll buzz upstairs for you."

"It's thirty-two D, but there's nobody up there. It's my apartment, actually. I'm Dennis Weeks."

The doorman helped Weeks to the elevators and went off to help the man with one leg bring in some luggage from the cab. There was a woman on board the elevator, but she didn't speak to Weeks. Charlie Stedman didn't try to be pleasant to strangers anymore. She'd been swallowing garbage all her life, but you didn't have to ask for it. She rode up to her floor staring into the surveillance mirror above the doors, at the reflection of the handsome bearded man. Maybe he couldn't see her. Still, he couldn't be completely blind, because there was no white cane. When the elevator stopped on her floor, Charlie started to get off.

"Excuse me," the man said, reaching out for her. He touched her arm, gently but firmly. She winced a little, because her arms were bruised and stiff. "What floor is this?"

"Thirty." There were no Braille numbers on the elevators buttons. "Going up?" For some reason she took a chance. "I'd be glad to ride up with you, if you'd like."

"Thanks. But that's okay. I can keep track now that I know. I lost count somewhere about sixteen. Wasn't concentrating." He smiled. "I was trying to figure out your perfume. It's Golden Lotus, isn't it? My sister used to wear it."

"They don't even make it anymore. But I save things," she said.

Somebody pushed past her and got onto the elevator and she stepped back. "Bye," said the man. "Thanks."

Upstairs on thirty-two, Sugar George, who had taken the freight elevator, had needed about eight seconds to pick the lock on the door of Apartment D. And as David, our newborn Dennis Weeks, complete with false beard and dark specs, went inside with George, a woman entered the lobby downstairs. She had black hair tied in a long ponytail, wore a gray uniform and a brown cloth coat well-worn at the elbows, and carried a clunky imitation leather purse. "Has Mr. Weeks arrived yet?" she demanded in a heavy Irish accent. "I'm to be his cook, y'see."

"Oh yes, ma'am. Shall I buzz him?"

"I got to make a phone call first." She marched over to the pay phone and dialed long distance.

A few moments later, I was just declaring Krish the winner of the cribbage match when Hannah, our Faculty Sec, came in to call me to the phone. "Winston Sherman here," I said.

"It's Alex. I mean, it's not me, I'm Mrs. Jack. I mean I'm wearing her clothes. If I weren't so mad, I'd be enjoying it."

"Alex, do calm down."

"I followed D. He's wearing the Uncle Vanya beard and the shaded glasses, the ones from that awful Vietnam thing he did Off-Broadway. George is with him. They've simply moved into the Weeks apartment. D.'s claiming to *be* Dennis Weeks."

"What the devil's the matter with him? Charlotte Stedman could recognize the pair of them, disguise or not. And George can't very well disguise anything."

"You know actors. The right illusion takes care of everything."

"Alex, kiddo, go up and talk some sense into him. Bat him on the head if you have to, but at least get George out of there."

"Oh," she said, "I don't think any batting will be required. Seeing me in this wig would put the fear of God into anyone."

Chapter Fifteen

Next morning, Sarah, Teresa, and I once again took the early train into the City. I was wearing down, I don't mind telling you. I was never cut out for the life of a commuter.

Sarah went off to hound Equity again about Maureen, and Teresa went home to try to make some order out of the chaos in her apartment. As for me, I headed straight for The St. Claire, but not before that dowdy little female with the black fright wig and the pocketbook. Alex had returned bright and early and it was she who opened the door of 32D when I knocked.

"I recognized her by the freckles," said David. "Should've used heavier pancake, love. I never saw a black-haired girl with freckles." He looked at her with, I thought, considerable pride. "'New cook, sir, sent by the agency,' she said, in this accent straight out of County Cork." Well, there I was, fumbling round, squinting at her."

"I *have* been taking acting lessons for donkey's years, you know," said Alex. "I *am* good for something besides a designer's clothes rack."

I looked around the place. It was bare of furniture, except for one chair, a telephone, and an answering machine. "Did you bring the answering machine or was it here?" I wasn't ready to start yelling at David yet, but I had no intention of disappointing him. He was watching me closely, timing the explosion.

"It was here. Recognize the chair?"

"Yes, of course I recognize the chair." It was the one from John's farewell tape. I sat down on it and glared at

David. "What I do not recognize is your right to make unilateral life-and-death decisions, and take mortal chances without consulting people who care about you."

"I suppose it would be better if you took the chance, or Eddie?"

"May I suggest the police, who get paid for it?"

"Cops aren't actors. This is my business, Winston. I've had years of training for it. It's like being a new actor who steps into an old play. You need instant perception of the other fellow's mind. I can do that, it's an old habit by now. Do you really think Duffy can?"

I groaned with frustration. "This isn't a movie where you can yell 'Cut' and stop the frame, you know. Danson knows you. You saw through Alex's disguise, and he may see through yours. You're damn good, but don't fool yourself. You aren't perfect. And if you're caught, I don't fancy finding you with your shoes and socks off at the back of some elevator."

"Speaking of which," David said, adroitly changing the subject, "come out here." He slid open the doors onto the balcony. "Look down there."

He pointed straight down and my old tummy did a flip-flop as I looked over the railing. We were at the back of the square tower that constituted The St. Claire. The floors were neatly divided in four, and Weeks's place faced out on to the alley at the back. It was daylight now, fairly early morning, and delivery men were bringing groceries to some of the apartments. Apparently the service elevator was back there somewhere. There was a paved pad of parking places for delivery vans, and next to it, where a small snowplow had worked, was a heap of piled-up snow that had been cleared. Now it was dirty and sunken and mostly ice, but on Tuesday night, when the City had just finished digging out from under the storm, that heap of snow would've been deep and fairly soft.

"I see what you mean," I said. "He might've fallen with his body on that concrete and his face in the snow. The force of the fall would've caused the skull fracture, but the snow would keep the face from too much exterior damage. And that alley would be the perfect place for Freiling's van to pull in, pick John up, and drive away. Naturally, Charlie Stedman couldn't leave him anywhere near here, because she'd be an obvious suspect, living in the building."

"Whether she did it or not," said David.

"And if they got the connection with *this* apartment, and Weeks, the whole scam was spoiled, so the others had motives to move the body as well. How do we know John didn't fall from Charlie's place?"

"It's on the street side. Sixty-ninth is busy even at two-thirty in the morning. Anyway, look at this." He took a photograph from his pocket. "There, you see that?" He pointed to something in the picture. "Alex took it this morning." It was a shot of the back of the building. David showed me the ledge of the terrace four floors down from the one on which we stood. Something was stuck on the point of one of the arrowhead-shaped spikes. It looked like a man's shoe. "He must've lost it during the fall. Teresa said he never tied it tightly because the orthopedic one was so uncomfortable. And we phoned the Weather Bureau to get the wind velocity that night. It was gusting up to sixty miles per hour, and clocked even higher between the buildings. That's high enough to blow the shoe back toward the terrace."

I fingered one of the sharp, wrought iron spikes of the paling on the terrace wall. "The tear in his sleeve," I said. "Whose place is that, with the shoe?"

"I checked the mailboxes downstairs," said Alex. "And George spoke to the doorman. It belongs to some people named Vandenburg, and they've been in the Orient since October." She was crawling along the floor at the edges of the room, like a cat hunting mice.

"What on earth are you up to?" I said.

"Looking for a cache. The character in D.'s new film, the spy chap? He cut out a square of carpet and put his getaway things under it, false passports and things."

David looked at me and smiled, and I smiled smugly back. Ah, bless her little English heart, she thinks she's Miss Marple. We left her to her charming game.

"So even if they saw the shoe up there, they couldn't have gotten it down unless they scaled the building. Nobody leaves keys to these places floating around. They add half a dozen locks without telling the super, and they certainly wouldn't entrust them to a part-time doorman who couldn't speak English."

"So to make it less likely somebody would keep looking for that missing shoe and happen to find it, they took off the other shoe as well. But why the socks?"

"Has anybody got a screwdriver?" said Alex. "And don't you dare ask if one of mine is loose."

I tossed her my Scout knife with the spoon, can opener, corkscrew, nail file, and screwdriver attached, and went on ignoring her. "Naturally, we can't keep this shoe evidence to ourselves. We'll have to get Duffy and put the whole business in front of him." Maybe it would put an end to David's masquerade, once the police moved in.

And then we heard a clang and a crash, and Alex gave a squeak. The grate in front of the heat register along the baseboard was lying on the rug beside her, and she was waving a fistful of papers at us. "What did I tell you? A cache, just as I thought."

David joined her on the floor. "I think you'd better see these, Winnie."

I came to stand above them, and David held open a passport. Inside was a photo, not very good, but the old on-camera smile was unmistakable. Only the name didn't read "John G. Falkner." What it said was "Max Fleming." He'd renamed himself for the one character he'd never been able to shed, the hero of his first novel.

"There's a bankbook in the name of Max Fleming, too," said David. "With a two hundred thousand dollar balance."

"Getaway money?" asked Alex.

"Hopewell money?" asked David.

"John's life savings," I told them. "According to Sandy Hoffman, he's got everything in trust for Mickey, and when I called his bank about an account for the estate, they told me he'd closed out his personal account, all in cash. This is where he put it, apparently. Alex is right, it's getaway money, from the looks of these passports. And these." There were two airline tickets, one in his own name to Cairo, Egypt, and the other, in the name of Fleming, to Montreal.

"Why two tickets?" asked Alex.

"A feint," David replied. "The kind you use in fencing. You lunge one way and then cut back the other. He would've gone to the airport and checked an empty briefcase on board the Cairo flight, then doubled back and taken the plane for Montreal as Fleming."

Some writers want to set up shop on a South Sea island, but John wanted the North. Go to the woods to live completely, said old Thoreau, and John believed the dream. It was all tied up with his mother's childhood in the cool, idyllic beauty of Quebec. But he'd never gone. He went everywhere else, but never Canada, as if he were keeping it clean for this, his last escape. I stood looking down at the bleary passport picture. When he was a kid, I'd promised to take him and Louise back to Quebec for a visit. It was one more promise I hadn't kept.

I closed the passport and looked around the empty apartment. It made me homesick for the old dead who died in quiet houses and sensible beds. This was not a place where anyone should die, or even live. It was a shell through which only money passed. It smelled of money and felt of money and you could taste money in its stale, complacent air. It had sold Johnny and made him die a tarnished public man, still planning the impossible escape to the clean, unravaged North.

I told David my plan for confronting Danson and Sommers at the Valentine's Gala. "But," I said, "I don't know how it'll work out with this scheme of yours."

"You do want me to keep it up, then?" he said.

"I don't like using you as bait, but with the cops close by, yes. So long as Sugar George keeps out of sight, Charlotte Stedman may not get wise. Where is George, by the way? Making funeral arrangements for Sonny?"

"Oh, Sugar has all kinds of arrangements under way. Did you happen to notice a bag lady in the door of the apartment house across the way?"

"Matter of fact I did, thought it was an odd part of town for her. Funny they don't give her the bum's rush in this neighborhood."

"That's Irma. Down the block there's a girl selling

flowers out of a plastic pail. She'll shift this way once Irma's moved on. Her name is Nita."

"Nita the hooker? The kid George took to Covenant House the night John died?"

"Sugar has a lot of friends, and so did Sonny. He's organized them into a real team, sort of the Times Square Irregulars. Some are watching Freiling's shop." He smiled. "Though I rather think George is keeping an eye on Teresa himself."

I got up and put my coat on. It was freezing in the joint. "All right, Davy, bundle up those golden tonsils and come on. We've got to see the cops about that shoe. You go down first, and I'll meet you in the park."

When he was gone, I took Alex's arm for a moment. "Kiddo," I said, "forgive me if this sounds like a slam, because it isn't one. But you seem so—"

"Unmodelish?" She laughed. "Is that a word?" She walked across the room in her best runway style, Mrs. Jack's wedgies and all, hand on slim hip, cheeks sucked in. Suddenly she stopped. "Know how old I was when Mum decided I could bring in a quid or two being a living mannequin at Brownlow and Frye in Piccadilly? Fourteen. From then on, if I broke a fingernail, it was an international incident. You don't belong to yourself, Winston. You can't, because you aren't anybody. You only exist in photographs. When I was in London last fall, I was asked to do the new styles, you know, all the Princess Di stuff. Only I couldn't. I got up there, I don't mean I was afraid. But I walked out after two dresses. They were livid, poor things. But I had to do it. It was something I'd always wanted to do. I'll never go back now, not ever. Maybe I'm not anything else. I don't really know yet. But I'm more than a damn photograph."

"Of course you are," I said. "You're the cook sent by the agency and your fright wig is slipping."

We arranged for Duffy's men to bug the Weeks place and lurk in one of the empty apartments down the hall, and then Sarah and I were free to go back home. On the train she filled me in on her progress in the search for David's mother.

"I spoke to her agent, and she's living in Toronto, all right. But she does touring shows booked out of New York, musical comedy, you know. It was always her sort of stuff, I think she did it because Erskine hated it. Anyway, she went directly from that flop in Toronto into a long tour. That silly thing you read the reviews of not long ago, what was it again?"

"Not the musical comedy version of *Anna Karenina?*"

She nodded solemnly. "It's to play all across Canada, and go from there to England. If we don't catch her soon, she'll be halfway across the world. We may lose her again entirely. Shouldn't I tell David?"

I thought for a moment. "No. Would you tell him if he were about to open in *King Lear?*"

"Of course not, you nitwit, it would ruin his concentration."

"Well, he's got another opening coming up," I said, and took the plunge. Once I'd told her what he was up to in the Weeks apartment, she just sat glaring at me for twenty miles or so.

Finally she said, "I shall leave you, if anything happens to him, you know that. It's you and all this mystery nonsense. I couldn't go on if anything went wrong, not the two of us. I'd always be thinking of it."

"I see."

"It's irrational, but there is it."

"Shall I call him off?"

"Could you?"

"Probably not."

"We didn't bring him up to be called off, did we?"

"No."

"So it's my fault too, I suppose."

"I suppose so."

"Then I guess we'll have to stick it out together, whatever happens."

"We always have, kiddo. We always have."

Once again, the man with the shaded glasses and the Uncle Vanya beard happened to get into the elevator just after Charlotte Stedman, who was coming home from work that night. "Hello again," he said, and turned vaguely in her direction with a smile. "You're wearing the Golden Lotus."

"Hello," she said. "How're you doing?"

"Settling in. What's a good restaurant around here?"

"Here? I don't know. Belle Epoque, I guess, or Mariano's. I don't eat out."

"I hate it myself," said the bearded man. "But I'm not much of a hand with a frying pan, and the woman from the agency was a dud. The guy who works for me took the week to visit his sister in Albany. So." He shrugged. "Look, I know you don't really know me. But I could use a navigator getting to this restaurant. Have you had dinner?"

"Oh," said Charlie. She thought about saying she'd eaten. You always got looks in restaurants, especially when you ate alone the way she usually did. She even thought about offering to cook. "Oh, I don't know."

"I put it badly," he said. "I should've said, will you please give me the honor of your company at dinner?" He paused. "I'm sorry. You're probably married or something. I didn't think."

"No," she said quickly. "It's not that. But I'd have to change first and everything."

"Why?" He brushed a hand unseeingly over her shoulders. "You look fine to me." He laughed.

"I don't even know your name," she said, and laughed too.

"I don't know yours either, but I'm on intimate terms with your perfume."

Charlie felt excited. In spite of everything, she was almost happy. "I'd like to know your name, though. Really," she said. "I'm Charlotte. Charlie."

"I like Charlotte." He said it again, but in French. "All right, are you ready for mine? Please bear in mind that my mother spent two years studying Classics in college. It's Demosthenes."

"Jesus." She laughed suddenly, like an explosion.

The elevator was about to reach her floor, and she realized this was a chance to pull back. She liked him too much. And after John, she didn't want to like anybody much.

"Come on, how about dinner?" he said. "This is your floor, isn't it? You get ready, I'll go up and get my stuff and stop down in ten minutes."

"No, I really don't—"

"Fifteen minutes. That's my final offer," he said. His eyes behind the glasses were a dark, intense blue and they looked toward her but not at her, unable to focus, as if she were too far away to be seen and had to be remembered. "Going, going, gone," he said. His voice was serious. She knew he wouldn't ask again.

"Okay," she said. "Okay."

They ate at La Belle Epoque, the snobby place in the penthouse of the York Regency Hotel. The first waiter put them behind a bunch of palm trees in pots; Charlie figured they didn't want her to spoil the atmosphere of ritzy European class. But D., as he told her to call him, signaled for the head waiter and rattled something in French, and before long they had a table with a perfect view of the Manhattan night and Central Park stretching off into the distance. "I like a room with a view, don't you?" said D., feeling for his water glass.

"Were you in Vietnam?" She didn't understand how he could make jokes.

"Right to the end," he said.

"I'm sorry."

"There're all kinds of wars, Charlotte. What's yours?"

"I don't know. Keeping myself out of messes, I guess."

"What kind?"

"Just . . . messes."

"People are pretty messy commodities."

He dropped the subject then, but he picked it up later, when they were walking through the snowy park after dinner. "Was it a man?" he said. "The aforementioned mess?"

"Why do you want to know?"

"Sorry. I'm a nosy bastard. Take me home and I'll leave you alone."

"No. It's—It was two men, really." She walked on in silence, but not too fast, because his hand was on her shoulder, so she could lead him. It was damp and cold, with a fine mist beginning, and it felt cool and good against her hot face.

His voice sounded grim. "Want to tell me, then?"

"Not yet. Let's walk."

They walked on through the light rain. It was beginning to freeze into a thick, wet snow when they reached The St. Claire. They rode silently up in the elevator together. David walked with Charlie, hand still on her shoulder, to stand in front of her door. He let his hand find her face and stroke it, and his eyes closed involuntarily, as if the deception was too much, too unkind, if he looked at her now and still pretended not to see. He bent his head to her, eyes still closed, and kissed her gently on the mouth. "I won't ask to come in," he said. "Not this time."

"Please. Please come in," said Charlie softly, and unlocked the door.

They had coffee, and then some brandy, and they sat for a long time listening to Mozart's *Jupiter Symphony*. Suddenly Charlie took his hand and put it to her face again, and he felt her lips brush the fingers and the palm of his hand. "You're so nice," she said. "I wish I'd known you a long time."

"What was it?" he said. "Tell me now."

"I was so stupid. This guy. He paid attention to me. At work. I've worked there so long, and I never get promoted, and I do everybody's work for them but it doesn't help. But he noticed me. And I thought—I thought—"

"You thought he was in love with you. And he wasn't."

"He used me. I should've known. I mean, what would he want with me? This Bus. Ad. type, with the fifty-buck tie, and the future locked up in his portfolio, what's he want with me?"

"What did you want with him? Sounds like a smug twit."

"But I needed him. I thought I did. And I did things for him, at work. And now I can't get rid of him." She began to cry, great heaving sobs that would have made another woman, even Alex, very ugly, but that brought Charlie's ugly face to the verge of a perverse beauty, like the shadowy, formless faces of Michelangelo's late statues. She seemed uncreated and wailing to be made, to be born. David pulled her gently against him.

"What about the other man, the second man? You said two." He was dull-voiced and relentless.

"I was mixed-up. After the other. He was kind to me. That was all. Do you know what that feels like? When all a man can be is kind to you?"

"Maybe he loved somebody else. Maybe he couldn't love you."

"But *I* loved *him*. I did. And now he's dead."

She leaned hard against David, the sobs shaking her body. He held her slumped against him on the couch as the snow began to pile up on the balcony outside, and he kissed her once or twice, until at last she lay asleep, her arm thrown around him, holding on for dear life.

Chapter Sixteen

There followed two days of blissful rest from the whizzing train trips of the week before. Duffy was busy retrieving shoes from railings, commandeering empty apartments, setting up surveillance equipment, and dusting the Weeks apartment for prints. Almost everything had been wiped clean as a whistle, including the phone and the glass of the balcony doors, but inside the trapdoor of the answering machine, where you put in the tape, was a nice clear thumb print that turned out to be unmistakably John's. Lincoln, who'd volunteered to help out with the undercover stuff when he was off duty, came in dressed up as a carpet cleaner. He went over every inch of the balcony rail and came up with a gray thread pulled tightly into one of the curlicues. This turned out to match the tear in John's overcoat sleeve. Even Duffy, who'd still been more than willing to accept a suicide theory, had to admit now that John hadn't jumped off that balcony entirely of his own choice. A jumper would choose a place with a clear fall, no messy sharp railings to get over. Even a man who wants to die will try to avoid causing himself pain in the process. The thread had been tightly wedged, as if the rest of the fabric had been forcibly pulled away. But at least there was no doubt now. John's death had taken place at the Weeks apartment. One of our big questions was answered.

Mickey was not to go back to the Wildwood School until after Sonny's funeral on Friday, so while his mother and Sarah were in the city completing the repairs to the ravaged homestead, the kid and I rattled around the old house together. I got one somewhat curious phone call from Merriman down in Savannah on the Wednesday morning, while I was making pancakes for Mickey's breakfast.

"Winston?" shouted Merriman. "Can you hear me?"

"No," I yelled, "you've just broken my eardrum."

"Oh, Listen. Randolph's in a tournament, the Cluck-Cluck Open, I believe it is. Cluck-Cluck Frozen Fried Chicken, family firm, he began the tourney and he plays in it every year. He's in it, and he simply won't come out, Winnie."

"Well, pry him out, then. Use your noodle. Think of something."

"He's invited me to play through a round with him, and what else can I do? I do not wish to be sitting in this motel much longer."

"Plumb making amorous advances, is she?"

"Don't laugh, Winnie. I sense the growth of expectations, and you know how I react to those. And something else. What does one wear to a golf tournament?"

"You're asking me, a man Sheffield once accused of having the clothes sense of Attila the Hun?"

"But, I mean to say, last time I played golf, the operative costume was plus fours!"

I could see smoke billowing out of the kitchen. "Wear your pale blue chiffon with the lace collar and your Granny's pearls, and for heaven's sake, do you have any real news? Will the Gala be at Clinton?"

"Don't know."

"Then call me when you do. My pancakes are burning!"

It was one of my teaching days, cold and clear without much ice left on the streets, so I brought out the bikes and Mickey and I pedaled together to campus. He wanted to get to work through the campus computer—the Frumious Bandersnatch—trying to find the records of the phony grant payments. And I meant to see what I could do about Tommy's mid-life crisis. That's why I mapped our bike route to swing by the Roman Holiday Motel. Sure enough, there was his little yellow car, still parked outside Cabin 13. Trust Tommy to draw the lucky number. I sighed. Credit for bringing the Danson Gala to campus might just save his bacon with the Board, but his marriage was something else again.

I ducked into the lounge to check out the faculty grapevine, and found Hilda Costello sitting with Hugh Jonas. Now between these two, they could supply the *Enquirer* with at least a month of front-page stuff. I plonked down with a cup of dishwater coffee under the vigilant eye of Alvin the stuffed Moose and started priming the pump.

"Well, I guess the production of *My Fair Lady* is officially off, isn't it, Hilda?" (Hilda, who has the dubious honor of being a Faculty Wife, as well as a Faculty, was to play Henry Higgins in the all-girl cast, to the dithering Eliza of Lady Di.) "What with Lady Di's divorce and all? Or have you recast the part? Mizz Barnes-McGee, now there's a possibility. Not exactly a Faculty Wife, but you could stretch a point."

Hilda's always been a staunch supporter of Women's Studies, including La Mizz. But then, like Lady Di, Hilda wasn't just a Woman, she was a Married Woman. "Hmmmmmph. Somebody ought to read that girl the riot act," she said.

"But I thought you'd approve. Fulfilling her sexual needs and all, down with the double standard."

"I do not approve of a woman using her body to get promotions."

Tess Jonas stirred beneath the pages of the *Times* and seemed to feel the breath of life along her keel. "I don't mind if she uses *her* body," he announced, "but she's using Tommy's, and it's shooting the whole place to hell. We're falling apart around here. Oh, I've seen it coming for a long time. The Humanities are a doomed profession." And he pulled his head back under the newspaper.

"So The Mizz has her eye on a promotion, does she?" I'd figured it was something of the kind. Mizz Alison Barnes-McGee is barely twenty-seven, and though she would no doubt hamstring any male who complimented her thereon, has a most attractive outer husk. What she wanted with a balding, overmeticulous, academic politician like Sheffield could only be explained if she had something nice and tangible in mind, and from what I'd seen of her, it certainly wasn't a split-level and two ready-made step-kiddies. "She wants early tenure, is that it?"

"It's ridiculous," snapped Hilda. "*I* had to wait the full six years. Why shouldn't she?"

Tess popped out again. "She can't. The budget cuts. Women's Studies as a discipline is down eighty percent in registration nationwide. As long as she's not tenured, she's expendable."

Ah. That explained it. As Chairman, only Sheffield had the power to drop the time limit on tenure. Our Mizz wanted a sure thing, even if it cost Tommy whatever it was he had.

At lunchtime I brought Mickey a burger and fries in the lair of the Bandersnatch. He looked as if he'd been fighting the thing bare-handed. His shirt was sticking to his back with sweat, his hair was standing up in a dozen directions, and his eyes had a sort of glazed look.

"So how's it going, kiddo," I said. "Any luck?"

"She's good, all right," he told me. "I found the erasures, at least a bunch of them. They've banked a lot of personnel files over them."

"Can you reconstruct the stuff that's underneath?"

"Don't know yet," he said, and shoved half a burger into his mouth. "When you come back, bring me a couple candy bars, okay? I need the sugar." He disappeared into the Bandersnatch again, with a slight beeping sound and a flashing of lights.

Next I met Krish outside the Faculty Cafeteria, and we filled our gray, pimply-looking plastic trays with the haute cuisine of Clinton—Velveeta sandwiches, globs of cottage cheese, and quivering rubber tiaras of crimson Jell-O, topped with a solitary green grape. I gazed around, spotted The Mizz, and took off, steering Krish ahead of me like a small cowcatcher on a very large steam engine. "Golly, sir," he said, "this is very personal. I think I would prefer not."

But it was too late. "Hello, Mizz Barnes-McGee," I said, taking root at her table. "You don't mind if I call you

Alison, do you? You're an old hand at familiarity. Of course, this isn't quite as good a spot as the Roman Holiday Motel."

"That's none of your business."

"You are most mistaken," said Krish. "The morality of marriage is a matter of public concern. I myself intend to marry as soon as a suitable lady shall occur."

I placidly ate a piece of geometrical Jell-O. "My friend here is a moralist. I, on the other hand, am a pragmatist. I'm interested in the future of Women's Studies on this campus. It hasn't got one. And unless you lay off Tommy Sheffield, neither have you, old sweetheart."

"Are you threatening me?"

"Naturally. You want tenure. You think you'll romance Tommy into giving it to you before the Budget Committee can give you the ax. But just getting Tommy's okay gets you nowhere, old love. We still have to vote on it. And *I'm* Chairman of the Tenure Committee."

She sat back. "Since when?"

"Since old Joe Philby in Classics got the glanders after Christmas and went out to grass. I am the Oldest Living Specimen on regular employment, thanks to the mysteries class, and that makes me automatic head of the Tenure Committee, by immemorial departmental custom."

"The old gentleman is quite correct," Krish assured her.

"Well this is just typical," said Mizz. Her face was unbecomingly purple. "Typical male chauvinist entrapment."

"If you got your big toe in a bind, little Mizz, you put it there yourself trying to shove it in Sheffield's door. Admit it. You used old Tommy. Not very nice."

"Women have been enslaved and used for centuries. We have a right to use any method at our disposal to break those chains."

"Including a little female chauvinist piggery? And what about Diana? Must say I'm not much impressed by the manner in which you've broken *her* chains."

Her chin jutted out. "If you try to block my tenure, I'll bring you before the Faculty Senate. I'll charge you with discriminatory practices."

"And I'll charge you with immoral behavior. I'm sure Diana'd be glad to testify."

"That morality clause is outdated claptrap. I could name you half a dozen faculty members—"

"Ah," said Krish. "But they already have this tenure. You, on the other hand, are at the moment wanting it."

"All right, I'll charge *you* then. After all, everybody knows you and Sarah Cromwell have been bed partners for years. They can take tenure away for immoral behavior, too, you know."

"Not as long as I'm Chairman of the Tenure Committee. Oh, look, you really don't get it, do you? It's Catch-22. It's the nature of bureaucracy. I've served my time. I paid for my little shred of power, and at the moment I'm finding a damn good use for it."

"Yes. Intimidating me."

"You pay your share, darling Mizz, because that's the way it is. You don't jump the turnstyle and get on without a subway token, just because it's quicker to tumble the driver than wait in line. The phrase is 'give and take,' not 'take and take.'"

"You also must take your chance, as with the rest of us," said Krish firmly, and sank his teeth into the Velveeta, after which he spake no more.

"You're not the only member of that committee," she said. She was almost out of buckshot.

"No. At least one other member thinks you ought to be fired out of hand."

"A man, naturally."

"Well, *I* wouldn't say so. It's Hilda, actually, Hilda Costello."

Mizz's mouth was set in a grim line. "If I break off with him, you won't vote against my tenure?"

"Oh, I really think you can forget about early tenure, even if you break it off. But I will suggest that there are other classes that might need your attention, although Women's Studies is no more." I thought a year or two of Remedial Composition from nine to five might do her the world of good.

"All right," she said. I took my foot off her coattail and she got up.

"Oh, one thing," I added. "Let the poor idiot down gently, will you? I think you owe him one break, don't you?"

That afternoon, while Mickey continued to battle the Frumious Bandersnatch and I taught my mysteries class, Teresa saw Sarah off for the station and walked Bea to the subway. The apartment was back in order and she wanted some time alone to get used to her new cello. She'd just sat down with the score of a Beethoven trio before her when the phone rang.

"This here's Fresno," said a man's voice. "Who's this?"

"Teresa. You sure you've got the right number?"

"Yeah. George said call you up. I got your guy Freiling. See, I work Third Avenue, I'm what you call your cash-flow engineer." Translation, pickpocket. "I been watching the music store, and this morning the guy comes charging out, so I get in my van—I got this van, I live in her, she's a 'sixty-two Volkswagen Microbus, dark blue, she's in great shape, 'know."

"Where is Freiling's brother?"

"Oh. So I tailed the guy to this Seaman's Hostel down on Jane Street and Washington."

"Where's George?"

"Said he'd meet us there."

"I'm on my way," she said, and hung up.

The cab, with a little encouragement from Andrew Jackson, made it down to Jane Street in record time. George was waiting in the doorway of a meat market, along with a giant of a man with pale red hair, who was munching on a hot dog with the works.

"Fresno and me are going in," said Sugar George. "You wait by the bus stop. When it's okay, Fresno'll come get you."

"I didn't come down here to sit by a damn bus stop. I'm coming in."

Sugar took her arm. His grip hurt a little, as it was

meant to. "Lady, don't gimme a hard time. You remember what the guy did to your cello?"

"Yes. I also remember what they did to my husband. You'll hit. And maybe he'll hit harder. I'll talk. I'm going with you."

So they made a strange little procession into the Seaman's Hostel, where a neat, gray-haired woman kept the register.

"Martin Freiling, *bitte?*" The signs in the place were all in German, and then the word for please was Teresa's entire vocabulary.

"Sorry," said the little lady in flawless Bronx. "No Freiling."

"Martin Gleich?"

She checked the register and shook her head.

"How about Thomas Mann?"

"Oh sure. Tom's in the library with his uncle. Right through there."

When they got to the doorway, George motioned to Fresno, who took up a position blocking the exit. Then he yanked Teresa back and planted her firmly behind a notice board in the hall.

Martin Freiling saw George the minute he walked into the room, but didn't seem to recognize him. Andreas, his "uncle," did, though. He said something in German and the younger man, perhaps six feet three or four and a couple of hundred pounds of solid muscle, jumped up and took off for the door. George raised the crutch and landed a nice whack across his knees as he ran past, and Martin went down heavily with a cry of pain. In another minute George had his own knee on Martin's chest and the crutch across the young German's throat.

Andreas dragged at George's shoulder. "Stop! You break his neck!"

Teresa was beside them. "Fresno! Get in here!" She wrapped both arms around George's body from behind and pulled as hard as she could. Martin Freiling lay on the floor choking and gasping. Fresno came lumbering in, looked the situation over, and silently picked Sugar George off, setting him down a couple of feet away on the floor.

George didn't get up. He sat bent deeply over. Teresa knelt behind him, her arms around him, hands locked tight across his chest. "He thinks your brother killed his friend," she said, looking up at Andreas. "In the street, with a gray car."

"He killed nobody."

"My husband?"

Andreas Frieling shook his head. He sank down into a chair, too tired to hold himself up any longer. "Nobody," he said. A group of sailors had gathered during the fight, and one of them helped Martin Freiling up. They spoke briefly in German and then the inquisitive sailors gradually dispersed. Sugar George touched Teresa's locked fingers and she set him free.

"After I left Austria," began Andreas, "my brother joins his crazy bunch."

"Red Thursday."

"He was just a boy. He didn't remember when the Reds marched in after the war. Communists, they are all God to him. I tried to tell him he was a fool. It was the sixties. A delusion, worldwide. Everybody travels with pink glasses. Anyway, finally, they try to blow up a print shop. A man gets killed in the street. Martin wakes up and tries to break off with them."

Martin began to speak and his brother translated. The younger man's voice was thick with emotion, but it didn't seem to be fear. "I got married, a nice girl, in Vienna. We had a little house, her Papa bought it. They came and put red signs on my door. They paint her bicycle, pour red paint on it. They blow up our garbage cans with a bomb. My wife gets scared, she goes. I don't hear from her now, ten years."

Andreas took over again. "By the police he's wanted as Red. By the Reds, he's a dirty revanchist, they want to send him east for a trial. What can he do? He takes other names. He gets to France and they track him down. So he buys another name, signs on a boat, and comes to me. I have a friend, the man on Staten Island. His wife knows somebody. A girl, her mother is German, married to a G.I. She speaks also good German, she can get Martin a job to help out. Doorman at a fancy building."

"Was her name Charlotte Stedman?"

Martin nodded, and again spoke in German. "I knew nothing about the man who fell, madame. I was in front, sweeping snow. It had begun to blow, the wind was bad. It was late, maybe three o'clock. She comes down in the elevator. 'Come with me, I need you.' What can I do? She's kind to me, she gets me a job. I go. Around the back there is this man, in the snow. Dead. Smashed up." He sat hugging himself, the big workman's arms folded tight to his chest. Sugar George was watching Teresa closely as the story got grimmer, nearer to John.

"'We have to move him,' she says. 'We have to take him away. Get your brother's van.'

"'Call the cops,' I tell her. I think she maybe killed him herself, maybe she's crazy.

"She just sits down in the snow by him. 'They've got to pay,' she says. 'If they find him here, they'll say he was drunk and fell. I want them to pay, the bastards.' I say again no, and she says, 'You want to get deported? Help me, otherwise I call Immigration on you.'"

"If he gets deported to Austria, Martin goes to jail," put in Andreas. "In jail, he maybe disappears. So he does this terrible business for her. She brings him in her car and he takes my delivery truck. I hear nothing, at night my hearing aid is on the table. Nothing, madame, even when they bring the dead man into my shop."

Teresa grabbed suddenly for George's hand and held onto it. Fresno, guarding the doorway, noticed the move, smiled to himself, and looked away.

"We had to drag him in," Martin said. "One shoe was off. We dragged him into the shop. I didn't know where else. I thought he would fit in the big crate with the harpsichord. But on the floor was varnish from a new cello, still sticky. I hadn't been home to clean up yet. It gets on his sock when we drag him, and onto his shoe. I burn the shoe and socks and I clean off his feet, and then we put him in the crate. That day, in the morning, we take him to the concert hall."

"I knew nothing," said Andreas. "We had no idea who the man was, madame, or that you might find him. It was

azard, nothing more. When we open the crate on the
tage, I see those feet. That I shall never forget. Martin
ooks at me, a sick dog, so I take the Konzertmeister off and
ve talk music a little. Martin puts the body in the elevator
nd sends it down to the cellar, and we get the devil out. I
now it was wrong. But what does one do for a brother,
nadame?"

"So your alibi was faked?"

"Yes. An old friend. He learned to lie under Hitler."

"And why did Martin go back to The St. Claire and
vork for two nights before he dropped out of sight?" asked
eresa.

"When they made him go to your apartment, madame,
nd break things, to scare you, that was the end of it. He
vas afraid they would next say kill somebody, and then kill
im. He came here to wait for a ship. China, maybe. Aus-
ralia."

"What kind of a car did she drive you in?" said Sugar.

Andreas translated for them. "I don't know cars. But
lue."

"Not gray?"

Martin shook his head. *"Blau,"* he said decidedly.
3lue.

"You said *they* made him break into my place. Did he
ee anyone besides Charlotte Stedman?"

"Niemand," said Martin. Nobody.

Teresa looked at Sugar. "Guess we'd better call Duffy."

Fresno's big ears flapped. "Cops?"

George turned to Andreas. "When's the next ship out?"

"I came to say good-bye. A ship goes to South America
omorrow morning."

"Tell him to watch his backside," he said, and limped
way.

They left the hostel and walked up Jane Street toward
ohn's old neighborhood. Fresno took off to return to his
ash-flow engineering, and George and Teresa walked along
a silence. Finally he stopped.

"I'll get you a cab," he said.

"Where will you be?"

"Around."

"Trying to find out who drove that gray car."

"Maybe."

"I don't suppose I can stop you."

"Nope."

"Please, I need to know something. John left a message, a line of poetry. I gave a book to Sonny last week. Any idea where he put it?"

"Could be anyplace by now. He didn't have it at David's."

A cab finally pulled over for them. George opened the door for her. "Mickey's still up at Sarah and Winnie's. I'm alone tonight." She got into the cab, leaving the door open. "I don't want to be."

"Be sure," he said quietly.

"Get in the damn cab," she told him, and he did.

It was almost six when I pried Mickey away from the computer and we biked home in the dark together. The kid looked frazzled and pooped, but unusually animated and bright-eyed. And, I reflected, I hadn't heard his pet obscenity in days.

"I rebuilt part of her program, using those codes Miss Plumb lifted from the Danson office for us." Plumb had spent an hour and a half on the phone with Mickey the night before, while he typed her smuggled codes onto the Commodore up in my Cave. "Maybe I got something wrong. I want to try a couple of new algorithms. Can we go back to the college after dinner?"

"Can't you try using the Commodore, kiddo? I don't like you wearing yourself out on this. Work at home tonight, and tomorrow we'll try again." I wanted to be able to shoo him off to bed before he fell asleep at the switch.

He clammed up the rest of the way home, either disappointed or brooding on his algorithms, whatever the hell they were. Sarah was practicing at her Steinway when we came stamping and sniffling in, and she came to meet us.

"Mickey, your mother just phoned. They've found Mr. Freiling's brother." She relayed the story of the raid on the Seaman's Hostel. "And Martin Freiling seems to have escaped before they could call Lieutenant Duffy."

"What about the John Donne poems? She was going to check her copy."

"She said there was nothing in the hardcover at the apartment, but she'd given the paperback to Sonny. She wanted to ask George, but apparently he didn't remember—"

"Doc, I gotta go home. *Now*," said the kid suddenly.

"Tomorrow, kiddo."

"Not tomorrow, now. Right now. When's the first train? I gotta find my Mom. I think I know where that book is."

So we phoned to tell Teresa he was on the way. When she turned around, Sugar George had gone. "Damn," she said into the phone, and I heard her door slam.

"Trouble?" I asked.

"George. He just took off. He thinks he's going to find the driver who hit Sonny. If it's Danson or Dean Sommers, George is way out of his league."

"Does he know who owned that car?"

"How do I know? He's got more sources than the CIA, and a lot of them in places you wouldn't expect. But Danson could buy a lot of protection, Winnie, and George isn't exactly Muhammad Ali, you know."

"Don't underestimate him, Teresa."

"Oh, I'm the last person who'd ever do that," she said.

Two and a half hours later, just about the hour Times Square begins to really cook, Teresa found herself being dragged along the dark of Forty-third Street into an alley next to a condemned building with its windows and doors boarded up.

"Walk faster, Ma," said Mickey. "Keep in the dark."

"Mickey?"

"Yeah?"

"You don't have to go back to Wildwood."

"I know. I wasn't going anyway."

They were about halfway down the alley now, and Mickey squatted to find the hinged entry hatch. "Stay here,

Ma. Don't be scared," he said, swinging his legs through the hatch.

"Jeez, not another protective male ego," she muttered, and slipped through the opening behind her son.

They dropped to the basement floor, Mickey in front of her. A candle was burning, and it was very cold. Two cans of Sterno gave off some faint warmth and a heavy smell of paraffin. In one corner, a woman was asleep in a hodgepodge of cardboard cartons. In another, an old man was finishing off a bottle. Near the Sterno cans, two young girls watched the intruders with big eyes. "You from Social Services?" said one. She didn't seem to care very much who they were.

"We're friends of Sonny's," said Mickey. "Any you guys know old Sonny?"

The old woman, ensconced in about six sweaters and a couple of pairs of men's pants, kicked and wriggled her way out of the cardboard boxes. She looked about Teresa's age, not really so old, but without a tooth in her head. "Everybody knows Sonny ya dumbhead," she told the kid. "He's croaked. Went uptown and wound up croaked. I told him, uptown ain't safe. Stick with the Square, where you got pals. Go uptown, you wind up pushin' daisies. What's *your* name, princess?" She was nose to nose with Teresa.

"Teresa," she said, meeting the stare. "What's yours?"

"Isabella of Spain." She held out her hand to be kissed.

"You old bat, you ain't never seen the backside of Brooklyn, let alone Spain," said the old man with the bottle. "You keep still, old fool, let the lady talk some."

"Sonny was our friend. I gave him a book. My husband died this week too. I think maybe he put something in that book for me."

"It's here, I know it's here. I saw Sonny put it down right over there, the day we came in here," said Mickey. He went to an old shelf, then dropped to his knees, scrounging among some newspapers. A rat squeaked. Mickey yelled, and the rat scuttled away into the dark.

"Hush up, boy, you want cops in here?" said the old man. "What you figure's in that book? Money?" His eyes glittered with interest.

"A letter," said Mickey, "maybe a letter, to tell us who killed my Dad. Maybe who killed Sonny, too."

"Okay, you children," said the old man, whose name was Jimmy, "get looking."

"I don't like rats," said one of the girls.

"Do like you're told," screeched Isabella, "or I'll have you beheaded!"

Slowly they plowed their way through the litter of the cellar, until at last Isabella picked up a wad of newspaper and shook it out. Something heavy landed on her feet and she jumped up and down with a shrill squeak.

"Rat? Where'd the bastard run to?" cried Jimmy, wielding his piece of iron pipe.

"I got it," singsonged Isabella. "Button, button, I got the button." She had the paperback in her hands.

"Let's see it," said Mickey, grabbing for it.

"Off with your head!"

She flipped through the pages. "Crap!" cried Isabella. She pulled a piece of paper out of the book. "Nothin' but junk." Disgusted, she tossed it away, and Mickey dived for it. The others gathered round. The candle was about to gutter.

"It's some kinda ticket, lady," said Jimmy. "Lottery, maybe." There were several numbers on the bottom half, but the top half, with the identifying name, was torn carefully off.

"Wrong color for Lotto," said one of the girls. "All this crapola for half a claim check."

"She's right," said Teresa, "it's a baggage claim, but where the hell did he put the half that tells where it's checked?"

"How about Doc's clue?" said the kid. "The banishment of what's-his-name."

Teresa gave her son a hug, much to his chagrin. "I think we'd better call him, right now."

I'd spent most of the evening in my Cave, trying to grade a batch of quiz papers. I really don't know when it dawned on me. I think it was looking at the row of windows and remembering Johnny standing there. I suddenly realized he'd had ample time to locate my copy of Shakespeare, then come back before he left and plant a clue in it. He'd even walked along, running his fingers over the books. I'd assumed *his* copy had to be the hiding place, but of course this would explain why he'd wanted to pick up Mickey here, and hadn't taken him directly from school. He had to get into my Cave to plant his final clue to the location of that file. I reached up and got the heavy old blue volume down, flipping it to the first act of *Cymbeline*.

I still had the torn claim check in my hand when the phone rang.

"Winston?" said Teresa. "We've found the John Donne. Go and look in your—"

"I know," I said. "I have the claim check half here."

"What does it say? Where do we go?"

"You're not going to believe this, kiddo. But that file full of goodies is sitting in the coatroom of Stuyvesant Hall."

Chapter Seventeen

Next morning, Thursday, which in New York was shimmering with February frost, was bright and sunny and seventy-eight degrees down in Savannah, as Eddie, clad in canary-yellow golf pants, strode along with Plumb toward the sand trap. It was round two of the Cluck-Cluck Open, and Randolph Danson was stuck in the rough. Dolph was a diminutive fellow with a puffy light gray moustache and salt-and-pepper hair. He looked up and spotted Plumb, and his brown eyes acquired a wicked twinkle.

"Pudding!" he cried. "Plumb Pudding!" Undecided, he took a last squint and waggle, then dropped his club on the sand. "Aw, shoot," he said. His voice was the amused whine of a man who takes almost nothing in life seriously and never has. "Cummere, Plummy," he said, and opened his skinny brown arms to enfold her. "How I've missed you, you old slave driver!"

"You could get that ball out of the sand, you know. You give up too easily, Dolph, you always did."

"I do, without you to make me dig my heels in," he said.

Plumb yanked Merriman forward. "This is my *friend*." She gave the word the kind of emphasis that could mean anything. "Edward Merriman, Randolph Danson. Dolph, we've got to talk. Andrew's made a mess, and you've got to help clean it up. Come along now." Then she just picked up his golf clubs and marched toward the clubhouse.

"Aw," whined Dolph, and followed her like a small boy with a killer nanny.

In the frigid, air-conditioned clubhouse, Dolph Danson stood the three of them a round of drinks with green leaves floating on top, while Plumb and Eddie quickly filled him in on the situation. When they were finished, he wiped his moustache, fluffed it out on the ends with his fingertips and gave them a quizzical look. "Andrew? I don't believe it. You pulling my leg, Plummy?"

"I assure you, it's true. We have a considerable amount of evidence, and we'll soon have more." (Naturally, Eddie couldn't have known the Weeks file was now safe in the hands of the New York cops.) "Problem is, we're not sure if your son was at fault. May've been one of his employees. A Miss Charlotte Stedman, for instance."

"Never heard of her."

"Computer expert, rather ugly child?" said Plumb.

"Computers?" Dolph shuddered. "God no."

"How about Mr. Dean Sommers?" Neither Plumb nor Eddie was certain Dolph knew about his son's extracurricular family.

"Oh, don't look so nervous, for pity's sake," said Dolph. "I know all about Andy's kids. Who do you think got the boy into Harvard? Oh, it was very well concealed, had to be, didn't it? Andy wasn't about to marry his Darlene Zadravic, even if good old Cella had bowed out gracefully. Which she wouldn't have, bless her heart. Though mind you, I think Andy did love this Darlene. For a while. She died some time back." He shivered slightly. "Andy put the children through school. That was about as much responsibility as he was able to muster. Gets that from me, I guess. You see, Mr. Merriman, we're hood ornaments, the bunch of us. We don't run the world, we just sort of ride along on top looking shiny. When he was a kid, Andy had the idea he was born to be an artist, or a writer, or something, because he didn't like the business. Chicken makes him break out, did as a kid. Guess it was prophetic. He didn't realize. He wasn't born to *do* anything. Andrew looks shiny, but he wouldn't have it in him, anything like this. It's too much for him."

"Andrew's not stupid, Dolph," Plumb reprimanded him.

"Neither am I. That's not the point. Point is, it doesn't

make any difference whether he's stupid or not. He's too rich to need to fight the battles, and if you don't fight the battles, you can't win the war."

"So he couldn't be an artist, because he didn't have to pay the price? I could name you any number of fine writers and so on who were stinking with the stuff," said Eddie.

"Hell no. He just couldn't do it. Always stopped a little short. You have to take chances in art. He wouldn't. Tame stuff, tight little pictures, constipated fiction. He could've saved Kenwood if he'd taken a few chances. Instead he keeps it for a write-off."

"Will Andrew inherit the fried chicken business?"

Dolph looked at him, then stared at the green leaves in his drink. "No. Everything goes into the Foundation."

"I see."

"He didn't want it. He never wanted the business."

"Does he know he's not to come into the majority of the family money?"

"Yes. It was a deal, when he took over the Foundation. He got his mother's fortune, and the Directorship. My money goes into the Foundation when I peg out." He drained his glass. "How bad is it, Plumb? Straight poop."

"National Endowment funds have been siphoned off into those accounts. Two men are dead, Dolph."

"Damn it, Plummy, what should I do?"

"Come back with us. Pack a bag and come to New York."

He glanced longingly out toward the green, where well-tanned people were tooling by in golf carts with little awnings over them. "I'll be up when the Cluck-Cluck's over. I promise, Plummy."

"Randolph! Shame on you. What would your father say?"

"Papa wouldn't like it, the whole thing going in the toilet, would he?"

"No, he would not. Nor would he like his grandson being charged with murder. Possibly two murders."

Danson shook his head. "Andy could not murder anybody. Now that boy of his is another thing. Helluva thing to do to kids, leave them hanging like Andy did. I'd be inclined to kill, in his place." He sighed. "Okay. I'll come."

Plumb nodded, satisfied. "When you get back, we shall go straight to the police and tell them everything. Oh, and another thing. Can you see to it that the Valentine's Gala at the Foundation is held at DeWitt Clinton College, up at Ainsley?"

He laughed. "That's only a week, kid. They've got things set up by now. Andy's probably hired Pavarotti and Beverly Sills already."

"Then let him unhire them. Waiter!" she cried. "Bring a telephone. Mr. Danson's about to make some calls."

"Aw, shoot," said Dolph, and winked at Eddie over his mint julep.

Not two hours later, I got a phone call from Tommy. He sounded a little nervous and very out of breath.

"Winston, Andrew Danson just telephoned me. Himself. Personally."

"Are you having the receiver bronzed?"

"He says his father is on the college Board. Is that true?"

"Certainly it is. Really, Sheffield, do keep informed."

"He wants me to arrange for the Valentine's Gala to be held in Gould Theatre. Of course, I'll have to get the seats removed, arrange the decorations, all that. Allie can help me a great deal with it."

Evidently The Mizz had not yet kept her end of the deal. "I should think it's more in Diana's line. Sheffield, listen—"

"As Chairman of Arts and Letters, he felt I was the right person to serve as his liaison."

Liaison, forsooth. I didn't have the heart to tell him whose idea it really was. "Just don't mess it up. It could save your tail around here, you know."

"Oh, I know, I know. It's much better than having you mention me on television. Of course, I understand perfectly why you didn't. Under the circumstances."

"Big of you."

"I wondered, since you and Sarah have the largest house, if you could offer hospitality to some of the people from the Foundation on the night?"

"Sarah's pretty choosy about who she lets in here." I paused for effect. "But she'd agree to two people I know of."

"Just let me get a pencil."

"Oh, I think you'll be able to remember them both. Andrew Danson and Dean Sommers. I want them, Sheffield." But he didn't know the half of it.

Next I called David's and sent him a message through Alex that the final scene of the Weeks impersonation—a blackmail payoff, and, we hoped, attempted murder—must be set up on the Clinton campus and not in The St. Claire. And finally, I dialed the office at school and asked Hannah for Mizz Barnes-McGee's extension.

"Not weaseling out on the deal, are you, Mizz? Sheffield's still laboring under the delusion that he's half of a twosome."

"I haven't had a chance. I do teach more than one class here, you know, unlike yourself."

"Not for long, old love, unless you get cracking. And remember, no unnecessary spite. Don't have to drop the baby on his head, do we?"

"Why the hell not?" she said.

By that afternoon, as promised, all Duffy's equipment had been set up. There were minuscule listening devices in every room of the Weeks place, a tap on the phone, and multiple tape recorders in the commandeered place down the hall. A bored resident cop was camping out in there, too, to watch over the equipment and, only incidentally as it turned out, over David. "I'm glad we're moving. There was too much business," David told me on the phone that night. "I didn't like it. Too damn many props. Plays with too many props always fold."

When the witching hour came at last and Duffy gave the go-ahead for the blackmail calls, it was past four in the afternoon, and David had had enough. He took control.

"Right, gentlemen," he said to the lingering cops. "Everybody out. Curtain time."

"No way," said Duffy. "I'm right beside you, that was the deal."

"The deal was," said David, "that I know how to do this and you don't. So why not clear out and let me do the thing properly."

He shooed them out and they sat around the tape recorders down the hall, waiting for the tapped phone to begin the calls. But David didn't make quite the moves they expected.

The first call was to Sommers's office at the Foundation. "Dean Sommers here," he answered briskly. "May I help you?"

"I think perhaps I can help you," said David, using the same scratchy voice as before. "I have all of John Falkner's evidence against you. It's quite considerable, actually. I think we should discuss it, don't you?"

"I don't know what you're talking about," said Sommers. He had no trouble keeping cool. You'd have to work hard to make him show his anger and even harder to make him act on it. "I'm going to hang up now," he said.

"Oh, I don't think so, or you won't know where to meet me, will you?"

"What do you want?" He sounded more involved.

"I'm not a philanthropist. Nor am I especially greedy. Five hundred thousand. A small sum, in view of the evidence. But sufficient." David was as cool and controlled as his opponent.

"I have no idea what your game is, but I don't know anything about this evidence. I have no intention of paying you anything."

"I see. Sorry to have bothered you."

"Wait," said Sommers abruptly. He might've been giving a command to a well-trained dog, for all the emotion he displayed. "I'll come to your place."

"Oh no. A public place. Lots of people, I think. The Valentine's Gala the Foundation is giving. I'll find you."

"What the hell's he doing?" shouted Duffy, pulling off his earphones.

"Shh," said one of the cops. "He's on again."

The phone was ringing at the Danson apartment in

Gallup Tower. A servant, probably the grandson of Jeeves, answered and there was a wait while he relayed the name of Dennis Weeks to his boss.

"Who is this?" said Andrew Danson. He showed more emotion than his son, but not anger. Not yet. "Winston, what game are you playing? I can call the police if you continue this farce, you know."

"I don't know anyone named Winston. But I don't think you'll be calling the police, Mr. Danson. Will you?"

David repeated the appointment for the Gala and then, without giving Duffy time to burst in on him, he dialed Charlotte Stedman's number downstairs. He knew he wouldn't be home from work yet because he'd been timing her for days so as to choreograph their little meetings in the elevator. He hung up, dialed again, then took a dime out of his pocket and scraped it across the mouthpiece of the phone.

In the next apartment, Duffy's ears felt as if he'd fallen into a gravel pit. "Jesus!" he said, and ripped the earphones off.

David stuck his head in the door. "Something wrong with the phone," he said. "Why don't I go out for some air while you see what you can do with it?"

"Hold it, mister," yelled Duffy. "What do you think you're doing, dammit? We get this all set up and you blow the whole thing with this Valentine's Gala crap. I can pull you out and put in one of my own guys, you know."

"Of course you can. If you want to lose him. They've heard the voice I've been using. They have it on tape. If you think one of your men can imitate me imitating James Mason, by all means go ahead. And there is the risk of entrapment, if you use an actual police officer. Resign yourself, Lieutenant. It's my neck. It's my set of rules."

So like a harried director confronted with a recalcitrant star, Duffy caved in.

Before the cops could check out the nonexistent trouble with the phone, David was downstairs, complete with shaded glasses and beard. He knew which direction Charlotte came from when she left her bus, and he waited for her on the sidewalk.

"D.? What's going on? What're you—"

"Come on." He grabbed her arm and hustled her toward the park. About halfway there she dug in her heels.

"Damn you. You can see me. Can't you? You could see me all that time? You go to hell." She turned back toward the building.

"My name's David Cromwell, and I'm a friend of John Falkner's. Now are you coming?"

She stood looking at him, the strange, monkeyish little face strained and tight, the large eyes uncertain. David took off the glasses and held out his hand to her. "I don't think you killed him," he said as they went on into the park. "Did you?"

"No." She kept her face turned carefully away from him now.

"But you know who did?"

"I think so."

"You weren't there?"

"Not in the same room. I was in the bedroom. In the closet."

"Did the killer know you were there?"

"Yes."

"Did John?"

"No. I was supposed to think he was in Philadelphia, like the rest of them did. Only I followed him. I saw him meet the man with one leg. I followed them to the airport, and I saw John come up here. That's when I called Dean."

"You helped set it up, then?"

"Yes. But I didn't think they'd kill him."

They sat down on a bench. It was getting dark, and rapidly colder. David sat with his hands in his coat pockets. Charlotte was silent for a long time. "I liked him," she said. "He asked me to help him. I didn't think he knew I was part of it. But I gave him too much. He must've known."

"That you were also helping to run the fiddle on the computers?"

"Dean promised me a promotion. Director of Computer Services. All I had to do was run the phony applications for them, and when the grants came through, I would order the checks paid out. Then I'd erase the amounts for those checks from the memory as soon as they were in the Montserrat account. It was easy. I'm very good at it." She looked up at him. "You know what it's like, watching little blonde ditzes getting jobs by the height of their goddamn heels? Hell, of course you don't. Look at you. What do you know about being ugly? It's a perfect society, and only the perfect belong in it, so the rest of the world is disposable. They were going to throw me away. Use me and then throw me away."

"Let you take the blame for the scam?"

"Sure. I figured, if I knew it, I could get out in time. Take what I had and make sure they got left holding their own bag. It was a calculated risk."

"So that's why you helped John. To cast the blame on them and away from you."

"At first. To protect myself. He knew so much already. But afterward, I just wanted to. I loved him. He said we'd get out, go away together. I actually believed him." She fell silent again, then went doggedly on. "I guess I'm not very smart after all."

"You found he didn't intend to take you?"

"I wanted to kill him."

"But you didn't."

"No."

"Who did?"

"Andrew and Dean were both there. And another man, just a voice. I didn't recognize him. I heard them arguing. Not the words, just the voices, louder and louder. John was goading them, you know how he was when he wanted to get under somebody's skin. He was trying to pick a fight. With Andrew, I think. I heard Andrew shouting. Dean never shouts. Neither did John. But he laughed, and then Andrew shouted, and the man I didn't know, and then Andrew said, 'Sweet Christ, he's gone,' and then the door slammed. When I got out into the living room, everybody was gone, and John was—down there. I looked over the railing and somebody was bending over him, but I couldn't see who, it was too dark. I got the doorman, Martin, to help me move John, he was the only one I knew who was big enough to lift him alone, and I didn't want to risk more than one person."

"Besides, you had a hold over Martin, didn't you? He was illegal."

"I thought I could still get away and make them pay for it. If everybody knew it was murder." She paused. "I really loved him. I think I did."

"And so you watched the music store and tried to scare the one-legged man with your car, so we'd keep digging even if the police gave it up or called it suicide."

"It wasn't my car. It was John's. He bought it for his son, a going-away present. He never had time to give it to him, but he'd left the keys with me."

"What kind of car does Creighton drive?"

"I'm no good with cars. Silver gray. Some foreign make."

David took her hand. "Charlotte, listen to me. I have to find out which one of the three men you heard actually killed John. I want your help. I'm not making any promises. I can't. Except that it will be better if you tell us everything you know, than if you don't. What about it?"

"I think he really wanted to be dead," she said softly. "I do."

"So did I, once." He took the hand she held and put it on the side of his face. "Feels odd, doesn't it? It's plastic, most of it."

She stared at him. "How?"

"Somebody cut me up and threw me away. And afterward I thought, what the hell, why not? Why not die? People looking at you and then looking away in a hurry so they won't get caught. Going round their houses taking down all the mirrors just to be kind. Didn't seem worth the effort, at first."

"But you didn't die."

"Oh no. Nor will you." He stood. "Come along now. You are going to learn how to fight for yourself."

And that night, in the presence of all Lieutenant Duffy's little machines, she told them everything she knew. But it still didn't include the identity of John Falkner's murderer.

"She threw me away, Winston," moaned a pie-eyed Tommy, as Krish and I hauled him out of the backseat of Krish's shark-fin Plymouth.

"Push harder, sir," said Krish, "I think his arm is becoming entangled between his leg."

"I think his head's been entangled with the sand, and
Mizz Barnes-McGee jerked it out rather harder than was
called for."

"Ooooooooooh . . ." moaned Tommy.

Between us we lugged the guts into Cabin 13 of the
Roman Holiday Motel. It was a dingy little joint with kitchenette attached, which meant it had a beer cooler and a hot
plate. Tommy flopped across the bed and Krish and I
straightened him out. "I must be going now," said my little
friend. "Mrs. Megrim is not permitting entrance after
twelve P.M." (Krish has taken over Eddie's old stand as
Blanche's one and only lodger.)

"Okay, Krish," I said. "I'll get the patient a bottle of
Perrier and a Tylenol and put him to bed." I couldn't find
anything else in the place, but Tommy's never without his
guppiewater.

"How could she do it, Winston? Alison. She threw me
away, just like that." Sheffield rolled over, groaned, and lay
still on the bed.

"You can be glad I have friends among the minions of
the law, or you'd be cooling your heels right now." Agate
had phoned me to pick up the sozzled Tommy, whom he'd
found passed out on a bench in the Ainsley City Park, waiting for the robins to cover him with leaves. "Really,
Sheffield. When are you going to snap out of this? I mean,
just look at this place."

The general motif was puce and red, with a touch of
watermelon pink. A painting of some antlered critter pawing the turf of a black velvet forest adorned the wall above
the Magic Fingers bed. On the night table, looking distinctly uncomfortable in pristine white lace, were Lady Di
and her daughters Frick and Frack, in a carefully polished
gold frame.

"I can't go home," he groaned, holding his head.
"Diana won't let me."

"I'll have a talk with Lady—with Diana."

"Would you? Really?" Hope began to dawn dimly in his
bleary eyes.

"On one condition. You promise to keep hands off the ladies from now on. Look, but don't touch."

"On my mother's grave," he said solemnly.

"And Thomas. Lose the wig. The piece. The Taiwanese peruke. It'll help your rapport with your wife, I guarantee you."

He looked doubtful. "Well. If you say so, Winston. I'll do anything you say. Anything."

It was tempting to try him out, but I restrained myself. "And don't worry about Mizz. She's young." But not, I thought, oh never, even in her bassinet, as young as Tommy.

"Winston? I'm worth something. Aren't I?"

"Of course you are," I said, wincing at his contractions.

"How could Alison just throw me away like I was nothing?" He sat looking at me with big bovine eyes, rather like the critter on the black velvet. "Just throw me away . . ."

"I don't know, Thomas. But there seems to be a lot of it going around these days," I said.

Chapter Eighteen

onny's funeral was held on Friday morning at the tiny hapel of St. Jude, near Times Square and all of Sonny's iends. Sarah, Eddie, and I left the Volks in a car park and alked the couple of blocks to the Chapel. Eddie and the hers had flown back very late the previous night in Dolph 'anson's private plane. Merriman looked completely ushed, and the air-conditioning had given him a sinus at- ck, but he'd insisted on coming.

A couple of doors down from St. Jude's we passed a uilding covered with orange and blue neon lights that ad: SEXATERIA—GIRLS, GIRLS, GIRLS! Grinding drumbeat usic blared out over the pavement, and around the entry ere were pictures of very young girls in several stages of ndress, with large children's eyes and ludicrous, artificial uting lips painted heavily for the camera. An oily article ressed in white, with white straw planter's hat and gold ains from neck to navel, shouted at Eddie and me as we ssed. "This way to the girls," he cried, "inside, gents, n't cost a dime to look, Sexateria, something on the menu r everybody, man, just step inside."

"What sort of customer do you get in here, vegetable · mineral?" I asked him. "You'd have to be a radish or a ck to need that much titillation."

"Hey, man," said Oily, "these are first-class girls here." hen he repeated his spiel. "This way to the girls, inside, n't cost a dime to look, something on the menu for every- ody."

"Come on, Winston," said Sarah. "For heaven's sake."

I noticed a dog tag around Oily's neck, buried among the chains. "Were you in the War?" I said.

For the blink of an eye, I thought he was going to answer me as a real person, but he switched on again. "Sexateria, something on the menu for everybody, just step inside."

We walked on, Sarah marching ahead. But I couldn't get Oily and his dog tags out of my mind.

He was near Sonny's age, and David's and George's, around the age of Dean Zadravic, too, and of Charlotte Stedman. They were a generation of takers and taken, the sold-out and the bought-out, without much middle ground, except that one thing. Mention the War to any of them and they never asked you which one. There was only one, the one they'd lost. They'd fought it in Vietnam, some of them, and some of them in Canada. But they'd only really lost it here. They'd gone into it as children, and when they woke up there were no more children. There were Sexaterias.

"'The best lack all conviction, while the worst/Are full of passionate intensity,'" I intoned. Then I realized people were staring, as they'd probably stared at Sonny. "'You blocks, you stones, you worse than senseless things,'" I railed, giving them the Bard. A bug-eyed woman in John Molloy suit, orange hair, and sneakers veered off the sidewalk into the street to avoid me. I noticed she hadn't bothered to do as much for Oily in the white suit. I zeroed in on her.

"'Twit, twit, twit,'" I said. "'Jug, jug, jug, jug, jug, jug.'" In Sonny's honor, it seemed the only thing to do.

The Times Square Irregulars had turned out in force, and the aisles of the Chapel were crammed with folding chairs. Young hookers in daylight uniform sat next to old women who'd wheeled in shopping carts and baby buggies loaded with plastic bags. There were transvestites with trailing scarves, and spike-haired adolescents, and cops, both in uniform and out. Among these I picked out Lincoln and Lloyd Agate, who'd journeyed in from Ainsley. Mickey and Teresa found places with Her Majesty, Queen Isabella and her court, and Sugar George sat up front with Alex and David, who was supposed to give the eulogy. George was wearing his old fatigues; there was no pretense here, no dressing up or down. We were what we were. People talked quietly among themselves, and nobody played sentimental music to shut them up. It was a gathering of friends, like no other funeral I've ever attended.

Father Myles gave a brief prayer and we sang a hymn, and then David stood up, propelling George in front of him toward the altar rail. David spoke conversationally, as if he were talking to a single person, and he might've been. The Times Square Irregulars had a lot in common.

"Sugar doesn't want to talk," he said, "but I made him stand up here with me, because he knew Sonny better than I did." There was a mumble of approval. "I knew him longer, though."

"What's he talking about?" whispered Sarah, and I shrugged in puzzlement.

Davy went on. "When I first met him, I was about nineteen, I guess. We were both at Columbia. He was a couple of years ahead of me. I didn't know him very well, but all the girls were nuts about him."

"Girls always been hot for old Sonny," said George, with a quick smile. There was a soft ripple of laughter from the rest.

"Anyway," David continued, "I wanted to be an actor." He looked over the room. "Me and about ninety-eight percent of Manhattan, right? Come on, come clean now. How many?" About two dozen hands went shyly up. It was like an Actors Anonymous meeting. "My mother was an actress, I guess. She took off when I was three, but maybe she put acting into my head. Maybe I wanted to prove something to somebody, I don't know. So I tried out for a lot of plays. The year Sonny graduated, they did *Hamlet*. I got to carry a torch around the castle, but Vincent Emerson—that was his name then—played *Hamlet*. It's about this guy who gets in trouble because people, other people, want more than they've got any right to, and he's left out in the cold with nothing but ghosts to talk to. In some ways, he's a lot like Sonny. He reads a lot." He smiled. "Talks a lot."

"Sonny never did shut up," muttered George, and everybody laughed.

"What I remembered was the way he said other people's words as if they were his, and he'd make them up on the spot. Somebody else might've written them, but he owned them and he used them. Sonny was a damn fine Hamlet." David paused. His eyes seemed vacant, unfocused, and his voice, like John's, might've been talking to itself. "I was still in school back in 'sixty-eight when Vince Emerson got drafted. Next time I saw him he'd turned into Sonny. That was last week. It took me a while to recognize him. But it didn't matter. The words were still there. And he was still a damn fine Hamlet."

The burial took place in a small cemetery across the bridge in Queens. Only a few of us traveled out beyond the pale of Manhattan. After the brief ceremony, I saw David walking off through the trees with Sugar George, deep in conversation; in another direction, Mickey, all by himself, scuffing at the snow, was all but out of sight of our parked cars already. Teresa was about to go after him herself, but Sarah stopped her. "Let Win do it," she said. "He's had a lot of practice."

So I took off at a brisk toddle and when I cleared a small rise, I saw the kid sitting on a bench all by himself. I heard a cough and a gurgle and I knew he was crying and trying to pretend he wasn't. Crying, apparently, was not cool. I clumped over, brushed the snow off the other half of his bench, and sat down.

"I'm not going to say anything dumb."

He choked and coughed and swallowed hard. "Like what?"

"Oh, 'It's all right for men to cry.' I don't cry a lot myself. Never seems to accomplish a great deal, and it makes my head ache." I felt as if I could use a couple of aspirin right now. "By the way, your nose is running, kiddo."

He wiped it on his coat sleeve. "Doc?"

"What?"

"I was going to take off."

"I figured as much."

"I get mixed up. I can't figure a lot of things out."

"Oh, I'm not sure it's a very good idea to try. With some things."

"But I do try. I get all screwed up. And then I take off."
He wiped his nose again.

"I wouldn't mind taking off myself, now and then.
What say we do it together?"

"You and me?" He looked dubious.

"I don't think I could swing Africa on my salary. But
have you ever been to Iowa?" He shook his head. "Then I'll
take you. When school's out."

"I'm not going back to Wildwood."

"No. But how about coming up to stay with us, and
finishing your year in Ainsley? Not a bad school system. You
might even get to like it."

"You mean it?"

"I said it, didn't I?"

He looked a little stunned, but not unhappy with the
idea. "Doc?"

"Yes?"

"About my Dad. About Sonny." He choked again, and
coughed. "I still don't understand it."

"No kiddo," I told him, "neither do I."

Meanwhile, in another part of the forest, George and
David were nearing the cemetery gates. "I didn't know you
knew old Sonny before," said Sugar. "I just asked you 'cause
I figured you could talk better'n me."

"I recognized him that first day, when he dived under
the desk."

"That all true, the stuff you said?"

"It's true."

"Me, I picked up with him in Chicago, and we came on
east together in 'eighty-five," said George. He stopped,
leaned against a tree, pulled a cigarette stub from his
pocket and lighted it, striking the match with his thumb-
nail. He looked over at David and grinned. "Know how long
it took me to learn to do that with one hand? Two years.
Sonny, he taught me how."

"You get it in Nam?"

"Hell, I wasn't never in Nam. Sonny, yeah. Not me. I

split for Vancouver in 'sixty-nine. 'Bout two jumps ahead of the Baton Rouge draft board."

"Sorry. I figured—"

"'Cause of my physical challenge?" He laughed softly. "That's what this ol' social worker used to say, she called it my physical challenge. Nah, I got this one night on the road up in Rapid City, South Dakota, when I was hitchin' home from B.C. after the amnesty in 'seventy-seven, you know, feeling real good. Goin' home. Here comes this party animal all juiced up on about four six-packs, headed for the big football game in his four-wheel drive. He lost his license for about six months, I got physically challenged. So he gets this big hairy case of the guilts afterward, he buys me a fancy fiberglass arm and a leg. Cost him a bundle, so I let him buy the crap. Threw 'em away up in Detroit. Made me feel like a goddamn Tinkertoy." He paused, then walked a few steps and pitched the cigarette. "When I first met Sonny, I used to fake it. You know. Pretend I got zapped in Nam, just like him. One morning I wake up, he's scrapin' the whiskers off and singin' 'O Canada' at the top of his lungs. He had me figured all along. Only he didn't give a shit *where* I got it."

They walked on through the trees. "So who you figure was drivin' that gray car?" said Sugar, stopping abruptly.

"We won't know until after the big showdown. Maybe not then."

George took his arm. "I wanna be there. I want to see the sonuvabitch that killed Sonny."

David nodded. "George. Why was it Sonny? That car could've taken all three of us out. But the green car went for you and swerved off on purpose, because Charlie had no intention of killing anybody. The gray one only wanted Sonny."

Sugar George looked closely at David. "Man," he said, "they killed him because he was up there. Sonny was up there the night John took the fall. He saw what happened, and he freaked. I didn't want no cops, I know cops. Sonny was the one they'd lock up. He hated it in those places, man. He died in those places, and I'd have to bring him back, every time they let him out." He slid down the trunk

f a huge old oak and sat crumpled in the snow. "So I tried
o shut him up, but damn him, damn him, Sonny wouldn't
hut up. He wouldn't ever just shut the hell up."

"So whoever drove that car followed him when he ran
rom The St. Claire and waited his chance to get rid of a
vitness."

"Sonny got lonesome when I was gone. He went look-
ng for John. He'd been to that ritzy apartment with me
vhen I took John his fake passport."

"You got him the passport?"

"I knew a guy that made good ones, you could trust
iim to keep his mouth shut."

"So John was planning to disappear. And instead of
;oing to Philadelphia, he sent you, and went to the Weeks
.partment to get his fake papers from the cache. Charlie
potted him, called Dean Sommers, and he and Danson
ame up to confront John, pay him off and get the evidence
ie had on them, something. John was drunk, he baited one
f them, or both, and one of them or both—or neither—
:illed him. And Sonny stumbled into being a witness."

"By the time I found him, man, he was way out of it,"
aid George. "I had to put it together myself. He was having
lashbacks, you saw him. By that time he'd calmed down
ome. But he wanted to tell you."

"And we still don't know which one of them killed
ohn."

"No."

George sat slumped against the tree. When David
ooked up, Teresa was behind him.

"He'll be all right," she said. "I'll take him home now."

We talked David and Alex into bringing little Gemma
ip for the weekend, partly to lay our plans for the Danson
hindig, but mostly to give David a salutary dose of nor-
nalcy. So far, it wasn't doing much good. Alex sat with us by
he living room fire with Gemma on her lap, but David
iad disappeared into my Cave with a bottle of my best and
iadn't been heard from in hours. Alex kept glancing over at
he stairs as she filled us in on his state of mind.

"I'll be relieved when this is over," she said. "His behavior's less and less predictable. And he feels awful about Charlotte Stedman."

"Of course," I agreed. "It's the part of crime solving I like least. Even in the Hyde books, I can never write a villain I don't like, or at least understand, and that makes running them off the road a bit painful. Still, crime and punishment seems to me to be better in general than crime and reward."

"I agree." Alex got up and carefully picked up her sleeping daughter. "I think I'd better go and pour my husband out of that Scotch bottle and take him to bed. He's got to talk plans with Lloyd Agate tomorrow, and a hangover won't help."

When she'd gone, I scuffled off to the kitchen in search of Merriman. I found him in his sitting room with a Kleenex shoved up his nose, trying to mat one of his watercolors. As usual, it was a view of the Hudson from our bluffs, and rather nice, though I wouldn't tell him so.

"You dow what, Widdie?" he said. "I have had a braidstorb."

"Well, don't tell anybody else, and maybe it'll go away. And do blow your nose."

He snuffed at his Vicks inhaler. "Ahhhh. I was thinking. Why would Dean Sommers murder John? I mean, according to Lloyd's information, he has neither kith nor kin except the sister and Andrew. No wives, no lovers, no children. He could simply have taken a powder and enjoyed his money."

"You mean he has nothing personal to lose by being found out."

"Of course. You can't enjoy half of fifteen million and still be who he is at the moment. He'll have to spread his wings a bit, become virtually a different person anyway. No old life to leave in ruins. No real life at all."

"Andrew, on the other hand, has a good deal to lose. If Othello's reputation's gone, no self-respecting culture vulture will hobnob with him on that yacht of his."

"He will cease to exist," said Eddie. "From what I gather of Andrew, he's got no insides, to speak of. It's a thing

ve never understood, but some people simply have none.
ike being born without ears."

"Oh, I think his feelings are there all right."

"All right. He *may* care for the boy and his sister, but
hat sort of love can they have for him, being hidden away
ke soiled linen all those years?"

"Extremely mixed ones, I should think. Sommers may
ave had ambition, but hardly love. And then there's the
1otive of Randolph's money. When the old boy dies, nei-
1er Danson nor his son will see a penny, unless they steal
. So they've engineered a way to get the money before the
1ct, thinking, I suppose, that it would be replaced at the
ld man's death with what would've been inheritance."

"Johnny was right," said Merriman. "Money has a life
f its own. Once it exists, it passes out of all control."

"'The Prince of Darkness is a gentleman.'"

"Sonny has certainly had his effect on you, Winnie.
)ecipher please."

"It's what Sonny told David. Davy said, 'Tell me,' and
onny said, 'The Prince of Darkness is a gentleman.'"

"Andrew Danson is nothing if not that."

"And Sommers doesn't quite pass muster. Those imita-
1on preppie clothes, the fake Harvard accent. Aspiring to
1e oligarchs, but he'll never make it, no matter how many
1illion he siphons off."

"I doad't dow, Widdie," Merriman said, and blew his
1ose. "But my bets are entirely on Danson. Never trust a
ybarite. Intensive luxury fills the mind with chimeras and
orrupts the will. If Andrew Danson found himself cor-
1ered, he wouldn't run. He'd have to fight. Leaving his
1ower would be leaving himself."

Next day was a Saturday almost like the ones I used to
ave with Davy when he was a kid, but with the addition of
ttle Gemma, just skidding round the corner of her terrible
wos and ready for anything. We spent the morning in the
ttic, exploring the heaps of stuff David's father had left be-
ind, things too good to pitch and not rare enough to sell off
1uring our periods of red ink, when I was between books,

Sarah was off the concert stage, and the roof needed fixing or the basement was shipping water. Gemma was enjoying an old rocking horse out of David's Lone Ranger and Tonto period; I'd found a stack of aged *Harper's* from the days when the print was small and the articles ran longer than six pages. David was over in one corner, pulling out a ratty-looking cardboard suitcase with the remnants of its lid mended with masking tape. I watched him out of one corner of my eye. He looked, predictably, a little hung over this morning. The usually graceful hands were somewhat unsteady, too, and he dropped the suitcase and spilled its contents onto the floor. He got down on his knees and began to sort through the stuff. "Remember this, Winnie?"

"Maureen's, isn't it?"

He nodded. "I used to come up here. Maybe once a year, till I was about twelve. Go through it. Try to figure it out."

"Yah!" said Gemma, getting up to a good gallop. "Yah, horse!"

"Why she took off? Not too hard to figure," I said. "She wasn't very happy. She wanted to be."

"I always wondered why she didn't take me." He smiled, rummaging through the things on the floor. "I mean, look at what else she left behind." There was a 1940s vintage dress, a small leather diary she'd never bothered writing anything in, half a dozen buttons strung together on a red thread, and a straw hat the mice had been into.

"So you cleverly equated yourself with the leftovers, did you? But Mo didn't know where she'd end up, David. Or with whom. She had no money of her own and she never asked Erskine for a dime when she divorced him. Under those conditions, would you go waltzing off into the sunset with Gemma under your arm?"

"Yah!" shrieked the kid. "Yah-ha!" The horse was rocking wildly.

"Okay, okay," said David, and grabbed her off a minute before she flew over the saddle horn. "Okay, Monkey." Her face puckered up with frustration and he began to tickle her without mercy. In two minutes she was happily playing house in an old oak wardrobe.

"Did you ever wish Mo *had* taken you with her?" I said. It was a question I'd had at the back of my mind for years, always pushed away and buried with practical concerns like whether the kid had clean gym shorts and how short the barber cut his hair the week before school started. But it had never gone away. I wasn't his father, no matter how much I loved him. I wasn't anybody's father, not even in the way Andrew Danson was.

"Most of the time, no. I couldn't have been happier, you know that." He pitched an old sofa pillow at me, the stuffing leaking out and filling the place with a bright drift of fibers. "But sometimes I did wonder."

"What if she walked up and rang the bell this afternoon?" I said. "How would you feel?"

"Curious."

"Not angry."

"Not anymore. I think—I'd just like to meet her. Probably we'd bore each other to death. In a way, I think that would be rather a relief. But I'd like the chance to find out."

"Someday I hope you do," I said.

"Pfu!" said Gemma, and waddled out, wafting Eau de Mothballs in her wake.

Near noon that same Saturday I had a phone call from John's old publishers. A Mr. Gary Banyon, Literary Editor, sounded excited and rather urgent. Certainly something had brought him to work on a Saturday.

"I'm told by Sandor Hoffman that you're the person to speak to about John Falkner's new novel. What's it called again?"

"*Dance of a One-Legged Soldier.* What about it?"

"Great title. You *are* his executor, I take it?"

"You take it correctly." I wasn't impressed.

"Well, we're very much interested in publishing the book. Is there a copy I could look over before I make my contract offer and take it to the Chief?"

"Interested in publishing? But he brought it to you first. You *have* read it. As I recall, you rejected it out of hand. Not competitive in today's marketplace was the phrase, I believe."

"Well. It's been some time ago. I've been doing some rethinking."

"Marketplace changed, has it?"

"Oh, constantly, of course, sure."

"Especially now that John is a dead celebrity."

"It was always a fine book, you understand. It was purely the—"

"But it's a lot finer since he's dead."

"Naturally there are certain new promotional possibilities. The public has been tuned in by the media."

"And why not exploit it? After all, that's what it's there for, eh? Something good might as well come out of a bad situation."

Banyon sounded relieved. "Of course, sure. I was thinking around eight."

"Thousand?"

"Sure, of course."

"Let me see, how much was it you paid for Shane McAuley's book? Million dollar advance, wasn't it?"

"Yes, but—"

"I know. That was low, first novel by an unknown, young fellow, no experience. I'd say at least eight."

"Thousand?"

"Hundred thousand. John's first novel is a classic now, after all. Oh yes. Eight hundred big ones, at least."

"Well," he gulped. "Let's talk about this. When will you be in Manhattan? Let's do a lunch."

"Oh hell," I said, "let's not." And I hung up.

Next I dialed the number of my own publisher and asked for old Cliff Munson, who likes to work on Saturdays when he can sip a little gin while he gleans the slush pile. "Cliff, it's Winston."

"Oh," he said, bracing himself. After all, we hadn't parted in the best of humor after his hatchet job on my new book. "How are you, Winnie?"

"Nicely recovered, thanks. Rejection-slip shock is nasty, but it doesn't take long to get over at my age. Listen, Cliff, I'm calling because I want to make a deal. I'm willing to revive old Hyde, but I want something in return."

"Let me guess," he said. "You want a contract for John Falkner's new book."

"A fair one. And I want you to take another look at that book of mine. Well?"

"Done." He laughed. "So Hyde lives again. Tell you a secret, Winnie. I was supposed to call you today anyhow and make a bid for John's book, Hyde or no Hyde."

"You're a tough old egg, Cliff," I said. "Let's do a lunch."

On Sunday night we took our three houseguests to the station and I steered Sarah past the Roman Holiday Motel to check on Tommy. There sat his yellow car, alone and palely loitering in front of Cabin 13.

Sarah chuckled. "Remember the time I threw you out?"

"You did not throw me, I rode my bicycle." One of our legendary tiffs had occurred about fifteen years back, over a gentleman called Kendall Dinsbury, whom Sarah had met on a London tour. "I had a right to be suspicious of that Doonesbury fellow. Slippery specimen."

"Dinsbury. You spent one entire night in the Lucky Clover Motor Inn, and came hobbling home with a terrible case of sciatica."

"And you didn't speak to me for three weeks."

"Two. Winston. Do you think it'll last? Alex and David?"

"I never thought I'd say this, but I hope so. Did you think we would?"

"I don't know that I thought about it at all. I just dived in, more or less, and kept swimming. You?"

"More like pedaling, in my case." I puffed on my Turkish Delight, deep in consideration. "Sarah, do you know Diana Sheffield?"

"Not very well. Why?"

I sighed. "This divorce of hers. Tommy's got no business on his own. The woman has to be made to understand a few salient facts. But it's difficult. After all, Tommy did stray."

"Hah!" Sarah exploded. "That shouldn't bother Diana too much. After all, what about Skip Winthrop?"

"The sci-fi professor? You mean he and Lady Di—"

"Winston," she laughed, as we pulled into our drive, "don't you ever pull the wool off your eyes?"

"Oh, believe me, they're wide open now," I said, scenting a juicy bit of blackmail. "Make way and lead me to the telephone." I paused to open the car door for her. "Oh, by the way, old kiddo. That case of sciatica fifteen years ago?"

"What about it?"

"I was faking," I said, and made for the front door.

Chapter Nineteen

The days that passed between Sonny's funeral on Friday and the Valentine's Gala the following Tuesday night were cram-packed. Whenever I happened to steer my bike past Gould Theatre, the parking lot was full of delivery vans, and Tommy Sheffield's trendy yellow car was always in the midst of them. Inside, the theater seats had been taken out and a crew of students was draping what looked like tinfoil all over the walls. On Monday, Valentine's Eve, Tommy gave me the grand tour.

"Never knew you had a flair for inferior decorating, Sheffield. What's the glitzy stuff on the walls?"

"It's silver lamé," he said reproachfully. "It'll make a perfect background for the floral garlands. Diana's idea, actually." He smiled and patted my shoulder. "I don't know how to thank you, Winston. Really."

"Oh, I'm sure I'll be able to think of some little thing," I told him, licking my chops.

"If only this gala has some effect on the Board." Tommy surveyed his handiwork. "Really, I do think it's beginning to look rather elegant, don't you?"

"My yes," I fibbed, and walked away muttering. "Like a Victorian whorehouse expecting the Prince of Wales."

On my way out I stopped for a look round. Our murderers wouldn't try anything at the dinner dance. Five hundred people listening to the Clinton Orchestra under the direction of Arlo Steinfeger would be bored enough to welcome any distraction, let alone an attempt to polish off a blackmailer. No. If they tried anything, it'd be elsewhere in the building, far from witnesses.

I don't mind telling you, it was a real relief to have the business moved up here to Ainsley and out of the bailiwick of the Delightful Duffy. Lloyd's steady, competent methods would be sure to keep David out of harm's way.

Looking at the building directory in the lobby, I took stock. The backstage would be crawling with people, and around here there were no such animals as private dressing rooms, so that was out. Upstairs were the drama class-rooms, and downstairs the furnace rooms and storage, but a steel grille expanded to lock off both stairways during public occasions. On the main floor there'd be the locked faculty offices, the rest rooms, the ticket booth, and a coatroom run on the honor system, without attendants. (Academics never officially believe in the existence of theft on campus. Educa-tion, like poverty, makes us all pure of heart.) But the Dan-son partygoers would be rich folk slumming for charity, and naturally they'd turn up in their furs to dazzle the locals. So I figured even Sheffield might take off his blinders and station someone in there. The ticket booth would also be soundly locked, since the Gala was advance tickets only. So nothing but the men's room was left.

I toddled down the hall and pushed open the splintery wood swing door. And what should I see but the small, meddlesome figure of Lieutenant Cornelius Patrick Duffy, doing his duty. Which in his case was sticking a small piece of metal with wire antennae onto the gooseneck of one of the washbasins. Our Duffy was planting bugs.

"Why, Lieutenant," I said, "I thought we'd got rid—that is, you're a bit out of your territory, aren't you?"

"No way, José. I got a local liaison up here, this guy Agate. But it's still my bust. We're setting it up here in the john. It's the best place."

"But how about the furnace room in the basement? Plenty of space for reinforcements, just in case anything goes wrong. Nobody likely to stumble in and spoil things. I'd say it was ideal."

"Nope. Too big. Can't wire it right."

"You mean these gizmos? What if they don't work?" I

picked one up and read the label on the back. MADE IN SRI LANKA.

"Look, I know what I'm doing. Relax. We got a bug on every sink in here, and one in every stall. We'll pick it up clear as a bell down the hall there in the Chairman's office."

"And if you don't make it down that hall before somebody breaks David's neck?"

"Just keep cool, Sherman. Go home, knock off a couple chapters, forget about it."

"What if some poor duck has to use the head?"

"We put up a Out of Order sign in the hall. Mr. Cromwell tells Danson and Sommers to ignore it and go on in. I tell you, this is perfect here. Small, contained. Listen to the sound in here, everything echoes. Reception's gonna be great."

"This isn't a radio show, Duffy, it's David's neck. I don't like all these gadgets, and neither does he."

"This isn't the first setup I ever ran, you know. It's gonna be fine." He whacked me paternally on the back as I left.

Out in the parking lot, I spotted Lloyd's squad car. He saw me, too, and came to meet me. We walked together up the snowy hill toward Grosvenor Arboretum, whose firs and hemlocks make an ideal setting for the Neo-Palladian swank of the old theater. The path climbed steeply upward toward the bluffs, and we stopped on a bench to catch our breath.

"I thought you'd wanna know," Lloyd began. "Lincoln's been digging into Kenwood. They've got two company cars, both gray Audis. Monday morning one of them was missing. The secretary reported it to the cops. Later she found one set of keys missing. Danson has access to the cars as head of the company, but so does Sommers. Doesn't drive much, unless he wants to go out of town. He checked it out the weekend after Falkner died."

"To buzz up and plant his answering machine in the motel so he could threaten me long distance."

"Thing is, the secretary doesn't remember him turning in the keys after that weekend."

"So he could've gone down to the Kenwood garage, used the set of keys he'd never checked in, taken the car, killed Sonny, and ditched it, then pretended the car was stolen. But he didn't get the keys back to the office before the secretary discovered they were still gone."

"And no car thief breaks into a place and rattles around looking for keys. He hot-wires. There was no sign of the ignition being jimmied. Whoever drove that car had the keys."

"So Sommers is our killer. At least Sonny's."

Lloyd shrugged. "Maybe. But every car comes with *two* sets of keys, Doc."

"If Danson used the car that was checked out to his son, he must've known he'd make the boy look guilty. Would he do that?"

"Depends on how he feels about his son, I guess."

"So we're really no further ahead than before. In fact we may have a setback. I assume you know Duffy's brilliant plan. Trust him to set the climax in a men's room," I said.

Lloyd laughed, without much conviction. "He's a frustrated spook. He tried for the CIA and didn't make it, so now he just plays with all their toys."

"Well can't you tell him to go play somewhere else? I thought you'd be in charge yourself."

He shook his head. "Can't. Got a deal with the NYPD. They scratch our back, we scratch theirs. Only they've got a lot bigger back."

"But Lloyd, no self-respecting murderer is going to go for his man in a public rest room where five hundred people will come running if the victim so much as sneezes."

Now a place like this Arboretum, I thought, would be much better. Private, inaccessible, and the victim could yell his head off out in these woods without being heard. Danson was no fool, and he was sure to smell a setup if we did things Duffy's way. It had to be open enough to make him sure of himself.

"I think we'd better talk to David," said Lloyd. "I'll give you a lift."

I bailed into the squad car and we drove up the winding road to the Monastery of the Renunciation once again. On Sunday night Davy had left his two girls with us and checked in to spend the remaining time until the big night in the safety of Brother Felix's electronic fence. Partly it was because he didn't want to take the risk of the Danson people buzzing in and trapping him before he could get ready. Mostly, though, it was David's usual need to get away and isolate himself before a performance. And at the moment concentration was difficult enough, even before the arrival of the dogged little Irish cop.

Duffy had checkmated his effort to get free by coming up to Ainsley. David could feel every one of those little wires waiting to trip him up. Too many props always made him blow lines. Then there was that balcony where John had gone off the edge of the world. The image of it never left David now, the presleep sensation of bottomless fall when consciousness is torn away. For three nights Alex had lain beside him and felt his body jolt helplessly as he fell asleep. It made no difference that he was no longer in the trap of that high-rise at The St. Claire. He was still hopelessly in the control of other people, namely the tenacious Duffy, whom he simply didn't trust.

Then it dawned on him. Duffy was merely the director. And no director ever born is in control once the curtain goes up. It would be David's show then, he could take it where he wanted it, rearrange the blocking and change the lines to suit himself. He'd made more than one turkey fly that way. You just had to know what to choose, and trust your instincts. He began to think about his options.

And that was what he was still doing when Lloyd and I got to the monastery. We found the kiddo in the garden with a broom rake, pulling dead leaves off a patch of early snowdrops. I told him the latest on the gray Audi, and he looked interested. I told him my idea about the Arboretum, and he looked relieved.

"I'd be a duck in a shooting gallery in that setup of Duffy's," he told us. "One thing, though. He wants me to wear a wire." He grinned at Lloyd's amused expression. "At least that's what we TV private eyes call them. But if he hears me making new arrangements, he'll probably blow the whole thing. I won't be able to ditch the mike in public. How can I disable it?"

"Easy," said Lloyd. "They'll tape it to your back or your

chest. Buy yourself a nylon undershirt and run it through the dryer first. That stuff rubs on the face of a wire, there's so much static Duffy'll think you're popping corn in there."

"Right." David turned to me. "How's Mickey getting on with the computer work?"

I knew what was on his mind, and it wasn't numbered bank accounts. "So far, everything jibes with what Charlotte's been giving the cops. She's not holding back. Make you feel better?"

"Not particularly," he said.

Lloyd scrutinized him. "You got the guilts about her?"

"To be honest, I feel like hell. I know, I know. Don't get involved."

Agate stamped a little circle in the mushy snow and came back to us. "If you're any good at this job, you start to understand them. Even the screwed-up ones. Some you even like. You feel like a bastard when they go down. Till one of them tries to blow your head off. Just remember, if it hadn't been for her, two men might still be breathing now. So quit putting yourself through it, and keep your guard up."

It was the longest speech I'd ever heard Lloyd Agate make. I think he rather embarrassed himself, because he said good-bye to Davy soon after and strode off to his car to hide out. I hung around a few moments more.

"Guess this is it, kiddo, till the grand finale."

"You'll be there. Won't you?"

"With my hair in a braid. Lloyd and I and as many of the Ainsley cops as we can fit behind those trees."

"But aren't you expected at the Gala? How will you get out of it without making Danson suspicious?"

"Oh, I have a feeling I'll be contracting a sudden case of my sciatica that night."

"Thanks. And Winnie?"

"Something the matter, kiddo?"

"No, No. Just tell Alex I don't think I was really meant to be a monk."

Lloyd and I went back to town, and David spent the afternoon rereading John's novel. That night shortly after the evening meal in the refectory, the buzzer at the front gate went off, and in about five minutes Brother Felix knocked at the door of David's room.

"There's a man named George Antoine at the gate who says he knows you. Shall I let him come in?"

David was surprised, but cautious. "Is there a camera on your security system?"

"Yes. The monitor shows a man with one leg and one arm."

"By all means let him in. He's a friend."

In half an hour they were sitting alone in the cavernous kitchen, while the brothers attended service. "How did you know where I was?" David asked, as George wolfed a sandwich and a glass of milk from the fraternal cows.

"Teresa."

David smiled. "I'm surprised she's not with you. I doubt that even a community of cowled monks would intimidate that one."

"I don't think nobody's gonna keep her away tomorrow night at that bash. Kid neither."

"She's smart. She won't put her foot in it." David considered a moment, refilled the glass with milk, then asked cautiously, "You do love her. Don't you?"

"Don't know. I guess."

"Then what the hell're you doing here, man? Why aren't you with her?"

"I guess you got the answer to that."

"If you mean your physical challenge, Teresa doesn't care a damn about it. And you can't blame everything on that for the rest of your life, every time you duck out on people."

"I meant Sonny. You know who hit him, don't you? You know whose gray car it was."

"Yes. I think so." Sugar's connections were good, but they didn't reach into the DMV. He hadn't come up with the name of Dean Sommers. "Suppose I told you. It still wouldn't prove who was driving it that night."

George got up and swung angrily across the expanse of the huge kitchen. Then he turned and looked at David. "They take too goddamn much," he said quietly. "They didn't have to take Sonny."

"Will it help to hurt them? Or kill them?"

"Maybe. Maybe it will."

"What about Teresa? Don't you think she's lost enough already? Do you have to start taking from her too?"

"What would I be takin' from her?"

"You, you bloody fool," said David. "And I'm not telling you a damn thing."

Next morning, Valentine's Day, began with a package in the mail. Merriman came in with it while Sarah and I were still at breakfast. "Look at that handwriting, Winnie," he said, eyes dancing wth excitement.

It was John's. Sarah slit the tape with a knife and I unwrapped another cartridge of videotape, with a note in John's writing attached. I read the note out loud.

"'Winnie. Please look at this tape alone. No other audience. My thanks. John.'"

"Well, I call that pretty hard," said Eddie. "Creating all this hoo-hah and then shutting the rest of us out at the climax. Still, you must respect the man's wishes, absolutely."

"Where's the nearest tape player? The one at school's on the fritz."

Eddie sighed. "Tommy *will* buy video equipment on sale at Walgreen's. Well, I hate to say this, but I believe Mrs. Megrim has one, the better to adore Leslie Howard. If you wish, I shall make the supreme sacrifice and call her."

And so it was that I watched John's final message to me on Blanche Megrim's big-screen TV in the musty parlor of her old house, while she and Eddie drank tea in the kitchen, and Krish, upstairs, typed out long letters to prospective brides in Pakistan.

As before, John seemed to have been alone in the ill-fated Weeks apartment at The St. Claire. He stepped in front of the camera and sat down, pushing the unruly hair off his forehead. He seemed more nervous than on the other tapes, and just about drunk enough to be really articulate.

"Hello, Winnie," he said, eyeing the camera which was me. There was the familiar tinge of suspicion, the faint paranoia in the glance that ricocheted off the lens. "I had Sandy Hoffman mail this and swore him to secrecy. Feels damn funny, but I wanted you to see me, not just get a letter. Thought I owed you. Got you in the middle of my mess and all. So if you're watching this, I'm probably gone, one way or another. Promise you won't get any phone calls asking for plane fare. I left you the mystery. Best going-away present I could think of, even if I'm the one who's going."

He laughed and the gold eyes glittered. He yanked off his tie and opened the collar of his shirt. It was soaked with sweat across the chest. He touched the sodden fabric gingerly. "See that? Panic. The characteristic disease of American civilization. Salved by television, conspicuous consumption, and the occasional invasion of third-world countries. And booze. Oh yes. When I break out in a cold sweat, it's ninety proof.

"'Panic you say? What're you afraid of, Falkner?'" He did a creditable impression of me at my stuffiest.

"Don't like being outnumbered. You don't either. Why do you think I picked you? You *know* how it is, Winnie. They own the damn world. They're turning us all to gold.

"'*They* is a paranoid's word, Falkner. Who the hell is *they?*'

"The Ant People. The Lotos-Eaters. Troglodytes, Sybarites, Catamites. I always had a helluva vocabulary." He paused, as if he were waiting for a reply, but none came. "We are superfluous men, Winnie. We've been replaced with plastic. Like those plastic hearts. They throw the real one away and the new one beats and they hear it and they think the poor bastard's still alive. But he isn't. Not really. Only it takes a while to figure it out. And I'm not willing to wait around till they do. Can't, as a matter of fact. Hell, another day, another brain cell. They're checking out on me like Israelites out of Egypt. When they say liquor is quicker, old friend, they're telling no lies." He closed his eyes and continued. "If you tell this to Teresa or Mickey, I'll haunt you to your dying day and then some. But you see, the concentration is gone. Sometimes I can barely read. Which is why it took so long with the new book. I can still hold out for, oh, a paragraph at a time. Maybe two. Before long it'll be a sentence. Finally a word. Which I shall puzzle over for days. Bloody thing is, you're entirely aware, you sit there watching yourself fumble, like a schoolmaster with an idiot child."

He sat quietly, looking away from the camera, then faced me again. "I could've taken the Weeks business to the police. But it wasn't enough. Charlotte or somebody else would've paid, not Andy. And even if he had, it wouldn't be enough. Not for me. You see, at first I just wanted to punish Andrew. Then I wanted Andrew to punish me. Now—well, at the moment I guess I'm past both of those. I can see myself falling. And the best I can do is bring the house down with me."

He got up quickly and switched off the machine. The screen flickered and then went black.

I heard the phone ring in Mrs. Megrim's kitchen, but I ignored it. I walked aimlessly around that front room, crowded with plastic-covered chairs that no one ever came to sit in, and china statuettes of dancing girls where no one had ever been known to dance. I felt lonely and scared, and what scared me most was that I understood every word he'd said. I knew exactly who *they* were. They were Alison Barnes-McGee and King Brat and Oily with the Gold Chains, they were all those people who kept empty palaces waiting for them in The St. Claire. And I was the old pterodactyl who'd sworn to go down flapping.

But when it came right down to the bottom line, I knew I wouldn't. I would roll with the punches, I would adapt, grumbling all the while, I would turn in Shakespeare for Agatha Christie and take my paycheck home like always, while I complained about the state of things and quoted *Hamlet* in the shower. And I knew why. It was because life mattered to me, however limited its possibilities. And it hadn't to John Falkner. I'd been hoping all along that his death wasn't suicide, but that depended on your definitions. I remembered his goading of young McAuley. What if it had been a rehearsal for that night on the balcony? What if John had found a way to make Danson pay for more than a mere fraud?

Eddie poked his head in. "That was Sarah on the

phone. The Danson entourage has pulled in, lock, stock, and limousine. In fact, three limousines and a clutch of servants."

"What, already? But it's not even noon yet, for pity's sake."

"I know. Hoping to catch us with our knickers down, probably. Naturally they suspect you had something to do with old Dolph's sudden passion to move the Gala up here."

"I wanted them to. Danson thinks I'm just an old meddler out of a TV series, poking around for the hell of it. But if he keeps his mind on me, even just a little, maybe I can keep him off balance enough to help out David."

"By the way, Sarah says Mickey and Teresa have also arrived, complete with cat. She promises not to interfere, but I think she was afraid the boy would dash up here alone if she didn't bring him. Well, come on then. We're to make haste to Mr. Untermeyer's for some of that choice Camembert, and you have a beef Stroganoff to concoct for lunch. Tommy and Mrs. Tommy won't be along for drinks till around four, so we've got a bit of time to reconnoitre."

"Eddie, I'm depending on you to keep Mickey and Teresa away from those woods tonight. We don't need a mob scene up there. And if there's anything you can do to stall Duffy, by all means, do it."

"Right-ho. Winnie, dare I ask? Was there anything on John's tape you feel like talking about?"

"A lot of things. But first I have to think about them."

He nodded and sucked at his pipe in silence. In a moment Blanche Megrim, her head wrapped as usual in a beaded turban, opened the living room door. "Can I tempt you boys to stay to lunch? We're having Tuna Surprise."

"Sounds lovely, Mrs. M.," I said. "But we've got people coming to lunch."

She smiled her Pepsodent smile. "Anyone I know?"

"Oh, I doubt it," I told her, and added as we left, "just a murderer or two."

When we got home, we found Dolph and Miss Plumb installed in the living room with Alex, who looked relaxed and at her stylish best. Instead of wife Cella, Andrew had brought the photogenic Tiffany, who sat diddling at the piano, playing something that should've been "It Had to Be You," but wasn't. Sarah was at the sideboard in the dining room, gnashing her teeth over the silverware. She hates diddlers.

"Where's Danson and son?" I said.

"In Erskine's study. I heard the door, but I haven't had a chance to eavesdrop."

"Teresa and the kid?"

"Upstairs. She's trying to fit David's old dinner jacket onto Mickey, but it goes around twice. Never mind the Stroganoff. I don't care if they eat scrambled eggs for lunch. Go and see if you can hear what they're talking about."

So I went into the hall and when I passed Erskine's study I could hear voices, all right. Sommers and Danson were having an animated talk about something, and they didn't sound happy about it either. I couldn't hear enough because the door is solid oak and the walls in the hallway are lath and plaster. But the hall closet, which wasn't built as part of the original house, was partitioned off from the study with wallboard. I knew you could hear through it, because I'd done it once or twice when we were keeping an eye on some other suspicious houseguests. So I pushed aside the coats and galoshes and got my shell-like ear against the wall.

"What did you use, Dean?" Danson's voice sounded calm, even a little subdued and deliberate.

"Old magazines. What difference does it make?" Sommers's voice rose shrilly and cracked, brittle as a stick. He hadn't his father's discipline, nor his self-control. If he showed nothing, it was because nothing was there. Andrew, on the other hand, contained a great deal more than he was willing to demonstrate. "Why play this game with him? Why can't we just pay the man off?"

"Because there is a certain pleasure in the end of a game. The man we're meeting tonight isn't a fool, Dean. But he doesn't know how far we're willing to go. That's our advantage."

"How far *you're* willing to go, you mean. All I want is to get the hell out."

"Dean, you're wired. Go and have a drink. You'll feel better."

"Don't patronize me, dammit. It's all going crazy, this whole thing, ever since you stuck your nose in it. It was smooth as silk, until you started meddling."

"You asked me to meddle. Falkner was getting too close, you said. Charlotte was pulling out on you."

"But I didn't want this. Why can't we just pay him off?"

"Because that wouldn't end the game, it would only confuse the moves. Trust me, son."

"Don't call me that."

Danson's voice sounded suddenly weary. "You remember that trip we took, before your mother got sick, the four of us? Before your sister left? You remember Barbados?"

"Yes."

"And I taught you to swim. How I'd put my hand under your belly and held you into the surf and let you kick? You were afraid of the fish, and I told you that you only had to worry about very big fish, not little ones. Because if you kicked hard enough, you could kick the little ones into the middle of the ocean and the big ones would eat them. This blackmailer isn't a big fish, whoever he is. We just have to kick hard enough."

"He isn't a fish, he's a man."

"You have to trust me, Dean. You used to."

"I used to be five years old. I used to think you really were my father."

"What else am I?" The voice was dull and full of pain.

"A man who got my mother pregnant."

There was a jolt on the back wall of the closet and a crash, as Danson knocked his son into the study wall. Then Sommers's voice, empty now, and without emotion. "Are you going to kill him?"

"Don't tell me you've developed a moral code, at this late date."

"Are you?"

"Possibly. Why?"

"I don't want to be there. Get me away from it, that's all. I don't want to see."

There was a long silence.

"Go and have a drink, Dean," said Danson slowly.

I couldn't take the chance that they'd come out and open the closet with me in it, so I dived out into the hall, faking a nice limp from my mythical sciatica attack. They were just coming out of the study.

"Been plotting treasons, stratagems, and spoils, you two?" I said.

Danson looked as tired as he sounded. There were dark circles visible even through the heavy tan, and frown lines etched on the forehead. Otherwise, he was impeccable as ever. Sommers looked exactly the way he sounded, badly frayed. His pseudo-preppie accent had all but disappeared, his Businessman's Special three-piece suit looked as if he'd slept in it, and one of his shoes was untied. At last his sense of the counterproductive seemed to have deserted him.

"Winston," said Andrew. "Don't tell me somebody's stepped on your toes. That's what will happen when you put your foot in the door."

"It's my sciatica, I'm afraid. I don't know about that shindig of yours tonight. Love to be there, but you never know, do you?"

"You've never liked parties anyway. I remember you on that cruise years ago. Completely miserable, like a fish out of water."

"And not a very big fish either," I said. "Oh, Mr. Sommers. Sorry to hear somebody swiped that gray Audi you drive."

"I don't have a car," he snapped. He stood with his hands stuffed into his coat pockets, the fists like round balls making the fabric bulge.

"Didn't say you did. Too bad though. Nice car. No honor among thieves, is there? If they'd had any, they'd have taken someone else's car. Before they killed a man with it."

Danson bailed him out. "It's shaken Dean up pretty

badly, Winston. The thieves must've been headed for Jersey when they hit that poor fellow up on Central Park West." He turned toward the stairs. "Haven't seen David. Back to the TV series, is he?"

"Davy?" I said airily. "Oh, he's researching a new part. Ought to be the role of his life."

I only hoped it wouldn't cost him his life to play it.

Chapter Twenty

went to school that afternoon and taught my class as usual,
hough nobody was paying much attention, including Yours
ruly. I'd taken along my old diamond willow walking stick,
nd when Krish dropped me off after class, I was leaning
eavily on it as I pegged up the front walk. After some per-
nctory chitchat with the others, I trudged pitifully up the
tairs to my Cave, only to find Danson in the hall outside
y door.

"Well, Cinderella," he said, "it looks as if you'll have to
it this one out."

"That's life. You never can tell when something will lay
ou low."

He smiled and went off to be fussed over by the hulk-
g Jamaican manservant he'd brought along, and I went
to the Cave, where I could be sure to avoid the bevy of
aids who'd been pressing gowns and doing hair and gen-
rally treating Tiffany like the Empress Josephine. I sat
own in my chair and opened a book, but I couldn't concen-
ate. Something was nagging at me. Then suddenly I real-
ed what it was. The top of my desk had been rearranged!

Now, I am not an orderly person as you'd usually think
f it, but in chaos I have a system of my own, and among the
eaps of papers on the desk I could put my finger on any
pecific one, providing other people keep their mitts off. I
ad left a student term paper on Wilkie Collins, with a
reen paper cover, parked on top of a heap of notes from the
l-fated novel, and under the notes were several other term
apers. One of these also had a green paper cover, but the

subject was Josephine Tey. And it was this paper from the bottom of the pile that was now on top. Somebody had searched through the papers, but had replaced the wrong one on top. I looked around to see if anything was missing, but could spot nothing. If they'd been looking for the Weeks file, they'd been sorely disappointed.

About seven that night, I stood in the hall leaning on my cane to see everyone off. Mickey looked like a scarecrow invited to a high-tone wedding in Davy's old suit. Teresa was in basic black and the diamonds John had given her, which I'd never seen her wear before. Miss Plumb was trying to catch her Edward's eye with a sort of formal jumper made of something shiny and silvery. She looked a bit too armor-plated for my taste, and Eddie handed her off to old Dolph Danson and squired Sarah, who had no expectations. Leaving his son to the company of a newly blonded Tiffany, Andrew took Alex's arm. She was resplendent in floating white silk and the antique garnet necklace Sarah and I gave her when she and David married. Danson was about to swoop her out the front door when she stopped short.

"Oh bloody hell! I've left my bag upstairs. Go on Andrew, I'll catch you up."

When he'd gone, she came over and yanked up the hem of her skirt, to show me the jogging pants underneath. "Miss Plumb's got my running shoes in her carryall," she announced. "I shall spill something messy on my gown and say I've gone home to change. I'm going to be up in those woods with you. No arguments."

"You've got no business up there. Anything could happen."

She put her arms around me, which came as a bit of a shock. "Last time David needed me, I ran. He felt I'd just discarded him, and maybe I had, out of cowardice. I won't do it this time as well."

There wasn't a lot I could say, after that. She sped off and the cars pulled away one by one, until I was alone with the maids and the Jolly Jamaican Giant. They were all still infesting our upstairs bedrooms. I had no idea how much

ney knew, or whether I might be spied on when I left, so I
ad to take precautions.

I never learned to drive a car, you know. Well, after a
ew early efforts with an old stick-shift Nash, I gave up—
fter I broke off the stick—because my way of dealing with
raffic jams was to un-jam them, employing the front end of
ne Nash. But a bike ride to campus would take too long,
'rieda Fritz's cab was too visible and she probably would've
nowed down half the trees in the Arboretum getting up
nat path, and Krish, bless his heart, was escorting Blanche
Megrim to the Gala as a special treat, so his shark-fin '59
lymouth was previously engaged. My best alternative for
peedy, effective transport up that hill seemed to be—you
uessed it—Lance "The Bull" Carmichael and his famous
notorcycle.

Leaving the lights on and the radio blaring in my Cave
o confuse the lackeys, I crept down the back stairs,
rrapped in my old overcoat, my touring cap tied onto my
ead with one of Sarah's woolly scarves knotted under my
hin. Lance, sweating like a trooper though it was barely
en degrees, pushed his machine silently up our back drive
o the portico, where we couldn't be seen from upstairs.
Ie'd rented me a sidecar, and he swore the path through
ne woods was wide enough for it.

"I'm not sure it's wide enough for me," I said, putting
ne leg in and trying my bulk in it. It wobbled dangerously,
nd Lance began to poke and pry and shove. "Couldn't we
ust put wheels under my bottom and tow me up there?"

But finally the elephant, as pudgy Dorothy Sayers used
o say, was crated. We coasted down the snowy hill in total
ilence, then burned rubber all the way through town. I
ode with my eyes screwed tight shut, but as I felt the ter-
ain rise beneath us, I opened them. We were zooming up
ne narrow path through Grosvenor Arboretum. I looked
own at the theater parking lot. It was nearly full. Danson's
mos were lined up near the door, and off to one side, away
om the lights, I could just make out the dark, gleaming
nape of David's Olds.

Lloyd was already waiting for us, and with the help of

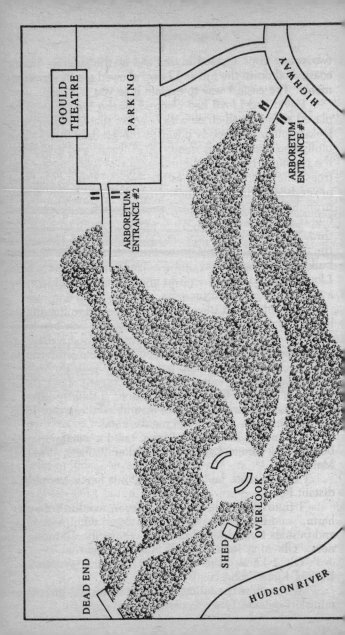

two young cops I pried myself out of the sidecar. Lance coasted off down the hill and Lloyd showed me the arrangements. The easiest way to explain it to you is a map.

David and Lloyd had planned for the big scene to be played at the paved circle with benches that forms an overlook through the woods down to the Hudson River. The bluffs here weren't too steep, but isolated, and except for the gardner's toolshed, there was no real cover except the trees. They were old and mostly pines and spruces that had never been trimmed. They dragged their heavy lower branches onto the snow-covered ground, making ideal blinds for Agate and his boys. Lance had brought me up through the main entrance off the highway, but David and the others would come up by the path from the theater building. It was shorter and quicker, and the shed where Lloyd had hidden his Jeep was invisible from it, hidden by a planting of luxuriant junipers.

"See this?" said Lloyd proudly. There were floodlights hooked high onto two of the pines opposite the overlook, where their light would hit the benches perfectly. "When we're ready, we can just hit the light switch and clean things up."

Suddenly the branches of a huge spruce about thirty feet from the bench stirred and lashed, and out popped a tall young man with a camera strapped to his shoulder. "Bingo," he said, and offered me his hand.

"He means his name's Bingo," said a woman's voice behind me. "Bingo Lynch. I'm Jennifer Wallace, WMTN, Manhattan."

I couldn't see her in the dark, but her voice rang a distant bell.

"I figured a little News at Eleven wouldn't do any harm," said Lloyd. "Pretty tough to argue with news film, and besides I owed Jenny one." He remembered his manners. "Oh. Miss Jenny Wallace, this is Doctor—"

"Oh, I know," she said. "His name is Ozymandias, King of Kings." She laughed.

"Why, you're the sausage casing! I mean, the girl in the miniskirt outside Teresa's apartment the day—"

"Right," she said, "but this time I'm not leaving till I've got the whole story."

"Bingo's got infrared in that camera," said Lloyd. "He can film all night under there and they'll never see him."

"But Lloyd. Cameras. Film. You remember what happened last time we tried an operation like this." I'd got the crooks on film and then proceeded to burn the stuff to a crisp in the projector. "You're sure that film's all right and the camera works?"

"No sweat," said Bingo.

"Not out here," I agreed with a shiver, and we retreated to the shed and Lloyd's thermos of hot coffee. It was going to be a long, cold wait.

Inside Gould Theatre it was certainly warm enough. Arlo Steinfeger and the Clinton Orchestra had murdered just about everything from "My Funny Valentine" to "Feelings" while the glittering guests milled round the auditorium sipping vintage wines and munching the Norwegian dilled salmon Danson's caterers had flown in. Tommy's Diana had done herself proud with the decor, all right. Garlands of red and white polyester carnations cascaded down the tinfoiled walls and rose in monumental pyramids from the double-knit lace that shrouded our old cafeteria tables. Tinsel arrows quivered in the bows of red foil cupids and stuck out of honeycomb paper hearts.

Well, I suppose it made a change, after all, from the usual grind at the Plaza, all that Waterford crystal and Limoges and orchids flown in from Maui. Because the guests seemed to be enjoying themselves thoroughly. There were even more than the promised five hundred, and Tommy was about to split himself in two, trying to round up extra seating and still stay within troweling distance of old Dolph and the Board of Trustees.

There were so many people that Alex didn't really see the man with the Uncle Vanya beard threading his way through the crowd until he was almost on top of her. She had her arm through Danson's, doing her "charm bit," as she told me later, when the bearded man came up to them.

Alex had to catch her breath. His shoulders hunched, David looked about two inches shorter than his real height, and he'd changed the dark glasses for ordinary black-rimmed specs. The beard and his hair were faintly grayed, and he walked with his hands clasped behind his back in the European manner.

"How nice to see you, Andrew," he said casually. "Interesting affair, nothing like Kansas City. Will you excuse us a moment, my dear?"

"Of course," said Alex. She kept her eye on them, as they moved to the bar and stood talking with great concentration. Then she searched the room for Dean Sommers and found him trapped in a circle of faculty. Hilda Costello, looking like Chairman Mao out on the town in a cerise pillowcase with marabou feathers around the hem, was trying to get the inside track on a grant application.

"I've always known I could become a film maker. Your organization is so supportive of women film makers—"

"Do you have a script?" Sommers asked politely, looking nervously at Andrew and his bearded companion.

"Oh yes. Well, I will. I just have to write it." Hilda was looking a little overripe after her fourth glass of Burgundy, as Alex joined them.

"Dean," she said archly, "your boss has totally deserted me. Would you be a love and get me a glass of wine from the bar?"

"White or red?" There was a fine beading of sweat along his forehead and his upper lip.

"Oh red, of course. After all, it is Valentine's," she said, and smiled.

Sommers had just returned with the wine and handed it to her when Andrew came through the knots of revelers toward them. Tommy was leading Dolph toward the stage for the official welcome speech before dinner. He tapped the mike on the podium. "Testing, one, two, three, testing."

Andrew touched Sommers's elbow. "I'm afraid something's come up, Dean. I'll need you for a moment or two. Forgive us, ladies? Won't be long."

"Ladies and gentlemen," said Sheffield from the stage. "Please be seated. Be seated, ladies and gentlemen."

Merriman, scanning the crowd with a worried frown, spotted David heading out the doors into the lobby. Eddie bounded up, then sat back down and nudged Sarah. "There he goes. The game's afoot, as Hyde would say."

"That's Sherlock Holmes," said Mickey.

"What's the difference, what's the difference, what's the difference?" snapped Eddie. "Where are you going, young man?"

"Around," the kid said, getting up.

Eddie yanked him back down. "Oh no you don't. I have strict orders."

"There go the others," said Sarah. "Oh this is maddening. I want to *do* something."

The two men were trying to make their way through the mob of guests just finding their seats at the dinner tables. The timing had been perfect. David was out of range and out of sight and could make it to the overlook with time to spare.

Alex was also stuck in the crush, holding her glass of red wine. Suddenly she lurched against Hilda and squealed with chagrin. A long red stain was spreading down the front of her dress. "Oh Lord, look at that. It's ruined," she groaned.

"Slice of cucumber will take that right out," said Hilda tipsily. "Raw. Not pickled. I think I'd like some more of that nice wine."

"Well, I'll just have to pop home and change. Excuse me," said Alex, and she plowed through the mob toward the coatroom, where Plumb had deposited the running shoes on an inconspicuous shelf. In ten minutes Alex was sprinting up the snowy hill, her gown tucked inside her jogging pants, her red hair flying in the bitter wind.

Meanwhile, a small, irate Irishman had burst through the doors of the auditorium in search of the reason his Sri Lankan bug was only pulling in snap, crackle, and pop. He landed on Merriman. "What the hell's going on?" said Duffy. "I checked the bathroom, it's dead empty. Where'd he go?"

"I've no notion, Lieutenant," said Eddie, wide-eyed. "Perhaps the furnace room?"

"It's locked up tight."

"Rex Osborn's over there, he'll have the keys. Come on, Lieutenant. David may be in trouble down there," said Merriman.

"I think we'd better try upstairs too," Sarah said, jumping up, "just in case."

And they took off with Duffy at their heels, to play history's longest game of hide-and-seek.

It was dark in the woods, but there was a good moon and the lights from the parking lot reflected brightly on the snow. David arrived at the overlook several minutes before he heard shoes scrunching the snow on the path. He stood silent in the shadows, his back to the campus side of the clearing and well away from the drop down the bluff where we were hidden behind the junipers.

Andrew entered the clearing first, with Dean Sommers behind him, carrying a neat attaché case. Sommers's breath was more labored than his father's, and he slipped once on the snow and almost fell. Andrew laid the case on the bench and I could see a small flash and smell the smoke of a lighted cigar.

"Bad habit, smoking," he said. "I try not to have habits. Now. Who the hell are you?"

David moved farther into the moonlight. "Dennis Weeks."

"Balls. I don't believe in ghosts."

"Not even the ghost of John Falkner?"

"That was an accident," burst in Sommers. "He was drunk. He fell."

"Balls," said David. "I don't believe in fairy tales."

"Enough," Andrew said. "I assume the materials are with you. All files, tapes, photostats, everything John had collected. Including any copies. We have the money here."

"Once I have the sum we mentioned, I'll tell you where to find the files."

"No. You'll tell us now. My associate will go for them.

If they're satisfactory, we'll conclude the deal when he returns."

David paused a moment, thinking. Beyond his father, Dean Sommers was circling, circling, like a small anxious dog in the snow. If he got rid of the frightened, unpredictable young man, Andrew might make his move. But Sommers could circle around and come at him from behind. David could only follow his instincts, and they told him Sommers didn't have a good attack left in him.

"Take the path up the bluff to the dead end. There's a shelter with benches. Under one of them is a canvas flight bag."

"All right, Dean," said Andrew. He drew on the cigar and tossed it away in a small shower of sparks. "Go ahead."

Sommers hesitated. "It's not my fault. You keep telling me it's me, but you added things. You confused it. All I wanted was the money, but you had to prove something."

"Some of us have more complicated motives, Dean."

"Money was all you ever gave me. Why should it surprise you that it's the only thing I want?"

"Just go, Dean. Now!" barked his father.

Sommers didn't turn around. He backed slowly out of the clearing and onto the path up the bluff. Then I could hear his feet slipping and sliding as he ran. Lloyd gave a nod and a young cop took off silently through the woods parallel to Sommers to prevent him doubling back and trying anything. Because, of course, there was no shelter, no bench, and no flight bag waiting for him.

Danson offered David a cigar. "Were you a friend of John's?"

"No."

"Intriguing man. Dean's right, of course. The game was rather a way of demonstrating my inventiveness to him, once I knew he was on to it. I found the fiction stimulating. I've never really thought of myself as a businessman." His voice wavered, softened. "At times I thought he almost liked me."

"You not only wanted to own him, then, you wanted him to adore you for it."

Andrew laughed and his voice snapped back, cold and

controlled. "I'm curious. You know what's involved here—millions. Why ask for so little?"

"I have to be able to carry it. And I didn't really fancy a computer transfer. Under the circumstances."

Andrew moved to the bench and unlocked the case, opened it, then stepped back, waiting. As David came forward to look, I saw Danson's right hand reach inside his dinner jacket.

When David turned around, the knife was in Andrew Danson's hand, blade forward. I could just see the glint of it in the dark. It had a light handle, ivory or bone, and a long, thin blade, highly polished. From her vantage point in the trees behind David, Alex saw the knife too. She stuffed her hand in her mouth to keep from screaming, and bit down hard on it.

There are things you do when a knife comes at you. You can find a shield—your coat, a stick, a chair. You can crouch and wait, ready to roll away from the lunge. But being slashed is like being burned. The second time, no rules apply. David could've run, but he didn't. Watching the knife gleaming in the moonlight while Andrew moved in half arcs back and forth, back and forth, like a pendulum, David swayed slightly, as if the ground were giving under him. A small sound came from him, neither cry nor shout, but a release of breath that means, *Yes, I've been expecting this.* And he had, of course. In the same dream at least once a week since the slasher took half his face away. Now it was happening, and he could only stand and wait.

Andrew's athletic body arched over the knife and he moved forward. Davy backed a step, then another and another, until he was at the edge of the paving. Suddenly the arch of his foot hit the curbing and he fell, with Danson on top of him.

At that moment there was a thrashing in the undergrowth and a third figure came hurtling through the air from across the clearing. We could hear the sound of blow after blow connecting with Danson's body, as he rolled away from David, trying to shield himself from the dark shape balancing on one leg above him, raising the dully gleaming steel crutch again and again.

"Hit the damn lights!" yelled Agate, and Jenny Wallace did.

In an instant the clearing was washed with blue-white light, blinding against the snow. My eyes blurred, and when I could see clearly again, Lloyd had pulled Sugar George off Danson. David was lying on his back in the snow and Alex, skirts spilling out of her jogging pants and red hair streaming, was running toward him from among the trees.

Danson picked himself up, reeling in the blinding lights. No one had taken time for coats, and his silk dinner jacket had one sleeve torn loose. His arm dangled limply at his side. His face had a streak of blood from the forehead to the ear, and the carefully moussed hair was matted with snow and grime. He spun around, staggering precariously.

"Winston," he roared, "where the hell are you? Winston!"

I hoisted myself onto the pavement and faced him. "Here."

"I thought you were only a nosy old maid," he said.

"You shouldn't be so quick to write people off." Lloyd stood holding the would-be murder weapon. It was the paper knife from my desk in the Cave, an ivory-handled job Erskine gave me years ago. "So that's what you nabbed in my lair this afternoon. What did you think you were going to do, incriminate me?" I hadn't missed the thing because I never use it. It must've been buried under a heap of papers.

"You were in my way, Winston. You're a bulldog."

"What, not one of the little fish who get eaten by the big ones?"

He sank down on the bench and I went over to help David up. Alex was mopping the muck off his face, but he seemed unhurt, only shaken. "Of course," said Danson, "it was you who maneuvered the Gala up here."

"Surely you knew that."

"I suspected, but I thought it might work to our advantage, being out of the city, isolated. When our friend here suggested the woods, I was actually delighted. I could simply have bought John's evidence, but it wouldn't have been enough."

"It never was, was it, Andrew?" The voice was Teresa's. She and Mickey stood at the edge of the paving. From the upward path, Lloyd's young cop had herded Dean Sommers down to us in handcuffs.

"We assumed at first that John wanted money, too. When he called, we were prepared to pay anything. We offered him a full third, it would've amounted to millions. He refused," said Andrew.

"He was drunk." Sommers growled.

"He'd have refused if he'd been stone sober," I told him. "Money was beside the point."

"Then why call us? Why tell us what he knew? It was all on that tape he played for Andy, everything. Why not just take it to the cops? He wanted it all, not just a third. We didn't offer him enough."

"He wouldn't put a price on it," said Danson. "It was mad, a crazy thing to tease us with what he knew."

I couldn't say it in front of Teresa and Mickey, but Charlie Stedman had been right. John had wanted to die quickly. He didn't want to watch himself disintegrate somewhere in the wilds of Canada. And if he got Danson to help him off that ledge where he'd been hanging so precariously for such a long time, and me to keep chewing at it until I put the blame where it belonged, so much the better. He felt Andrew Danson had cheated him out of a life, and he wanted him punished not just for fraud but for the murder of what John Falkner might've been.

"He was very, very drunk," said Andrew. "He went out on the terrace staggering drunk. He had his overcoat on, it was cold as ice in the place. The heating had broken down and the whole building was freezing. John kept talking and talking. He took jabs. At my—my family. My life. He kept leaning over the railing, those sharp spikes. Saying I was nothing without my money. Saying I'd never really existed, except in my own mind and the society columns. 'If you looked in the mirror before the papers came, there'd be nothing to reflect.'" He sat with his head in his hands. "Christ, he was right."

"He wanted it. He wanted you to hit him," said Sommers. "It wasn't your fault." Somewhere the five-year-old boy remembered a father and wanted to protect him.

"So you punched John and he fell, is that the story?" I said.

"He was unsteady and just as angry as I was. I hit him. Yes. But he didn't fall right away. His coat sleeve caught on the railing and for a minute I thought he'd be all right. But the fool yanked it loose, it tore, and he fell."

"So nobody killed him?"

"Nobody."

"But Sonny thought you had."

"You mean the man in the fatigues? He came in after we were there. John shouted at him to go, and he began to shout too, having some sort of flashback, so it seemed. Something about firefights and boobytraps. When John fell, he suddenly got very quiet and he looked at Dean and me and said, 'You bastards, you just had to take him out, didn't you?' Perfectly lucid."

"Sonny was mixed-up, man," said George. "He wasn't stupid."

"He was right," I said. "You did have to take him out. Otherwise, what kept you in that apartment, once you knew he wouldn't be bought off? You didn't have to stay and take his insults. If he hadn't arranged the fall, you would've had to take him some other way. With your son's gray Audi perhaps?"

"One question," Lloyd said. "Why not go for the Stedman girl? She knew the whole operation."

"Charlotte went quite wild, of course, after John's fall. She insisted on moving the body, following you people about. And I suppose it was only a matter of time until we'd have had to do something about her. But she didn't actually see John's fall, and she knew she was as guilty as we were of the fraud. As for the other man, Sonny, was that his name? Well, Dean followed him from the apartment that night, but we lost him. So when you got involved, we began taking turns keeping an eye on all the apartments, hoping he would surface. When he turned up at David's place, we simply had to do something. It was a matter of choosing the time."

"Did you suspect David was the mythical Weeks?"

"Never. The voice was altogether different. Even tonight when we met, I'd have sworn you were twenty years older than you are." David had removed the beard and was standing close to Alex. "He is rather remarkable."

"So Sommers was watching the apartment on Sunday night in the gray Audi when George and Sonny came out. They were in the street and he just picked Sonny off, is that right?"

"Me? I wasn't driving that car." Sommers stared.

"It was checked out to you. You had the keys."

"I came up here and planted the answering machine in the motel. I drove the German to Seventy-sixth Street to wreck the apartment. I made some phone calls. I didn't kill anybody." He stared at his father. "Well? Tell them, damn you."

Danson looked up at me. "You haven't got a son, have you, Winston?" He wiped his hands across his muddy face. "Look at him."

"You wanted them to think it was *me*, didn't you? You bastard." Sommers charged forward, to be blocked by Lloyd. "Like you took Sherman's paper knife. You took my keys."

"Do you think it's true what they say?" Danson asked me. "That each generation tries to devour the one before it? He'd have eaten me alive. Wouldn't you, Dean?"

"So you took the car your son had signed for and used it to kill a man?"

"I wanted to be—in control again." He took a deep breath and smiled. "Besides, I couldn't very well have driven the limo, could I?"

As we trudged down the path to the parking lot, we met a red-faced and breathless Cornelius Duffy laboring his way up, followed by three of New York's Finest.

"What the hell?" he said, staring at the handcuffs on Andrew Danson and his son. "Agate, what's going on? We combed that building from top to bottom. What the hell they doing out here?"

"Getting busted," said Agate pleasantly. "Attempted murder. Come on Duffy. I'll give you a lift to my station. It ain't Manhattan, but it's warm."

The station Jeep came bouncing down from the woods with Jenny Wallace and Bingo the cameraman on board. There'd be News at Eleven that would come as a surprise to anybody watching the tiny TV in the elevator at Gallup Tower.

We'd all need to give statements, but Agate had said that morning would be soon enough, and I was glad. My leg, in revenge for the fib and the motorcycle ride, was hurting for real now, and Sarah and Eddie, who'd led Duffy and his boys a merry chase through the bowels of Gould Theatre, were worn out and frazzled. But they insisted on waiting while I went in search of old Dolph Danson and the loyal Miss Plumb.

"The old gentleman was watching when they drove Andrew and his son away," said Sarah. "Those awful handcuffs."

"Try the furnace room," said Merriman. "He turned that way when he went back inside, but I didn't see Plumb."

I climbed down the stairs to the basement furnace room, to find Dolph Danson sitting on a costume trunk, amidst some leftover props from a production of *Cabaret*— a megaphone, some tinfoil stars, and a canvas flat painted to look like a crowded audience. The one-dimensional faces leered and smirked over the old man's shoulder as I sat down beside him.

"Don't want to butt in," I said. "But my leg's killing me."

He didn't speak for a while, just sat there dangling his feet off the trunk. From upstairs came the music of Arlo's orchestra and the shuffling of five hundred pairs of dancing feet, broken now and then by causeless laughter and applause.

"He never liked me, you know," said Dolph at last. "I never expected enough of him, is why. Never made him try himself."

"He's certainly intelligent enough."

"But you see, he didn't need to be. I didn't either, I

ad Plummy, bless her heart. Didn't bother me either. I
idn't care if I went to hell. But Andrew did. He went to
aste."

"He wasn't the only one."

"You mean Falkner? Yes, I knew how Andy had fiddled
ie Prize Comittee that year. Stupid thing to do. John was a
ne writer, would've won on his own in a couple of years.
ndrew couldn't wait. But you know, I thought at the time
was a good sign. He was doing something. That's why I
idn't leave him my money. Thought it might make him do
>mething."

"I guess he did."

"What'll happen to him?"

I shrugged. "He's still a rich man. He killed a poor
aan. Unfortunately that makes a difference where punish-
ient's concerned. If they plea bargain, and they will, they
aay get it down to motor-vehicle homicide, and call John's
ll a suicide. Maybe two years on a nice white-collar prison
rm."

"And the boy? I feel real bad about the boy."

"Just write him into your will. I have an idea he'll be
erfectly fine. But what about you?"

"Oh, Dolph's coming back to the Foundation, to
raighten things out," said the voice of Plumb. She was
anding at the top of the stairs. "We have a lot of work to
>. Now come along, Randolph, you can't sit down here all
ight."

Obeying orders from long habit, Danson clumped up
ie stairs, and Plumb whispered to me behind his back as I
assed her.

"He's really quite intelligent, you know. But he had all
aat money. Nobody ever expected enough of him."

Except, I thought, for a short, gritty lady with a large
ocketbook and a wardrobe of jumpers who never, under
ay circumstances, would be found hiding out in a pent-
ouse, or anywhere else.

Naturally everybody had missed dinner in the commo-
on, so I made a giant platter of French toast, basking in

the pleasure of my warm kitchen, sciatica or no sciatica. We gathered there to talk things over. David had Gemma on his lap, but halfway through the meal she fell asleep. Alex stood up. "I'd better take her up, D. If she wakes up, she'll be awake right through the night."

"Let me," he said. He'd been quiet ever since we got home, hardly adding two words to my recounting of our adventure in the woods.

When he'd disappeared up the back stairs, I looked over at Sarah. "Now. Go and tell him now."

She nodded and followed him.

"Tell him what?" Alex looked worried.

"About his mother. Sarah located her up in Toronto."

Alex stood up suddenly and began stacking the syrupy plates, a housewifey thing I've never seen her do the like of before or since. "Go and find him, Winston," she told me. "He'll be wanting you."

"And you."

"No." She was firm about it. "Not for this."

I found them in my Cave, David stretched out on my rickety couch with a glass of whiskey and Sarah just on her way out. "Hasn't said boo," she mumbled as she sailed out. "You get it out of him."

I sat down in my creaky office chair, which has had the same comforting squeak since Davy was a kid and we sat here together cooking up Hyde plots. Then I poured some Haig and Haig into a glass and lighted a Turkish Delight as I put my feet up on my desk. Neither of us felt much like talking. That's one of the joys of being with David. When you don't want to talk, you don't have to. Sarah was right though. On top of the business with the knife out in the woods, the news about Maureen had pushed him into retreat; it's been my experience that thinking too hard and long about any one thing is something no human was built to do and keep his balance.

"I've been thinking about Danson," he said finally. "Those two children of his."

"He seems to have loved them. In his way."

"Wanted them. It's a different thing. The best he could've done for them was to keep away. No false emo-

ons. He wanted to be two people, a nice ordinary family
man who expects love in return, and a power broker with no
obligations money can't buy." He closed his eyes. "He
hould've stayed the hell away from them."

"Like Maureen did?"

"I don't know. Maybe."

"Will you go and find her?"

"I need time to think. I don't want to start something I
an't finish. Like tonight."

"You mean that knife? Kiddo, you're an actor, not a
udo master. You did damn well out there."

"I'm trained in fencing. I didn't even parry. I froze. I
as back in Manhattan, staring at the other knife."

"Some things get lived over and over, kiddo. Like John
nd that book of his."

He got up and refilled his glass. "I think I finally under-
and Sonny. It's a damn long war, isn't it, Winnie?"

"I'll drink to that," I said, and we did.

Chapter Twenty-One

The District Attorney arraigned Andrew Danson, Dean Sommers, and Charlotte Stedman on several counts of fraud; the federal charges involving the National Endowment funds were waived in view of the plethora of other counts. As for John's death and Sonny's, the charges seemed to balance out. The first, which had been a form of suicide so far as I could understand, was filed as unpremeditated murder. Sonny's, which had been a true murder, went down on the books as motor-vehicle homicide, with all kinds of evidence brought forth about the psychological instability of the victim and so on. It was hardly sufficient, but no worse a travesty than I'd expected. Andrew Danson himself shouldered both charges, absolving his son of all responsibility except as an accessory. They were both out on bail in forty-eight hours, with the trial date set for midsummer.

Two days after the arraignment I received an engraved ivory envelope in the morning mail, with a return address from Gallup Tower. Cella Danson requested the pleasure of my company at the lunch the next day. Just me, without Sarah as a buffer zone. Well, I couldn't in any conscience refuse. I got Krish to mind my class and took the train into New York once again. I had no idea whether Andrew would be present; he hadn't been mentioned on the invitation.

When I got off the elevator at the penthouse floor, the jungle was still flourishing as before, the bananas hadn't been harvested, and the Buddhas were still smiling mildly. But no Tiffany came to greet me. Instead a tall, thin descendant of Jeeves led me through the high-ceilinged galleries to Cella's radio room. At first I didn't see her. She was sitting on the floor in the far corner, between two of the radio sets, a pair of headphones over her ears. When I came in, she didn't look up, but remained concentrating on the sounds pumping into her ears. Her knees were pulled up under her chin and her hands locked around them.

"Cella?" I said.

She still didn't notice me. I followed the headphone cord to the proper radio and switched it off.

"Oh!" she cried. She pulled the headset off.

"Peking?"

"It's gone."

"Sorry."

"Andrew's gone."

"Is he?"

"I miss him."

"Since he's gone."

"Yes." She clamped the headset on again. "No more," she said, and pulled it off.

"Come on, Cella. Let's go into the living room."

"No!"

"Beautiful things out there. No matter who owns them. They ought to be enjoyed. Come on out."

"I can't. It's not right out there. Andrew's gone."

"Cella, how long have you been sitting in here?" As I came closer to her I could see that her sweater was caked with grime around the neckband and her hair hadn't been combed in days. "How many days have you been in this room?"

She replaced the headphones. "Turn it on again. Oh, please turn it on." She hunched down in the corner again.

I switched on the radio. As I walked out through the treasures in the spacious rooms, I found Jeeves waiting for me with a note on the same ivory paper as the invitation. It was from Andrew Danson.

Winston: I wanted you to understand. You
have seen what Cella really is. I couldn't leave her.
I offer that as fact, not excuse. But facts don't add

up to a human abstract, do they? I would have done anything to make Dean love me. You may not understand that. But then, you've never had a son. Have you, Winston?

Congratulations on the game.
A. Danson

Charlotte Stedman waived a jury trial and was sentenced by a judge to four years in Bedford Hills Women's Correctional Facility. David went up to visit her, just before he went back to California to resume his TV series. At least I thought that's where he was going.

"Charlotte's going to be teaching a computer course up there," he told me on the phone.

"Hopefully without any fancy flourishes."

"Most of those were invented by Sommers. She's a lot tougher than she thought she was. She'll be all right."

"Speaking of tough, will Alex be going out to L.A. with you?" David's stylish redhead had surprised herself up in the woods that night. I didn't want to see her give any ground now.

"She's going to London for a while."

"London? But I thought she was settling in to your place." Alex had given up her high-security apartment on Riverside Drive and brought Gemma to David's place. I'd thought everything was finally worked out between them.

He laughed. "She's gone to sell the London house, that's all. We're economizing. We'll both be in New York from now on."

"But what about California? What about the TV show?"

"I was going to wait till I got back to tell you. I'm just going out now to close up my place there. *Greyhawk*'s been canceled."

"Can't those great dodos at the network make up their minds?" The show had been canceled before and brought back, like old Hyde, by popular demand, a huge write-in campaign. Now they'd canceled the thing again!

"The programming boys at the network kept putting their fingers in the pie and making changes, till you could hardly recognize the thing," he said. Well, he was right, of course. Contract players who'd bombed out of six previous shows had turned up as semi-regulars for no apparent reason. Nick Greyhawk had ceased to solve crimes by rational deduction and suddenly become clairvoyant, and to top it all off they'd become so busy with the Social Problem of the Week that old Nick hardly ever got off a good smart crack anymore, for fear of offending the Mothers Against Ball-Bearing-Skateboards Association or the Freedom of Nude Bathing Society. "Really, they just saved me the trouble of breaking the contract," said Davy.

"Now what? More spy flicks?"

"I'm going back to theater. Take a while to line something up that's worth doing. But it's what Alex and I both want. And Winnie?"

"Kiddo?"

"I'll be going up to Toronto. Try to find Maureen. You won't be hurt by that, will you?"

"Hurt? Me? Why, kiddo, what're you talking about? Maureen's a mystery, after all. And you know me and mysteries."

It wasn't until the middle of March that Sarah and I returned to Gould Theatre for the all-girl *My Fair Lady*, presented by the Faculty Wives. It'd been postponed due to a round of flu that laid Hilda Costello low for ten days or more. (Personally, I chalked it up to all that wine at the Gala.) Eddie and Krish, one on one arm and one on the other, escorted bony Blanche Megrim, reeking of Tea Rose cologne and sporting more warpaint than was seen at the Little Big Horn. Tommy Sheffield, with Frick and Frack in tow, was sitting down front to cheer on Lady Di as Eliza, his balding dome shining bright.

How can I describe the performance? Imagine Chairman Mao in a tailcoat and spats singing "The Rain in Spain Falls Mainly on the Plain," and you'll have some idea of Hilda's Henry Higgins. As for Lady Di's Eliza, think of a six-foot adenoidal Margaret Thatcher with her beady eye trained on her husband in the front row, and you'll come close. We'd just lived through her funereal rendition of "I Could Have Danced All Night," when some kind soul on the light board figured we all needed a break and put up the house lights in the middle of a scene. The cast scuttled off and the audience, assuming it was intermission, began milling around in search of commiseration. Tommy stood up and put his hands to his eyes, scouting the terrain. Finally he found me and plowed his way up the aisle.

"Winston," he said, "I suppose you've heard." He was smirking ear to ear.

"Yes, Diana was a tad loud."

"About the Board meeting. The budget cuts. We went over it all at the faculty meeting."

"You know I'm allergic to faculty meetings."

"Well." He paused for another smirk. "Randolph Danson has given a large donation, earmarked for Arts and Letters. With special thanks to me as liaison for the Gala. Very generous of him, in view of all your poking around, and his son." He tried to frown, but he was feeling too far above it all.

"So you've kept your job, have you? And what about Women's Studies?"

"Oh. It's being retained. On a trial basis," he said.

Lady Di was taking her place on stage again, and the lights dimmed. "Well just keep this in mind, Sheffield," I said, nodding toward his wife. "So are you."

The audience was smaller, but considerably more mellow on a night two months later, toward the end of May, at Buster's, a small jazz club up near Columbia University. The sign outside read, SUGAR GEORGE ANTOINE, APPEARING NIGHTLY. Teresa's friend Buster was sitting in on the drums and George was at an old upright piano with the kind of sound I hadn't heard since I hitchhiked down to New Orleans the summer I turned eighteen. And it wasn't only the piano that brought back memories of my ever-dimming youth. My only godson had turned eighteen himself that day, and was about to graduate from Ainsley High. He was sitting with his mother, between Eddie and Sarah, and he couldn't take his eyes off Sugar. You'd have thought he invented the man and had just gotten the patent. "George is great, huh Doc?" he said, beaming.

Sugar was playing a version of "Satin Doll." With a little light work on the drums for backup, his one hand wove the melody round and round with variations as complex as the steps of a dance. I'm well known for my tin ear, but even I can tell a natural talent when I hear one. "He's fine," I said. "Just fine."

Sarah looked soberly over at Teresa. "How long do you think he'll stay?"

George finished his set and got up to join us. "I don't know," said Teresa quietly. "But it'll have to be long enough."

When George had found a chair and a glass of 7-Up—he never drank when he was working, I was told—I rapped the table with Eddie's pipe. "All right, you lot, listen up. I've got an announcement or two."

"So have I. If you break that pipe, I shall take you to Small Claims Court," announced Merriman, yanking the thing to safety.

I pulled a wad of paper out of my inside pocket and unrolled it. It was really several pages, legal size, with an official-looking blue paper cover. I handed it to Mickey. "Happy Birthday, kiddo."

"What is it?"

Teresa leaned over his shoulder. "Why Winston! It's a contract for John's new book."

"There'll probably be other offers, bigger ones. But Garner and Sloan are an old house, conservative, and they'll do it justice. If you want more money, hold out for it. You're the heir of John's copyrights, Mickey. Read the terms, think them over. It's a big responsibility, the future of your Dad's book."

"Garner and Sloan are your publishers, aren't they?" asked Teresa.

"What kind of deal did you make with them, Winnie, to get this offer wrapped up so neatly?" Eddie said, twinkling at me over his gin and ginger ale. "What did Cliff Munson stiff you for?"

"Nothing. Cliff was naturally glad I've decided to revive Winchester Hyde in a new trilogy."

"Aha!" cried Eddie. "Good old indestructible Hyde of blessed memory! I knew you couldn't get along without the old boy much longer."

"But it had nothing to do with John's book. They wanted that sight unseen." I buttoned my lip and sat wondering whether to produce the rest of my news. To be honest, I hadn't really made up my mind whether I'd done the right thing about it.

"On with it," said Sarah. "Don't sit there like a stuffed frog. What's the rest of the news?"

"Well, you have to promise not to rib me too much," I said. "But—I'm going to be in pictures." I gulped my booze for nerve. "That is, I'm going to be on TV. Every Sunday night. I'm taking over John's talk show, starting next month."

What is that line they used in the old novels? "And mirth was unrestrained." Well, I guess we were all in a mood for letting our hair down that night. The weather was warm, and I could smell the peculiarly appealing scent of rain on blacktop, mixed with drifting car exhaust, as I stood out in the alley behind Buster's, listening to the girls playing a jazzed-up version of "Deep Purple" with Buster on drums. The waiters were stacking up the tables and chairs and it was nearly three A.M. when Sugar George came to find me. I lighted him a Turkish Delight and we stood together in the faint mist that was still falling.

"About Sonny's book," he said, meaning *Dance of a One-Legged Soldier.* "Thanks."

"Thank John. He wrote it."

At the end of the alley near some Dumpsters from a restaurant, something moved and a dark shape circled. A man was sifting through the garbage, filling a plastic carrier.

"Well, you've certainly got a whole new life now," I said. "Things have changed."

"Sure," he said, his eyes on the man at the Dumpster. "Sure." He spun the cigarette onto the wet bricks with a hiss. "I think I know that guy," he muttered, and took off down the alley into the changeless, hungry dark.

Ropedancer's Fall is M. K. Lorens's second Bantam mystery featuring Winston Marlowe Sherman.* If you enjoyed this book, you will enjoy her third.

DECEPTION ISLAND

Here is an exciting preview of this suspenseful new mystery, available at your local bookseller in November 1990.

Sweet Narcissus was the first Bantam mystery by M. K. Lorens.

ONE

"Goddamn sonuvabitch!"

It was almost four o'clock on a breathless August afternoon, and my old stomping grounds, the little town of Ainsley, New York, had been stuck in the middle of a heat wave for more than a month. The rain had held off since the middle of May, and the temperature couldn't seem to drop below ninety-five. I had to agree with old Charlie Hull.

"Goddamn it to hell!"

He was parked beside me in his wheelchair, his good hand slapping down like an impatient heartbeat on the table edge, making the tower of shiny new paperbacked Winchester Hyde novels shiver dangerously.

"I—I—goddamn it, sonuvabitch!"

Charlie lapsed into a frowning silence, the mask of fine lines around his bright brown eyes like a crumpled road map. The thought was still there somewhere, but it had hit a dead end. Charlie summoned a final effort, tongue between his teeth, and his fist hit the table with a great *whack*.

But it was no good. Somewhere between Kate Hull's father and the rest of us a door had closed, quickly and finally. Almost exactly a year ago, in the heat of another muggy August, Charlie had suffered a damaging stroke. Now he spent most of his days here, in his daughter's small bookstore and travel agency, swearing blindly out the front window into space.

"Goddamn fucking bastard," he mumbled.

"I'm terribly sorry, Doc. I feel just awful."

Kate glanced over her shoulder at her lone customer, a stocky little man with the beginnings of a red-brown beard, and bit her lip in consternation. It looked red and sore, as if she'd bitten it more than once lately.

"Oh," I said, "Charlie and I understand each other. Don't we, kiddo?"

Well, of course it was a fib. I couldn't understand, I could only guess, like everybody else.

I steadied the tower of books as Charlie's furious hand slammed down again. After a year of washing him, feeding him, putting him to bed at night, and dressing him in the morning, not to speak of emptying her bank account to pay for his therapy sessions in Manhattan, Kate's anger, I thought, must be almost as great as her father's.

But nothing in her fair-skinned, lightly freckled face betrayed it. She just patted Charlie's shoulder and turned to ring up a sale for the man with the chestnut beard. He went out, letting in a blast of heat from the sidewalk, and Kate continued in her husky contralto.

"I wasn't apologizing for Pop's language. Hell, give me a swearer to a weeper any day. I just meant today's been a complete washout for you. That was only the third Hyde book we've sold so far. I was hoping for a grand-slam success." She smiled and stroked back her father's damp white hair. "After all, it isn't every day I get the great Henrietta Slocum in my place to autograph copies, is it?"

That grand old lady of the mystery novel, creator of the famous Gilded Age detective G. Winchester Hyde, had agreed to spend this sweltering afternoon signing some new reprints of her early novels. To anyone who really knew the old girl, the fact that the shirt under Henrietta's madras sports jacket had the sleeves whacked out of it, that her tie was peppered with ash from her favorite Turkish smokes, or that the washed-out jockey shorts under her twill pants suffered from a bad case of droopy elastic could've come as no particular surprise. One or two blue-haired old darlings had toddled in expecting a genteel, fluffy Miss Marple, and had gotten the rudest of awakenings when introduced instead to Yours Truly, Winston Marlowe Sherman, Ph.D., with a shape like William Howard Taft, grey hair like the wet tail feathers of a Plymouth Rock hen, and brows second only to those of the late Leonid Brezhnev.

After writing a score of Hyde mysteries under my alias, I'd finally killed off my famous sleuth. But a fervent write-in campaign from Hyde's adoring fans had trapped me into promising a resurrection. Already the publishers were beating the drums with a series of reprints—the books on the signing table before me. Glowing retrospectives had turned up in the *Times*, no less, and every guest on the PBS talk show I'd recently taken over seemed to ask about my new book.

How could I explain that, with my deadline less than six weeks away, I had nothing so far but a muddle of notes and some half-finished pages? My brain was as dry as the scorching August weather. It's ridiculously easy to kill a man, but bringing him back to life, even on paper, is a trick of the gods.

I had just mulled over and rejected my latest unworkable plot line, when the front door opened. The customer was tall and thin, almost entirely bald, with a long, equine face, small bright-blue eyes, and a short upper lip from which protruded two extremely white, extremely large front teeth.

Luther Morley smiled as he came past my table, leaning heavily on a mahogany cane with a horn head in the shape of a lion. Old Luther is usually said to be the richest professor on the Clinton College faculty. He's been with us for a dozen years or so, counting his inherited money and dabbling lightly in the mundane profession in which I've spent my life. I've been fighting off retirement for several years, but Luther—my age and then some—is cordially invited to "share his expertise" with the rising generation. He offers an annual seminar in art history, but he's mainly renowned for giving the infamous Arts Lecture every spring, rabbiting on for at least an hour about the cave paintings of the Burmese hill tribes. Otherwise he drifts into faculty meetings like Queen Victoria opening the Crystal Palace, and generally views academic serfs like myself as less than the dust beneath his chariot wheels.

He squinted down his nose at my pile of Hyde books.

always find paper covers so unaesthetic, don't you, ally? And these cheap, thick pages. I always feel I want to ash my hands afterwards."

"They're books, Lady Macbeth," I snapped. "You read em. If you want to tickle something, buy a sheepdog."

He smiled, the buckteeth gleaming, and moved off to ard the art section in back, leaning heavily on the fancy ane.

"He comes in here two or three times a week," said ate in an undertone, "but he never buys anything, just ands around reading the books for free."

"Naturally. How do you think he hangs onto all that oney, the way he lives? Probably goes through Food City ree times on Saturday collecting free pizza samples in his ggie bag."

At that moment Kate's phone rang and she dashed over yank the thing off the hook. I sat mopping my forehead, atching her out of the corner of my eye.

It isn't exactly a burdensome task, watching Kate. I've een doing it, off and on, ever since she popped up in one my Shakespeare classes back in the sixties. Now, twenty unds heavier and scraping the edge of forty, she'd lost one of that lucid, unassuming elegance she seemed un ware of. Her satiny light-brown hair was escaping in wisps d hairpins fell from her like the gentle rain from heaven, ut even in this weather she was a pleasure to look at.

As soon as she'd picked up the phone, though, some ing seemed to make Kate Hull uneasy, and it appeared to e Yours Truly. Her cool, brown eyes watched me watching er and she ducked away, swaying uncertainly on her high eeled pumps and gripping the receiver for dear life, nielding it just a bit with her palm. It was obvious that she idn't want me to overhear.

Always faithful to the principles of the great Hyde, I aturally pricked up my big ears.

"No," she said, in an urgent stage whisper. "I told you efore. Don't push me. I know, I know all that, but— Oh, l right. Tonight."

My curiosity was killing me. "Who was that, the CIA?" said, as soon as she'd hung up.

"Oh. The damn insurance." The answer came a bit too quickly and too loud. "They're raising my rates again."

Insurance? Well, I ask you. How do *you* tell when someone is feeding you a baloney sandwich? That call hadn't been from any insurance salesman, and we both knew it.

"If it weren't for the extra money I make working for Richard over at the gallery, I'd have had to close up and sell out six months ago," she announced, her fists stuffed in the pockets of her faded denim skirt.

I sat up a bit straighter. "Since when are you working for Richard Brant?"

"Oh, I just help him out with odds and ends. It hardly pays to burn the lights in this place most days anyway." She sighed. "I thought business might pick up during the Arts Festival. But just look out there. You could fire a cannon down that street."

She was right. Clinton Street was decked out with red, yellow, and blue plastic pennants that hung limp in the sultry air, and the big banners that proclaimed that night's annual street fair and outdoor art competition drooped low over the hot sidewalk. What tourist wanted to stroll the pavements with the temperature bumping a hundred?

"It's not just for the money, though. Richard's taught me a lot about art. I like it."

Kate tottered a bit on the success-conscious shoes. She was a true child of her generation; she hasn't felt entirely at home since her last pair of Earth Shoes gave up the ghost. I'd never seen her tricked out in high heels before, and now I knew the reason for them: Richard Brant.

He was a personable, energetic Englishman who ran Les Artistes, the classy little art gallery straight across the street. I'd met him a few times at the houses of mutual friends, a pleasant, knowledgeable fellow in his late fifties or early sixties, still handsome enough to rouse the slumbering matchmaker in any hostess.

"And I like Richard, too," she said defiantly. "Don't you?"

I hunched my shoulders and mopped my forehead again. When Kate decided to get married a few years ago,

...e came to me in just the same way, chin tilted back, hands
...uffed staunchly in her pockets, with a husky, pink-
...eeked adolescent of thirty-six named Brad in tow. I
...niled and shook hands and told her later what she already
...new perfectly well: Her Brad had the brain of a slightly
...eficient peahen, and they had nothing in common.

Two days after I delivered myself of that opinion, they
...ere married. They set up shop here, Kate running the
...ookstore and Brad the travel agency, till one fine day he
...ought a ticket on one of his own package tours and rode off
...to the sunset. Katie got a postcard from Tunisia, and next
...y she was up in my inner sanctum, hands in her pockets
...ain, defying me to say she shouldn't get divorced.

I glanced at Charlie. We'd always filled two different
...mpartments in Kate's life. Her Pop gave her unques-
...oned love, but it was always Yours Truly who had to tell
...r what she didn't want to hear. Since Charlie's stroke it
...as even more the case than ever. I sighed and charged into
...e breach, armed with the one thing that had always
...uzzled me about Richard Brant.

"That's a pretty expensive layout over there," I said.
...ll that flagstone and leather and etched glass. I don't see
...w he does it. Keeps the same stuff on display for months,
...om what Eddie Merriman tells me. Never seen a cus-
...mer come out of the place. Who's his backer, anyway,
...idas of the Golden Touch?"

"I don't think he has a backer. He isn't even incorpo-
...ted."

"Then how can he keep that place going?" I shook my
...ead. "He's always going on buying trips, but he never
...lls. Something fishy somewhere, kiddo."

Kate bristled. "I thought you, of all people, might be
...s friend, Winnie."

"I am, I guess." I lighted a Turkish Delight and sat
...uffing thoughtfully. "As much as anybody is."

"What the hell does that mean?"

I could see I was going to have to spell it out.

"It means Richard's a dark horse because he damn well
...kes being a dark horse. And although I admire good horse-
...esh as much as the next gambler, I've got sense enough to

put my money on a sure thing. Listen, Katie. Just how heavy are your own bets on Richard, anyway?"

She kicked her yuppie shoes into the corner with a vengeance, clearly wishing they were me. "He's thinking of opening a new gallery in the spring. In Manhattan I think. He may want me to come along and work for him."

"You're not seriously thinking of moving back to town, are you?"

Kate had put in several unhappy years in Manhattan, sweating away at a writing career that had never materialized. Then she'd tried publishing, and that, too, had been a washout. Manhattan was like those high-heeled shoes—classy, but uncomfortable and not at all her style.

"Richard will do fine in Manhattan," I said, fiddling with my autographing ballpoint. "After all, what have we got here for him? A one-horse summer art colony and a couple of refugees from SoHo. Brant's making a good move."

"But I'm not?" She forgot that Luther Morley was still padding around the place, and her voice rose angrily. "Your prize student will fall flat on her face, just like she's done for the last twenty years? Well, I've got news for you. I've already decided. I'll go if he wants me to; I'd sell this damn place and go with him tomorrow!"

She thudded off to the back room in her stockinged feet, mumbling to herself. I sighed and drew deeply on my Turkish Delight.

"What's our kiddo gotten herself into, Charlie?" I said.

The gleam in the old boy's eye was as good as a telegram. I lighted another smoke and stuck it in the corner of his mouth; he inhaled gratefully. His thick, stubby fingers found my ballpoint and brought it down against the writing pad on the table; I watched him expectantly, trying to read some meaning into the circle after meaningless circle he inscribed on the empty page. There was none.

"So Richard Brant will be leaving us." It was Luther, hovering over my shoulder. "I couldn't help overhearing."

"Couldn't you?"

"A loss to Ainsley, naturally. But the man's always seemed a bit shady to me, frankly." The intense blue eyes bored into me. "And of course his taste in paintings verges on the archaic."

"What you mean, Morley," I said, "is that he doesn't cotton to all that primitive stuff that makes you salivate. But that hardly makes him shady, now does it?"

I suddenly realized I was defending Brant against the same charge I'd made myself a minute before. But then, if Luther Morley had attacked bubonic plague I'd have found something nice to say about it. We were natural adversaries; I was the big, old, captious tomcat, and Luther the fussy, pretentious Pekingese.

He merely smiled, the buckteeth glittering. "If you and I were ever to agree about anything, Winston, one of us would have to be lying. Oh, by the way, don't forget the faculty party on Sunday night," he said, and made his way to the door.

I watched him move off down the block, just as the baby-blue bulk of Ainsley's one and only city bus creaked up at the curb outside. In a minute it pulled away, leaving a natty little man in a seersucker suit, starched white shirt, and red bow tie standing alone on the corner. He hitched up the brown cardboard portfolio he was carrying and toddled briskly toward the entry of Richard Brant's gallery. Hardly able to trust my eyes, I grabbed for my long-distance specs.

"Merriman? Oh, I don't believe it!"

"Good old Eddie!" Kate was back, looking over Charlie's shoulder, her bad mood entirely gone. "So he's finally taking the plunge with those watercolors of his! I told him to give Richard a crack at them. They're really damned good, you know."

"He's got enough to fill that ratty portfolio ten times over, and he never tries to sell them," I grumbled. "You know the man, he has no ambition; since he stopped teaching he lives for pleasure alone."

Since his retirement as Milton and Chaucer professor at DeWitt Clinton College, my former colleague and best friend does only what pleases him best—playing his ancient clarinet off-key, researching arcane trivia, and painting countless landscapes of our wooded Hudson River bluffs.

"He just figures they'll hang over there for a month or so," I went on, "and then he can take them home. I'll have to quit hounding him and give him some peace in his declining years."

But if peace and quiet were what Eddie was after, they certainly didn't turn out to be what he got.

He had no sooner disappeared through the handsome wrought iron entry of Les Artistes than a huge black limo pulled up in front.

"I had no idea Donald and Ivana were joining us for the Arts Festival," I said. "Look at the thing! An entire family of Chinese peasants could set up housekeeping in that back seat."

The driver, wearing Ludwig of Bohemia's cast-off dress blues, got out and stood at attention beside the passenger's door. When I saw who was inside, I was surprised there weren't a brace of footmen in powdered wigs riding shotgun on the back bumper. I groaned.

"Oh, no! Just what I needed to make my day complete! Another of my favorite people."

"Oh, that's Harold Divine!" Kate stood on tiptoe to get a better look. "He's supposed to be one of the judges at the Festival Awards tonight. But what can he want with Richard?"

"I don't know, but I don't envy Brant the pleasure of his company. The night he was on our show, the ratings hit absolute zero. The Divine Harold has all the charisma of a fruit fly."

Harold Divine, raconteur, aesthete, and longtime critic for *Manhattan à la Mode,* was best known for pumping up the reputations of two-bit graffiti artists and neocubists, and draping himself round the postmodern furnishings of any Manhattan gallery that happened to be handing out free booze and beluga. He made quite a sight, impeccably clad in the snow-white Colonel Sanders suit that was his trademark, plus peach silk shirt, silver tie, and Panama hat. He minced his way to the front door of Brant's gallery and disappeared inside.

"Winnie," said Kate, her voice breathy with excitement, "hold the fort for me. Keep an eye on Pops. I've got to get over there. Now!"

Before I had a chance to complain, she was out the door and halfway across the street, jamming her hair back into its few remaining pins. In stockinged feet on the sizzling pavement, she made record time, and she must've been in Brant's lobby no more than a minute or two after the Divine Harold himself.

I sat open-mouthed, staring after her.

"Fee, fie, fo, fum. I smell the blood of an Englishman. There's a mystery in the wind, Charlie, my boy. And it's got something to do with Richard Brant and that pompous twit who just blew in over there."

Charlie stared straight ahead of him out the window. "Sonuvabitch," he said softly.

And from everything I knew of the Divine Harold, I had to admit I agreed.

TWO

"Brant! Where's that unconscionable fraud, Richard Brant?"

Divine's voice was as mechanical as the voice box of a computerized toy. He stood in the exact center of the gallery lobby, looking neither to left nor right, his Panama hat still jammed firmly on his head.

When Harold Divine made his grand entrance, my friend Merriman was lost in the contemplation of a remarkable pair of large watercolor portraits in the display area. He had made no effort to find Richard Brant or to go upstairs to the little office. He hadn't come to sell his own pictures at all.

When he heard Divine's voice, Eddie ducked into the maze of Y-shaped paths formed by the converging partitions on which the pictures hung. The outer, containing walls were covered with smoked mirrors, gleaming discreetly in the cool, dim stairwell and the lobby. By tilting dangerously sideways and hanging on to a marble sculpture plinth, Merriman could just see the mirror image of the man in the Colonel Sanders suit as he moved across the reception area.

He also saw Kate come skidding up behind Harold Divine in her stockinged feet.

"I'm helping out this afternoon," she said, glancing nervously up at the office. "Is there something I can show you?"

He sniffed, looking her up and down, his gaze coming to rest directly on her toes in their ruined panty hose. He didn't even bother with a perfunctory insult, merely turned and marched off toward the hanging area, leaving her to trail behind him. Eddie made another quick dive for cover and scuttled round a partition; from his new nest he could hear everything.

"Brant!" The mechanical voice rose to a shriek. "Richard-bloody-Brant!"

Divine stopped in front of the same two paintings Merriman had been admiring. They were the best in the place. In the three days since Kate had found them in Richard's storage closet and hung them here, she herself had come back again and again to study these large, luminous watercolors.

According to the vetting papers from Ghent, the pictures had been painted in the 1940s by an unknown Belgian named Julien Phillipe. They were glowing, poignant character portraits of a slight, sharp-faced woman with black hair chopped off at irregular lengths in no discernible shape. She had large, disturbing eyes, almost those of an animal: wild and unpredictable, but at the same time gentle, mutely perceptive.

It was a hard face, but the parts were stronger than the whole. There was about the woman a sort of frangibility, like glass that will shatter with sound. In one painting she was young, sunlight touching the high, narrow cheekbones until they seemed to blaze with a light of their own. In the second portrait she was middle-aged, the shadows greenish and brutal, the lines even more angular. They were amazing pictures, the sort a buyer stumbles onto only once in a lifetime.

"These objects," announced Divine, "are fakes." He let his flat voice echo up the wrought-iron spiral staircase. "Either Brant's an idiot or he's a simple crook."

"Harold, my dear fellow, if ever I decide to become a crook, I shall hardly be a simple one."

Kate sighed with relief as the athletic figure of Richard Brant—a tall, graceful blur in the smoky mirrors in which Eddie glimpsed himself—came bounding down the last few steps of the iron spiral and landed beside her. It delighted him to rattle people; he never approached, he exploded out of nowhere.

Richard Brant had the kind of composed patrician bearing the boys in the theater used to call "presence." When he came into a room, you noticed him. His gray hair was brushed smooth from a perfect part at the left; the face was bold, the jawline squarish without being bulldog like my own. The skeptical slate-gray eyes took in everything and gave back only a hint of benevolent amusement, impossible to read.

Brant blinked at Divine over a pair of Ben Franklin glasses. Then he took them off, whipped out a silk handkerchief, and stood calmly polishing the lenses, rocking back and forth, back and forth on his heels. It wasn't the first time Kate had seen him play this game, stalling for time, hoping the other person would break from pure impatience.

Divine didn't. His glare and his silence were equally steady. Beneath the absurd caricature he presented to the eye, there was something in reserve. Not strength, precisely, nor conviction, nor even stubbornness. Harold Divine had the smug confidence of a man with a secret weapon.

At last Brant sighed, folded his glasses and put them away in the pocket of his jacket. He would be forced, it seemed, to make the next move himself.

"Kate, old love," he said, "I think Harry needs a drop of that lovely Pernod upstairs. I do believe the heat's short-circuited his nervous system; he seems to be babbling."

Kate could hear Richard's exploding laugh as she went obligingly up the stairs to his office where the hospitality booze was kept. When she got there, heart throbbing ferociously, she opened the office door and shut it again with a loud enough click for the two men downstairs to hear plainly. Of course it occurred to her that Eddie must still be somewhere in the gallery, but he would just have to look after himself. Kate crouched down at exactly the point where the curve of the stair would conceal her from sight. The voices of the two men funnelled neatly upward, thanks to the Y-shaped angles of the walls.

Merriman, just across the partition from Divine and Richard Brant, could even hear them breathing. Brant spoke first.

"What the hell do you think you're doing, talking like that in front of the girl? I've told you to keep clear of this place."

"You're finished, Ditch. You've gone over the line. I know about your little game."

"Balls, Harry."

"You'll never pull it off on your own. You haven't got the nerve for it. You need me."

Brant laughed again. "A sorry, aging pimp? Whatever credibility you got from the Leipzig operation went up your nose years ago."

"Too bad about poor old Peter Mellors, wasn't it?" said Divine. "Or hadn't you heard? Peter didn't have your style, or we might've made him the offer we're willing to make you. He was always a prissy idiot, Mellors."

All of a sudden Divine's paunchy body lurched into sight below Kate in the lobby, stumbling backward. His nose was bleeding, a smear of bright red on the white lapel. He didn't bother trying to stop the flow, just righted himself and came at Brant again, strangely unangered by the punch he'd taken.

"I don't give a puking damn what happens to you, Ditch. Not personally. But we can use you. Unless you go the same way as Peter, sticking your damn-fool neck out."

"All right. You think you know what I'm up to, do you? Who's your source, some gallery whore? He's feeding you swill," said Brant coolly. "I'm doing business as usual. I buy pictures as instructed and send them straight through London. By the Scriptures, all Ten Commandments. You have nothing, Harry. Nothing."

"You didn't buy *those* pictures anywhere." Divine read the card Kate had posted next to the two watercolors. "Julien Phillipe, my ass. You faked them, naturally, you're good at it. Didn't even bother to sign the phony name to them, they're still unsigned. We both know who painted the originals, though, don't we, the ones you copied from? They're phony Frances Woodvilles."

ABOUT THE AUTHOR

M. K. LORENS is a scholar and playwright who lives in a small town much like Ainsley. *Ropedancer's Fall* is the second Winston Marlowe Sherman mystery. The third, *Deception Island*, will be published by Bantam in the fall of 1990.